Murder

at

Bertram's

Bower

A BEACON HILL
MYSTERY

CYNTHIA PEALE

A DELL BOOK

Published by
Dell Publishing
a division of
Random House, Inc.
1540 Broadway
New York, New York 10036

Copyright © 2001 by Nancy Zaroulis
Digital Art by Melody Cassen
Cover photograph courtesy of Boston Public Library, Print Department
Cover design by Amy C. King

Dell® is a registered trademark of Random House, Inc., and the colophon is a trademark of Random House, Inc.

Library of Congress Catalog Card Number: 00-063877

ISBN: 0-440-23563-4

Previously published as a Doubleday hardcover in March 2001

Manufactured in the United States of America
Published simultaneously in Canada

April 2002

OPM 10 9 8 7 6 5 4 3 2 1

For
Katherine

Murder

at

Bertram's

Bower

❧

CHAPTER
1

BOSTON: THE JANUARY THAW, 1892. A WATERY GLOOM HUNG over the city like a shroud.

Day after day of heavy, relentless rain had threatened to submerge the new-filled Back Bay, and the miniature lagoon in the Public Garden had overflowed its banks. On Beacon Hill, streams of water pounded the brick sidewalks and cascaded down the narrow streets, splashing women's voluminous skirts, splattering horses with mud up to their blinkers. People clung to their firesides, waiting for winter to return.

In the South End, Officer Joseph Flynn of the Boston police was making his rounds. He had been on the force for less than a year, and he was eager to do well in this job which until recently would not have been given to an Irishman like himself. When he saw the shape on the ground halfway down the alley behind West Brookline Street, he paused. Because it was night, and very dark in that district, he could not immediately tell what the shape was. A heap of refuse, he thought, or a pile of rags. Or, at worst, some drunken tramp from the nearby railroad yards.

Still. Best be sure. On the lookout for rats, his bull's-eye lantern sputtering in the rain, he stepped carefully along.

When he came to it—to her—he could hardly believe what he saw. He had witnessed some serious mayhem during his brief time with the force, but he had never seen anything like this. Half crouching, holding his lantern close, he stared at her for a long moment.

Dear Mother of God. What monster had been at work here? He felt his stomach heave, and he heard the anguished cry torn from his throat. His lantern clattered to the ground. Suddenly overcome, he fell retching to his knees. Then he vomited onto the dirty, rain-soaked snow.

CHAPTER 2

"I WILL PUT MATTHEW HALE NEXT TO HARRIET MASON," said Caroline Ames. Her pencil hovered over the sheet of paper on which she had written names around a diagram of her dining room table. "He is so terribly shy with women, and Harriet can get conversation out of a lamppost."

Dr. John Alexander MacKenzie had been struggling through a life of Lincoln highly recommended by the clerk at the Athenaeum. Now he laid aside the heavy volume and rose to knock the ashes of his pipe into the grate where simmering sea coal warmed the parlor at No. 16½, Louisburg Square.

"Might she not frighten him?" he said, smiling down at her. She'd given him permission to smoke when he'd come to live here several months before, and he'd been grateful to her—for that, and for much else.

She was a pretty woman of some thirty-five years, a little plump, with fair, curly hair caught up in a fashionable Psyche knot and frizzy bangs partially covering her wide, smooth forehead. Her eyes were brown, her mouth a vivid rose, and although her cheeks were tinged with pink, he was almost certain that she did not use face paint. She wore a high-necked long-sleeved dress of soft gray, plainly made and slightly out of fashion because of its bustle. Her only ornament was a mourning brooch for her mother.

She had been fussing over this dinner party for weeks, and now it was nearly upon them. Although MacKenzie had been invited to it, he hardly cared about it—only to the extent that it was a worry for her. When she had first announced her intention to have it—"For Nigel Chadwick, who is coming from London, and every hostess in Boston is maneuvering to get him to her table!"—he had thought the effort would be too much for her. She had been wounded by a bullet in the shoulder the previous November, and while she had healed well, her normal strength and vitality had been slow to return.

And, too, he thought darkly, she was not an ideal patient, too quick to take up her multitudinous activities, many of which were good works. Only that morning she had been summoned on an errand of mercy for the Ladies' Committee at her church, and to his chagrin, she had gone.

"It is my turn to go, Doctor," she'd said.

He had protested as much as he thought he dared, for he was only a boarder, after all. "In this weather?" he'd said.

"They wouldn't ask me unless it was important. I know this family. The committee has been working with them for months—since last summer, in fact. The woman is an excellent person who is trying very hard to keep the family together. I must go—but to ease your mind, I will take a herdic."

He'd offered to go with her himself, or even in her place, but she'd refused, allowing him only to go down to Charles Street at the foot of the hill to find a herdic-phaeton for her and bring it to the door. These were small, fast cabs unique to Boston, whose strong, agile horses darted about the city at all hours.

Now, safely home once more, she'd been struggling for the past half hour with the seating for her party.

"I don't think so," she said in answer to his question. "Harriet isn't a frightening kind of person, just very chatty."

"Then by all means," he said, "you must seat her next to him."

She looked up at him, returning his smile. He was stockily built, not much taller than herself, and a few years older (she'd turn thirty-six in May). He had graying hair, a broad, honest face adorned by a not too brushy mustache, and kind, wise eyes. She'd liked him from the moment he had presented himself the previous September, bearing a note from Boston's most famous surgeon, Dr. Joseph Warren. MacKenzie, a surgeon himself with the army on the western plains, had taken a Sioux bullet in his knee; after the army doctors in Chicago had informed him that he must lose his leg, he had come to Boston, to Dr. Warren, to see if he could save it.

Warren had done so, and had recommended his neighbors across Louisburg Square, Addington Ames and his sister, Caroline, as a place for MacKenzie to board at not too great an expense while he recuperated.

The Ameses' elevator, installed for their late mother's convenience, had been a great help, particularly in the first days after his operation, when he was confined to his room on the third floor at the back of the house. Margaret, the all-purpose girl, had brought him his meals, and Caroline herself had come up once or twice a day to see how he did. Eventually, when he could hobble about, he sat by the window and enjoyed the view: down over the crowded rooftops of the western slope of Beacon Hill to the river, and to Cambridge beyond. On fine days, all the autumn, he enjoyed the sunsets, and as he recovered further and could go downstairs in the elevator, he had enjoyed the Ameses' company as well. He had become, he thought, not so much a paying boarder as a friend. Now, in the winter, he could not imagine a life apart from them. From her.

He moved to the bow window that overlooked the square. Its lavender glass was old, original with the house. Caroline had told him that it had been imported from Europe; imperfect, it had turned color when the sun first struck it. Her grandfather, a China trader and one of the first proprietors of the square, had been too thrifty to replace it. It gave the trees and shrubbery in the central oval an eerie, purplish cast; MacKenzie still wasn't used to it.

This day, rain lashed against the panes, making him glad to be indoors. He'd heard about the vagaries of the New England weather before he'd come, but rain in January seemed very odd indeed.

A tall, cloaked figure was striding through the downpour. In a moment more, he had passed beneath the window and they heard him coming in.

Caroline brightened. "There! That will be Addington. He is probably soaked to the skin—I can't imagine why he felt he needed to go to Crabbe's in this weather."

Her brother was a devotee of Crabbe's Boxing and Fencing Club down in Avery Street, beyond the Common. He went there nearly every day, sometimes very early in the morning after a night of stargazing. He kept a telescope on the roof of the house, but for the past several nights, the thaw, with its clouds and rain, had made stargazing impossible.

They heard him stamping in the vestibule, and after a moment he slid open the pocket doors to the parlor. He was a tall man, whippet thin, with dark hair combed straight back from his high forehead, dark, deep-set eyes in a long, clean-shaven face, and a pronounced nose. Ordinarily he was self-contained, not given to displays of feeling; just now, however, they saw from his expression that something was obviously amiss.

"What is it, Addington?" Caroline asked.

"Bad news, I am afraid." He carried a folded newspaper, which he gave to her. "Look at this."

As she opened it, MacKenzie saw that it was an "Extra," and he caught sight of the bold black headline: MURDER AT BERTRAM'S BOWER!!! And in slightly smaller type: VICIOUS CRIME!!! WOMAN'S BODY FOUND IN ALLEY!!!

Caroline quickly scanned the page. They saw her amazement—then shock, then horror. Deathly pale, she looked up at them, while the newspaper dropped to her lap.

"May I?" said MacKenzie, taking the paper and reading: Last night a young woman, Mary Flaherty, a resident of the well-known home for fallen women, Bertram's Bower, had been murdered in a South End alley not far from the Bower.

A brutal crime; robbery not a motive; Deputy Chief Inspector Elwood Crippen of the city police stated that "the crime was probably the work of a deranged person."

"I am sorry, my dear," Ames said to his sister. He advanced to the fire and took up his customary position, one slim, booted foot resting on the brass fender. "I know that Agatha is your friend."

Agatha Montgomery was the proprietress of the Bower.

"I must go to her at once, Addington."

"In this downpour? Surely she will be distraught, distracted—"

Just then Margaret knocked and announced lunch, putting a brief end to Ames's protest. But as they spooned up their leek and potato soup, and ate their minced beef patties and boiled beets, Caroline explained to Dr. MacKenzie about Bertram's Bower.

"It is a most worthy establishment, Doctor. And, unfortunately, a necessary one. Agatha takes in girls who—well, they are girls of the street, if you follow."

He did.

"If Miss Montgomery felt the need to speak to you," Ames said, "she would have sent you a telegram." He eyed his plate warily. He did not like beets.

"Not necessarily. She was never one to ask for help, even when she most desperately needs it. It is her brother, remember, who does all the fund-raising."

She turned to MacKenzie. "Agatha has been a friend of mine since we were children, although she is a few years older than I. The Montgomerys grew up around the corner on Pinckney Street. When Agatha was seventeen, her father went bankrupt. She never had a coming-out. She started Bertram's Bower about ten years ago, when an uncle left her a small inheritance. Now she and her brother, the Reverend Randolph Montgomery, support the place from donations."

"You go there regularly," MacKenzie said. Caroline had recently resumed most of her schedule: church meetings, Sewing Circle, Saturday Morning Reading Club, and, of course, the Bower.

"Yes. To teach the girls to read and write, and to sew and do fancy embroidery. They come to the city in search of work, and if they cannot find it, or if they find it and are then dismissed, they end up on the streets." She shuddered, and her brother frowned at her.

"Not a suitable place for you, Caroline," he said. "You know I have never approved of your going there."

"If Agatha Montgomery can devote her life to those poor creatures," she replied with some spirit, "surely I can give them one afternoon every other week."

She turned to MacKenzie again. "She is very strict with them, of course—and of course she must be. She must maintain the highest moral standards. The girls violate the rules at their peril, and well they know it. But they know, too, they are fortunate to be there, because a girl from the Bower can almost always find decent employment when she leaves. Agatha's reputation for high standards guarantees that. At first, when she had just opened the place, she used to go out at night, searching for girls on the streets. Can you imagine? She would talk to them, persuade them to go with her. She keeps them for three months, usually. Feeds them, gets medical attention for them at Dr. Hannah Bigelow's clinic. And she recruited all her friends—her former friends, that is—to teach them."

"Did you know this girl—the one who was—ah—"

"Mary Flaherty? Yes. Not well, for she already knew how to read and write when she came to Agatha, and she could sew a pretty seam. She was a lovely girl, bright and hard-working. You could see she wanted to advance herself in the world. And in fact Agatha kept her on when her three months were up, employing her as her secretary."

Her eyes held MacKenzie's in a steady gaze. "Sometimes I think the work that Agatha Montgomery does over there in the South End is more important than all our charity fairs and sewing for the poor and Thanksgiving baskets of food that the church gives out. We play at good works, but when our hour or two of service is done, we return to our comfortable homes. Agatha lives her charity, she works at it twenty-four hours a day. It is her life. Oh, dear, she must be devastated!" She turned to her brother. "And think of the harm such a scandal will do to the Bower's reputation, Addington. No one will want to volunteer, donations will fall off—they might be ruined because of this!"

"The Reverend Montgomery is a skilled fund-raiser," Ames replied. "I don't imagine this incident, unfortunate as it is, will crimp his style."

"Unfortunate!" she exclaimed. "Is that what you call it?"

"Unfortunate—yes. Hardly a scandal. It is not Agatha Montgomery's fault if some deranged person—as your friend Inspector Crippen put it—has murdered one of her girls."

"Do not call him my friend, Addington." She shook her head. "If Inspector Crippen has charge of this case, they might never find the man who killed Mary."

"True. But a random killing in the night—if it was random—is a difficult thing to solve."

"All the more reason for me to go to Agatha and see what I can do to help." Her face, ordinarily so gentle and sweet, hardened into lines of determination as she added, "So, yes, Addington, I am going to go to her. And I am going to try to bring her back here with me. She must be in a terrible state. It will do her good to get away, even just for overnight. We can put her in the front room on the fourth floor."

"You are not forgetting Wednesday evening," he cautioned, referring to her dinner party.

For a moment it was obvious that she had done exactly that.

"Oh—no, of course not. I have things fairly well in hand, and even if Agatha does stay until tomorrow, that is only Tuesday. Will you come to the Bower with me, Addington?"

"I would prefer not to."

She accepted the rebuff with only a slight tightening of her lips. "Doctor?"

"Well, I— Yes, of course."

MacKenzie sighed to himself. He'd become accustomed to a nap after lunch. But now Caroline Ames, for whom he had come to have feelings that went far beyond casual friendship, was asking him for help. He could not possibly refuse her.

"Good," she replied. "We will go at once."

Since it was obvious that nothing would deter her, Ames threw up his hands and set off in the rain once more to find them a cab. Shortly they heard the horse's hooves on the cobblestones outside, and Caroline and the doctor, stoutly protected against the weather with waterproofs, galoshes, and her capacious umbrella, bade Ames good-bye.

He stood at the parlor window and watched through the lavender glass as the narrow black cab wobbled its way to the end of the square and turned down Pinckney Street. It was early afternoon but already growing dark. What state Agatha Montgomery would be in—or what tale of horror Caroline would bring back to him—he could only imagine.

It was a bad business, this murder. Nothing for a lady like Caroline Ames to be involved in.

CHAPTER 3

In the cab, MacKenzie glanced at his companion. Beneath the brim of her dark gray bonnet, her face was strained and pale. Her hands in their black kid gloves were clenched in her lap, and although her gaze was directed toward the passing row upon row of redbrick and brownstone town houses that lined the streets, he doubted that she saw them. He cast about for some comforting thing to say to her, but he could think of nothing. For the time being she was estranged from him, and he acknowledged to himself that the very fact of her concern for her friend was part of the reason he had come to care for her: She was a woman of tender sensibilities, kindness and goodness personified, just as all women were supposed to be but were not.

Soon they crossed over the Boston & Providence railroad tracks and passed into the South End. This was a district much like the Back Bay and built around the same time, thirty-odd years before, but as it was literally on the wrong side of the tracks, it had quickly fallen into shabby disrepair. Its handsome buildings had been cut up into apartments, and, worse, single rooms for rent; many of them had deteriorated through years of neglect. As the cab rolled by, MacKenzie saw more than a few disreputable-looking characters who would never have ventured onto Commonwealth Avenue or Beacon Street or the Ameses' place, Louisburg

Square. But he noted, too, a number of churches. There must be some kind of faithful flock existing hereabouts, he thought.

Bertram's Bower, on Rutland Square, was one of a number of matching brownstones that curved around a small oval "square," a kind of miniature Louisburg Square. Here MacKenzie could see that some effort had been made to keep property values up: The high iron fence that encircled the little oval was intact and free of rust, the brass door knockers on the houses were brightly polished, the doors themselves freshly painted. Someone—Agatha Montgomery?—had seen to it that this little enclave, at least, would not succumb to decay.

They alighted, MacKenzie paid the driver, and sheltered by Caroline's umbrella they mounted the tall flight of steps to the Bower's door. He lifted the knocker and brought it down sharply twice.

It was opened by a frightened-looking young woman in a white bib apron over a plain dark dress.

"Yes, sir?"

"Hello, Nora," Caroline said.

"Oh! Miss Ames! I didn't—" She broke off, obviously embarrassed.

"Is Miss Montgomery in?" Caroline asked. She smiled at the girl, whom she knew from her embroidery class.

Nora hesitated. "No, miss," she said, not meeting Caroline's eyes.

"You mean, she is, but not to visitors?" Caroline said gently.

Nora nodded.

"Well, I imagine she will be in to me—to us," she corrected herself.

Nora's eyes slid unhappily to MacKenzie.

"This is Dr. MacKenzie," Caroline added. Standing on the stoop, they were getting thoroughly wet, and with a graceful gesture that waved the girl aside, she stepped into the vestibule, and MacKenzie, shaking out the umbrella, followed.

"Oh, but, miss—" Nora began, looking more frightened than ever.

"Never mind, dear," Caroline said. "I'm sure Miss Montgomery will see us."

She moved into the dim, bleak front hall, MacKenzie close behind. Two meager gas jets on the wall by the stairs provided the only illumination, hardly sufficient on this dark day. The place had an institutional smell: a combination of cooking odors, strong lye soap, and an indefinable smell that was the odor of many human bodies crowded together. But it was oddly silent, he thought. Surely now, at mid-afternoon, a place like this should be buzzing with activity? Or perhaps not; perhaps the girls were at their classes, and the noise and chatter would come later, when they were released.

"I will just go and see—" Caroline began, when suddenly, from the back of the hall, a woman appeared. She was middle-aged, of middling height, with a mannish look to her—broad shoulders, short, thick neck, and a coarse-featured face.

"I told you not to admit anyone!" she snapped, addressing the now thoroughly cowed Nora. Then, seeing Caroline, she caught herself. "Miss Ames," she said, but hardly in a welcoming tone.

"Matron Pratt," Caroline replied easily. "I have come to see Miss Montgomery. This is my friend, Dr. MacKenzie."

As Matron Pratt flicked her cold gaze over him and instantly dismissed him, his greeting died on his lips.

"She's not in," Matron said.

"She isn't? Oh, dear, I am sorry."

Just then they were aware of a movement at the top of the long, narrow flight of stairs. A young woman—another resident of the place, obviously—had started down, but when she saw Matron Pratt, she stopped.

"One demerit, Slattery!" snapped the matron.

"But I was just—"

"Back to your class! Or I'll give you two!"

Stifling a sob, the girl retreated.

Caroline tried again. "Mrs. Pratt, I know what a difficult time this must be for you, but I wanted to see Agatha, just for a moment."

"She's not fit to see anyone, Miss Ames."

"So she is here?"

"Yes." Matron Pratt's cold gray eyes never wavered as she met Caroline's anxious gaze. "But she's in no condition to see you. The police have been all over the place, all morning. I swan, I don't know how we are supposed to get on with our business here, with them poking and prying."

"Yes," murmured Caroline, aware that Nora was edging away from them toward the stairs. "But if she could see us, even for a moment—"

"Cromarty!" snarled Matron Pratt. "You were told not to allow anyone in! Two demerits!"

Nora stared at her, appalled. "But, Matron—"

"You heard what I said! Get back to class now, or I'll make it three!"

As Nora scrambled up the stairs, they saw a female coming down, and this time she did not flinch and flee at the sight of Matron Pratt.

"Agatha!" Caroline exclaimed, relieved to see her friend at last.

The proprietress of Bertram's Bower peered down at them, squinting a little, as if she could not see clearly. She moved aside to let the luckless Nora pass, and then descended slowly, clinging to the banister; once she seemed to stagger, but she caught herself before she fell.

"Oh, Agatha! I came as soon as I heard the news." As Miss Montgomery reached the bottom of the stairs, Caroline seized her hands. "And I have brought my friend, Dr. MacKenzie," she added.

He advanced and held out his hand. Miss Montgomery did not seem to see him at first, but then she took his hand—hers was icy cold—and mumbled a greeting.

She was as plain a woman as he had ever seen, with graying hair parted in the middle and pulled back severely into a knot. Her face was long and rather equine, with a prognathous jaw and thin lips; her complexion was muddy, and her eyes were a watery color that he could not put a name to.

He chided himself: This was not some would-be debutante, but a woman in severe distress whose looks hardly mattered. And so he spoke to her gently, and said he hoped they were not intruding.

She did not seem to understand him. Shock, he thought; shock and stress, and very little sleep last night, more than likely.

Matron Pratt hadn't moved, but her rather threatening presence did not deter Caroline.

"Dear Agatha," she said, "can we not sit someplace and talk for a bit? I could use a cup of tea, and—"

Suddenly Miss Montgomery came back to them. "You must pardon me, Caroline," she said with an attempt at a smile. "I—we—have been—most upset."

"Of course you have," Caroline replied warmly. "I came as soon as I heard the news. I could hardly believe it."

"Come," said Miss Montgomery, "we will go into my private room. And, yes, tea is a good idea. Matron, would you have one of the girls bring us a tray?"

Glowering, Matron Pratt pinched her mouth into an even tighter line than before. "You should rest," she said. MacKenzie wondered at her tone: Was she in the habit of ordering Miss Montgomery about?

"I have done that," Miss Montgomery replied. "And now I will take tea with Miss Ames. And her friend," she added.

She led them past a door labeled Office and back along the hall. At the end was an arched doorway that gave onto a good-sized dining room, empty now, the long tables laid with places for the next meal. Opposite was an unmarked door, which Miss Montgomery opened.

"Oh!" She stopped short, nearly causing Caroline to collide with her. Then she advanced slowly into the room—a small, chilly parlor—and Caroline and MacKenzie followed.

A young woman had risen from a chair by the window. She was of medium height, plain—homely, even, and with her eyes reddened by weeping. In her dark dress and white apron, she was obviously a resident of the Bower. Caroline recognized her, in fact, as one of the girls in her Thursday afternoon sewing class. She nodded at Caroline, but she addressed herself to Miss Montgomery.

"Excuse me, miss," she began. "I know I shouldn't be here—"

"No, Brown, you certainly should not," Agatha Montgomery replied grimly. "Whatever are you thinking of?"

"I'm thinkin' of Mary, miss."

They were—had been—roommates, Caroline remembered.

"We are all thinking of Mary," Miss Montgomery replied a little more gently. "But you should not be breaking the rules—"

"I just wanted a word with you, miss."

Caroline knew this girl, Bridget Brown, as dutiful and humble, the way Bower girls were supposed to be, and never one to make trouble. She was amazed that Bridget had the gumption to stand up to Agatha Montgomery like this.

"As you see, I am occupied just now," Miss Montgomery said. "So go back to your class, and if Matron sees you and tries to give you a demerit, tell her I said you were to be let off this once."

But Bridget was not so easily disposed of. "I need to speak to you, miss," she said. Although her eyes were cast down in a properly subservient attitude, her voice was steady and determined.

The proprietress of the Bower stared at her for a moment as if she were weighing something in her mind. Then: "You may come to see me before supper," she said. "But for now, you must return to your class."

Uncomfortably aware that she, too, was probably breaking one or another of the Bower's many rules, Caroline stepped forward and put her arm around the girl to lead her away. "Dear Bridget," she murmured, "this is a terribly difficult time for you. I came here today to see if I could do anything to help Miss Montgomery"—they were in the hall now, and walking toward the stairs—"but if I can do anything for you, as well, or for any of the girls here, you must let me know."

Bridget stopped and stepped away from her to face her. "I don't know how I could do that, Miss Ames, seein' as how we aren't allowed to use the telephone." She nodded toward the instrument on the wall by the office door.

An indisputable point. "What did you want to ask Miss Montgomery?" Caroline said.

Bridget bit her lip. Then: "I wanted to ask her—somethin'." Bridget's eyes flashed up at Caroline; then she looked down again.

Something private, obviously. Caroline didn't know the girl well enough to press her further.

"All right, Bridget. As she told you, you may speak to her later. But before you go back to class, I want you to promise me that you won't leave the Bower until the police catch the man who—who killed Mary."

Bridget had gone very pale. "You mean, because he might get me too?"

"Yes. That is exactly what I mean." Caroline did not want to frighten Bridget more than she was already frightened, but she felt it was necessary to speak so, to keep her safe. "He might get any of you," she added. "So you must stay here. Will you promise me that?"

"Can't stay in all the time, Miss Ames. You could go crazy, stayin' in this place."

"Well, then, promise that you will go out only in the daytime—and not alone! You must always go with one or two other girls."

Bridget gave her a last, imploring look. She was crying again. Caroline thought she was about to say something more, but then, without replying—without promising what Caroline had asked of her—she turned and ran up the stairs. Poor thing, Caroline thought. She is grieving for her friend, and neither Agatha nor I can be of much help to her.

Agatha Montgomery's parlor was furnished in what looked like cast-off items—probably from some of the same benefactors who supported the place, Caroline thought as she rejoined the other two. Miss Montgomery motioned her visitors to sit on a worn horsehair sofa, while she took a wooden rocking chair.

"I apologize for that intrusion," she said. "Thank you, Caroline, for dealing with her. It was good of you to come. In my experience," she added with some bitterness, "people often turn away at the first sign of trouble."

"Dear Agatha, can you talk about it at all?" Caroline said gently.

Miss Montgomery shook her head. "It is very hard," she said, and they heard the catch in her voice.

"Yes. I know it is. But if you could—"

A rap on the door, and a girl came in bearing a tray. No hot-water jug, Caroline noted; the tea was already brewing in the pot, then. When Miss Montgomery did not move to pour, she rose and did so herself.

"Here," she said, handing a cup to her friend. "This will do you good."

Miss Montgomery took a few sips of the steaming brew and then, seeming somewhat revived, set her cup and saucer back onto the tray.

"You knew Mary," she said.

"A little. She was always in the office, so I didn't see her much. A slightly built girl, with brown hair and a pretty Irish face?"

"Yes." Miss Montgomery grimaced as if she were in pain. "Yes, she was pretty. And very slight indeed—seriously underweight—when we took her in. In fact, she was near death. She had pleurisy, and she could not draw a breath without agony. Under our care, and with Dr. Hannah's help, she revived."

"Dear Dr. Hannah," breathed Caroline.

"But even as sick as she was, I could see right away that she was different from the others," Miss Montgomery went on. She paused to take a handkerchief from her cuff and dab at her watery eyes. "She was really quite bright, and surprisingly well spoken. She was about nineteen or twenty, but she seemed younger—hardly more than a child."

"And so after she had stayed her three months—" Caroline prompted.

"I asked her to stay on, to be my secretary. I had been managing without one, but the work never lets up, and I really thought I could not go on unless I had help. I asked Randolph about it, of course, because he oversees the budget and I needed his permission to pay Mary a small salary. It wasn't much—not nearly what she was worth." Miss Montgomery paused again and thought for a moment, lost in her memories.

Then she went on. "Eventually, Randolph came to see what a good investment it was. He even came to the point of offering to buy us a typewriting machine. All the most forward-looking businesses use them, and she was eager to learn. He'd bought her an instruction manual, and she was studying it. Oh, she was a wonderful girl! I cannot understand why—"

She broke off, and there was another pause. MacKenzie shifted uncomfortably on the hard sofa. Undoubtedly because of the weather, he thought, his knee had begun to ache.

Miss Montgomery began to speak again. "Last night, even though it was Sunday, Mary said she would work in the office to bring the account books up-to-date. Matron had gone to her regular Sunday evening religious service over on Columbus Avenue—with a Mrs. Mary Baker Eddy, do you know her?—and I was at evening prayers at Trinity Church in Copley Square. Miss Cox had come in to mind the girls, as she does when both Mrs. Pratt and I are out.

"I got back shortly before nine. The house was quiet. I did not see Matron, but I did not expect to because her Sunday evenings generally last until ten. Miss Cox gave her report—all was well, she said—and I said good night to her and she left. All the girls were asleep upstairs—or in their rooms, at any rate. The office was dark, so I assumed that Mary had finished her work and had gone to bed."

She paused, as if to gather her strength. They waited silently, caught up now in the drama of her story.

She went on: "So, seeing nothing amiss, I went to my room at the top of the house. I never heard Matron come in, and I was asleep when the policeman came. It was Officer Flynn, our neighborhood patrolman."

She drew a ragged breath, and when she spoke again it was haltingly, as if she were having to force out the words. "Matron came to wake me at once, of course. She said he wanted me to go with him. He would not tell her why, but somehow I knew it was some terrible trouble.

"I dressed as quickly as I could, and we hurried over toward Warren Avenue. As I came near, I saw three or four carriages—police vehicles, and a long black wagon. There were lanterns and torches, so that the place was brightly lighted. Over and over again, I asked Officer Flynn why he had come for me, but he would not tell me. Yet all the while, I knew—not that it was Mary, but that it was one of our girls, and some harm had come to her."

Her voice broke then, and with a great shudder she put her hands over her face while she choked back her sobs.

Caroline made small soothing noises to comfort her, and MacKenzie waited, uncomfortable as men always were in the presence of women's tears. Perhaps she should not go on, he thought, but as it was not his place to suggest it, he trusted in Caroline's judgment as to how much more emotional turmoil her friend might be able to endure.

Miss Montgomery, somewhat recovered, went on: "There was a crowd gathered at the entrance to the alley behind West Brookline Street. When I reached it, I saw another little group halfway down, four or five men and something lying on the ground. It was covered with some dark drapery, a blanket perhaps. When I approached the men, one of them spoke to me and introduced himself as Inspector Crippen."

"Yes," Caroline interjected. "I know him."

"You do?" Miss Montgomery seemed momentarily surprised—startled out of her grim recital.

"Yes. My brother—but never mind that. Go on. You were in the alley with the police?"

"Yes. It seemed that I had been summoned because a body—and that is what it was, a body—had been discovered by Officer Flynn. At first he thought it was a bundle of rags, but then he saw a shoe protruding and he realized it was the body of a woman. He recognized her as one of our girls. So he sent for help, and they told him to fetch me to give positive identification."

Her voice trailed off, and for a moment her face went slack with the memory of what she had seen. Caroline pictured it: the dark, the rain, torches and lanterns flickering in the raw night wind, the little circle of men's faces peering down at the girl's body. And poor Agatha, called out on such a dreadful errand . . .

"She had been badly cut up," Miss Montgomery went on. "Her dress was slashed to ribbons. Underneath it I could see her terrible wounds. The rain had washed away her blood, but the puddles by her side were dark with it. I never thought a human body could contain so much blood. Oh, it was horrible! Horrible! That poor girl! She didn't have an enemy in the world. Unless it was someone from the streets she came from, someone from her past. Or—some madman." Piteously, she looked at Caroline. "Yes, it must have been that. Some madman. Some lunatic, killing poor Mary and not even knowing who she was."

"Obviously, anyone who would commit such a crime—such a savage crime—was not in command of his faculties," Caroline replied. She did not want to seem callous, but— "Agatha, do you have any idea why Mary went out last night?"

"No. None."

"It is very odd, don't you think? Since she had said she would work in the office, and she was such a dependable girl?"

"Yes. It is odd. I can't think why—"

"And Miss Cox never mentioned that Mary had gone out?"

"No. She had the girls in Bible study"—a weekly undertaking, Caroline knew, mandatory for all residents but not, apparently, for Mary—"and when she left, she would have seen that the office light was not on, and she would have thought—just as I did—that Mary had finished her work and gone to bed."

Caroline cast a warning glance at MacKenzie. She didn't want him tattling to Addington about what she intended to say next.

"Agatha, perhaps we can help you. To find out why Mary left. To talk to the girls, perhaps, and ask—"

"No." Suddenly Miss Montgomery stopped weeping. She made a final swipe at her reddened eyes, blinked rapidly, and took a deep breath. "No, Caroline, it was more than kind of you to come, but you have your own affairs to tend to. The police will manage well enough, I imagine."

"Yes, but—"

"No. I insist. You must not trouble yourself anymore." She stood and walked to the window, moving stiffly, as if her bones ached, thought MacKenzie. In her dark, shapeless dress, lacking a bustle or nipped-in waist, lacking any kind of ornament, she seemed even taller, more gaunt than before. "It is still raining hard," she said. "I will send one of the girls to fetch a herdic for you."

"Then at least come to us for the night," Caroline persisted. "It would be no trouble at all. We could put you on the fourth floor and we have the elevator so you will be spared the stairs—"

"No." Miss Montgomery turned to face them, and now MacKenzie saw what he had not seen before, the strong-minded female who had brought this place—this refuge for fallen women—into being. "No," she repeated less vehemently. "You must go home, and I—I must deal with matters here."

Caroline made one last try. "Surely Mrs. Pratt can deal with any emergency—any further emergency—and she can send a telegram to you at our house if you should be needed."

"You do not subscribe to the telephone?"

"No. We have talked about it, but—no, we do not." So far, Ames had won, and a subscription had not been taken.

"Well, then," said Miss Montgomery, as if that settled the matter: If the Ameses had no telephone, she could not possibly stay with them. With somber courtesy, she held out her hand to MacKenzie. "Good day to you, Doctor," she said. And to Caroline: "You have been more than kind to come. But now, if you will excuse me, I must see to my girls."

CHAPTER
4

MACKENZIE'S SHATTERED KNEE, OPERATED ON IN LATE SEPtember, had healed well until November, when his recuperation had had a temporary setback in the business of the death of Colonel Mann. Now, in January, he still occasionally awoke in the morning to find that his knee had stiffened, making it difficult to navigate the stairs.

On those days he went down to breakfast in the elevator. Like all machinery, it made its own peculiar noises. He had come to expect them whenever he stepped in and pushed the brass handle either right or left, depending on whether he wanted to go up or down. Now, on the morning after his visit to Bertram's Bower, when he pulled shut the grille and grasped the handle to push it to the left, down, there was a heart-stopping pause—a hesitation that had never happened before. He was just about to let go of the handle and step out, when the elevator started its descent. But its soft moan and wheeze sounded different this day: more strained, somehow.

Nevertheless, since he had started to go down, he had to keep his grip on the handle or he would stop between floors. So down he went, past the second floor, where he could have alighted had he had second sight.

When the cab had just passed the second floor, the machinery shuddered to a stop. Here between floors it was gloomy despite the leaded glass skylight that topped the shaft; the cab's brass grille all around allowed a little more light to come from the stairwell. Still, it was pretty dim.

Worse, the elevator, great convenience though it was, was a space no bigger than four feet by four feet, and perhaps seven feet high. It was a small space to be confined in, particularly for someone like himself, who suffered from a mild form of claustrophobia.

This is a pretty pickle, he thought. After a moment, not knowing what else to do, he called, "Ames! Are you there?"

He heard Ames come out of the dining room and into the first floor hall. "Halloo! Was that you calling, Doctor?"

MacKenzie could hear him clearly; had Ames been on the stairs, he could have seen him through the grille.

"I'm afraid the thing has gotten stuck," he called. "I'm not sure what to do."

"Don't do anything! You might disrupt the machinery and go crashing down. Damn! Caro's down in the kitchen with Cook. Just wait a minute—"

It was Caroline who was the elevator expert, since she had had to learn the idiosyncrasies of the thing in the course of attending to her mother during that lady's illness. She had given MacKenzie a thorough course of instruction not only on how to operate it but also on its little quirks.

He tried to remember, now, precisely what she had said. "If you feel it start to shudder too badly" (he thought she'd said that) "you must grip the handle—so—and pull it neither left nor right but toward you. And if it starts to drop too quickly, push this button"—a large white ceramic thing above the lever with the word BRAKE embossed upon it. Installed next to it was what looked like an oversized red china doorknob that she had made no mention of, or if she had, he had forgotten what it was. "And if it stops altogether—I mean between floors, where it is not supposed to—then do—"

What? He racked his brain. Her other instructions he thought he remembered, but this most crucial one he could not recall.

He stood frozen in fear. What if the damnable thing dropped straight down to the basement, collapsing into a crumpled heap of brass and wood? He did not dare to touch either the handle-lever or the big white ceramic BRAKE button. He contemplated the large red—for emergencies?—knob, but he was even less inclined to touch that unknown. He could only stand stiffly, his knee throbbing, and wait for his rescue.

"Hold on! Don't panic!" called Ames. He was on the stairs now, right outside the cab. He himself never used the elevator; he didn't trust it, and incidents like this only confirmed his suspicions. "We'll have you out in no time. Are you all right?"

MacKenzie said he was, although in truth he was not sure.

"Good. Good. Now I am going to go down to the kitchen and fetch Caroline—ah! There she is now."

And he pounded down to the front hall, calling to his sister as he went.

In a moment she was there, speaking to MacKenzie from the stairway; he could see her through the grille. She gave him the crucial instruction—the one he had forgotten—and in no more than a minute or two he was safely downstairs.

"What a fright!" Caroline exclaimed as he emerged, shaken, from the elevator cab. "My dear Dr. MacKenzie! Such a dreadful experience! Thank goodness you don't have a weak heart! I am going to write out all the instructions for every conceivable occurrence, and post them inside the elevator so this will never happen to you again."

Flexing his knee a bit, he assured her that no harm had been done, and they proceeded into the dining room. He heard the dumbwaiter thumping and creaking in the back hall, and then Margaret appeared bearing the breakfast tray. What he needed, he thought, was a cup of strong black coffee to repair his nerves; the oatmeal that was their standard fare except on Saturdays, when they had bacon and eggs, seemed singularly unappetizing just now.

The morning *Globe* lay at Ames's place at the head of the table, and MacKenzie could see a bold black headline. Now

Ames picked it up, started to hand it to his sister, and then hesitated.

She had seated herself and was pouring his tea. "Here you are, Addington. Why—what is it? What is wrong?"

"More bad news for Miss Montgomery, I am afraid."

She put down the teapot and stared at him. "Oh, no. What is it?"

"Another girl from the Bower has been killed. And in the same way."

"Oh, *no.*"

MacKenzie thought he heard tears in her voice. For the moment she'd forgotten him, so he poured his own coffee. After a few sips, he felt much better.

She put out her hand and Ames gave her the newspaper. Rapidly she scanned it, uttering little exclamations of dismay as she did so.

"This is terrible, Addington."

"Did you know this girl?"

"Bridget Brown. Yes. She was in my Thursday class. She was quiet, never offensive. In fact, we saw her yesterday afternoon. Do you remember, Doctor? She was the girl who wanted to speak to Agatha. I made her promise she wouldn't leave the Bower after dark—and never alone. But she must have gone out, after all, and—" She broke off, trying to acknowledge to herself the horror of what had happened.

Then: "Oh, poor Agatha! After all these years, when she has worked so hard to make the Bower a respectable place—"

"It is not her fault that some madman is loose in the district, Caroline."

"No. Of course it isn't. But you know how people are. After this, when they think of Bertram's Bower they will think of these hideous crimes. They won't stop to consider— Oh, Addington, this will be the ruination of the Bower! People will never support it if it is associated with scandal like this. Agatha will have to give it up, and all her years and years of good work will have been for nothing!"

"From what you told me of your visit to her yesterday, she seems to be holding up fairly well."

"Yes, but that was before—before this second death."
She stared at him with anguished eyes.

He put out his hand and she gave the newspaper back to
him. Watching her across the table, MacKenzie could see
that she was struggling to contain her tears. Absently, he began to pull at one end of his mustache, a habit he had when
he was unnerved.

At length, composing herself, she rose, helped herself to
oatmeal, and returned to the table where, MacKenzie was glad
to see, she began to eat. After a moment she said, "Addington."

"Yes?" He did not look up at her. According to the
Globe's account, Deputy Chief Inspector Elwood Crippen
was assuring the public that the perpetrator of these atrocious crimes would soon be caught. People need have no
fear for their safety, but in the meantime, while the hunt was
on, he cautioned them, particularly females, to avoid walking alone at night in the South End.

Crippen. He felt a little shiver of distaste as he called up
into his mind's eye the image of the officious little policeman. Caroline was right: Crippen would bungle this case for
certain. Too quick to make an arrest, too quick to jump to
unfounded conclusions . . .

"Bridget Brown was Mary Flaherty's roommate," Caroline said.

He looked up. "I beg your pardon?"

"I said, 'Bridget Brown was Mary Flaherty's roommate.' "

"Are you sure?"

"Of course I'm sure! Otherwise I wouldn't say so. Don't
you think that is significant?"

He thought about it. "It might be, yes."

"And what did she want to speak to Agatha about, I
wonder." Her face suddenly became animated. "Addington,
we must help Agatha. Really we must."

He contemplated her from beneath his dark brows. His
look was stern, but MacKenzie thought he saw in it some
hint of apprehension.

"And how are we to do that?"

"I don't know. How would I know? You can go to the

Bower—go to Inspector Crippen, for that matter. Offer to help him."

"He does not look kindly on my help, Caro. You know that."

She waved her hand in irritation. "Nonsense. He is often mistaken, but he is not a fool. If you can save him from making a serious mistake—as you have done twice before—"

"And do not forget Cousin Wainwright," Ames added. That worthy, a cousin on their mother's side, sat on the board of police commissioners. He was jealous of the authority of the police and did not welcome unasked-for assistance from outside the ranks.

"Oh, Cousin Wainwright!" Caroline exclaimed. "He cannot possibly object to your talking to Inspector Crippen, or even visiting the Bower."

"Caroline, we cannot intrude ourselves into this case," Ames said flatly. He handed the newspaper to MacKenzie and rose to get his oatmeal from the sideboard.

His sister made no reply, but MacKenzie noted her rather alarming expression. Had he been asked to describe it, he would have said that it was one of mulish stubbornness. It did not quite fit with his image of her as the Angel of the Hearth, compliant always to the wishes of her older brother.

Ames returned to the table and began to eat. Caroline watched him for a moment, and then she said, "Remember Agatha's father, Addington."

"What about him?"

"Don't you remember that our own papa thought very highly of him? They were friends for years."

"Yes. I know."

"And before Mr. Montgomery went bankrupt, I believe I am right when I say that one time he helped Papa through some business difficulty. I don't know the details—Mama did not either, but she once told me—"

"Caroline." Ames had stopped eating, but he still held his spoon. "Listen to me."

"Yes, Addington, I am listening," she said, but her expression did not change.

"There have been two atrocious murders over in the South End. Both victims were residents of Bertram's Bower. The police have begun their investigation. I have no doubt that soon enough they will find their man. You and I"—and here he spoke with unusual sternness—"have no business interfering."

"How can it be interfering, simply to—"

"None," he snapped. "As regrettable an affair as this is, it is none of ours. I would ask you to remember that."

For a moment she held his gaze; then she looked down at her half-eaten oatmeal congealing in its dish.

"I have no time today or tomorrow," she said at last, "because of my dinner party. I cannot even attend Sewing Circle this morning. But after tomorrow evening I will be free to—"

"Don't say it," he warned, scowling at her.

"I will say it. Agatha is my friend. I have known her all my life. I work at the Bower two afternoons a month, as I have done ever since she started it. I have watched her build the Bower from a rented apartment into that entire house, which they were able to buy because of her brother's skill at fund-raising. That was a tremendous achievement, to buy that place. Think of it, Addington—think of how they have worked over the years. And now Agatha is in trouble. Through no fault of her own, but serious trouble all the same. What would you have me do? Turn my back on her? Refuse to help her?"

"Of course not, but—"

"Then you agree that I must do what I can."

"You must do nothing, Caroline. I forbid you."

She lifted her chin. Not an Angel of the Hearth, MacKenzie thought, but a warrior princess from some ancient myth. He had admired her tremendously from the day he'd met her, and never more than at this moment.

"Of course, what I can do is very little," she went on as if she had not heard her brother's last words, "compared to what you might accomplish. I—well, you know how people hate pushy, forward women. Agatha herself has often been accused of being forward, but really it is just her sense of mission that drives her. While I—well, I have never had much to be pushy about, have I?"

"Fortunately," Ames muttered.

For a long moment she contemplated him. Then: "I really do think you should go to see Inspector Crippen."

"And tell him what?"

"You don't have to *tell* him anything. But you might *ask* how the case is progressing."

"And what about Cousin Wainwright?"

"You probably won't see him, but if you do, send him to me. I will deal with him."

Ames could not repress a smile. He was four years older than she; he could remember the day she'd been born. From that day, he had been brought up to care for her as a gentleman should care for his sister, to protect her, cherish her, keep her from all that was sordid and vile in the world. He had done so as well as he could. It was not his fault that she had inherited the family stubbornness and, worse, its stern New England conscience that sometimes prompted her to act rashly for what she considered good cause.

"All right, Caroline." He shook his head. "I will go to see Crippen, and for your sake as well as Miss Montgomery's I will try not to antagonize him too greatly."

CHAPTER
5

HALF AN HOUR LATER, AMES AND MACKENZIE MADE THEIR way along Louisburg Square to Mt. Vernon Street and up Mt. Vernon to Joy. The rain had stopped during the night, but still the morning was damp and gray, the air filled with the sour salt smell of the sea. The redbrick town houses that lined the way, with their shining black or white doors, their brass door knockers, their shuttered windows, did not glow today as they did in the sun. The city had an air of grim expectation, as if it waited for the thaw to pass and winter to return.

"He'll be annoyed," said Ames, lifting his hat to a woman passing.

"I imagine he will," MacKenzie replied. He had met Crippen the previous autumn and had not liked him—not least because the man had seemed to want to pay suit to Caroline Ames.

"Still, Caroline is right," Ames went on. They trod carefully along Joy Street, down the steeply sloping sidewalk that led to Beacon; the bricks were slick with the wet, and often uneven. "She is very loyal, my sister. And it is true that Agatha Montgomery has devoted her life to her flock over at the Bower. It is too bad that it might all come to nothing now because of some madman."

They came out to Boston Common, dull and dreary on this dull and dreary day, tall, leafless elms lining the walkways, the grass dead and brown and patched with soot-blackened snow. Few pedestrians were about. There was skating on the Frog Pond in winter, but now the ice had melted and signs were posted warning would-be skaters away. Beyond the treetops, the tall spire of the Park Street Church rose into the pale gray sky.

They walked up the hill past the gold-domed redbrick State House, and down again past the forbidding brownstone exterior of the Boston Athenaeum. The morning traffic was heavy, carts and wagons and carriages and herdic-phaetons all jostling for passage. At the foot of Beacon Street, they had some difficulty, but then they were across, passing the oddly truncated King's Chapel and mounting the broad granite steps of the ornate Second Empire City Hall, going through the tall oak double doors and entering the hushed, thrumming atmosphere of the city's municipal offices.

They went up to the second floor, down a corridor, and into Crippen's lair.

"Not in, sir," said the young man guarding the inner office door.

"Really?" said Ames. "And when might he be?"

"Not for a while, I'm—"

The door opened and Crippen appeared. "Davis, did you find— Ah! Mr. Ames!"

He had been frowning at first, but now, seeing Ames, a smile spread over his ugly little face, and he held out his pudgy hand, its fingers stained with nicotine.

"Good morning, Inspector."

"And to what do I owe this pleasure?" Crippen said, shaking Ames's hand vigorously. He was short and plump, nattily dressed in a rather common way in a brown checkered suit, yellow vest, and a cravat in a particularly hideous shade of green. His watch chain, stretched across his paunch, looked as though it needed a few extra links. Although his clean-shaven face looked young, and was surprisingly unlined for a man in his position, his hair was gray.

MacKenzie, understanding that their dislike was mutual, did not offer to shake Crippen's hand.

"I merely wanted a word," said Ames.

"Ah! A word! Come in, come in." Crippen was all smiles, forgetting what he had been about to ask his clerk.

MacKenzie followed Ames into the inspector's crowded little office, and they seated themselves on rickety wooden chairs before the overladen desk.

"It's about these murders over in the South End," Ames began, removing his hat and gloves and placing them on his knees.

"The South End," Crippen repeated.

"Yes. The girls from Bertram's Bower."

"Bertram's Bower," Crippen repeated.

You are stalling, MacKenzie thought, and that means you have made no progress in the case.

"A couple of Irish streetwalkers," Crippen said. "I don't see—"

"The proprietress there is a great friend of my sister's, and as you can imagine, she—Miss Montgomery—is extremely distressed."

Crippen pursed his lips. "And well she should be, Mr. Ames. Well she should be. But we'll have the matter cleared up quick enough, seeing as how she's got a likely suspect under her own roof, so to speak."

"You don't say. Under her own roof?"

"That's right. Of course, we can't make an arrest yet, haven't got our case complete. But we have it well in hand, Mr. Ames. You can tell your sister I said so." Suddenly, alarmingly, he leered at them; a revolting sight, MacKenzie thought. "And how is she? Recovering well?"

"Perfectly well, thank you."

"I am going to call on her one of these days, you know."

"You are welcome at tea any afternoon, Inspector."

"Is that so? Well, now, I just might turn up sometime. You can tell her that too."

Ames cleared his throat. "About your suspect, Inspector?"

"Ah. Yes. Well, we must bide our time a bit. He'll come walking into our arms one of these days, and sooner rather than later, I should think."

"Indeed? But he must be some kind of madman, if the newspaper accounts were correct. Have you found the weapon?"

"Not yet."

"Some kind of knife—"

"Yes."

"There must have been a good deal of blood, from what I gathered from the account in the newspaper."

"Not really. There was severe mutilation of the lower abdomen, true enough, but—"

"Like the first girl, the night before," Ames interjected.

Crippen frowned. "How did you know that? It wasn't in the papers."

"As I told you, my sister is a friend of Miss Montgomery's. She went to the Bower yesterday afternoon, as soon as she saw the news. How did you manage to keep it from the early editions, by the way?"

Crippen grunted. "With difficulty, Mr. Ames. With difficulty. Those newspaper fellows would run over their own grandmothers to get a story ahead of the competition. Anyways, where was I?"

"You were saying there wasn't much blood. Because of the rain, I take it."

"Right. It was cats and dogs all night—and the night before as well. And besides, the fellow knew his business. He strangled 'em—garotted 'em—before he cut them up. So they didn't bleed as much as they would have otherwise."

"And the knife was some kind of hunting knife, or fish fillet—?"

"From what we can tell, in both cases it was a blade about one inch wide, six inches long. Probably a common kitchen knife. The Bower's cook says just such a knife is missing."

"But no idea who might have taken it?"

"Not yet."

"And it would be easy to dispose of."

"That's right. We searched the alleys thereabouts, and the train yards, but I doubt we'll find it. My guess is, by now it's at the bottom of the Charles."

"You have spoken to the residents of the Bower?"

"Naturally. I myself interrogated a dozen—ah—females there, and my men questioned everyone else."

"And what did you conclude?"

"Nothing, for the moment. These things take time. We don't want to arrest the wrong person and have the right one get away, now, do we? I will tell you one thing, however. Mind, it's strictly against the rules—but you say you are acquainted with Miss Montgomery? And her brother also, the Reverend Randolph Montgomery?"

"Yes. You have questioned him?"

"He was here earlier. He gave us some interesting information."

"About—"

"About an Irish boy who works at the Bower."

"Oh? And what did he say?"

"That it would be well to keep an eye on him, the Irish being what they are. And considering what the medical examiner has just put on my desk"—he lifted a sheet of paper and let it drop again onto its pile—"the Reverend Montgomery may be right."

"Why?"

"One of those girls was in the family way."

"You don't say. Which one?"

"Mary Flaherty."

"The first one to be killed."

"That's right."

"How far along was she?"

"About three months."

Ames thought for a moment. The police department's medical examiner was a thorough, meticulous man, a swamp Yankee from Worcester. He'd been with the department for nearly twenty years, and Ames knew the police took some pride in the fact that Boston had been one of the first cities in America to have its own forensic physician. "That is, of course, very interesting," he said, "and in a way it might simplify the case."

"Precisely."

"You suspect the Irish boy was—ah—intimate with her?"

"Yes."

"Do you have any information about her other than that she was a resident of the Bower? Anything about her family?"

"No. Most of them are from out of town, those—ah—women. They have no family here."

"Well, then, what about her friendship with the second girl—Bridget Brown?"

"How do you mean?"

"They were roommates."

"I know that."

MacKenzie detected a note of irritation in the inspector's voice, as if he thought Ames was wasting his time by giving him information that he already had.

"My men are right on top of this case," Crippen went on, "but even so, we have a good deal to see to otherwise. That North End gang, for instance. We've been tailing them for the past three years. They don't know it, but they are about to be brought to heel."

"I am glad to hear it," Ames replied easily, and, in an aside to MacKenzie: "The inspector refers to a gang of roughnecks, Irish boys. What do they call themselves, Inspector? The Copp's Hill Boys? Yes. They are a scourge upon the city, and we will be well rid of them. They have nothing to do with this case—right, Inspector?—but still, we will be happy to see them gone, once and for all."

Not for the first time, MacKenzie noted that when Ames spoke of Boston, he did so in a proprietary way, as if the city were his own personal responsibility, as if it needed him to tend to it, to keep it running smoothly. It was not surprising, he reflected, given that Ames's ancestors had been among the first settlers of the place, centuries ago, when they'd come over on the *Arbella* with John Winthrop. Caroline had told him that an Ames had lived in Boston ever since, and had been able to show him on a map exactly where.

"But to come back to the Bower," Ames went on. "The

second victim—Bridget Brown—was not—ah—in a similar condition?"

"No."

"But killed in the same way."

"That's right. Garotted, then cut up."

"Were there signs of a struggle?"

"Now, that's an odd thing, Mr. Ames. No sign at all. She was lying in a puddle—the drains in those alleys aren't kept as clean as they should be—but flat out on her back."

"And what do you make of that?"

"That she was killed elsewhere and dumped in the alley."

"I see."

"Usually in violent killings like these, you get some indication that the victim tried to defend herself. Superficial wounds on the hands and arms, and so forth. But since they were both strangled first, we didn't have that here."

"And what do you deduce from that?"

"Hard to say. I remember four or five years ago—not my case—a woman killed her husband over in the West End. Big brute of a thing, he was. She got him quiet by using chloroform on him first, to put him unconscious before she finished him off."

"And did you find any trace of chloroform on either of these girls?"

"No. But it's hard to find that anyway. It evaporates quickly, leaves no trace. And with all the rain to wash it away—but it's a possibility. 'Course, since he strangled 'em, he didn't need to chloroform 'em as well, did he?"

"It would seem not," Ames said. He stood up. "You have been very helpful, Inspector. We will not take up any more of your valuable time—"

"Wait!" Crippen exclaimed. "I almost forgot. One more thing. Have a look at this. If you hadn't come in, I'd have brought it around to you myself."

He pulled out a drawer from the oak file cabinet behind him and extracted something. Handing it to Ames across the desk, he said, "Damned strange, isn't it?"

It was a sheet of rough paper, creased where it had been

folded. Upon it were pasted cut-out, printed letters. Ames read:

VPZRYPMOHJYROHJYDJSTQYRAAMPPMR

"Well?" said Crippen impatiently. "What do you make of it?"

"Nothing, for the moment," Ames replied, handing the paper to MacKenzie. "What is its provenance?"

"Beg pardon?"

"I mean, where did you find it?"

"Oh! Yes, that's important. We found it on Mary Flaherty."

"Ah. She was clutching it?" But no, he thought, the rain would have disintegrated it.

"In the pocket of her skirt."

"And you have put your cryptanalysts right onto it, I assume?"

Crippen threw him a disdainful glance. "There's no money in the budget for cryptanalysts, Mr. Ames. That's why I thought you might like to have a look at it. You told me once that a lot of your friends over the river know strange languages. I thought perhaps you might recognize this, or that one of them might."

"That is possible," said Ames. "I will certainly have a go at it." He took out his small Morocco leather notebook and, retrieving the paper from MacKenzie, copied the letters.

"And if you can make anything of it—" Crippen said.

"Certainly, Inspector. I will notify you at once. I have your permission to show this to Professor Harbinger? He is a brilliant linguist, among his other talents."

"Does he know Gaelic?"

"Gaelic? I don't know. Why? Ah! The Irish connection."

"That's right. Well, see what you can do with it, in any case. If it isn't Gaelic, it may not be of any use to us."

CHAPTER
6

A SHORT WHILE LATER, ON NEWSPAPER ROW AT THE FOOT OF School Street, Ames and MacKenzie walked along until they came to a narrow doorway that gave onto a steep flight of stairs. At the top, down a corridor, Ames opened a door whose lettering announced the BOSTON LITERARY JOURNAL. MacKenzie knew the place, had been here before: It was the office of Ames's good friend, the proprietor of the publication, Desmond Delahanty.

"Desmond!" Ames exclaimed as they went in. They were in a small, cluttered office with every surface piled high with papers that looked like manuscripts. Behind a desk, one foot slung on its littered surface, sat a man with very red hair worn long over his collar, and a mustache whose ends drooped down near his jawline.

"Ames!" Delahanty replied, equally enthusiastic. He rose, threw down whatever it was he'd been reading, and held out his hand. "And Dr. MacKenzie—good to see you."

He was slightly shorter than Ames but equally thin, with bright blue eyes, an Irishman's beguiling smile, and a brogue to match. MacKenzie had known Irishmen in the army, but never one so charming.

"What brings you slumming?" Delahanty said with a grin. "D'you want to make me a present of some literary endeavor?"

Ames snorted. "Hardly. I want to exploit you, Desmond—and your connections."

"My connections?" Delahanty looked around in mock puzzlement. "And what might those be?"

Ames did not reply at once. He picked up a neatly bound periodical from one of the tables and waved it at his friend. "The new issue?"

"Dummy copy. And only a month late."

"Anything good in it?" Ames was a subscriber; every now and again he found something interesting.

"A story by a young lady that isn't bad."

"Not the young lady with the illegible handwriting?" Ames said, smiling. Delahanty was often besieged by hopeful scribblers, male and female alike, whose persistence mounted in inverse ratio to their literary talents.

"No." Delahanty rolled his eyes. "I haven't seen her since before Christmas, thank God. I think I finally managed to discourage her. Told her to take up some other interest, like decoupage or Berlin needlework."

Ames laughed, but then suddenly he sobered. "I have a more serious business, Desmond," he said. "The murder of the girls at the Bower."

"Ah."

"Miss Montgomery, the proprietress, is a friend of Caroline's."

"I see."

"Caroline holds to the belief that one must help one's friends when trouble comes. And so now she has it in her head that we must help Miss Montgomery by attempting to . . ."

To what? Find the madman who had murdered, in the most hideous fashion, two of the Bower's girls?

Crippen's ugly little face rose up in his mind's eye, and he went on. "To find who might be responsible for the deaths. Crippen is heading up the investigation," he added as if in explanation.

Delahanty nodded. "Your sister is a loyal friend."

"Loyal—yes. And perhaps rather foolish. But she maintains

that if the murderer is not caught—if, God forbid, more girls are killed—the Bower will suffer."

"Yes. Well, she is right about that, I'd say. And of course my fellow journalists hereabouts make as much sensation as they can out of such matters. Anything to sell their rags."

"Both those girls were Irish, Desmond."

"That they were." Delahanty's eyes were suddenly cold.

"We visited Inspector Crippen just now over at police headquarters, and I had the distinct impression that he has not put their deaths at the top of his agenda."

"Because they were Irish girls," Delahanty said. He glanced at MacKenzie. "To be Irish in Boston, Doctor," he went on, exaggerating his accent, "is to be less than human. It is the NINA effect. I'm sure you've seen it. 'No Irish Need Apply'—a motto found in every help wanted advertisement, every position listed at every Intelligence Office—"

Ames held up his hand. He had been friends—good friends—with this particular Irishman since they had met five years before. He did not need yet another of Delahanty's sermons on the iniquities of Anglo-Saxon Boston.

"Yes, Desmond," he said. "I imagine that is so—because they were Irish girls."

Delahanty waited.

"And so," Ames went on smoothly, "I thought perhaps— I don't suppose you knew them yourself, but I thought perhaps you might know someone who does. Did," he corrected himself.

"I might." Delahanty nodded. "Yes, in fact, I'm sure I do. My friend Martin Sweeney runs the Green Harp Saloon down on Atlantic Avenue. He knows nearly every Irish family in Boston."

"Crippen believes the girls came from elsewhere."

"Even so. They may have had some connection to the Irish community here, and if they did, Martin will know of it—or he will know of someone who does."

"Excellent. What do you say to lunch at Durgin-Park, and then perhaps you will be good enough to introduce us to this Martin Sweeney?"

Delahanty looked around his cluttered little office. "I don't—"

"Oh, come on, man," Ames said, reading his friend's thoughts. "It will do you good to get out for a bit. And if you have lunch at Durgin-Park, you won't need to bother with dinner. Unless they've shortened their portions since the last time I was there."

The Durgin-Park Market Dining Rooms opposite the Quincy Market were always busy at noontime: men from the neighboring financial district, seamen on leave, traveling salesmen—"drummers"—in town for a little recreation. There was no individual seating here; customers sat at long, communal tables and suffered the slings and arrows of the outrageously rude waiters whose insufferable manners were part of the attraction of the place, as Ames had explained to MacKenzie on their first visit some weeks before.

This day, the place was crowded as always, the waiters as harried and rude as ever as they dashed back and forth from the kitchen bearing platters of Yankee pot roast and boiled scrod and Indian pudding. The noise precluded any further conversation about Bertram's Bower or anything else, so Ames and his companions devoted themselves to their food—a bargain at fifty cents for the pot roast, less for the scrod—and in good time, well fed, stood outside once more in the busy Haymarket.

"Shall we call on your friend Sweeney?" Ames asked Delahanty, stepping out of the way of a farmer's wagon navigating the straw-strewn cobblestones. Behind them, the domed granite market building loomed into the rainy sky. Directly in front of them was the redbrick Faneuil Hall with its gilded cricket weathervane; farther on was Scollay Square and its notorious, illicit entertainments.

Delahanty waved down a herdic, and soon they were making their tortuous way through the city's narrow, crooked streets. The horse was balked at almost every corner, and more than once they heard the driver cursing, not at his horse but at the malign Fates that seemed to rule the city's traffic.

At last, however, they came to the waterfront, the neighborhood of Sweeney's saloon. It was only mid-afternoon, but the early winter darkness was fast coming on. In the rain, the streetlamps, sparsely spaced out, gave off a pale, ghostly glimmer. Faint gleams from the cab's sidelights glistened on the wet cobblestones, and the odor of the sea filled the air. Over the clop-clop of the horse's hooves came the melancholy clang of bell buoys in the harbor. Gone was the cozy residential neighborhood of Beacon Hill, the bustling streets of downtown. MacKenzie could see only the black hulks of warehouses and chandleries, the grim establishments of any working waterfront. Opposite the long row of their forbidding exteriors were the wharves and docks, and the bowsprits of fishing smacks tied up prow to street, arching over the heads of the occasional passersby on the sidewalk. Every so often they saw the dimly lit sign of a place like Sweeney's.

A little hush fell over the crowd as they entered, and MacKenzie was made uncomfortably aware that he and Ames, at least, were aliens.

"Martin, my friend!" Delahanty cried as he led the way to the long, polished mahogany bar. Behind it stood a tall, stout, gray-haired man wearing a spotless white shirt with sleeve garters, and an equally spotless white apron over his trousers. He nodded at Delahanty, but he did not smile.

"Desmond. It's been a good long while, man, since you've shown your face to us."

"Yes, well, I have a demanding profession that never lets me rest. But today I have brought you two new customers. Gentlemen, what is your pleasure?"

Ames and MacKenzie, introduced to the barkeep, ordered Guinness Stout, and Delahanty did the same. As they made themselves a little place to stand at the bar, talk rose up around them again; still, MacKenzie had the uncomfortable sensation that they were being watched. Like explorers coming into a native village, he thought, we are indelibly marked as outsiders.

Delahanty, however, proved to be a man of two worlds,

comfortable in both. In a little while he had chatted up his friend to the point where the saloon proprietor, poker-faced at first, actually gave Ames and MacKenzie a small, grudging smile.

"Oh, yes," he said. "I know Bertram's Bower."

"Do you indeed?" said Delahanty. "Might you know anyone there who could be of assistance to Mr. Ames?"

Sweeney observed them for a moment, his smile vanished. Then: "I know a lad who works there. A handyman, like. Jack of all trades. He comes here nights to help out, when he can."

Delahanty's thin face brightened. "Does he indeed? And who might that be?"

"Garrett O'Reilly. I've known his ma since she stepped off the boat, and that was twenty-five years ago if it's a day. Used to know his da as well—a good friend of mine, Jim O'Reilly was—till he died, two years ago now. Left his missus with eight little ones younger than Garrett. The lad's worked for Miss Montgomery over to the Bower since Jim went. The missus thought it was a bad influence on him, but they needed the money, so she's let him stay. He had th'infantile paralysis when he was just a little lad, so he's a bit lame, no good to th'army, or on the docks hereabouts neither. So when the Reverend Montgomery and his sister, Miss Agatha, offered him a handyman's place, he was glad enough to take it. His ma is always worried he'll take up with one o'them women, but I guess he's kept clean. I've not heard a bad word about him, an' I would'v' if any was bein' said. Talk to him, tell him you spoke to me. He might know somethin'."

"Will he be here tonight?" Ames asked.

Sweeney shrugged, expressionless. "Don't know. He doesn't keep a regular schedule. He might be, might not."

"Martin," said Delahanty, "did you happen to know either one of those girls?"

"No," Sweeney said. "I don't say that I don't know one or another of 'em over there from time to time. There's good Irish girls enough who've fallen by the wayside, or been ruined through no fault of their own. But those two—no, I didn't know 'em."

"But you'll keep an ear out for us, will you?"

"That I will." Sweeney nodded once, emphatically. Ames felt that he was a man of his word, and that once he had accepted your friendship, and given his own in return, he was your friend for life. "I hear a good deal one way and another," Sweeney added.

Ames produced his card. "A note to this address will always reach me."

Without looking at it, the barkeep tucked it into his shirt pocket. "All right," he said. "If someone's taken it into his head to kill Irish girls, I want to help put a stop to it right enough. But talk to Garrett. He'll know something the police haven't picked up, or I'm an Englishman."

He turned away to tend to business, for the place was filling up now toward the end of the day.

"Shall we wait for this lad?" Ames asked Delahanty.

"I can't stay—not tonight. I must dress for dinner at Mrs. Gardner's."

A smile of understanding passed over Ames's face, and to MacKenzie he explained: "Mrs. Gardner—Isabella Stewart Gardner, of the New York department store Stewarts and the Boston Lowell Gardners—has the most artistic and literary circle in the city. She is a noted collector—not only of objets d'art, but also of talented young men like Desmond here."

"None of your blarney now," Delahanty said, laughing. "The next time she gives one of her big 'crushes,' Doctor, I'll have her secretary send you a card. Addington is invited regularly, but he never comes."

"A waste of time, those big turnouts," Ames said brusquely.

"But you won't get better food this side of Paris, my friend."

Outside, it was full dark now, and still raining hard. A carriage light came bobbing toward them along the broad cobblestone street: a vacant hansom. They hailed it and climbed in.

CAREFULLY, BECAUSE SHE WAS A LITTLE ON EDGE, CAROLINE lifted the china teapot, poured the hot amber liquid into one of her second-best cups, and handed it with its saucer to her guest.

"It is so kind of you to call, Cousin Wainwright," she said. "I'm sure Addington will be home any moment now." For there was no need to maintain the pretense that Cousin Wainwright had come to visit her; it was Addington he wanted to see, and she had a good idea why.

On the other hand, she had promised Addington that she would deal with Cousin Wainwright, and she felt duty bound to do so now, while she had him to herself. The only problem was, Cousin Wainwright had a firmly settled opinion of woman's place, and interfering in a murder investigation was not it.

He was a tall, fat, balding man with none of the family looks. He stared into the depths of his cup as if he were looking for tea leaves to read. He seemed uncomfortable, she thought, far too large for the chair he had chosen, which was a delicate Empire piece with fluted legs and a worn brocade seat. Caroline hoped that his trousers were not damp, else the brocade would be ruined.

Ordinarily at ease in any social situation, for the moment she was at a loss. She hadn't seen Cousin Wainwright in ages—not since her mother's funeral well over a year before—and in any case, whenever she had seen him over the years, she'd never known quite what to say to him. He was stern and straitlaced, a man of impeccable rectitude, who had singlehandedly brought about great improvements in the Boston police force. This had included the hiring of a few Irishmen, somewhat lessening the tensions between the reigning Yankee class and the huge numbers of Hibernian immigrants. "Paddies," they were called, after St. Patrick, the patron saint of their benighted island. So many Irishmen were arrested, day after day, that the long black police wagons that carted them off to jail had become known as paddy wagons.

"And how is your boy, cousin?" Caroline asked a little too brightly.

"Well enough." Wainwright's boy—a boy no longer—was in his third year at the College, which was what Brahmin Bostonians called Harvard.

"Enjoying his studies?" she added, feeling slightly desperate. Try as she would, she could not summon up an image of the lad.

"I shouldn't think so," Wainwright said, looking up at her at last. "But I told him he had to stay on, and so he will."

"Oh, yes, you are quite right to tell him—"

She broke off as she heard the clatter of hooves outside, and prayed silently that it was a cab bringing Addington home at last.

"There he is," she said as she heard his voice and MacKenzie's in the front hall. Cousin Wainwright took a quick sip of tea and set down his cup. As he stood, Caroline glanced apprehensively at the brocade. It looked quite dry.

The pocket doors slid apart, and Ames and MacKenzie came in. "Well, Caro, we have had a most interesting—" Ames began. For a moment, Caroline thought he looked startled at seeing their guest, but he quickly assumed his usual sangfroid.

"Cousin. Good to see you," he said, advancing to shake Wainwright's hand. He introduced MacKenzie, and the men settled themselves. Caroline handed around tea, while MacKenzie helped himself to a piece of Sally Lunn cake.

There was a little silence. Then Ames, never one to flinch from an awkward moment, said, "I visited your place this morning, cousin."

"So I understand." Wainwright scowled at him.

"Things seem to be going fairly well, wouldn't you say?"

"Well enough—if we can be free of outside meddling."

Oh, dear, thought Caroline. So it was going to be an unpleasant encounter after all. Well, it couldn't be helped.

And Addington was certainly capable of standing up to anyone, even Cousin Wainwright.

"Oh? Who has been meddling?" Ames asked. His face was bland and smooth, but Caroline thought she saw a hint of amusement in his dark eyes.

"I shouldn't think you'd need to ask that," Wainwright said. "Inspector Crippen—"

"Good man," Ames interjected.

"Yes. He is. And he doesn't need civilians coming in to interfere—"

"Oh, now, I wouldn't say it was interfering, simply to pay a call—"

"That is exactly what it was," Wainwright said. His jowly face had taken on a pinkish color, which made the contrast with his starched white shirt collar all the greater as it cut into the folds of his neck. "Interfering with police business. I cannot understand why you believe that you can manage our affairs better than we can manage them ourselves. Hah? Why is that?"

Ames bit back the sharp retort that sprang to his lips: because Crippen works hind foremost, deciding upon the solution to a case and then finding evidence to fit it. "I am not trying to manage anything," he said.

Caroline was proud of him. Ordinarily he did not trouble to hide his irritation, but at the moment he was hiding it very well.

"Then why did you take up an hour of Crippen's time this morning?" Wainwright demanded.

"It was more nearly fifteen minutes. Did he complain?"

"What with the Copp's Hill Boys ripe to be got," Wainwright went on, "and now these murders over in the South End—"

"It is my fault, cousin," Caroline put in. She knew she shouldn't interrupt, but she had to deflect his anger before it boiled over with who knew what consequences for poor Agatha Montgomery.

Sharply, he turned to look at her; he seemed to have forgotten her existence. "What?"

"I said, it is my fault that Addington went to see Inspector Crippen. I urged him to do so."

"And why did you do that, pray?"

"Because Agatha Montgomery, the proprietress of the Bower, is a friend of mine. She grew up just around the corner on Pinckney Street. She has been the heart and soul of the Bower ever since she started it, and it seemed to me that with these dreadful murders, she stands to lose it all. People will no longer support the Bower if scandal attaches to its name, and poor Agatha would be—"

"And what does that have to do with Crippen?" Wainwright demanded. His face was redder than before, and he was blinking rapidly, as if her putting herself forward in such an unladylike way had unnerved him.

"Why—I asked Addington—and Dr. MacKenzie too—to pay a call on him to see if they could help him in his investigations. It was not meant to be an interference—or meddling, as you put it. It was meant to help. The sooner we—you—find the person who killed those girls, the less danger the Bower's mission will be ruined."

Wainwright looked baffled. "You think that Addington can outwit the police in a matter like this?"

Caroline lifted her chin, and her face took on the look of steely determination that MacKenzie had come to recognize.

"It is not a question of outwitting anyone, cousin," she said. "It is a question of helping Agatha. And if Addington—or even if I—can assist her in any way, we intend to do so."

Wainwright's jowls, bright red now, flapped like a turkey's. "You!" he exclaimed, fixing her in his hard little eyes. "You don't mean to tell me that you would involve yourself in a murder investigation!"

"Yes," she said. "I do mean to tell you exactly that. If any of us here"—her gaze swept over her brother and MacKenzie—"can do anything at all to help Agatha in this terrible affair, we will do so. And I might add, cousin, that it would not be the first time that Inspector Crippen owed us—owed Addington—a debt of thanks. You will remember the business at the Somerset Club—not to mention the death of Colonel Mann—"

"Enough!" Wainwright shot to his feet, startling them all. He stared down at Caroline, momentarily speechless with outrage. "I did not come here to listen to such drivel," he said at last. "I came here to warn you—all of you—to stay out of this business once and for all. I would advise you to heed that warning. Good day to you."

And before she could answer, he stalked out of the room, pulling the pocket doors shut behind him with unnecessary force. They heard him in the vestibule, and then the front door slammed and he was gone.

"Well!" Caroline said, managing a little laugh. "I certainly didn't keep my promise to you about dealing with Cousin Wainwright, did I, Addington?"

"Don't worry about it." He emptied his lukewarm tea into the slop dish, poured a fresh cup for himself, and stood at his accustomed place before the fire. "He will calm down soon enough. I suppose Crippen complained to him, although I must say, Crippen seemed happy enough to see us."

"What did he say?" Caroline asked. "Did he tell you anything useful?"

"Yes, as a matter of fact, he did." Briefly, Ames recounted what they had learned. MacKenzie was shocked when he spoke so matter-of-factly about Mary's pregnancy, but Caroline seemed neither shocked nor surprised at that particular piece of news.

"Agatha has had to deal with something like that before," she said. "There have been at least two girls who have had to leave because they were in the family way. One of them, I believe, was already *enceinte* when she came to the Bower, and the other—well, they have pretty close supervision, but some of them manage to evade it all the same. You have met Matron Pratt, Doctor, and you can see for yourself how strict she is. She must be, under the circumstances—strict, and always vigilant. Agatha went through two or three matrons before Mrs. Pratt came to her, and none of them was satisfactory. Those girls need a good, strong hand to guide them, and whatever else you may think of Mrs. Pratt, her hand is very strong indeed."

MacKenzie nodded. "Too strong, do you think?"

"Why, how could she be too strong? It is a houseful of girls—there are twenty at least, and sometimes more—many of whom have never had proper guidance in their lives. And she has only three months to guide them, don't forget, before they must go back into the world, with all its temptations and possibilities for error. Even if she must sometimes seem unfair—the way she did yesterday, for instance, with that poor girl who answered the door—I have no doubt that she has the best interests of the girls at heart."

MacKenzie was not so sure about that, but he let it pass.

"Look at this, Caroline," Ames said then. He took out his pocket notebook and showed her the jumble of letters he had copied in Crippen's office.

"What is it?" she said, staring at it.

"Some kind of note found on Mary Flaherty's person. It wasn't written—it was letters cut out and pasted together."

"How very odd," she said, handing the notebook back to him. "Some kind of code, or cipher?"

"Yes. Crippen thought it was either that or some esoteric language. But it isn't any language I've ever seen. And so much for Cousin Wainwright's pique," Ames added. "Crippen was planning to come to me for help, so I don't see how Wainwright can object if I call on him, in turn, to find out what he knows."

Caroline met MacKenzie's eyes and smiled. "Did you have an interesting day, Doctor?"

"Indeed we did. And not the least of it was our excursion down to the waterfront."

"The waterfront! Why did you go there?"

MacKenzie deferred to Ames, who told her of their visit to the Green Harp Saloon.

"Garrett O'Reilly!" she exclaimed. "Yes, I know him. I see him sometimes when I go to teach the girls. He's a good boy, very dependable."

Ames contemplated her. "Is he the kind of boy, do you think, who would—ah—get Mary Flaherty in the family way and then murder her to keep her quiet?"

She went a little pale as she set her cup and saucer onto the tray. "No, I don't think he is," she said.

"Crippen seems to think he might be," Ames replied.

At that, she blazed up. "Then Crippen is wrong!" she said vehemently. "Again! He was wrong before, and he is wrong now! Why, Garrett O'Reilly is a perfectly wonderful boy, Addington! He is as nicely mannered as any young man over at the College—better, in fact—and bright and capable. I cannot believe he is involved in this business. Oh, dear! And Inspector Crippen will arrest him, and he will charge him with the crime—"

"Crimes," Ames interjected. "There have been two deaths, remember."

"Yes, and all the more reason to believe that Garrett had nothing to do with them! Why would he kill Bridget if it was Mary whom he—"

Her vocabulary failed her, and she broke off as a knock came at the pocket doors.

"Excuse me, miss," said Margaret, looking in, "but Cook is wanting to speak with you about the dinner."

She meant, Caroline knew, not tonight's repast, which would be something plain and easy to prepare, but the dinner for the following night, when a dozen people were coming to meet her "lion," the British journalist. Caroline had thought every detail of the menu was settled, but apparently not.

"All right, Margaret. I'm coming." And when the maid did not immediately withdraw: "Is there something else?"

"Yes, miss. When I took out the big serving platter, I found it cracked right through."

The potted grouse, thought Caroline. Potted grouse was heavy—too heavy to risk a disaster. Fortunately, they had twenty-four hours to repair the damage.

"The recipe for china cement is in my household book," she said. "I will be down directly, but you can begin to prepare it. Beaten egg white, quicklime—and it will need some old cheese, well grated."

The maid withdrew. She'd been with them for more than ten years, with never a day off more than her half-Sunday every other week. When she'd asked permission to visit her sister in Fitchburg, Caroline hadn't had the heart to refuse. She was to take the train on Saturday night, and somehow they'd survive until she returned.

"I must go to Cook," she said to the men, "before she works herself up into a state. And tomorrow is hopeless. I must be here all day, getting ready. A hired girl is coming in to help, and the pastry cook arrives at dawn. And you, Addington—"

He smiled at her, understanding. "I will be well out of your way as soon as I finish breakfast. And Dr. MacKenzie will be with me."

"You will go to the Bower," she said, and it was not a question.

"Yes, Caro. I—we—will go to the Bower."

CHAPTER 7

AT BREAKFAST THE NEXT MORNING, CAROLINE SIFTED through her letters—the bills went first to Addington, although she was the one who dealt with them in the end—and extracted one, a thick pale blue envelope with a stamp far too beautiful to be American.

"At last!" she exclaimed, smiling. And, at MacKenzie's quizzical glance, "From Val in Rome. I haven't heard from her since she sent me that one brief note just after she arrived. Oh, I do hope she is having a good time! You don't mind if I read it, Addington?"

He waved a hand at her, his face hidden behind the morning *Globe*. MacKenzie made do with his oatmeal, resigning himself to a breakfast without conversation, but, after a moment Caroline said, "Listen to this, Addington!"

Ames put down his paper. "What?"

"Val and her set have taken up with the crowd that visits the artists' studios, and they go two or three times a week to the museums. They even went to Florence last week. I am so glad she went abroad after that horrid episode with George Putnam. His mother passed me in the street the other day and cut me dead."

Their cousin Valentine, recovering from a broken engagement, had fled to Italy for the winter. She had invited Caroline to join her in the spring, in the South of France, but MacKenzie, realizing his selfishness, hoped Caroline wouldn't go.

"Good," said Ames, returning to his newspaper. But after a moment he put it down with a small *tsk!* of irritation. "They are bungling it," he said.

"Crippen?" MacKenzie asked.

"Of course Crippen. Who else? He promises the public that the killer of the Bower girls will be apprehended 'swiftly'—his word. Meanwhile he promises—as he has done for weeks now—that the Copp's Hill Boys will be behind bars any moment."

Caroline left off reading Val's letter and tucked it back into its envelope. She was too busy to fully savor it. Tomorrow, she thought, when I have more time.

"You are going to the Bower this morning, Addington?" she asked.

"Since I promised you that I would—yes."

"I've been thinking," she went on.

At once he was on his guard. Caroline, thinking, was always problematical.

"I want to invite Agatha for this evening," she said. "And her brother."

"Really? Are you sure that would be wise?"

"Yes, I am."

"Won't people think it odd for a woman in Miss Montgomery's situation to show herself at a social occasion?"

"But that is the point, Addington. It is important for people to see that she has not been banished—that the people who have supported the Bower have not turned away from her. Don't forget that Imogen and Edward Boylston are coming. He sits on the Bower's board of trustees."

He grunted, still skeptical.

"So I will write a note to Agatha," Caroline said, "inviting them both, and if you would deliver it to her—?"

Ames rolled his eyes and retreated behind his newspaper once more, and Caroline met MacKenzie's glance with a little smile of triumph.

Half an hour later, Ames and MacKenzie made their way

down the steep slope of Mt. Vernon Street to Charles. Pedestrians hurried by, tilting their umbrellas against the rain, while delivery boys and errand boys hurtled past, dodging in and out. Over all rose the strong odor of the sea and the ever-present smell of horse dung.

They found a herdic in front of the S. S. Pierce grocery store, and at last, with a crack of his whip, the driver found a way clear and they set off.

"As Caroline says, Miss Montgomery is a most admirable woman," Ames said. He did not look at MacKenzie as he spoke but gazed out at the row of brick and brownstone town houses along Beacon Street.

"Yes, she seems to be." MacKenzie put a hand on the seat to steady himself as they took a sharp corner at Arlington.

"And unfortunately, her work at the Bower is sorely needed," Ames went on. "Down near Crabbe's, at certain hours of the evening, it is becoming impossible to walk twenty paces without being set upon by some poor drab in search of a customer."

Ames's wide, thin mouth drew down in an expression of distaste, and MacKenzie had a brief mental glimpse of the austere, proud and proper Bostonian who was Addington Ames being accosted by a woman of the streets.

They crossed the railroad tracks near the Boston & Providence station and came into the South End. A newsboy was crying a late edition at the corner of Columbus Avenue: "Read all about it! Bertram's Bower! Vicious crime!"

"The journalistic community seems to be making a good profit out of this affair," Ames said sourly.

"That is their business, I suppose," MacKenzie replied. He had a memory of his landlord threatening bodily harm to a prying reporter, two months before, in the case of Colonel Mann.

At length the herdic turned into Rutland Square and they alighted at the Bower. As Ames paid the driver, MacKenzie looked up at the tall brownstone. All the blinds were drawn, giving it the look of a house of mourning—which it was. No wreath adorned the front door, however. Probably they did not deem it wise to draw attention to themselves, he thought.

They mounted the steep steps, and Ames lifted the knocker and brought it sharply down.

No answer.

He tried again, but still no one came. Just as he raised his hand to try a third time, the door flew open, and they were confronted by the forbidding figure of Matron Pratt. MacKenzie had come to think of her as a dragon matron, hostile to all outsiders.

"No visitors allowed," she snapped.

"I beg your pardon, madam," Ames said, "but we are not visitors in the usual sense of the word. I am a friend of Miss Montgomery's. Is she in?"

Over the past four months of his acquaintance with the Ameses, MacKenzie had learned that Addington Ames could be curt to the point of rudeness, but he could also be the image of controlled, ever so slightly condescending courtesy, as he was now.

Matron Pratt looked them up and down as if they were the most disreputable type of interloper—traveling salesmen perhaps. "No, she is not!" she snarled, and before Ames could speak again, she slammed the door in their faces.

"Well, Doctor, it seems that we are not welcome here," Ames said mildly. He was not offended, or even surprised, at Matron Pratt's behavior. He'd never met her, but he'd heard a good deal about her from Caroline.

"Shall we try again?" he said, once more lifting the brass knocker and bringing it down hard.

Instantly, the dragon matron confronted them for a second time. "I said—"

"We heard what you said." Ames braced his hand against the door to prevent her from slamming it shut. "I understand that you are in crisis here," he went on. "I simply want a brief moment with Miss Montgomery, and I promise you—"

"What is it, Mrs. Pratt?" came a voice from within.

As the dragon matron turned, they could see beyond her the tall, angular figure of Agatha Montgomery.

"They want to talk to you," Matron Pratt said.

"Who does?" Miss Montgomery advanced. "Oh—Mr. Ames."

"My sister would have come again herself," Ames said, "but she was unable to. So she asked me—us," he corrected himself, "to come instead, to inquire if there is anything we can do to help."

Miss Montgomery shook her head. "She is very kind to worry so about us," she said. She seemed about to say more, but she was interrupted by the sound of a crash from the rear of the house, followed immediately by a loud wailing.

Miss Montgomery turned to Mrs. Pratt. "Matron, will you— No. Never mind. I will go myself." She left them and hurried back along the hall.

Ames took this opportunity to step into the vestibule. Matron Pratt stared at him in amazement. Obviously, thought MacKenzie, stepping close behind, she is not accustomed to having her dictates opposed. Ames shut the outer door, and then he moved into the hall and MacKenzie followed. The place seemed as deserted as it had been the day before, and it carried the same institutional smell. They would never rid themselves of that, MacKenzie thought; probably the girls carried it with them when they left.

"You are trespassing!" snapped Matron Pratt, recovered from her astonishment. "I will call the police!" There was a telephone on the wall outside the office door.

"Please do," Ames said smoothly. "They are friends of mine. I would be delighted to see them."

Miss Montgomery was approaching them from the back of the hall. "It was an accident," she said distractedly, as if she were speaking to herself. "Coughlin dropped some plates."

Matron Pratt narrowed her eyes, no doubt calculating the cost of the breakage, MacKenzie thought.

"Now, Mr. Ames," Miss Montgomery said, "you wanted to speak to me."

"If you can spare the time."

"At the moment, I cannot. But Matron will help you, and then perhaps I can—"

"I have the schedule to attend to," Matron Pratt protested.

"Yes, well, that can wait," Miss Montgomery said.

A look passed between them. Then Matron Pratt said nothing more, merely muttering an assent and opening the door to the office. "In there," she said sharply, but then, as if she remembered something: "I haven't had my paper returned to me!" she called to Miss Montgomery.

They heard the reply: "I have already spoken to everyone except O'Donnell and Fletcher. You might question them yourself, Matron, at the noon meal."

Matron Pratt slammed shut the office door and turned to face the visitors. Her face was rigid with anger, and her mouth worked for a moment before she spoke.

"They are thieves, here, along with everything else," she said then.

"Thieves?" Ames replied. "How do you mean?"

"I mean, they steal things!" she snapped.

"You have lost something?" Ames asked.

"No! I didn't lose it! Someone stole it! My tract—one of my papers from my Sunday evening meetings." As she came into the room, she flexed her broad, thick hands.

"And you think that one of the—ah—young women here has taken it?"

"I don't think it! I know it! How else could it disappear?"

Surely, thought MacKenzie, the "Mrs." in Matron Pratt's name was a courtesy title, for what man would marry such a harridan?

She went to the front windows and peered out from behind the blind. "There he is again," she said.

"Who?"

"One of those newspapermen. They are like a plague, worse than the police. They haven't left us alone for a moment."

She came back to them, but she did not take a chair. Neither, therefore, did they.

MacKenzie looked around. It was a fairly large room, linoleum-floored, with a good-sized desk facing the door. Rows of oak filing cabinets and glass-fronted bookcases lined the walls. On the bookshelves, neatly arranged, was a set of what looked like account books, each with its year stamped in gold on its spine. On the desktop were stacks of bills and correspondence, an in box and an out box, a glass pen tray and two bottles of ink, a sheet of green blotting paper—fresh, unmarked—and a tall spindle impaled with a thick stack of notes. The top one had the notation: "Mr. Boylston, 10 A.M."

"What do you want?" Matron Pratt said abruptly, addressing Ames.

"I want—if possible—to help."

She surveyed him for a moment, and he surveyed her back. "That's what we try to do here," she said. "We try to help. *Them,*" she added, casting her gaze upward; they took it to mean the young women housed on the upper floors.

"Indeed," Ames replied. He felt a fleeting moment of compassion—no more—for Elwood Crippen, forced to deal with this gorgon and not having the option, as Ames did, of walking away from her if she did not cooperate.

But he would not walk away, he thought. The more this woman defied him, the more he wanted, perversely, to pry from her some small item of information; he would keep at her until he did.

"And I am sure that you do help them," he added.

She glared at him. "The ones as want to be helped," she said. "Some don't."

"How do you mean?"

She shrugged her massive shoulders, which were encased in a black dress of some cheap-looking stuff. "A lot of them just take advantage of *her,* if you ask me." She meant Agatha Montgomery. "They know they can get fed, and get to a doctor if they need to—and most of 'em do, as you can imagine—and rest a bit from their labors, if you take my meaning. We give them a little vacation here, and then out they go, back where they came from, looking for men to make their living off of."

"You mean they do not take the employment that they might get after their—ah—lessons here?"

She threw him a glance of contempt. "If a girl gets work in an office for four or five dollars a week, she won't think that's such a grand thing, will she? When she can make that much in a night—on her back."

MacKenzie had never heard a woman speak so crudely, and he was mightily offended by it. Ames, however, seemed not to notice—or, if he did, not to mind. "Yes, well, I take your point," he said. "But about the two girls who—ah— Mary Flaherty and Bridget Brown?"

Matron Pratt sniffed contemptuously. "Brown was humble enough. Never caused trouble. Did her work."

"And Mary Flaherty?"

Instantly, a look of pure malice crossed the matron's face. "I couldn't say."

"Was she well liked?"

"By some, I suppose."

"But not by you?"

"I couldn't say," she repeated.

"Try. Could you tell us anything about her?"

"I've already told it all to the police."

"Even so."

Again the woman's heavy shoulders rose in a shrug. "She was getting above herself."

"You mean because of her position as Miss Montgomery's secretary?"

"Yes. She gave herself airs."

"In what way?"

"About the typewriting, for one thing."

"How do you mean?"

"The Reverend Montgomery said he was going to buy a typewriting machine for the office. He bought her a manual so she could start to learn about it. And when she talked about it—and she did talk about it till you were sick of hearing her—it was always 'When I get my typewriting machine.' Like that. With her nose in the air, as if learning to pound away on one of them things was going to make her all of a sudden better than the rest of us."

Ames nodded. "So perhaps some of the girls resented her?"

"Yes. 'Course they did."

"Did you?"

It was a thrust that went home. Her mouth twitched, and she clenched her hands again.

"It isn't my place to resent any of the girls here."

He let it pass. "Was there anyone in particular who disliked either Mary or Bridget?"

"Brown—no."

"But Mary Flaherty?"

She frowned. They waited. She wants to tell us, thought MacKenzie, but she cannot quite bring herself to do so.

"Verna Kent," she said at last. "Miss Montgomery expelled her last week," she added.

"Because?"

"She was a thief. I told you, we have our share of them here."

"What did she steal?"

"One of Flaherty's petticoats. Flaherty found out about it and told Miss Montgomery."

"Did this girl admit it?"

"She could hardly deny it, could she, when the petticoat was found under her mattress?"

"So then?"

"She was angry with Flaherty, of course. She went after her—right here in the office. A terrible scene she made. She went for Flaherty's throat, crying that she would kill her. I hauled her off," she added.

"And then she left?"

"Yes."

"And you saw nothing of her afterward?"

"I didn't, no. But the next day, when Flaherty went out, Kent was waiting for her over on Warren Avenue. She went

after her again—set right on her. Lucky for Flaherty there
was a policeman nearby."

"And the girl was arrested?"

"Yes."

Easy enough to check, he thought.

"Do you know where she is living now? Assuming that
she is not in the lockup."

"On Chambers Street, in the West End."

"Did Mary have any other enemies that you know of?"
Aside from yourself, he thought.

Matron Pratt shrugged. "I don't know about enemies, but
she didn't have many friends. She thought too well of herself,
if you can imagine it. And she was far too free, coming and
going. I don't know why Miss Montgomery allowed it."

"How do you mean?"

"She didn't keep to a schedule like the others. She'd
work here in the office at night, and then she'd go out during the day. She had to run her errands, she'd say. Errands! I
ask you. And often enough she'd go out at night, too, without signing out. Where was she going at all hours? Aside
from everything else, it isn't safe for a girl to go wandering
about in this district. I guess she learned that lesson in the
end," she added with grim satisfaction.

"Did you ever speak to her about it? About her comings
and goings?"

"Oh, yes. I spoke to her all right. But she never thought
she had to listen to what I said. 'Never you mind about me,
Mrs. Pratt,' she said. And gave me such a look! I'd have
taken a switch to her if I could. The little baggage! Well, she
went out one last time, didn't she? And she never came
back." Her face had taken on a gloating expression that
Ames found repulsive.

"Did you see her go?" he asked.

"No. Sunday night is the night for my meetings over on
Columbus Avenue. I go out at a quarter to seven every
week."

"And you return when?"

"Not before ten."

"I see. Was Sunday visiting day, perhaps? Were there any visitors to the house that day—anyone strange, I mean, whom Mary might have met? Fathers of the other girls—brothers or uncles perhaps?"

"No men!" she snapped.

"No men visitors? None at all?"

"Men are the cause of all their troubles, Mr. Ames." Matron Pratt's face had darkened into an expression of pure hate.

"But surely—"

"Men are vile creatures through and through. I should know—I was married to one of 'em once." A sneer had enhanced her expression, so that she looked more forbidding than ever.

"Surely there are some men in the world of whom you approve," Ames said. "The Reverend Montgomery, for instance."

"Not him either."

"But he comes here, does he not?"

"Yes," she muttered darkly.

Against your wishes, MacKenzie thought.

"All men are worthless if you ask me," she added. "And so are the girls who go with them."

MacKenzie felt slightly ill in the face of this woman's implacable animosity toward all his sex.

There came a tap at the door: one of the girls, come to announce that Miss Montgomery would see the gentlemen now.

In her private room at the rear of the house, Agatha Montgomery sat in her rocking chair before the low fire. At her murmured word, the two men sat opposite her on the same worn horsehair sofa where MacKenzie had sat with Caroline two days before.

"It is good of you to see us," Ames began.

Miss Montgomery inclined her head. She looked somewhat more composed than before, but still there were lines of tension around her mouth, and a haunted look in her pale eyes.

"You should not have troubled yourself, Mr. Ames."

"As I said, Caroline wanted us to. And—" He reached to his inside jacket pocket and withdrew the envelope containing his sister's note. "She invites you to dinner this evening—you and your brother. She is entertaining a 'lion' from London, and she thought he might amuse you."

She did not at first seem to understand what he said. "How . . . kind."

"You will come?"

"I—I don't know."

"Just a dozen or so people, a congenial company. She thought it might—ah—divert you a little."

"Caroline has always been a good friend to me, and now she still—" She broke off, thinking. "All right, Mr. Ames. Yes. We will come, and please thank her for her thoughtfulness. She has always, over the years—I remember when my father—well. That was a long time ago, was it not?"

She fell silent, staring at her hands clasped in her lap.

Then Ames said: "Miss Montgomery, can you tell us anything about the second girl who was killed?"

"You mean Brown." She did not look at him.

"Yes."

She shook her head. "No. Nothing. She was a good girl, quiet, obedient. I thought that when she left us, she would have no difficulty in finding a position—a decent position— to support herself."

"Was she from Boston?"

"No. Fall River."

"No family locally?"

"Nor in Fall River either, as far as I know."

"I see. And no enemies?"

"No. She was far too inoffensive to have enemies, Mr. Ames."

"Did she have any particular friendships here?"

"Only Mary." She used the girl's Christian name, he noted. Was that significant?

"So Bridget would have been upset about Mary's death?"

"Oh, yes. She was very upset. She—" Miss Montgomery

pressed her lips together, as if she were trying to keep back what she had almost said.

"Yes? She what?" Ames prompted softly.

"She . . . went out. In the late afternoon, after her sewing class. She came to me to ask permission, and of course I refused it. How could I have agreed to let her go out after what had happened to Mary only the night before?"

"But still, she went."

"Yes. I remonstrated with her—"

"You mean you argued."

Ames had a mental image of poor Bridget, inoffensive, humble, arguing with Agatha Montgomery. The girl must have had a very good reason indeed to defy her, never mind wanting to leave the safety of the Bower.

"Yes. But short of physically restraining her, I could not stop her. After she left, I thought that perhaps she wanted to go to church—to find a priest perhaps."

"So what did you do then?"

"I followed her."

"And did you ever find her?"

"No. I went all the way to the cathedral, but I never saw her."

"Did you go in?"

"Yes. She wasn't there."

"So you came back?"

"Yes. It was raining hard." She shivered as if she were still cold and wet, as she must have been last night, hunting for Bridget Brown through the dark streets of the South End.

"And when she didn't return?"

Miss Montgomery's gaunt face crumpled for a moment, then she regained control. She met Ames's eyes steadily as she said, "I will tell you frankly, Mr. Ames, it is not unheard of for one of our girls to go missing. I was frantic, but of course I could not let it be seen. The girls were upset enough, what with Mary's death."

"You did not think to notify the police?"

Miss Montgomery looked a trifle abashed. "I cannot go to the police every time one of our girls fails to turn up for supper. I would have gone, yes—if, say, in a day or two she had not come back."

She pressed her handkerchief to her eyes as if to forestall her tears.

Suddenly restless, Ames stood up and began to pace the little room. He thought of Crippen's revelation that Mary had been pregnant. Did Miss Montgomery know that? It was too delicate a question to put to her at this point, he thought; if he went too far beyond the bounds of good manners, she would refuse to talk to him altogether.

But the coded note—yes, he could ask her about that.

She stared at the copy he'd made. "I have no idea what this is."

"Or who could have sent it?"

"No."

"Did Mary receive the Bower's mail?"

"Yes. She dealt with it every day."

"So we cannot know if this was sent to her through the mail or if someone here"—she looked up at him sharply—"gave it to her."

"Who would do that?" she said. "Anyone here who wanted to send a message to her could simply speak to her."

"Then, for the moment, at any rate, we must assume that this was sent to her from outside. So even if Bridget had no friends or family in the city, Mary probably did."

Do you know, he thought, watching her. Do you know that Mary had someone who was more than a casual friend, someone who had put her in the family way, and then, very possibly, killed her to silence her?

Miss Montgomery handed back his pocket notebook. "Did the police have any idea—"

"No. None. Inspector Crippen asked me to look at it because he thought I might be able to translate it."

"And can you?"

"No."

She blinked several times, as if absorbing what he said, and then she stood up.

"I must thank you again, Mr. Ames, for being so kind."

She was dismissing them. No, he thought, not yet.

"I wonder if we could impose on you a little further, Miss Montgomery."

She'd put out her hand to bid him good-bye, but now she took it back. "Yes?" she said warily.

"I would very much like to see Mary and Bridget's room."

She hesitated. "I am afraid that isn't possible."

"Because—?"

"Because—it isn't clean."

"But that is nothing. Clean or not, it doesn't matter. I simply want to see it—just for a moment."

Still she hesitated. As she looked down at the tips of her worn boots protruding from beneath her dark skirts, she seemed to be waging some internal struggle. MacKenzie wondered if she, like Matron Pratt, harbored a dislike—a hatred, even—toward men.

At last she gave in and looked up at Ames. "All right. If you insist."

She led them out and up the stairs. As they went, MacKenzie glanced behind, down to the hall. He saw the office door cracked open, and he knew that their progress was being observed by the dragon matron.

It was mid-morning; some of the Bower's residents were in the second-floor hall, changing classes. MacKenzie noted that all of them, dark or fair, tall or short, looked more or less the same, and not only because of their plain dark dresses and white aprons. They all had a look of defeat about them, he thought, and in girls so young—most of them did not look more than in their early twenties—such a look was painful to see.

Now, catching sight of the two strange men, a few of them stifled little cries of alarm, and all of them looked frightened. MacKenzie had a sudden urge to speak to them, to reassure them that he and Ames meant no harm, but of course he could not.

Miss Montgomery led them on, up to the third floor. She stopped before a door numbered 37. Without knocking—for who would answer now?—she turned the knob and pushed open the door.

The room was dim, the blind at the single window pulled down. Only a little light from the gas fixtures in the hall penetrated to the interior. Then Miss Montgomery turned up the gas by the door and suddenly the room was filled with a harsh, bleak illumination.

They saw a bare linoleum floor; two cots, both neatly made; two night tables; two small bureaus topped with basins and ewers; one small bookcase. A door ajar halfway along one wall showed the presence of a closet. Over one cot hung a lithograph of Jesus; over the other, a small crucifix. Not clean? thought Ames. Despite Miss Montgomery's objections, the room looked as if it and everything in it had been freshly scrubbed and polished.

He stood still for a moment, looking around. "Do you know what the police took with them, if anything?"

"No."

He went to the closet door and opened it: a small, shallow space. A few items of clothing hung from hooks; on a shelf were two flimsy cardboard hat boxes.

He turned back to the room as if he expected something—some telling thing—to announce itself. But the room was as anonymous—as unrevealing—as a vacant room in a cheap hotel.

He went to the bookcase, which held perhaps a dozen volumes. He took each one and flipped through its pages to see if something might fall out—a note, a clipping, anything to tell him something about the two girls who had shared this barren chamber.

"Did the police examine these?" he asked Miss Montgomery.

"Not that I saw."

A few dime novelettes; a book on etiquette; a *Life of*

Jesus; a cheap edition of *Little Women;* the memoirs of Mary Livermore, who had been a nurse during the Civil War. This last bore an inscription: "For another Mary, from one who admires her very much, in the hope that it will inspire her to be a good girl."

He held it out to Miss Montgomery. "Do you know who gave her this?"

She looked at it. "No."

"Were you aware that she possessed it?"

"No."

"So you do not know whether she brought it with her when she came, or—"

"She didn't do that. She came—" Her voice roughened, and she cleared her throat. "She came with no more than the clothes on her back. And those we disposed of immediately, since they were not fit to wear."

He glanced at the inscription once more and then returned the book to the shelf. He opened the bureau drawers, riffled through the contents of each one. Nothing. Remembering the tale of the stolen petticoat, he turned first to one cot and then to the other and slid his hand underneath the thin mattresses. Nothing there either.

Miss Montgomery stood like a sentinel at the hall door, watching him. When Ames finished, having found nothing, MacKenzie thought she looked secretly pleased, as if to say, I told you so.

"Thank you," Ames said to her. "As you said, there is nothing here to help us."

"No."

"One more thing," he said.

She had started to turn down the gas, but now she stopped.

"Yes?"

Sooner or later, MacKenzie thought, she will have had her patience tested long enough, and we will be asked to leave.

"You have a boy who works here. Garrett O'Reilly."

"Yes?"

"Might we have a word with him?"

"How did you know—"

"We heard of him yesterday from a mutual friend."

A look of distaste came over her face, as if she thought that such an association, even at one remove, was not proper for a man of gentle birth like Addington Ames.

When she did not answer, he said again, "I would like to see him for just a moment. He works here regularly, I believe. Might he be here now?"

"I am not sure. I will ask Matron."

"You will ask Matron what?" said the man who had suddenly appeared in the doorway.

CHAPTER 8

HE WAS TALL, THOUGH NOT SO TALL AS AMES, AND STYL-
ishly dressed in a dark brown coat, finely tailored, with a
velvet collar and bright gold buttons. Across his pale yellow
waistcoat stretched a heavy gold watch chain ornamented
by several talismans. He wore a fine gray silk cravat, and his
feet were shod in shining leather boots that looked expensive. His thinning, pale brown hair was long at the sides,
with impressive sideburns, and brushed back over the
crown to give a luxurious, bouffant effect. In one hand he
carried, incongruously, a half-eaten sweet roll.

Miss Montgomery, startled at first, went rigid. Then,
when she realized who had come, her face assumed a look
of loving pride—adoration, even, thought Ames—that
seemed unsuited to her. She gazed greedily, hungrily, at the
newcomer, as if his presence gave her some much-needed
emotional nourishment.

"Randolph! I never heard you on the stairs."

For a moment, he ignored the two men. As he looked
into his sister's eyes, he laid the flat of his free hand against
her sallow cheek in a gesture that was oddly intimate.

"How are you, my dear?" he said softly.

"I am all right. And you?"

"You needn't worry about me. As long as I know how
you do, I shall be fine."

Despite his dandyish appearance, it was his voice that captured attention: a rich and mellifluous voice, a true preacher's voice. He must be impressive in the pulpit, thought MacKenzie; he must sway his congregation as the wind sweeps over a wheat field. He was intrigued. The Reverend Randolph Montgomery was very different from the preachers he had known in the Midwest, and was probably very different too, he thought, from most of his brother ministers in Boston.

"And what was it you were going to ask Matron?" the reverend asked his sister again.

"If Garrett has come to work today."

"Ah. Garrett. I have not seen him, but then, I have been in the kitchen with Cook this past half hour." He smiled at Ames. "Mr. Ames, how are you?"

Ames introduced MacKenzie, and the reverend offered his left hand. An odd handshake, MacKenzie thought, letting go at once.

"I am a bachelor, living solitary," the reverend continued, "so I have taken it upon myself to make friends with Cook here. She is a kindly soul. She often feeds the folks hereabouts who come begging at the kitchen door, and she feeds me up very faithfully as well."

And, indeed, he looked sleek and well fed, MacKenzie thought, far more so than any of the Bower's girls.

"I am acquainted with your sister, Ames," Montgomery went on. "Is she well?" His handsome face showed a courteous smile, but his eyes were chilly. Handsome, but weak-looking, MacKenzie thought, with not quite enough chin and the eyes a trifle too close together.

"Yes, thank you."

"And you have come here because—?"

Still those chilly eyes, despite his smile.

"Caroline was most distressed at the news of your trouble."

"You mean the death of two of our girls."

"Yes."

"And so she wanted you to come to offer help?"

"Yes."

"It is very kind of you." The reverend contemplated Ames for a moment. "I cannot imagine what you could do for us, but I am grateful to you—and to Miss Ames—for your concern."

But you do not seem grateful, thought Ames. You seem—what? He could not put a name to it, but he felt very strongly that the reverend did not want him here.

"But why are you here in Mary's room?" the reverend went on. "Surely the police have done a thorough job of searching it."

"I told them that, Randolph," Miss Montgomery said quickly. "But they insisted—"

Did I insist? wondered Ames. Yes, I suppose I did.

The reverend arched an eyebrow. "Do the police approve, Mr. Ames?"

"Of my coming here? I have no idea. But when I visited Inspector Crippen yesterday, he made no objection to my helping in a general sort of way."

"A general sort of way," the reverend repeated. "I see. Well, then! If the good inspector has no objection, I can hardly object myself. In fact—" He moved away from the threshold, down the hall toward the stairs, and they followed, Miss Montgomery closing the door of Mary and Bridget's room behind her.

"Why not come along to the rectory, where we can speak without interruption?" the reverend said over his shoulder as they began to descend the stairs. "It is not far, and I can offer you some small refreshment."

Garrett O'Reilly, it seemed, had not been seen at the Bower that day, and so shortly Ames and MacKenzie found themselves outside in the rain once more, accompanying the Reverend Montgomery to his rectory three blocks away.

This proved to be an imposing mansion house made of stone like the church next door. A wrought-iron fence surrounded a small front garden whose few winter-dead plantings were half covered in dirty, icy, rain-pelted snow.

The reverend opened the gate and led them up the path to the door, where, beneath the cover of the porch, he shook the water off his umbrella, closed it, and produced his key.

"You won't find me standing on ceremony," he said as he ushered them in. "I am a plain and modest man, and I live the same."

You are neither plain nor modest, thought Ames, but as he looked around, he saw that the reverend spoke the truth—about his house, at least.

The wide entrance hall beyond the vestibule was barren, no pictures on the walls, not a stick of furniture. Their footsteps echoed on the bare tile floor as they followed the reverend into the parlor. Here they saw a worn, threadbare carpet, a sagging serpentine-backed sofa, and three ancient upholstered chairs. Several straight-backed wooden chairs surrounded a large round table in the center of the room which was laden with books, newspapers, periodicals, and a messy pile of manuscripts.

A bachelor's place, indeed, thought MacKenzie, and he had a brief, poignant memory of the welcoming parlor at No. 16½ Louisburg Square, with Caroline Ames giving them tea, and a sea-coal fire simmering on the hearth.

Here, a few charred sticks of wood lay cold in the grate. The reverend threw off his overcoat, tossed it onto a chair, and bent to put in a handful of kindling. As he touched a match to it, a small, inadequate flame appeared.

Then he turned up the gas, and they saw even more clearly than before that this was—in contrast to the man himself—a place that looked most desperately poor. The plush upholstery on the sofa was worn down to the nub, the seats of the chairs were lumpy, and a film of dust covered every surface. Better to leave the lights low, thought Ames as he and MacKenzie seated themselves at the table.

The reverend swept off the clutter, dumped it onto the sofa, and said, smiling, "Do you know, Doctor, someone told me about you only the other day. Addington Ames has taken on a boarder, my friend said—a veteran of the Indian wars in the West. So already you are acquiring a little reputation here in Boston, which, despite appearances, is a village at heart, full of gossip."

MacKenzie did not know how to reply to this, and so he said nothing, but merely nodded.

"And your bad knee?" the reverend went on.

"Healed well, thank you."

"Good. I am glad to hear it. Nothing so tiresome as not being able to get around. I get around myself a good deal, as you can imagine." He chuckled, inviting them to share this glimpse of his busy life.

"Now, what can I offer you?" he went on. "I have sherry, or a drop of Scotch whisky. It's a bit early in the day for stimulants, I grant you. Or if you would prefer tea, I can whip down to the kitchen to put on the kettle."

They declined any refreshments. Ames took out his pocket notebook and opened it to the page that held the copy of the coded note. "Have a look at this, Reverend," he said. "Crippen can make nothing of it. Your sister couldn't either."

"What is it?" Montgomery took it and squinted at it so that MacKenzie wondered if he needed reading glasses but was too vain to produce them in front of strangers.

"It is a copy of a note that was found in Mary Flaherty's pocket on the night she was killed. Some kind of code, obviously. Crippen thought it might be some foreign language, but it isn't that."

The reverend gave it a final glance and handed the notebook back to Ames. "I have no idea what it is," he said dismissively.

Ames watched him for a moment. Then: "You knew Mary Flaherty."

"Yes."

"How well?"

Montgomery smiled with what MacKenzie thought was rather irritating condescension. "Fairly well, I suppose. As well as anyone did. She was—how shall I put it? She was a very inspirational kind of girl."

"How do you mean?"

"I mean, when you looked at her, you saw the real possibilities—the very real hope and promise of what Agatha is trying to do. Here was a girl"—his rich baritone rolled over them—"who had been on the streets. I will not mince words: Mary was selling herself to any man who would buy. Agatha found her, took her in, healed her in body and spirit—a task in which I had some small part—and let her see that her life need not be one of shame and degradation. Under Agatha's care, Mary—and many like her, make no mistake—blossomed. The world was no longer for her a place of fear and violence and foul disease and miserable death. In fact—"

"Do you know of any enemies she might have had?" Ames broke in. "Or the other girl, Bridget?"

"No." The reverend shook his head slowly, thinking about it. "Well, there was the business of the girl who was expelled a week or so ago—"

"Yes. Matron Pratt told us about that."

The reverend allowed himself a small smile. "She is a perfect dragon, is she not? But she is a strong right arm to Agatha. She lacks a certain finesse, it is true, but I do not believe Agatha could operate the place without her, as rough and ready as she is. Before she came, Agatha had a difficult time of it, maintaining order. But now Mrs. Pratt keeps a steady hand—"

"Do you think that this girl—the one who was expelled—might have been angry enough to kill Mary?"

"I don't know."

"She threatened her—accosted her in the street."

"I know she did. But still, it seems highly unlikely, don't you think?"

"Yes. Particularly in light of the fact that a second girl was killed also, and as far as we know, the girl who was expelled had no quarrel with her."

"Correct. No, I think—" Montgomery pursed his lips. "I think, if you are looking for a more likely suspect, Mr. Ames, that you might look in the direction of one Fred Brice."

"And who is that?"

"He is a young man who sells typewriters. He brought a machine to the Bower one day last fall to give us a demonstration. So that Mary could see it, you understand, since she was the one who would be using it."

"And—?"

"Well, he made Mary's acquaintance, of course. And I must say, anyone who met Mary—any likely young man, I mean—was quite liable to fall in love with her. She was a very pretty girl, was Mary."

"And did he? Fall in love with her, I mean."

"Oh, I think so. Yes indeed. He came around quite often after that, Agatha told me. Several times he came when I was there—I am in and out, you know."

"You are the only male whom Mrs. Pratt allows regularly on the premises," Ames remarked.

"The only—well, yes. If you put it like that."

"Aside from Garrett O'Reilly."

"Aside from—yes."

"You warned Inspector Crippen about him."

The reverend's eyebrows rose. "Did I?"

"So he says."

"Yes, I remember now. I did pass that along to the police."

"And did you also pass along the fact that Mary was in the family way?"

There was a little silence while the reverend absorbed it. Then: "Really?" He seemed surprised.

"Yes. Really. According to the medical examiner."

"You don't say."

"And so if this typewriter salesman was in love with Mary—"

"Yes. I see what you mean. Very possibly he was—ah—the man responsible—"

"And very possibly he did not want to make an honest woman of her, so to speak. You are certain he was infatuated with her?"

"He seemed to be. Matron spoke to me, once or twice, about what a nuisance he was, always hanging about, sending Mary notes and so forth."

"Given her attitude toward men, I am surprised she allowed him entry," Ames remarked. "And as for notes, we saw none in Mary's room."

"I doubt she would have kept them. She had—how shall I put it?—higher aspirations than Fred Brice."

"How do you mean?"

"I mean that Mary probably thought that even a likely young man like him was not good enough for her, although to be Mrs. Fred Brice might not be such a bad thing for a girl from the Bower."

He laughed, but without sound. MacKenzie thought it an unnerving sight.

"At any rate," the reverend went on, "and I was not present to witness it, you understand, I was told that on Saturday last—"

"The day before Mary was killed."

"Yes. On Saturday last, Brice came to the Bower and made one hell of a scene with Mary. You didn't hear about it? Agatha was not there either—we were together, as a matter of fact, at a convention of Presbyterians over at the Mechanics' Hall—but Mrs. Pratt certainly was. Brice found Mary at work in the office and made some kind of proposal to her, apparently. Things worked up into a very loud and acrimonious argument. Finally, Mrs. Pratt threw him out—literally. She is quite strong, as you may have noticed."

"Have you told this to the police?" said Ames.

"Yes."

"So you think this typewriter salesman, rebuffed in his advances to Mary, worked himself up into a murderous passion, not at the time, but—what?—more than twenty-four hours later?"

"I have no idea, Mr. Ames. I am merely trying to be helpful."

"Yes. Of course. Well, now you have given us another person who held a grudge against Mary, but neither this typewriter fellow nor the girl who was expelled had any grudge against Bridget Brown, as far as you know."

"Right."

Ames leaned forward in his chair, resting his elbows on his knees. "What do you think, Reverend? Have you any notion of who might have killed those girls?"

The reverend looked away as he considered the question. "Not really," he said at last, meeting Ames's eyes again.

"But—?"

"But you know as well as I do, this district is not what it was when it was built, some forty years ago now. This district went from brand-new and as elegant as the Back Bay to what it is now, a place where some streets are handsome and well kept and some are not. We have—how shall I put it? a rather more—ah—diverse population than what you have up there on Louisburg Square or on Commonwealth Avenue. You should see the stream of Irish who pass through in the summertime on their way to the Braves' ball field off Walpole Street alongside the railroad tracks. And all year round we have tramps, hobos—all kinds of riffraff. Oh, yes, we have quite a problem here with the transient and homeless population."

"Some of whom come begging at the Bower's kitchen."

"Yes."

"One of the cook's knives is missing."

"Yes, she told me that," the reverend said.

"It may be relevant. Probably it is, in fact. Do any of these—ah—transients ever bother the Bower's girls?"

"Not the ones whom Cook feeds, one must assume. But the others? Indeed they do." The reverend frowned, remembering. "They ride the rails, you know, back and forth between here and who knows where—Springfield, Albany, all number of places. Looking for work—or for handouts. When they are hereabouts, they prowl the neighborhood and beg. They are most annoying—and dangerous. Several times over the past few years they have accosted girls from the Bower. Only the other week, an inebriate tried to—well, fortunately she got away. Two girls were raped last year, however."

"By the same man?"

"Yes."

"And was he caught?"

"Yes."

"A drifter?"

"That is correct. He drifts no more, however, since he was sentenced to a term in the state prison over in Charlestown."

"So he is not our man in this case."

"It would seem not."

"And there have been no further assaults since his arrest?"

"Except for the one that was averted, none that I know of—and I would know, of course. Very little happens at the Bower that I do not know about. Agatha—and I speak in all modesty—Agatha relies upon me, as of course she should, in most matters concerning the running of the Bower, quite aside from financial details."

Raising the money to run the place is hardly a detail, Ames thought.

"You helped her draw up the rules?"

"I did. I saw no reason why such a worthy enterprise should be deprived of Christian counsel."

"Of course."

There was an awkward little silence. The reverend looked around the room as if he were seeking some new topic of conversation. Ames cleared his throat, but the reverend did not seem to notice; now he was studying the large gold ring that he wore on the small finger of his right hand.

That's the end of it, Ames thought; he'll give us nothing more. He cast about for some way to keep the conversation alive, but before he found it, the reverend spoke again.

"You have been very kind, Mr. Ames, to trouble yourself about this wretched business."

"Yes, well, as I said—"

"I understand—your sister encouraged you."

Caroline. "That reminds me, Reverend. Caroline is holding a dinner this evening for Nigel Chadwick—do you know him? He is a London journalist touring America to promote his latest book. I took a note from her, just now, to Miss

Montgomery, inviting you both to join us this evening—if you will forgive the lateness of the invitation."

The reverend blinked. "Indeed? How very kind."

"Will you come?"

"Why—yes. I—we—will be happy to join you."

But he did not look happy, MacKenzie thought; he looked puzzled.

"Caroline thought it would do Miss Montgomery good to get away from the Bower."

"Yes, I imagine it might."

The reverend got to his feet. Now, at last, the interview was definitely over. He started toward the door, and Ames and MacKenzie followed.

"I am sure that in a matter of days," the reverend was saying, "the police will have brought this distressing matter to its conclusion. I have every confidence in them," he added as they came to the vestibule. "Inspector Crippen is one of their best men, don't you agree?"

The front door was open to the pelting rain. Ames stepped out and rescued his umbrella from where he had left it on the porch. "Yes, I do," he said with a small smile that Montgomery did not return. "That's what troubles me—that Crippen is one of their best. Good day to you, sir."

In the herdic-phaeton, Ames let out an exasperated laugh. "A smooth customer, is he not, Doctor?"

"The Reverend Montgomery?" MacKenzie shook his head. "Yes, indeed. But very effective for the purposes of the Bower, I imagine."

"Yes. I am sure he is that. They don't run that place on a pittance, and from what Caroline tells us, they exist entirely on what he can bring in. I can just see him, making his case to a parlor full of ladies, any one of whom is wearing a piece of jewelry that would support the Bower for an entire year. Did you happen to notice the pages on his table?"

"No."

Ames grunted. "I couldn't be sure, but I thought the handwriting matched the dedication to Mary Flaherty, written in a book in her room."

"Really?"

"Yes. But I could hardly steal a sheet to make sure, and beyond that, I don't know what good it does us. Or not at the moment, at any rate."

He fell silent, brooding. The cab made its way through the rain-drenched streets, past the Boston & Providence railroad station, down Charles Street between the Common and the Public Garden. Perhaps the reverend had been right, he thought; perhaps Crippen, for all his faults, would be able to catch the man responsible for the Bower murders. Perhaps he, Addington Ames, did not need to involve himself further.

And yet . . . Caroline's reproachful face rose up in his mind. She was right, of course. Agatha Montgomery did the city much good with her refuge for fallen women, and he and Caroline should do what they could to help her, even indirectly, to keep the place going. As it would not, if the scandal grew.

"He was filled with helpful suggestions about a possible suspect, was he not?" MacKenzie said, jarring him out of his reverie. "Drifters, hobos, baseball enthusiasts—not to mention the typewriter salesman and the Irish lad. And yet, despite what he said, I would put my money on that dragon matron."

"What? The estimable Mrs. Pratt? Why do you say so?"

"I can't give you a particular reason. But she seemed so filled with anger, so—resentful, is that the right word?—so resentful of the girls, and particularly Mary. Do you not think it odd that a woman like that, so bristling with hostility, would seek employment in such a place?"

"But you heard what Caroline said, and the reverend also. Mrs. Pratt does her job and does it well. Besides which, she claimed to be at her religious meeting on Sunday night. Do we know if she was at the Bower on Monday, when the second girl was killed? I agree with you, Doctor. The woman is hardly a sympathetic figure. Whether that makes her a murderess, I doubt we can say."

At Beacon Street, the herdic suddenly lurched as the driver took his opportunity and whipped his horse across, along Charles Street to Mt. Vernon. Rapidly, they went up the hill and came into Louisburg Square, and then they were home; a tall, redbrick, swell-front town house, with lavender-glass windows and a shiny black front door, fanlight above it and a brass door knocker in the shape of a hump-backed sea serpent—a reminder of the origins of the Ames family fortune, rather depleted now, when Ames's grandfather had been one of the foremost China traders in the city.

Ames paid the driver and they mounted the small flight of granite steps, scraped their boots on the iron boot-scraper beside the door, and went in. The odor of spicy pea soup greeted them, and in the next moment Caroline appeared from the dining room.

"Addington! I am so glad you're home. Margaret is just serving lunch. And this came." She held a small yellow envelope: a telegram.

Hanging his cape on the hall tree, Ames took the telegram and opened it as he went into the dining room.

"Well?" she said, seating herself at her place at the table and ladling out his bowl of soup. "What is it? Something to do with Agatha?"

"I don't think so." He read it again, just to be sure. And it was only a few words after all:

> Can you call this afternoon stop.
> Serena Vincent

Serena Vincent.

He tucked the telegram into his breast pocket and waited until his hands were steady before he lifted his soup spoon. Suddenly, the dreary day had brightened, a fact that had nothing to do with the weather.

"What is it, Addington? Or is it something personal?"

The soup was thick and hot, one of his favorites. "It is Mrs. Vincent. She wants to see me this afternoon."

Instantly Caroline froze. MacKenzie understood her reaction. She was wary of Mrs. Vincent: a notorious—and very beautiful—actress who had once, some years earlier, been a member of the Ameses' social circle. But she'd been caught out in an adulterous affair and disgraced, divorced by her husband, her name never mentioned again in proper Boston households. Instead of having the decency to commit suicide, or at the very least to move away, she'd stayed on in the city and made a successful career for herself on the stage. Only last fall, after not having seen her for some years, the Ameses had made her acquaintance once more.

"Why?" she said, more sharply than she had intended.

"I have no idea. I assume that I will discover why when I go to see her."

Caroline forced herself to change the subject. "How did your morning go at the Bower, Addington?"

He shrugged. "Not as badly as it could have, I imagine." And he told her of their interviews with Matron Pratt and Agatha Montgomery.

"You saw Mary's room! I am surprised that Agatha let you do that."

"Yes, well, perhaps she is more upset than we know. At any rate, there was nothing helpful to be seen there. And then the reverend came—"

"He did? How did he seem?"

Ames glanced at MacKenzie. "What would you say, Doctor? He didn't strike me as being terribly distraught."

"No," MacKenzie agreed. "But then, all these men of the cloth are disciplined to hide their feelings, wouldn't you say?"

"Hmmm." Ames thought about it. "Perhaps. At any rate, he assured us that Inspector Crippen and the police are perfectly capable of apprehending the man responsible for the murder of the Bower's girls, and he has every faith that they will."

Caroline made a little moue of distaste. "Do you mean he asked you not to involve yourself?"

"Yes. I would say he asked exactly that."

"But you won't stop—"

"No. Not yet, at any rate."

"Did you deliver the invitation to dinner?"

"Yes. They will come."

Ames wiped his mouth with his napkin and pushed back his chair. Serena Vincent, he thought. He was eager to be out of the house and on his way to see her. More eager, perhaps, than was prudent.

"Can I be of assistance to you this afternoon, Miss Ames?" MacKenzie asked.

"Oh—no, I don't think so. But thank you."

Ames paused. "In that case, Doctor, perhaps you would like to hunt up Verna Kent? A girl who was expelled from the Bower last week," he explained to Caroline, "and who threatened to harm Mary Flaherty."

MacKenzie nodded with what he hoped was sufficient enthusiasm. "Yes, of course."

Margaret appeared in the doorway. "Cook says to come, miss. The boy from S. S. Pierce hasn't delivered the order, an' the aspic isn't takin' right either."

As Caroline rose and hurried out to see to this latest domestic crisis, Ames said to MacKenzie, "We are well away from here, Doctor. I wish you luck."

And I you, MacKenzie thought.

CHAPTER
9

AT SERENA VINCENT'S FASHIONABLE APARTMENT HOTEL ON
Berkeley Street, the concierge, forewarned, ushered Ames in
and directed him to the elevator. As the uniformed operator
clanged shut the door, Ames realized that he was sweating a
little, and his heart was beating fast.

Stop it, he told himself as the brass and mahogany cage
rose slowly upward. She is an actress: beyond the pale. The
fact that her husband had been far too old for her, and,
worse, a mean and vicious man; the fact that her punishment—banishment from Boston Society—had turned into a
kind of victory for her; the fact that since he'd met her the
previous autumn she had lived in his dreams—all of those
facts were irrelevant. No woman could be an actress and
still be thought of as decent. By rights, he should think of
her only with contempt.

But that was not the way he thought of her: not at all. He
was honest enough to admit it, to himself if to no one else.
The last time he'd seen her, in the fall, she'd been jailed in
the Tombs, dressed in prison garb which did nothing to
lessen the impact of her stunning beauty. He remembered
how he'd briefly put his hand on her shoulder and felt her
warmth through the cheap, flimsy cloth.

The elevator stopped, the door clanged open, and he

stepped out into the thickly carpeted hall. He was admitted by the maid, a middle-aged woman who, as he knew, was more duenna than maid. She took his hat and gloves and Inverness cape, and then she showed him into the parlor, where Serena Vincent awaited him.

She rose as he entered. She was tall for a woman, some years younger than himself—about thirty, he thought—with auburn hair and wide, greenish eyes set in a stunningly beautiful face. He realized with a little pang that he'd forgotten just how beautiful she was, and how could he have done that? She wore some kind of tea gown of grayish-green silk, with—apparently—no corset or, indeed, undergarments of any kind to encase her voluptuous figure.

"Mr. Ames," she said, advancing and giving him her hand. He caught a whiff of her scent—something French, no doubt. "How kind of you to come."

Her voice was low, with a husky, sensuous undertone, but as he knew, she could project it seemingly without effort to the last row of the second balcony.

"Not at all," he said. He was relieved to hear that his own voice sounded steady, reassuringly normal.

A small Yorkshire terrier on a silk pillow by the fire lifted its head and growled softly at the intruder, but at a word from its mistress it subsided.

She motioned him to a chair and took a seat opposite on a brocade settee. He was conscious of not knowing what to do with his hands; he still heard his heart pounding in his breast, and he wondered if she could hear it too.

"I have read in the newspapers about the trouble over at Bertram's Bower," she began. She spoke with grave formality, as if the moment of closeness—intimacy, almost—between them in the Tombs had never happened.

"Ah." So it was not some personal thing, then, that she'd wanted him for. He felt a small stab of disappointment.

"And since you were so helpful to me last fall, I thought perhaps, since it is Inspector Crippen who is in charge of the investigation—"

She didn't need to say more. It was Crippen who had arrested her—mistakenly—for the murder of the infamous Colonel William d'Arcy Mann.

"I understand." He smiled at her. Looking at her was like looking at some glorious work of art created by an artist who specialized in sensuous femininity.

"I wonder if you do." She did not return his smile. "You are familiar with my story, are you not?"

Her story. Did he want to hear that? "Yes, but—"

"I married foolishly, too young. Then I took a lover—yes, I admit it, I have always admitted it. And then my husband divorced me."

"I don't see—you needn't go into it—"

"Ah, but I must, Mr. Ames. You see, when my husband banished me, it was without a penny. I had no money of my own. My own family would not have me back, not after the disgrace I had brought upon them. I was literally without a soul in the world to turn to. I had no place to live, no way to survive."

The amazing thing was, he thought, that she said these things so calmly, only the shadow of remembered pain in her eyes to show that she spoke of her own disgrace, and not, say, that of some heroine in some play.

"It was Agatha Montgomery who took me in," she went on. "Does that surprise you?"

"Yes." It did, very much.

"It shouldn't. I was as destitute as any of the girls she finds on the streets. I very likely would have been on the streets myself if she hadn't helped me."

She paused, remembering. Then: "It was a day toward the end of March. Just after lunch. I knew my husband had learned of my—indiscretion—but I didn't know the end would come so quickly. He handed me my hat and cloak, and a small valise with some clean undergarments and—always with an eye for detail—a bar of lye soap. He took me by the arm and literally pushed me out of the house. I remember that I stood on the doorstep, looking up and down Marlborough Street and wondering if I should throw myself under the wheels of the Green Trolley that was just passing by."

She reached for an enameled box on the table beside her and took out a long, thin brown cigarette. "Do you smoke, Mr. Ames?"

"No, thank you."

But he sprang to his feet to light it for her with a match from a silver matchbox.

She inhaled deeply a few times, seemingly lost in thought. Then she went on: "But even at that blackest moment of my life, suicide did not appeal to me. So . . . for the last time, I walked down the front steps of that house where I had been so unhappy. I walked and walked—I don't remember where. At last I found myself in front of a pawnshop over on Tremont Street in the South End. I realized that I did not have a dollar to my name, but I did have—I was wearing a pearl brooch. I went into the shop. The proprietor took my brooch and gave me ten dollars for it—can you imagine? It was a fine piece, worth much more. But it was ten dollars more than I'd had before, so I accepted it. I suppose I was still in a state of shock, too dazed to bargain with him for a better price. I found a rooming house that did not look too disreputable, and I took a room. For twenty-four hours I sat in that room, contemplating the wreckage of my life. At last I got up, I went out, and I found a café where I had a bowl of soup and a piece of bread—ten cents, coffee included." Her mouth twisted in a bitter smile at the memory.

"As I was leaving, a woman came in. She was tall, ugly, very determined-looking. Yes—Miss Montgomery. She must have seen something in my face that led her to speak to me. She did not recoil when she learned who I was, as if merely to speak to me would soil her beyond redemption. She had heard of my scandal, of course—everyone in Boston had heard of it—but she did not judge me. She offered me a place to live—at Bertram's Bower, yes. Do not look so surprised, Mr. Ames. It was a warm bed, a safe place, a place where I could gather my wits about me and think how to start my life over again, as I needed to do."

"But—" He thought of the sad, defeated girls he'd seen that morning; he could not picture a woman like Serena Vincent among them. "How did you fit into the population there?"

"I didn't—not very well. The matron—this was before Mrs. Pratt—was a kindly woman, far too lax with the girls. So I was able to avoid the classes in reading and sewing, which in any case I hardly needed. I stayed in my room, mostly, for the brief time I was there. Miss Montgomery often came to talk to me. She helped me to see that I was, after all, a child of God like everyone else, and that even though I had transgressed, I was young, I could make something of my life."

She stubbed out her cigarette in a china dish, and then she met his eyes with a somber look. "I wonder, Mr. Ames, if you could understand me if I tell you that Agatha Montgomery is a kind of saint."

Saints were papist things, not part of his own upbringing, which had been Unitarian.

"She is a truly Christian woman," Mrs. Vincent went on, "a rare soul. She labors day after day with the outcasts of this world, with girls who would never be admitted to the decent homes of the city, not even as servants. She gives herself to them, she slaves for them, she rescues them from a life that is worse than death. I know she is hardly an attractive woman. Many people would call her unladylike, unfeminine. She is too driven to be ladylike. All people with a true mission in life are like that, I think—heedless of surface appearances, of the niceties of so-called polite society. She doesn't care what the world says about her, because she has her work to do, and she will do it, come what may."

"You would like me to help her."

"Yes. She needs help now, and I have very little faith—as you can imagine—that Inspector Crippen is up to the job."

"You and my sister both," he said, "agree on that point."

"And did she—your sister—urge you to involve yourself in the case?"

"To do what I can, yes. She feels that if this man—this murderer—is not apprehended quickly, the Bower will suffer scandal that will make it impossible for the place to continue, depending as it does on donations."

"From the respectable people of the city." She made "respectable" sound like a slur. "People who would not allow any of Miss Montgomery's charges into their homes but who feel it their Christian duty to support her in her work. At a respectable distance," she added with some bitterness.

He shrugged. "Hypocrisy does not necessarily cancel out people's desire to do good."

"No. It does not. But I believe your sister is right, Mr. Ames. People will not want to be associated with the Bower if this man—this killer—is not found quickly."

She shuddered. Did she see herself, he wondered, night-walking the streets, as degraded as any girl whom Agatha Montgomery took in? But no, Serena Vincent would never have stooped to such an existence. True, it was scandalous of her to have gone on the stage, but at least it was not too unpleasant a life, and from what he saw around him, she made plenty of money.

Unless she had found a lover to support her. He hated to think that; forcibly he pushed the notion from his mind. She'd recently had a lover, he knew, but the fellow had killed himself last fall, and in any case he'd not been wealthy. Had she mourned him? Did she still? He couldn't tell. But she made a fine high salary at the Park Theater, where she was the resident star; she didn't need some man's fortune to live well. He thought that most women earning so much would have been coarsened—unsexed—by that fact, but she was not. Far from it.

"Do you—now—support Miss Montgomery in her work?" he asked.

"Of course. I give as generously as I can. I can hardly do otherwise, considering what she did for me."

"Her brother does well at raising funds."

"Yes." Her face had suddenly gone blank.

"You know him?"

"I—yes. A little."

"Do you"—it seemed intrusive, but he wanted to know—"give your donations to him, or do you give directly to Miss Montgomery?"

"I give to her."

Tell me more, he thought, but apparently, she was not about to. The moment passed; she was smiling at him.

"Well, then," he said. "Since not only my sister, but also the most acclaimed actress in the city, asks me to involve myself in the case, I can hardly do otherwise, can I?"

He was not accustomed to delivering gallant little speeches, and certainly not to a woman like Serena Vincent, but the words had come to him effortlessly, due, no doubt, to her somewhat intoxicating effect on him.

Yes. He felt intoxicated. He realized it—and realized, too, that he should probably take his leave. Allowing oneself to be intoxicated by any woman, but particularly by a woman like Serena Vincent, was a dangerous business.

But he didn't want to leave. That was the very devil of it: He would happily have stayed in this luxurious little bijou flat for as long as she would have him. Just to sit here across from her and watch her, and catch a whiff of her perfume, and listen to her low, sensuous voice—it hardly mattered what she said—was like some amazing gift.

Just then the maid brought in a tea tray, and so he did not need to take his leave just yet. He accepted a cup and allowed Mrs. Vincent to charm him further with a lively patter, her painful memories apparently forgotten, but all the while, as he watched her, he pondered in a small corner of his mind the story she had told him. Amazing, that she'd been so destitute, that she'd had nowhere to turn for help. She'd been born and bred a Boston Brahmin like himself, but in her hour of need, it had not been any of those folks who had helped her, but another castoff from that same cold, insular tribe, Agatha Montgomery.

". . . and so, of course, we had to demand a rewrite," she

was saying, her beautiful face illuminated with laughter just barely contained. "No one—and certainly not I—could stand before an audience and say lines like that."

"Of course not."

There was a little pause. She set down her cup and clasped her hands—slender and long-fingered, the nails shaped to a perfect oval and buffed to a high polish (and who gave you that stunning emerald ring? he wondered; and what favor did you bestow on him who gave it?)—clasped her hands before her swelling bosom and said, in what he was sure was her best tragedienne's voice, "Mr. Ames, I have never adequately thanked you for what you did for me in the business of Colonel Mann's murder."

"No thanks necessary."

"Ah, but I think they are. If you had not persevered—why, I might have been on trial for my life. And now I am asking you for help once more. I am shameless in my asking, because I ask not for myself but for Agatha Montgomery. If it were for myself, I would not ask at all—but you understand that."

"Yes." Lovely woman, he thought—and where would you turn, should you yourself ever need help again?

She rose, and he did also. "It is late," she said, "and I must get to the theater." She walked to the door, opened it, and went before him into the foyer. The maid was nowhere to be seen, but Ames had the sense that they were being watched.

Mrs. Vincent took his things from the hall tree and handed them to him. When he'd thrown his cape around his shoulders and was reaching for his hat and gloves, she held out her hand to him and he took it. He felt the impact of her touch rocket through him. She fixed him in her lustrous eyes. "If I can be of any help, you will tell me," she said. "I am tied to the schedule of my performances, but otherwise you can find me here."

"Of course."

"And you will let me know how you do?" She was holding his hand in both her own.

"Yes."

His heart hurt a little when she released him. And then he was out in the hall, her door closed behind him. Too late, he wished he'd managed to say something more. As he waited for the elevator, as he went down and out into the street once more, as he stood on the sidewalk and gathered his wits, deciding what to do next so as to avoid returning home and getting in Caroline's way—during all that time he realized that he had the sense of having narrowly escaped some dangerous episode. If he had stayed, if he had kissed her hand instead of merely holding it . . .

Stop it.

She had asked him for help. That was enough—for now.

The rain had lessened, but the chilly damp of the thaw still blanketed the city. He took a deep breath of the salty air and began to walk.

AT NO. 16½ LOUISBURG SQUARE, DR. MACKENZIE ALIGHTED from the herdic. As always when he returned to this place, he felt his heart lift at the thought of seeing Caroline Ames. She would be busy now, of course, because there were only a few hours until her guests arrived, and he'd have no hope of a word with her, or a cup of late afternoon tea by the parlor fire. But still, he would know she was near, he would feel her presence in the house, making of it the home he'd never had, not since his childhood. And even then, that childhood home had not meant to him what this one did.

He took off his hat and gloves and hung his overcoat on the hall tree. His cane stood, unused, in the umbrella stand. He hated it, was glad he didn't need it anymore. Caroline was just coming up from the kitchen as he went into the front hall.

"Oh! Dr. MacKenzie! I thought it was Addington."

Her hair was disarranged, and a grease spot soiled her apron. The cuffs of her sleeves were turned up, revealing a smear of flour on one forearm.

"He has not returned?"

"No." A frown creased her smooth white brow. "I know it sounds selfish of me, but I don't like to think of him with that woman."

He understood: For all her kind and generous heart, Caroline Ames, like all respectable women, was deeply suspicious of actresses. Even actresses like Serena Vincent, who had come from her own class.

"He will be back soon, no doubt." He tried to sound reassuring. Despite her beauty, Serena Vincent was not the kind of woman he himself would ever be attracted to, but he did not yet know Addington Ames well enough to judge Ames's susceptibilities. The man had hidden depths to him, a romantic side to his temperament that MacKenzie had been surprised to discover: Only last fall, Ames had been scheduled to travel to Egypt, to the Valley of the Kings, on an archaeological expedition with one of his former professors at Harvard. The professor had broken his leg, and so the trip had been canceled.

Caroline had reverted to her immediate concerns. "The blancmange did not come right," she said, almost as if she were thinking aloud. "And the hired girl cannot seem to understand that I do not want the napkins laid flat, but folded to stand straight, as I showed her—and she cannot master the folding."

Suddenly she slumped against the wall. MacKenzie, alarmed, put out a hand to steady her.

"My dear Miss Ames, if you will allow me to speak in my professional capacity—you need to rest a bit. You are working yourself up into a nervous state over this dinner, and if I were your physician, I would order you to stop."

She gazed into his kind, worried eyes and managed a smile.

"You are not my physician," she said softly, "but I know you are right. Let us have tea together, Doctor, and you can tell me of your afternoon's adventures."

He slid open the pocket doors to the front parlor, and

Caroline pulled the bellpull by the fireplace to summon Margaret. Then she sank onto the sofa and smiled at MacKenzie again.

"You see how reasonable I am, Doctor. Twelve people coming tonight, and yet I obey you because I trust your opinion."

He heard the sound of hooves on cobblestones, and he went to the window to look out through the lavender-glass panes. In the gathering darkness, the bare trees in the little iron-fenced oval seemed like twisting arms ready to snatch the unwary interloper, and the shrubbery, shriveled in the winter cold, looked as if it hid goblins ready to pounce. The lights in the tall redbrick town houses across the way glimmered with the suggestion of sanctuary.

A four-wheeler clattered by. He gave himself a little mental shake. He reminded himself that aside from being reluctant to spend even the smallest sum on something (like a cab) that he found unnecessary, Ames was a dedicated walker. He roamed the city at all hours, loping in his long stride, thinking, thinking—about what? MacKenzie hardly knew. Ames was a man of many interests, most of them intellectual. In a way, although he had graduated from the College years before, he'd never stopped being a student. He was an autodidact, always studying some esoteric subject or other, a faithful patron of the Athenaeum, visiting his former professors across the river for conversations that lasted long into the night.

Margaret appeared with their tea, and Caroline poured and offered MacKenzie his cup as he came back to her.

"And what did you discover this afternoon, Doctor?"

He settled himself into what had become his own chair, a Morris rocker. "Not much."

"You found the girl who was expelled from the Bower?"

"Yes." He frowned at the memory.

"And?"

"I doubt she could have been responsible for the crimes. She was very ill—with pneumonia, I think."

"She was bedridden?"

"Yes." In a stinking room in a stinking tenement, although he would not tell her that. "She was very weak, with a high fever. She did not want to talk to me at first, but then, when she realized what I was asking her, she vehemently denied any involvement in Mary Flaherty's death. It seemed unnecessary to ask her about the second girl."

"Well, at least you have discovered that much—that she is one less person we need to consider."

He caught the "we," and he met her gaze, which had suddenly turned defiant.

"Yes, Doctor. *We.* I know Addington does not want me to involve myself in this matter, but how can I not? Poor Agatha! I do hope she will come this evening. You're sure she said she would?"

"Yes. And the reverend as well."

MacKenzie was torn. He understood—and applauded— her urge to help her friend. But her brother was right: Bertram's Bower was no place for a lady like Caroline Ames.

But he understood, as well, that despite her charming exterior, she was a woman made of stern stuff. Underneath her pretty coiffure lay a mind as keen, in some ways, as her brother's, despite the fact that it had never been educated beyond Miss May's School for Girls. And her character, too, was steely and determined, infused with a fierce sense of right and wrong. He knew that the Ameses' formidable aunt Euphemia, who lived over on Chestnut Street, had been a stalwart in the fight for abolition decades ago before the war; some of her blood ran in the veins of this delightful woman before him now, and inevitably, it would find a way to announce itself.

She smiled at him again. "You will think me strong-minded," she said.

"Not at all."

"Oh, yes. I can see it in your eyes. You think I am an Amazon, and at any moment I will start to agitate for the vote."

He cringed a little. Given the opportunity, would Caroline Ames join the suffragists?

"No," he said. "I do not think that."

She laughed at him. "Well, to be perfectly frank with you, Doctor, I do not care if you do. But woman suffrage is not our problem at the moment, is it?"

Despite her laughter, her voice was strained. He watched her for a moment, and then he said, "Miss Ames, do you not think you should go up to your room to rest for a while before you dress for dinner? I am sure that Cook has everything well in hand—"

"But I am not," she retorted. "Dear heaven, that reminds me—the blancmange! She said she'd do it over, and she sent down to the market for another two dozen eggs. I don't even know if they've come. Please excuse me, Doctor."

As she sprang up, they heard the front door slam. Ames, home at last, thought MacKenzie. Well, that should ease her mind a bit.

She slid open the pocket doors.

"Addington! I am so glad you're back! Cook is in a temper, and we don't have our blancmange yet, and—"

She broke off. Through long years of experience, she knew better than to bother him with her domestic concerns; this was no time to begin.

She hesitated, torn between her need to tend to affairs in the kitchen and her desire to hear what he might have to report. And so when he came into the room, she followed him.

"Well?" she said. "And what did Mrs. Vincent want?"

He accepted the cup of tea she handed him and took his accustomed place by the fire.

"She wanted what you want, Caro," he said.

"How do you mean?"

Should he tell them the story he'd heard from Serena Vincent—her abandonment, her disgrace, her rescue by Agatha Montgomery? No.

"She is a strong supporter of the Bower," he said.

"She is? You mean financially? I never knew that."

"Yes, well, I imagine she and Miss Montgomery both wish to keep it quiet. Her money is not quite so pure as some."

They heard the unmistakable note of sarcasm in his voice.

"And so she asked you to help?"

"Yes."

Caroline struggled with it, and her better nature won. "I am glad she did that. Good for her. I never would have thought that someone like Mrs. Vincent—"

"Had an altruistic bone in her body?" Ames finished for her.

She lifted her chin. "No, Addington. That is not what I meant. What I meant was, she left the world of good works behind when she took up her life on the stage. I always think of actresses and artists and such as rather selfish, self-absorbed creatures. Which I suppose they have to be. I never would have thought of her as being concerned for women less fortunate than herself."

"You call Serena Vincent fortunate? When she suffered disgrace that would have killed many women?"

"Yes, but she turned it to her advantage, didn't she?"

"Yes," he replied softly. "She did."

There was a silence as he stared into the fire. Then MacKenzie said, "I found that girl, Ames."

"Ah." Ames came back from his reverie and turned his dark eyes on his lodger. "And did she confess?"

"Hardly. She was very ill. I doubt that she could have been up and about two or three nights ago."

"Hmmm. Well, then, at least we have eliminated her. After I left Mrs. Vincent, I went across the river. I took the electric cars"—a new wonder, a marvelous improvement over the horse-drawn omnibuses—"to visit Professor Harbinger."

"Your Egyptologist friend at Harvard."

"Yes. I thought he might be able to tell me something about that very odd note that Crippen showed us."

"And did he?" MacKenzie asked.

"No. It was like nothing he'd ever seen before. We went through all kinds of possibilities—a simple transposition code, the cipher wheel, the Vigenère Table, the St. Cyr Slide, a cipher square with a key word—"

"Excuse me, miss." The pocket doors slid open to reveal Margaret, looking harassed. "If you could come down—Cook's sayin' she's goin' to leave this instant, and the hired girl's takin' a fit—"

And so Caroline's moment of respite came to an end, and with an exclamation of alarm she hurried out.

CHAPTER 10

THEY WERE FIFTEEN THAT NIGHT AROUND THE SHINING MA-
hogany table, and as Caroline surveyed her guests, she felt
a sense of well-deserved triumph. It was going to be all
right—more than that.

The hothouse flowers (expensive, but worth it), the tall
candles glowing in her heirloom silver candelabra, the spar-
kling crystal, the china adorned with the Ames family crest
brought over by her grandfather from Whampoa in '27, the
silver epergne laden with fruit—yes, it was a picture-perfect
scene. No hostess in the city could have offered a more elegant display of hospitality. She glanced at the portrait of that
same grandfather gazing down at them from its place over
the mantel. He'd been a stern man, very old when she was
quite young and never given to showing his feelings, but
he'd be proud of her tonight, she thought, if he were here.

The candlelight—so much more flattering than gaslight—
glowed on the women's shoulders and, here and there, dé-
colletage, and glittered on the discreet displays of jewelry,
much of which, like Caroline's china and silver, was heirloom. Imogen Boylston was wearing her mother's pearls;
Edith Perkins was almost too showy in a matched set of
emeralds; Harriet Mason's grandmother's ruby earbobs dan-
gled and sparkled every time Harriet uttered a syllable,

which was frequently. As Caroline had hoped, Harriet had taken the shy Matthew Hale under her wing. He could hardly get a word in edgewise, but he looked enthralled at Harriet's ceaseless chatter.

The guest of honor, Nigel Chadwick, sat at Caroline's right. He was a small, fastidious man with pale hair and a closely clipped mustache. He wore gold-rimmed spectacles over his bright, canny eyes, and he spoke in a high-class accent that every now and then slipped into what must have been his native cockney. He had the air of a man touring the former colonies—ever courteous, and only occasionally condescending. Caroline could see, from the way her female guests hung on his words (the men were less enthralled), that she was having one of the triumphs of the social season. Her friends, she knew, would be envious for a time, but eventually they would forgive her, and as the evening slipped into legend, Chadwick's bons mots would be passed along, and embroidered upon, and everyone would say how clever Caroline Ames had been to snare him, and how beautifully she had carried it off.

The hired girl, looking smart in her black dress and white ruffled cap and apron, was handing around the salmon mousse. Caroline met the eyes of her friend Imogen Boylston, who lived in a grand house on Commonwealth Avenue and was known for her elaborate entertainments. That lady arched an eyebrow and smiled as if to say, congratulations.

Next to Mrs. Boylston sat the Reverend Randolph Montgomery. He seemed in fine form this evening, chatting wittily on any number of topics, always ready with a quip or a question, all the while devouring with gusto the food that was placed before him. His pomaded hair shone in the candlelight, his handsome face radiated goodwill, his demeanor was that of a man without a care in the world.

But as Caroline watched him, she thought, he knows these people here tonight hold his fate in their hands. He is putting up a good front, but all the same, he must realize the need to extricate the Bower from scandal as soon as possible, so that these people, and others like them, will continue to give generously to his appeals.

His sister Agatha looked less at ease. She sat down the table at Ames's left, next to Desmond Delahanty. She spoke very little and ate less. She should try to seem more tranquil, Caroline thought, to reassure people that she can bear up under the strain of the past few days.

Chadwick was talking about his adventures in America. "I landed in New York—oh, two weeks ago now," he said. "And d'you know, I was delighted to see it in every book-shop. Amazing!" "It"—his book, which he was assiduously promoting—was a slightly scandalous work about Queen Victoria.

"You people over here may have fought a war to separate yourselves from us," he added, "but I believe you miss us all the same. You can't seem to get enough gossip about the Royals."

"Indeed, Mr. Chadwick," chirped one of the ladies. "Tell us something delicious about the Queen."

He paused for effect. Then, with a conspiratorial smile: "For one thing, she is extremely superstitious."

A little murmur of excitement went around the table.

"Do go on, Mr. Chadwick," chirped the same lady. "Don't torment us—do tell!"

"She cannot tolerate a broken mirror," Chadwick said. "And as for spilled salt—a catastrophe! And she lives in dread of certain dates of the month—the thirteenth, of course, but the fourteenth as well. Her beloved husband, Prince Albert, died on the fourteenth of December back in eighteen sixty-one, and"—another dramatic pause—"only last week, on the fourteenth of January, her grandson Prince Albert Victor died."

An audible gasp came from the ladies.

"Yes," Chadwick went on. "Very odd, is it not? But there is more, much more. I should refer you to my book, but—well, I can tell you this much at least. She is a confirmed spiritualist."

A few of the ladies squealed with delight. The hired girl took away their plates and stepped aside for Margaret bearing Cook's potted grouse. Caroline, thinking of the mended platter, mentally crossed her fingers, but it was all right, it held.

Chadwick waited for Margaret to leave the room before he continued. "She used to indulge in table-turning with Prince Albert—her husband, I mean. And after he passed on, she took part in spiritualistic séances with her Scots gillie, the notorious John Brown. He died some years ago, and I have not been able to determine whether she has since made contact with him, wherever he is now."

Chadwick basked for a moment in the admiration of his audience, but then, as if he feared giving away too much from his book, he turned the conversation back to his adventures in America.

"I have been to Philadelphia, to Baltimore, Washington—a strange place, that—and Richmond. I returned to New York for a few days, and then I made my way north, to your fair city."

"And you return to London when?" MacKenzie asked, picking at his grouse. He'd never had it before, and he didn't care if he never had it again.

"Next week—from New York."

"And how do you find us here in Boston?" asked Edward Boylston. He was a stout, balding man, a pillar of strength to the Bower, where, twice a year, he audited the account books.

"How do I find you?" Chadwick allowed himself a small smile. "Why—very well. Very well indeed. You are so very—ah—democratic, don't y'know."

Delahanty met MacKenzie's gaze and quirked an eyebrow. "Democratic" was the last word he'd have used to describe this assembly of upper-crust Bostonians.

"I'm sending back a regular report to my newspaper," Chadwick went on. "I want to give 'em a good sense of you. I've been to the theater in New York, I've visited reformatories and prisons, I saw a hospital in Baltimore, and tomorrow

I am to have a tour of your medical school here at Harvard. I've gone to the big department stores in New York, and to Wanamaker's in Philadelphia. I saw your Congress in Washington—amazing, the oratorical powers of some of those gents. They could give our fellows in Parliament a run for their money any day. I even went to an auction when I first landed in New York. I have a weakness for eighteenth-century stuff, and they'd advertised a little Watteau for sale."

"How fascinating," said Caroline. "Did you get it?"

"No, worse luck. I stopped just in time before I bank-rupted myself. I never saw the fellow who did. He had a straw bidding for it. Someone told me later he was a Boston man, in fact."

They felt that he was chastising them. Was he holding them collectively responsible for doing him out of that painting? wondered MacKenzie.

"We have many noted connoisseurs here in Boston," Delahanty replied, smoothing over the awkward moment. "If you have time, I'll take you to meet Mrs. Gardner over on Beacon Street. She's been buying up half the treasures of the Continent, and she even has a smart young man to help her choose what is best. Her collection is a bit of a jumble, but you might find it interesting."

Caroline threw Delahanty a grateful smile. In the little silence that followed, Matthew Hale, perhaps emboldened by the three glasses of wine he had drunk, leaned around his neighbor, the voluble Mrs. Mason, to peer at the reverend. "Speaking of New York, Reverend, I saw a friend of yours there last week."

"Oh?" replied Montgomery. He did not seem particularly interested.

"Yes, indeed. A most charming lady."

Montgomery did not reply, but a wary look came over his face.

"And she had a most interesting secret to tell me," Hale went on, smiling merrily now. He was flushed, and his eyes were shining brighter than Caroline, who had known him since childhood, had ever seen them.

"I don't think—" Montgomery began, but Hale was too quick for him. He prattled on, chuckling a bit, glancing around the table to gauge the effect of what he said.

"She gave me to understand that she is your fiancée, Reverend. You sly dog," he added, grinning broadly. "I told her that half the single females in Boston had set their caps for you. It was too cruel, I said, that you went to New York to find a bride."

As Montgomery, for once, seemed at a loss for words, they were startled by the sound—and sight—of his sister choking. At once, MacKenzie jumped up and began to pound her on her back.

During this distressing episode, Ames noted that the reverend sat perfectly still, his eyes fixed on Matthew Hale. It was not a look of a man who has had his secret revealed but who doesn't mind very much. Rather, it was the look of a man who would like to murder the person who revealed it. Montgomery's eyes burned with anger, and he did not appear even to notice his sister's difficulty, eased now by Dr. MacKenzie's efforts.

"Well," Hale said cheerily, oblivious of the effect of his revelations on the reverend. "Is it true, sir? Will you soon be entering the sacred bonds of matrimony with that charming lady from New York? Or is she, shall we say, allowing her own hopes and desires to triumph over the facts of the matter?"

The Reverend Montgomery's face had gone from pale to pink to an odd shade of puce. He was clutching his fork in a death grip; had it been his wineglass, he would have shattered it. "I—it is a personal matter, sir," he managed to get out at last.

MacKenzie sat down. Agatha took a sip of water. Harriet Mason asked someone a question about the new exhibition at the art museum in Copley Square. Margaret returned bearing the next course—a melange of vegetables. And so, somehow—Caroline never remembered exactly how—they got past the moment that had threatened to ruin her party.

By ten o'clock they were finishing the blancmange, which

had turned out splendidly after all. Fruit and cheese appeared and were consumed, and then Ames suggested that the men remove to his study for their coffee and port and cigars. A question had come up about ancient Athenian red-figured pottery; he could show them a very fine example, he said, that he'd picked up in Sicily several years before. The ladies, he added with a look at Caroline, could proceed into the parlor, where the men would join them shortly.

Everyone rose. Ordinarily, Caroline should have led the women first out of the room, but when she saw that Agatha had remained seated, as if the effort of standing were too much for her, Caroline asked Mrs. Boylston to take the ladies out. The men left, then, as well, and Caroline and Agatha were alone. When the hired girl looked in to see if she could clear, Caroline asked her to wait.

"What is it, Agatha?" she said. "Are you all right? The evening went well, I thought, and I am so glad that you and the reverend could come—"

Miss Montgomery was visibly trembling. "I do not feel well, Caroline. But as you say, it is very good for Randolph to be here. I don't want to take him home just yet. The men often have much to say to one another away from the women. If I could just lie down for a few moments . . ."

"But of course!" Caroline was alarmed. Her friend really did look ill, her muddy complexion pale, her eyes watering. "I will take you up to my room—we will use the elevator—and you can rest for a bit. Should I ask Dr. MacKenzie to see you? He is very kind, and very wise, I think. Perhaps he could—"

"No—no," Miss Montgomery gasped. "I just need to rest for a bit—perhaps I laced too tightly."

Caroline put her hand under Miss Montgomery's elbow to steady her, and as she did so, her eye was caught by a gleam of gold on the carpet.

"Why—what is that?" she said.

"What?" asked Miss Montgomery. "Oh, goodness, it belongs to Randolph. He wears it on his watch chain."

Despite her momentary faintness, she managed to stoop

and retrieve it. Caroline had glimpsed it for only a second; she thought it was some kind of coin.

"It must have dropped off when he got up from the table," Miss Montgomery said. "I will give it to him later," she added, opening her small, shabby reticule and slipping it in.

After Caroline settled Miss Montgomery upstairs, she returned to the front hall, where she paused for a moment. She heard a burst of masculine laughter. Good.

In Ames's study, the question of the vase settled, he offered port and cigars to his guests. One of them, a man whom Ames did not know well but whose wife was an associate of Caroline's in many of her charities, offered the Reverend Montgomery his condolences on the trouble at the Bower.

"It will pass," the reverend said. "With the good Lord's help," he added.

Chadwick's ears had perked up. "You and your sister have been the subject of the sensational reports I have read in your local news sheets," he said to Montgomery.

"Yes," the reverend replied slowly. He seemed not to want to discuss the matter.

"Do you think—but no, you wouldn't know that, would you? I was going to say, do you think the man is targeting your—ah—place specifically, or may these be random murders like our own case a few years ago?"

"Your own case?" Ames asked before the reverend could reply. "You mean—"

"Yes. He called himself Jack the Ripper, but of course we never knew who he was really."

"Never caught," said someone.

"No."

"I hardly think—" the reverend began, but he was interrupted by Delahanty.

"Did you report on the case for your newspaper?" he asked the Englishman.

Chadwick paused before he replied. "I did, yes."

"And since the police never caught the man—never even came close—he is still at large?"

"At large? I am not sure about that. Let us say that he has claimed no further victims."

"All of them in the slum district of Whitechapel—the East End of London."

"Yes."

"A curious fixation, was it not?" said the man who had first spoken. "Not really killing at random, was he, since he always chose as his victims—ah—ladies of the evening, shall we say?" He smiled in an unpleasant way.

"Yes. Five women, possibly six. From August to November, three years ago."

"And then nothing," said Delahanty.

"Right. It was as if he went away."

"Or died."

"Or died, yes. Or was incarcerated for some other crime. It was a baffling case. There were several suspects, each with his fervent adherents. A local butcher, some said. A demented barrister, some said, who killed himself just when the murders stopped—a convenient coincidence perhaps. Some people even thought that the murderer—and his victims—had some connection to the Crown. I touch on that aspect of the case in my book about the Queen. Her own physician had a very vocal claque supporting his nomination as the Ripper."

"The Queen's physician?" said Ames. "But that is extraordinary, is it not, to suspect such a man?"

"Sir William Gull, yes. Preposterous on the face of it, of course. There was a scurrilous story about one of the Queen's grandsons having some involvement with a woman, a child born, blackmail, et cetera. And because the victims were all—ah—extensively carved up, it has been held that the murderer knew something of surgery."

"Or butchery."

"Or butchery, yes. But may I ask, Mr. Ames—does your killer here send notes to the newspapers the way the Ripper did?"

"No. Not yet, at any rate. But he—"

The reverend loudly cleared his throat. "Do you think it

necessary to burden our visitor with the tawdry details of a minor local case?" he said to Ames.

But the Englishman's eyes had lighted up, and he seemed eager to hear every detail of the murders at Bertram's Bower—to hear them from Ames, if not from the Reverend Montgomery, in the hope, perhaps, of learning some detail that the newspapers had not reported.

"The two women were both residents of the Bower, were they not?" he asked Ames. "I should think that was of some importance."

"It may be, yes."

"And the police have no idea—? Of course not. The police in Boston, no doubt, like the police in London, have far too much to do, and too few men to do it. Has the weapon been found?"

"No."

"Not surprising. A knife is an easy thing to dispose of. Well, I will say this: One thing you can count on is that if the killings continue, as they probably will, there will be a public outcry. Even though the women involved are—ah—of the lower orders, as they were in Whitechapel, there will be panic. Just as there was panic not only in Whitechapel but in all London. The idea of some lunatic stalking the streets and bent on brutal murder is simply too horrifying for the public to bear, no matter who his victims are. Two women dead already, and then a third, and a fourth . . . Oh, yes."

"How do you mean?" Ames asked. "Are you insinuating that—"

"I am not insinuating anything. I am stating flat out that a man who kills in this way will not stop at two. He will kill again."

Not everyone in the room had been paying attention to the conversation with Chadwick, but now, suddenly, all eyes were on him.

"Why do you say that?" Delahanty asked.

"Because it is the nature of the beast. Consider: The bodies of these two women were found not far apart in the same district of the city—a poor district, yes? Although not the slum that Whitechapel is, I daresay. They were both reformed prostitutes. I would wager that some Boston man with a grudge against them, or women like them, has decided to start killing them. In some twisted fantasy of revenge perhaps—or in a hideously misguided attempt to rid the city of their kind. Unless—"

He smiled, not pleasantly. "Unless our man has come over here to America."

There was an appalled silence.

"You mean—the Ripper?" Delahanty said at last. "Here in Boston? But how could that be?"

"Easy enough. Quite a few people in London held to that view—that the Ripper had escaped. Never proven, of course. And so if you assume, as some people have, that the Ripper did not die, did not kill himself or meet with some disaster, and so eluded Scotland Yard's net, you can at least entertain the possibility that he may have bought passage away from London. Where? Anywhere. South Africa, India, the Orient. Or any city in America, Boston included."

"That is absurd," said Edward Boylston, frowning.

"Absurd?" Chadwick removed his spectacles, flicked a speck of dust off one lens, and replaced them. "How is it absurd, sir?"

"Because the Ripper must have been mad, and how could a madman plan so rationally to make his escape?"

"Madmen's twisted minds can come up with diabolical, insanely logical plans," Chadwick said. "Madmen can decide upon a course of action quite as readily as you or I can. That course might be mad—probably will be, in fact—but it is a plan that can be acted upon, and will be acted upon, just as you or I would act upon our own." He waved a hand dismissively. "But we gain nothing by idle speculation. What is needed in these tragic cases is evidence. And that, unfortunately, is the hardest thing to come by. Facts. Information. Physical evidence—those are the difficult things in cases like these. In any event—yes, I understand that it is time to return to the ladies—in any event, gentlemen, I will say to you once more: Your killer, whoever he is, Ripper or not, is not done with his work. He will kill again."

On this dispiriting thought they joined the ladies in the parlor, and shortly afterward the evening came to an end. As the guests took their leave, MacKenzie stood with the Ameses in the front hall, saying good night. Then, his head stuffy with cigar smoke and too much port, he stepped outside and stood at the top of the little flight of granite steps, watching the last of the carriages make their way down the square, their red taillights blurred in the fog that had come with the dark. A damp night, with a raw, penetrating chill. Suddenly, he shivered, but not from the temperature. This is a night for murder, he thought. He remembered Chadwick's warning, and in his mind's eye he saw the shadowy, faceless man who had killed two of the Bower's girls, slipping from door to door along the dark, deserted streets of the South End, searching for another victim.

He turned and went back into the house, grateful that he had such a warm and welcoming refuge as No. 16½ Louisburg Square.

It was the middle of the night, and Caroline lay wide awake, listening to the bells in the Church of the Advent tolling the hours.

Addington had told her about Nigel Chadwick's prediction. She couldn't believe it. Another murder of another Bower girl was not possible—it would be too cruel for poor Agatha, who, on leaving earlier, had looked so exhausted and despairing that Caroline almost regretted having invited her. Perhaps the evening had been too much for her after all. Perhaps she would have been better off back at the Bower.

No. The Bower, now, must be a place of torment for Agatha. Every room in it must remind her of Mary. Poor Mary—a pretty girl who had wanted to better herself.

Who had killed her—and Bridget too?

Why?

Caroline turned over on her side, and then, her mind racing, turned back again.

Who had killed Mary?

Was it the unknown someone who had sent that odd, coded note? Who would send a note like that? And why? And what was the key to the code?

Suddenly a thought blazed across her mind. After a moment, stunned, she sat bolt upright.

Could it be?

She slipped from her bed and turned up the gas, wincing in the light. On the bookshelf by the fireplace. Her own collection of novels by Diana Strangeways, England's premier lady novelist of sensation stories. Diana Strangeways was Caroline's secret vice. Caroline belonged to a Saturday Morning Reading Club, whose members read uplifting works to improve their minds: the poetry of Alfred, Lord Tennyson, the essays of Ralph Waldo Emerson. But no matter how much improving literature she read, she maintained her devotion to the thrilling stories annually produced by Miss Strangeways—tales of love and adventure and fabulous derring-do, whose heroines were always beautiful and strong-willed, the dashing heroes always handsome and gallant.

And always, there was a little trick to the plot—a secret, discovered usually by the heroine in the nick of time.

Caroline was thinking of such a secret now as she took one worn volume from the shelf and then another. Oh, where was it? In *The Curse of the Wigmores*? In *The Second Lady Mandeville*? In *The Velvet Glove*?

Ah. She'd found the right volume at last. Heedless of the chill of the room, she sank down into the little rose velvet slipper chair by the cold fire and eagerly flipped through the pages until she came to it. Yes. There it was. Her heart pounding, she read it once, then again.

Perfect.

She'd not wake Addington now to tell him, but in the morning—

She thought she'd be too excited to sleep when she went back to bed, but she was wrong. She fell asleep at once and slept until her usual time to rise, which was seven-thirty. And when Ames came down to breakfast, she was awaiting him with her news.

CHAPTER
1 1

"MISS STRANGEWAYS?" SAID AMES. HE TOOK HIS PORRIDGE from the tureen on the sideboard and came to sit at the table. "Good morning, Doctor," he said to MacKenzie, who was just coming in, and then, turning back to Caroline: "I hardly think she will be of help to us."

Caroline heard the disapproval in his voice. He had never actually forbidden her to read Diana Strangeways' novels, but she knew he thought of them as no better than trash.

Which, perhaps, they were—but such fascinating, such diverting and elegant trash that even if he had forbidden them, she would have found some way of surreptitiously continuing to read them, year after year, as they appeared regularly from across the Atlantic to a horde of eager, devoted readers in America.

"But just listen, Addington," she said. She'd already tried to explain the discovery that she'd made in the middle of the night—the revelation that lay in the pages of one of Miss Strangeways' torrid, lurid narratives—and she'd botched it. He hadn't understood her at all.

He doesn't want to understand, she thought, because it is coming from Diana Strangeways, of whom he does not approve. Ridiculous. Pry open your mind, dear brother, and *listen*.

She tried again. "Two lovers, Addington. From feuding families—like Romeo and Juliet. Forbidden to communicate with each other, they must contrive to do so secretly."

He was scanning the morning *Globe,* hardly paying attention to what she said.

"So romantic!" Caroline went on, smiling at MacKenzie. Her eyes sparkled as she recalled the story. "Miss Strangeways certainly knows how to make you want to turn the page. At any rate, the solution they—she—came up with was to provide each of them with a copy of the same book of poetry. Love poetry, of course. And they wrote their notes in code, using numbers. Page and line and so forth. Don't you see, Addington?"

He put down the newspaper, and now he was staring at her, his teacup halfway to his lips. He fixed her in his dark, brilliant eyes as if he would see through to her soul—as if he were trying to read in her mind something that even she might not know was hidden there.

"How do you mean?" he asked.

"Two people, working from the same—oh, I don't know what to call it! The same key. Isn't that what a code is? Or a cipher? Or what if—what if, instead of a key, what if there were some kind of cipher machine? Like a telegraphy machine that sends the Morse code—?"

"You must have been reading Jules Verne, Caroline, not Miss Strangeways. A machine? But Mary did not have a machine."

"No, but she had the key to one, Addington. She had the typewriter manual. And would not such a manual have a diagram of the keys?"

Carefully, he put his cup back onto its saucer. He held her gaze still, his mind working furiously.

"Yes," he said as if to himself. "The manual for a typewriting machine." And then, more forcefully: "By God, Caroline, I think you've hit on something!"

She flushed with pleasure. "It was not I, Addington, it was Miss Strangeways."

"Then I am not only in your debt, but in hers as well. She

will never know how she helped us. A typewriting machine! Of course!"

And before she could reply, he had leapt up and dashed out of the room; in another moment they heard the front door slam.

"Now where has he gone?" Caroline said to MacKenzie. Her porridge lay cold and congealing before her. She pushed it away. She'd eaten far too much last night to be hungry now.

MacKenzie didn't answer. He'd risen, too, and had gone through the hall into the front parlor, where he stood at the lavender-glass windows, looking out onto the square. A dull day, no rain yet but no sunshine either; he couldn't remember when he'd last seen the sun.

He caught a glimpse of Ames's tall, dark-clad figure across the square, pounding on Dr. Warren's door. After a moment, a maid let him in.

"Dr. Warren?" said Caroline when he returned to the table. "Why Dr. Warren?"

"You have put into his mind the idea of a typewriting machine. No doubt he hopes that Dr. Warren will have one."

"Ah. Of course."

But Ames's hope was misplaced, as he reported when he came back not five minutes later. "He didn't have one," he said without explanation, as if he assumed they would understand. "But downtown—yes. Are you finished with your breakfast, Doctor? Come along, then. Typewriting! And who of all the people involved in this case would have been familiar with a typewriting machine?"

"The salesman," said MacKenzie.

"Right. Who had a nasty argument with Mary Flaherty the day before she was killed. And who—if my knowledge of traveling salesmen is correct—may have had a way with him, may have been accustomed to seducing the young women he met in his travels. Yes, Doctor? What do you think?"

"I think we'd better see if we can decipher the note before we jump to any conclusions."

"Right again."

They walked rapidly along the square and over the hill to the Common, where they cut across on one of the long paths. In no more than ten minutes they had arrived at Proctor & Moody's Stationery and Office Supply Store at 37 West Street. Proctor greeted them personally, all smiles, hoping no doubt for a good sale. His shop was a wilderness of paper, pens, pencils, bottles of India ink, bottles of glue, letterhead in all sizes (engraving extra), account ledgers, receipt books, blotting paper, green eyeshades, and all the other dozens of items necessary to the modern office.

"A typewriting manual?" he said, his face falling a bit. "Why—yes. Right here. Perhaps you wish to buy a machine?" he added, brightening. "They are very useful, very useful indeed."

"No," Ames replied shortly. "Just the manual, if you please."

He flipped through the pages until he found what he sought: a diagram of the keyboard.

"What a devil of an arrangement," he muttered. "Why did they design it like this? Q W E R T Y— It makes no sense."

"I believe it was done deliberately in that way so that the typewriter—the person who uses it—would not jam the keys," Proctor offered. "But it is not difficult to learn."

"Yes, well, I have no intention of learning it," Ames replied, fishing for his coin purse. "But I will purchase this booklet. Ten cents? No—I don't need a receipt. Come along, Doctor."

Shoving the manual into his pocket, he exited the store, MacKenzie following behind, and went along three doors to a small coffee and tea shop, still busy at this early hour. Settled at a table toward the rear, Ames took out his notebook, opened the manual to the diagram of the typewriter keyboard, and began to puzzle over the code. MacKenzie ordered coffee for both of them and waited.

"No," Ames muttered, scribbling. "It doesn't work. Damn! But perhaps—yes—perhaps this way—"

Their coffee came. Ames pushed his away and went on

working. The shop was overwarm. MacKenzie wanted to remove his coat, but he didn't want to make any movement that might distract his companion.

For some few minutes longer, Ames remained hunched over the materials in front of him, studying them intently, uttering little grunts of satisfaction—or frustration—as he looked from one to the other, made a note, looked again, made another note. Then he scribbled furiously.

"Yes," he murmured. "Yes, I think so."

At last he gave a little cry, causing several of the other patrons to stare at him. "Look here, Doctor," he said. He slid his notebook across the table, narrowly missing MacKenzie's cup, and pointed to the open page. "Look at this—and this! You see? Just as I thought."

Just as your sister thought, MacKenzie amended, but he kept the notion to himself as he scanned Ames's printing:

COME TONIGHT EIGHT SHARP TELL NO ONE

"You see?" said Ames, his face alight with triumph. "Mary Flaherty's death was no random murder—nor Bridget's either, I'll wager. Someone lured Mary to her fate. Someone who very cleverly composed a code that not many people would know how to break. Look here—you see how it goes? It is the letter to the immediate right of the letter desired, so that C becomes V and O becomes P and so forth. He excluded punctuation marks—used only letters, which made it more confusing at first."

"Very clever," said MacKenzie. And indeed it was, he thought, depending as it did on such a relatively new and unfamiliar thing as the keyboard of a typewriting machine. Few people had ever seen a typewriter keyboard; almost certainly none of the girls at the Bower had seen one, except for Mary Flaherty. And it was not something that came readily to mind when one faced the task of solving a cipher. No wonder Professor Harbinger had been stumped. Undoubtedly, it would be years before the scholars at Harvard began to use the machines.

"Come on," said Ames, scooping up his papers. "I must show this to Crippen immediately!"

He proceeded up Tremont Street at a good clip, MacKenzie struggling behind. When the doctor reached the Parker House, he saw Ames just disappearing into City Hall; when MacKenzie finally arrived at Crippen's office, he found the two men deep in conversation.

"I don't see how this helps, Mr. Ames," Crippen was saying. He glanced at MacKenzie coming in but did not greet him, and returned his attention to Ames's pocket notebook, which he held open before him.

"But of course it helps, man!" exclaimed Ames. He paced nervously back and forth across the narrow space between Crippen's desk and the door. "Don't you see? This note was sent to Mary Flaherty by someone who wanted to lure her away from the Bower, secretly, to meet him. At a time when she was supposed to be working in the office—"

"A romantic assignation," said Crippen. "What of it?"

"What of it?" cried Ames. He was nearly exploding with frustration. "Only this—that Mary Flaherty was pregnant! And the man who sent that note—"

"And how do you know it was a man, Mr. Ames?"

"Because one thing we can be sure of is that no woman impregnated her. The note summons her to a romantic assignation, and who else would summon her in such a way except the man who was—is—responsible for her condition? And also because it is so clever a cipher. Far too clever for a woman to have devised."

MacKenzie thought of Caroline Ames, and then he thought of Diana Strangeways, but he kept silent. This was not the moment to distract Ames in a discussion of the mental powers of the so-called weaker sex.

Crippen, exasperated, tossed Ames's notebook onto his littered desk. "I am not arguing with your translation," he said, "just your interpretation."

"Inspector, listen to me. There is a man named Fred Brice who sells typewriters. He is known to have struck up an acquaintance with Mary Flaherty. The Reverend Montgomery told us that Brice was probably in love with her. He is known to have visited her at the Bower on the day before she was killed. They had an argument. Are you telling me that you see no connection between those facts and the fact of this note?".

"I am."

"But you said yourself, Inspector, when you showed it to me and asked me to look into it—"

"Yes, well, that was then. This is now, and the investigation has taken a different turn."

"How so?"

Crippen shrugged. His ugly little face was closed—secretive. And stubborn, thought MacKenzie; he is a stubborn man, jealous of his prerogatives.

"I know where this case is going, Mr. Ames, and it has nothing to do with this note. What is more, I know how important it is that we move quickly. I have had word, this morning, from my superiors. They have warned me about a piece that is to appear in this afternoon's edition of the *Boston Star.*"

"A cheap penny sheet—"

"Cheap it may be, but it has the biggest circulation in the city. Its proprietors practice New York journalism here in Boston, and very successfully, I am sorry to say. And in this afternoon's edition, they are going to run an article saying, in effect, that we have Jack the Ripper right here in our midst. I know it sounds unbelievable, but it's going to stir up trouble all the same."

Ames glanced at MacKenzie; each saw the thought in the other's eyes. "Who wrote it?" Ames asked Crippen.

"A visiting Britisher. A fellow who has done some investigating of his own, apparently, into the Whitechapel murders."

"Nigel Chadwick," Ames said.

"I don't know his name. They didn't say. All I know is, that piece is going to cause a commotion. People are going to be upset—even more than they are already. Only last night, one of my men had to rescue a fellow over on Columbus

Avenue from a pack of screaming women, claiming he was going to murder one of 'em."

"And was he?"

"Of course not. He was a perfectly respectable fellow, just stopped a girl to ask directions of her, and she became hysterical."

"You have ascertained where this man was on the night Mary Flaherty—"

"Yes, yes, of course. We checked him out. He was with his family in Dorchester, a dozen witnesses to attest to it. But about this newspaper piece, Mr. Ames. We have to move quickly, before the entire city gives way to panic. Not to mention the possibility of copycat crimes. I've no doubt we'll have at least one of those before we're through if we don't catch this fellow soon. I have to tell you, I don't think this business of the note moves us along at all. With all due respect—and I appreciate your help, Mr. Ames, don't think I do not—but with all due respect, I have a hunch we're going to resolve this case, and very quickly too. That young Irish fellow at the Bower—"

"Garrett O'Reilly."

Crippen's eyebrows rose. "You know him?"

"I know of him, yes. And you told us the Reverend Montgomery brought up his name."

"Well, then. There you are."

Where are we? thought MacKenzie, struggling to keep his expression free of the dislike he felt for the little police inspector.

"Look at it this way, Mr. Ames," Crippen went on. "We have already agreed that whoever put Mary preggers was in all likelihood the one who did her in, isn't that so? Yes. Now I ask you, who is more likely than that young Irish fellow to—ah—succumb to the temptations all around him in a place like Bertram's Bower?"

"Yes, but—"

"And, consequently," Crippen went on; he was puffed up now, warming to his theme, "if he succumbed, and if he then became frightened of being found out, what was more likely than he'd try to—ah—eliminate the person who could name him as her seducer? And consequently ruin him, hah? The sole support of his widowed mother, isn't he? Wouldn't like to be discharged from his place at the Bower, would he? Couldn't afford to be, in fact. So there you have it. I'm bringing him in anytime now. We'll soon see what kind of story he makes up to try to defend himself. One thing I'm sure of—he won't know anything about typewriting machines."

Ames stared at the little inspector, his lips pressed together as if to forcibly stop some angry retort from spilling out. Then, quietly: "I would ask you to keep an open mind, Inspector."

"Open mind? Of course I have an open mind, Mr. Ames. That's my job. You're leaving now? Just stop by my secretary on your way out, will you? Have him make a copy of that note. I'll put it in the file, even though I can't see what good it does us. But I thank you for bringing it."

Ames looked dreadful, MacKenzie thought—angry, and deeply troubled. They waited for a moment by the secretary's desk while the young man copied the decoded note, and then they were out in the corridor once more, their footsteps echoing on the worn marble floor. Municipal employees hurried by, including a few young women in dark skirts and high-collared white shirtwaists, with celluloid sleeve protectors over their cuffs. MacKenzie hated to see them. Females who ventured into the working world would inevitably be coarsened by the experience; they belonged at home, Angels of the Hearth, presiding over their proper domestic sphere. Like Caroline Ames.

"I want to see Delahanty," Ames muttered. But in Newspaper Row on Washington Street, Delahanty's office was empty. A note on the door instructed callers to go inside and make themselves at home; Delahanty would be back within the hour. Since there was no time noted, it was impossible to tell how long that would be.

They had been waiting for only ten minutes or so, however, when Delahanty appeared. At once he apologized for keeping them. "I've had the devil of a time with my printer—I needed to go to his plant to make my corrections for the next issue. How are you, Addington? Any news? That was a nice time your sister gave us last night, even though I think that English fellow is off on the wrong tack when he talks about the Ripper coming over here."

"Yes, well, listen to this, Desmond."

As Ames proceeded to tell his friend of the interview with Inspector Crippen, MacKenzie saw the Irishman's face, ordinarily cheerful and bright, darken into anger.

"That man is a pox on the population," he exclaimed. "It's always the Irish, isn't it? We are responsible for every petty theft, every assault, every murder—"

"Can you get hold of the lad?" Ames interrupted. "Send him a message—either at the Bower or at his home?"

"Yes. What shall I tell him?"

"What I told Martin Sweeney—that he must come to me if he has any trouble with the police. You must insist that he do so."

Delahanty flushed a little, and he hesitated, biting his lip. He looked almost hostile. "Now, why would a man like yourself, Addington, do a favor for an Irish lad? The Irish being the plague on the city that they are."

"Not as much a plague as an incompetent police force. God damn it, Desmond! Do you think all of us are blind bigots?"

Delahanty shook his head. Suddenly, he seemed embarrassed. "No, I don't. It is just that—well, I don't want to see an innocent lad hanged because he happens to have come from the wrong place."

"Nor do I. Will you tell him?"

"Yes."

Ames's face brightened. "Will you come to the St. Botolph for lunch?"

Delahanty—educated, charming, "literary"—was a member, thanks to Ames's sponsorship and over the objections of some of the older men.

"Not today, thanks. But—" Delahanty put out his hand, and Ames took it. "I beg your pardon, Addington," the Irishman said, his voice a little rough. "I did not mean to—"

"I know what you meant. Don't give it another thought. But do get word to that boy that he must come to me for help if necessary."

"He might not want to. For a lad like Garrett O'Reilly, Louisburg Square is alien ground."

"Nonsense. If his situation grows desperate enough, Louisburg Square will seem a safe haven."

It was nearly noon. In the street, boys were crying the early editions of the afternoon newspapers. All their high, shrill voices cut through the dank air like sharp little knives, but the *Star*'s boys were getting the most business: "Read all about it! Jack the Ripper! Police stymied! Jack the Ripper here in Boston!"

With a muttered oath, Ames plunged through the crowd, threw down a penny, snatched up a paper, and began to read. MacKenzie, seeing the big black headline—JACK THE RIPPER HERE!!!—did the same. Heedless of the throngs swirling around them, they stood on the sidewalk and read the columns of badly set type that contained the poisonous drippings from Nigel Chadwick's pen:

> . . . *brutal evisceration . . . women of the streets . . . a faceless, nameless terror . . . a monster who, unsatisfied in London, has come across the sea to prey on the citizens of Boston . . . the beast will strike again, for his thirst, far from being slaked, only increases with the blood of each new victim . . . a warning to the gentler sex—do not walk at night, do not venture from the safety of your hearth. . . .*

"What rot," muttered Ames. He looked around. All up and down the sidewalk, people were holding the same newspaper, reading, transfixed by Chadwick's reckless scribblings, glancing up with frightened eyes, murmuring in low voices to their companions, looking about them to see if, even now, the killer stalked them.

"Crippen was right to be concerned," MacKenzie remarked as they started to walk. Jostled by the crowd, he bumped into a woman absorbed in the Ripper story. She started, threw him a frightened glance, and quickly moved away. Several men nearby glared at him threateningly.

Ames seized MacKenzie's arm and shouldered his way through the crowd. They turned up Bromfield Street in search of a herdic.

"Damn the man for his mischief," muttered Ames.

MacKenzie was shaken. He'd seen the look in the men's eyes—fierce and hungry, hunters' eyes, eager to seize him and—what? Beat him? Lynch him perhaps? In any case, exercise some rough justice, frustrated that they could not catch the real murderer who now, thanks to the traitorous Nigel Chadwick, had terrified the city and would continue to do so until he—or someone supposed to be him—was caught.

CHAPTER 12

JANE COX LIVED IN A THREADBARE APARTMENT ON PHILLIPS Street, on the back, less affluent side of Beacon Hill. She was a small, neat woman whom Caroline knew only slightly, since they did not travel in the same circles. However, they had in common Agatha Montgomery and Bertram's Bower, and so Caroline was able to dispense with the formalities and get to the point at once.

"You didn't see Mary go out last Sunday night?" she said.

Miss Cox frowned. She sat perched on the edge of a Windsor chair with her hands clasped in her lap. "No. I had the girls in Bible study in the reading room."

"Which Mary was not obliged to attend."

"No. She had"—Miss Cox's frown deepened—"extraordinary privileges."

"So I understand. So when you came in, she was working in the office."

"I did not see her. I saw only that the gas was turned up—the door was ajar—and I assumed she was there."

"You did not speak to her?"

"No."

"And nothing unusual happened during the evening?"

"No. Nothing."

Caroline shifted slightly on her chair. Her corset was too

tight—it was always too tight—and her head ached after the excitement of the previous evening. Perhaps she should not have come out this morning, but she had been restless after Addington and Dr. MacKenzie left, and she hadn't wanted to stay in.

"And after Miss Montgomery returned, you passed the office on your way out, and it was dark?"

"Yes. I have told all of this to the police, Miss Ames, and I don't see—"

"I understand. And I don't mean to press you, but it is such a dreadful thing for Agatha—Miss Montgomery—to have to bear, and if any of us can be of any help to her at all—"

"I will not go there again until this man is caught," Miss Cox said with an air of prim dismissiveness.

"Oh, but you must! It is very important that all of us stand by her—"

"And be murdered for our pains?" Miss Cox exclaimed. "We do enough for her as it is. I hardly think that we need put our lives in jeopardy as well. I do not even want to leave here"—with a frightened expression she looked around the small, poorly furnished room—"and walk to Charles Street, never mind going over to the South End. I will not visit the Bower again until they catch this man. No woman is safe on the streets of the city until he is behind bars."

Caroline bit back the angry retort that sprang to her lips. People like Jane Cox—she thought of her as a sunshine patriot, a summer soldier—were too infuriating. Coward, she thought as she rose to take her leave. You can stay in this miserable little room for the rest of your life for all I care.

But as she descended the stairs and came out onto the street, she could not repress the thought that Miss Cox's sentiments were probably shared by most of the people—the good people of the city—who were connected to Bertram's Bower. Despite her own efforts of the previous evening, demonstrating her loyalty by inviting Agatha and the reverend to her home, most people would probably take the path of least resistance and turn their backs on Agatha while this terrible trouble persisted. Just as she'd foreseen.

This afternoon was one of her afternoons to teach at the Bower. Even more than usual, she looked forward to it. She'd speak to Matron Pratt, she thought, and to some of the girls.

LUNCH AT THE ST. BOTOLPH CLUB ON LOWER NEWBURY Street was always more or less the same: some kind of soup, cream of pumpkin in season, clam chowder or consommé otherwise; some kind of overdone fish or fowl or meat, wet cod or dried-out chops; soggy vegetables; Boston cream pie or Indian pudding for dessert.

This day, the dining room hummed with conversation, as it always did, members trading gossip, trading family news and financial information. Ames and MacKenzie could hear the convivial voices as they came into the lobby, and through the open doors they could see the large communal dining table ringed with men.

Before they could go in, however, someone emerged from the members' room opposite.

"Ah! Ames! Have you a moment?"

It was Edward Boylston, who last night with his wife had attended Caroline's dinner party.

"Yes, of course. Doctor, would you wait?"

MacKenzie said he would, and set about studying the announcement board, where there were often listings of some interest.

Boylston led the way to a quiet corner. He seemed upset, Ames thought.

"It's about the Bower," Boylston said.

"What about it?"

"I had another look at the account books this morning."

"And?"

"And something doesn't add up. I've had my suspicions for some time now, but—"

"How do you mean?"

"David Fairbrother told me last week what he'd given to the Bower in December. And on Monday, Harry Venn said he'd given—well, quite a large amount. But the books don't show it. They show something from both those men, but not the right amount."

"You assume they were telling you the truth?"

"Of course. Why would they lie?"

Ames shook his head. "No reason. What do you propose to do about it?"

"I don't know. I had planned to speak to the reverend, since he does the fund-raising, but in view of the trouble they have just now—"

"Yes. I understand. Well, perhaps you'd better wait until the police make an arrest in the murders."

But this did not satisfy Boylston; he seemed to want to say something more.

"You know the police, Ames."

"Some of them, yes."

"And your cousin—"

"Yes. Sits on the board of commissioners."

"I've never had much to do with the police myself, thank heaven. So I didn't know— You see, Ames, I am wondering if this—ah—irregularity in the books has to do with that girl's murder."

"Which one?"

"The first one—Mary Flaherty."

"How do you mean?"

"Well, she worked in the office, didn't she? I used to see her there myself. She had access to the account books. What if she spotted something wrong and spoke about it to someone who didn't want it known?"

"If, as you say, a lesser amount was noted in the account books than was actually given, how would she have known that?"

"Hmmm. That's true enough."

"I think you should wait for a few days," Ames said. "Let

us see if the police can make an arrest in the murders, and then you can take your concerns to an attorney."

"Yes. You're right. This is no time to start some new trouble over there. I must say, Miss Montgomery looked poorly last night. I suppose she takes it very hard, all this trouble. My wife thinks the world of her, you know."

"As does Caroline," Ames replied. Account books, he thought. Why hadn't he looked at them himself? But it wouldn't have done any good; he wouldn't have known the correct amounts to look for.

He parted from Boylston with a promise to meet again the following week, and then he joined MacKenzie and they went in to lunch.

MacKenzie examined the plate of soup that the waiter placed before him. Clam chowder. Well, that was all right; in his time in Boston, he'd grown fond of clam chowder. As he began to spoon it up, he looked around.

Desultory talk rose and fell. He listened for any mention of the murders at Bertram's Bower, but he heard none. The newspaper that carried Chadwick's poisonous article was not one these men read, and in any case, it had just come out; most of them would have missed it on their way here an hour or so earlier.

No, the murders of two poor girls over in the South End would not concern the members of the St. Botolph Club. Their lives were safe and secure, well removed from poverty and scandal—particularly now that the blackmailing Colonel William d'Arcy Mann and his scurrilous gossip sheet, *Town Topics,* had been done away with. The men here had been glad enough of that, MacKenzie knew; some of them had paid up to the Colonel, and some of them, thinking Addington Ames had killed him, had congratulated him for doing so.

As the main course appeared—roasted fowl of some kind with cranberry sauce and mashed potatoes—a new arrival came in. He was of average height, neatly attired, with a high, domed forehead, a small beard, penetrating blue eyes, and a businesslike manner. Professors were popularly supposed to be absentminded and rather vague, but William James was just the opposite: precise, brilliantly focused, ever alert.

Ames nodded to him across the table. Professor James was just the man he wanted to see, and so, half an hour later, lunch over, the members scattered to their afternoon's business, he and MacKenzie and the professor retired to one of the club's private rooms.

"I must be in Cambridge at three," James said, "but yes, I have a little time. How are you, Doctor?"

MacKenzie said he was well enough. Although he had met William James several times, he was not yet accustomed to speaking easily to this world-renowned professor of psychology—a new discipline, not yet considered legitimate by many in the academic world.

"What is it, Ames? These murders over in the South End?"

"You know about them."

"Yes."

"My sister—" Ames began.

"Has she recovered fully?"

"Yes, I think so."

"Good. A nasty thing, a bullet wound. But you would know about that, Dr. MacKenzie, would you not? So what interest has your sister in these crimes, Ames?"

Ames told him.

"I see. Admirable. She wants to protect her friend and her good work."

"Yes."

"And she thinks her brother is the man to do it."

"Yes."

"She may well be right." James smiled. "So what did you want to ask me?"

"There is a rumor, scurrilously being spread in the newspapers today, that Jack the Ripper has come to Boston."

"I know. I heard the newsboys as I came in."

"As you can imagine, this irresponsible notion—that we

have such a madman in our midst—has put considerable pressure on the police."

"Of course."

"And so I was wondering—I hardly know how to put it. Everyone describes the Ripper as a homicidal lunatic, and that is how they refer to this man here in Boston as well. What the public does not know, because the police have not released the information, is that the first girl who was killed was pregnant. So her condition might have been a motive for her murder."

"But the second girl was not?"

"No. And because her death seems motiveless—"

"As far as you know."

"As far as I know, yes. But if—I repeat, *if*—Mary Flaherty's pregnancy was not a motive, then the killings may in fact have been random acts committed by some madman. But he is not obviously mad, not raving and conversing with voices in his head, or he would instantly call attention to himself."

"No," James replied, "I would think he is not that."

"So what kind of madman are we looking for? Can you venture a guess—make some kind of hypothetical description of him?"

James sat back in his chair, steepling his fingers.

"It is an interesting question," he began. "And you—and your sister—have more than, shall we say, an academic interest in the answer."

"Yes."

"You would like a psychological profile of the man who killed those two girls—leaving motive out of it?"

"Psychological profile," Ames repeated. It was not a term he had heard before, but it fit. "Yes. That is it precisely. What is such a man like, Professor? In his mind—in his emotions—in his soul, if you will? A man who attacks women in the streets at night for no obvious reason other than that they have crossed his path?"

James thought for a moment. Then: "I have no idea."

At once he saw Ames's face drop with disappointment,

and he added quickly: "Which is not to say that I won't try to answer you all the same. What is this man like? Why, I would say that he is like the character in Robert Louis Stevenson's tale *The Strange Case of Dr. Jekyll and Mr. Hyde.* Have you read it?"

"No."

"Fascinating. The great writers—the Greek tragedians, Shakespeare, Dickens—are very wise about the human psyche. I am not sure that I would classify Stevenson as the equal of Sophocles—I would not, in fact—but nevertheless, in that story, he created an unforgettable character, a man who could well be your murderer."

"Or he could be Jack the Ripper," MacKenzie offered.

"Or Jack the Ripper, yes."

"So you are saying—what?" Ames asked.

"I am saying that he is probably a man who is someone like us. An ordinary man, showing no hint of the sickness within himself—a mental sickness rather than physical, and therefore sometimes difficult to see. A softening of the brain, perhaps, that like a recurring fever periodically erupts and drives him to violence."

This is hardly helpful, Ames thought.

"In the story," the professor went on, "Dr. Jekyll becomes more and more deranged—and it shows physically. But that need not be so. This man here in Boston may well seem perfectly normal, whatever that is, with no change in his appearance. The change, you understand, being Stevenson's way of dealing with the mind-body relationship, his way of showing, externally, Dr. Jekyll's mental and spiritual deterioration. Caused by a potion—again, symbolic, used for dramatic effect. I would say that he—your murderer here—is probably fairly low-key. Inoffensive, mild-mannered. But underneath—yes, underneath he is a sadistic killer. It is possible that he gets sexual satisfaction from what he does. I gathered from the newspaper accounts that the girls were pretty badly cut up. Around the female organs? Yes? Well, that fits with what I am telling you."

"So he could be anyone," MacKenzie said uneasily.

"Yes."

Ames gave a short laugh. "Crippen will not be happy to hear that."

The professor shrugged. "That is his problem, not mine. I am simply trying to answer your question."

"Of course. And do you think—since we are assuming that both girls were killed by the same man—might we assume also that he will find a third victim?"

"Or even a fourth or a fifth," James replied.

"Like the Ripper, in fact."

"Yes. Until somehow he is stopped."

Which is what Chadwick said last night, Ames thought. "The Ripper was never stopped—or not by the police, at any rate. The killings stopped, but the police never caught him."

"Is there any record of such a case?" MacKenzie asked. "Other than the Ripper, I mean. A man who kills repeatedly for no apparent motive? Again and again—"

"Serially," James said. "One, and another, and another, and another. That is what I would call him, in fact: a serial killer." The phrase had an ominous ring to it.

"The Ripper was that, of course," James added. "And I suppose Bluebeard would qualify, if he existed. Otherwise I know of no example, nor of any way to predict such behavior, much less prevent it. We have much to learn"—and here he smiled at them—"about ourselves and our darker impulses, which we hide under the rather thin veneer of civilization."

Much indeed, thought MacKenzie. And meanwhile—

Professor James stood. "I must go. My students await me. But listen, Ames. If this man is caught—"

When, Ames thought. It must be when.

"—I would be glad of an hour's conversation with him." James tapped his high, domed brow. "To discover, perhaps, a little of how his mind works. Fascinating, is it not? The workings of the mind—a secret world, each man's mind hidden from every other. Good day to you, gentlemen. I hope I have been of some little help."

CHAPTER
13

THAT NOONTIME, WHILE AMES AND MACKENZIE WERE lunching at the St. Botolph, Caroline ate a hurried, solitary meal at home. Then, well protected against the elements in galoshes and waterproof and carrying an umbrella, she set off for Bertram's Bower, where, half an hour later, she was admitted by a girl she didn't know.

"Is Matron in?" she asked.

"Yes, ma'am." The girl was a dark, bold-looking little thing with slightly protruding eyes. Almost at once she disappeared down the back hall.

Caroline knocked on the office door.

"Come!" was the brusque reply.

Matron Pratt sat at what had been Mary Flaherty's desk. She was wielding a pen, her brow knotted in fierce concentration.

"Good afternoon, Matron." Caroline had never felt quite at ease in Mrs. Pratt's company, and she felt even less so now.

" 'Afternoon, Miss Ames."

"How are you?"

"I'm well enough."

"And the girls—how are they managing?"

A faint sneer crossed Mrs. Pratt's face. "Not so saucy nowadays."

"I was wondering—" Caroline had approached the desk, and now she stood before it, as much a supplicant as any poor Bower girl.

"Yes?" barked Mrs. Pratt.

"I—I would like to talk to some of the girls. I'll start my class on their work, and then I'll have a little while free. Would that be permissible?"

Mrs. Pratt blinked. "Talk to the girls? What about?"

"Why, about Mary and Bridget."

Mrs. Pratt sniffed. "I don't see what good that would do. They don't know anything they haven't already told the police."

"Yes, but—" Caroline's gaze strayed to the bookshelves as she struggled to find a way to make her case. A row of account books, a dictionary, a volume on deportment, and—

"What is that, Matron?"

"What is what?"

"May I?" Without waiting for permission, Caroline stepped to the bookshelf and slid out something that was little more than a pamphlet: an instruction manual for the Remington typewriting machine.

"This is what the Reverend Montgomery gave to Mary," she said, "so she could study it before he bought the machine itself."

Mrs. Pratt regarded her with hostile eyes. "Yes."

"Has it always been kept here?"

"Mostly. Sometimes she took it up to her room to study it. Much good it did her."

"I see." Caroline slid the little pamphlet back into place. The coded note, she thought: And this might be its key. Just as—thanks to Diana Strangeways—she'd thought. Well, she'd have to depend on Addington to decipher it, as she was sure he would.

"As I was saying, Matron—I'd like to talk to some of the girls who may have known Mary and Bridget. Can you give me any names?"

Mrs. Pratt thought about it. Then, grudgingly: "All right.

They might not be so eager to speak to you, what with the police asking questions all over the place. But, yes, go ahead. Say I gave permission."

"Mrs. Pratt—" Had the woman been less hostile, Caroline would have seized her hand; as it was, she clenched her own hands into fists in an effort to strengthen her determination.

"You understand that we—my brother and I—are trying to help you."

To her surprise, Matron Pratt's grim visage softened. "I know that, Miss Ames. You're a good friend to Miss Montgomery. Not like some," she added bitterly. "And Lord knows she needs her friends now. She's built this place up from nothing over the years, she's given her life to these girls, and to see it all disappear, just because of some madman— Well. I made up my mind the day I came here, I would stand by her come what may. I know the girls think I'm too hard on them. Of course I'm hard. That's what I'm paid to be. I don't do it for them in any case."

To Caroline's astonishment, the matron's eyes glistened with tears, and she paused for a moment to regain her composure. Caroline had never thought Mrs. Pratt had the smallest chink in her armor, not the tiniest soft spot in her adamantine heart. But she did: Agatha Montgomery.

"No, I don't do it for them," Mrs. Pratt repeated. "I do it for her. She gives herself night and day, works herself to the bone for them—and do they appreciate it? No. They come in here straight from the streets, and the first thing you know, they're complaining about me. About the discipline, about the fact that I make them keep clean and abide by the daily schedule and do their work—oh, yes, I know they don't like me. But do I care? Not a bit. I work for Miss Montgomery, not for them."

Will wonders never cease? thought Caroline. I can never again think of you with dislike, Matron Pratt, not after this little confession.

"And you are indispensable to her, Mrs. Pratt. I'm sure you know that."

"Yes." Matron was her former grim self once more, all show of emotion gone. "I am. And she knows it too. Now. You wanted the names of girls who knew Flaherty and Brown. You should speak to Quinlan—and O'Connell, I suppose." She glanced at the large Seth Thomas clock on the wall. "They should be in the reading room. You're taking your class today as usual?"

"Yes—yes, of course. I'll just start the girls on their work, and then I'll find—ah—Quinlan and O'Connell." She hated Matron's use of last names only, but she supposed there was a reason for it.

Upstairs, she settled the eight girls in her class into their work. Nine, she thought; there should be nine. Bridget had been in this class. Her empty chair was by the window. As Caroline's throat tightened, she coughed, but the tightness didn't go away. The girls were working on the satin stitch. Most of them were embroidering handkerchiefs—little squares of cloth that Caroline had bought, cut to size, and brought to class. They had hemmed them, and now they were embroidering their initials.

"Go on with it," she said to them, "and I will be back shortly."

They gazed at her with sad, wary eyes. Most of them had succeeded in learning the satin stitch, but in the larger world, when they left the Bower, success at anything would be chancy, she knew. She supposed they knew it as well. Poorly paid clerking in a store, even worse paid factory work—such would be success for them.

She left the classroom, closing the door behind her. She was on the second floor. The Bower was quiet, everyone at her assigned place. She'd need to look in on Agatha before she left, if only to make sure that her indisposition of last night had cleared up. But just now she wanted to find the girls who had known Mary and Bridget.

The reading room was at the back of the second floor. Its shelves were filled with mostly self-improving tomes: *A Young Woman's Guide; A Treatise for Young Ladies; Mrs. Smallwood's Manners and Morals*. Diana Strangeways would have no place here, thought Caroline, which was too bad. Her stories were sensation stories, yes, but at least they gave one some enjoyment; these stuffy preachings could put a girl off reading for life.

A few young women were sitting at tables, books spread open before them. At least one, resting her head in her hands, seemed to be asleep. The girls Caroline sought were sitting side by side, whispering—something that was forbidden by the list of rules posted on the wall: no talking, no whispering, no exchanging of notes, no eating, no sleeping. . . .

They seemed startled to see her, but then they recognized her as one of the good women of Boston who regularly came to teach them. And when she asked them to come with her, they promptly obeyed—glad, perhaps, to leave the reading room and its stultifying offerings.

Where to have a private word with them? They suggested the dining room at the rear of the first floor. It would be empty now, and they probably would not be disturbed.

Quinlan—that was Liza—was the more forthcoming of the two. She was brown-haired, plain, with a scar across her upper lip where once, perhaps, it had been split. She'd taken a penmanship class with Caroline several weeks before, and Caroline had liked her; she'd seemed bright, with a fair amount of gumption. Now, in fact, she showed a remarkable amount of spirit as she answered Caroline's questions.

Yes, she remembered the fight between Mary and Verna Kent. Verna had threatened Mary—oh, yes. She'd screamed and yelled something terrible. Matron herself had had to forcibly put her out.

And then on the street—yes, Verna had found Mary the next day and had threatened her again.

"But in the end, she didn't actually do Mary any harm?" Caroline asked.

"No, miss." Liza's eyes grew round as she considered the implications of the question. "Do you think it was Verna who done it, miss? Mary an' Bridget both?"

"No. In fact, I am fairly certain it was not. We found Verna. She is very ill. I don't believe she could have been well enough to get up in the night and walk out into the pouring rain."

Liza nodded, somewhat reassured.

Why? Caroline wondered. Because of the notion that it was, after all, some stranger who had done these terrible crimes rather than a girl who had lived among them? Yes: A stranger they could understand, menacing though he might still be. But to believe that a girl like themselves had killed someone she'd known at the Bower—that was too unnerving.

"Did you know Mary well, Liza?"

Liza shrugged. "Some."

"Katy? Did you?"

Katy was pale: eyes, hair, skin—all of it. She licked her lips nervously before she replied. "A little, yes, miss."

"And do you know if she had any enemies? Anyone who might have wanted to do her harm?"

Katy let out a nervous laugh. "Nobody liked her much, miss."

"Why not?"

"She was—" Like the others, Katy had a vocabulary too limited to express herself well. "Uppity, like."

"You mean, she gave herself airs? Thought she was better than everyone else?"

Katy nodded, relieved to have been understood. "That's it. Like she was too good for us. An' she used to say how she wouldn't be here for long."

"Because she was going to find another position someplace else? Or—"

Katy's face twisted with the effort of remembering precisely. "I think—well, she didn't come right out an' say it, but I think she had it in mind to get a husband."

"Really? And did she say who he might be?"

Katy shook her head. "No. But I heard her say"—she affected a high, mincing voice—" 'I'll have a ring on my finger before long. An' good riddance to all of you here.' "

She lifted her chin. "I ask you, miss, who would marry one of us?"

Her simple question—the bleakness of it, the premise upon which it was based—wrung Caroline's heart. Who indeed?

"But you never knew who the man was? She never mentioned a name?"

"No, miss."

"We didn't see much of her," Liza offered.

"Because she worked in the office?"

"Yes."

"And that was another reason she—ah—gave herself airs? Because she had that position?"

"Yes."

Liza seemed to want to say more, but she was having trouble with it.

"Go on, Liza," Caroline prompted.

They sat before her, eyes downcast. What is it that they are not telling me? Caroline wondered. And how can I persuade them to divulge it? She felt like a bully, but she pushed on nevertheless. "Because she worked in the office for Miss Montgomery," she said, "and because—"

"Because of *him*," Liza said very low.

"Who?"

The two girls exchanged a glance. Liza sniffled. "I don't like to say, miss."

"Oh, but you must tell me, Liza. If Mary knew anyone—any man, I mean—who might have wanted to do her harm—"

"Oh, I don't think that, miss. I don't think he wanted to do her harm. But she was friendly with him, like, an' she gave herself airs on account of it."

"Who? Who do you mean, Liza?"

Again the two girls glanced at each other. Katy bit her lip, shifted uneasily in her chair.

"Himself," Liza said then. "The Reverend Montgomery."

"Ah." There was a brief silence as Caroline absorbed it.

"But of course—he promised her a typewriting machine, didn't he?"

The coded note, she thought. But no, that must have come from the elusive typewriter salesman.

Liza nodded. "You'd never believe the way she carried on about it." Her eyes were hostile, remembering. "Oh, she was little Miss Princess, bragging about it. Who'd want one of them things anyways? *I* wouldn't! It would hurt your hands somethin' awful to use it."

"But about the reverend," Caroline said, steering the conversation back to more pertinent paths. "She was friends with him?"

Katy threw her a sly glance—a glance far too knowing about the world and its wicked ways, Caroline thought.

"Maybe more," Katy said. "Maybe she was more than friends with him, if you know what I mean."

Caroline struggled to keep her expression noncommittal. Mary was pregnant, the medical examiner had said; but surely not by the Reverend Montgomery?

"No, Katy, I am not sure I do know what you mean."

Katy shrugged. "Goin' out at all hours, an' where did she go, if not to him? I seen her once, comin' out of his place. She was all—like—flummoxed. But happy—she looked real happy. 'What'r' you doin' there,' I asked her, but she wouldn't say. She just got that look on her face, like 'That's for me to know and you to find out.' An' when he came here, just happenin' to run into him, always givin' him the eye." She batted her eyes in an exaggerated imitation of a flirtatious look. "Like that. 'Oh, yes, he's goin' to buy me a typewritin' machine. He's my special friend. He's such a handsome man, isn't he? An' a real gentleman.'

"That's the way she went on, miss. Enough to make you sick. As if a gentleman like the Reverend Montgomery would ever give her a second look."

Liza had been troubled during this last, and now she said, "But he did, didn't he?"

"Give her a second look, you mean?" Katy replied.

It was a dialogue now between the two of them, with Caroline watching on the sidelines.

"Yes. He didn't seem to mind, the way she made up to him."

"I seen them one time when they didn't know I was there," Katy said. "I was comin' down the stairs, an' the office door was open a bit, an' they were standin' inside." She giggled and flushed a little, and threw a half-ashamed glance at Caroline. "An' he had his hand—oh, I daren't say it, miss. He had his hand *here*—" And she gestured toward the insignificant swell of her bosom.

Really, thought Caroline, I do not believe this. The Reverend Montgomery may be no better than he should be, but surely he has some sense of decorum.

"She wasn't the only one neither," Katy added.

"How do you mean?"

"I seen him once in the back hall with—what was her name, I can't remember. She's gone now. It was just after I came here, an' she was in her last week or two. I knew who he was because he talks to each of us before Miss Montgomery takes us in."

"He does?" Caroline was surprised. "I didn't know that."

"Yes. We all have to have a private talk with him, like, beforehand."

Times had changed, then, Caroline thought, from when Agatha roamed the nighttime streets looking for candidates for her charity—girls who would immediately be taken in, fed, tended to, given a bed. Perhaps it was understandable that now she asked her brother to interview the girls first, since her reputation had spread, and there were so many more, it seemed, needing her help.

Or perhaps she hadn't asked him to do it. Perhaps he had insisted.

"So you saw him with a girl?"

"Yes."

"And what were they doing, together there in the back hall?"

"He was—I don't know. She was pushin' him away."

"And did she succeed?"

"Yes, miss. She got away from him."

"And did he see you?"

A sudden look of fear crossed the girl's face. "No, miss."

"You hope," Liza said.

"He didn't. I know he didn't," Katy said firmly, but still she looked frightened.

Of course Katy could never have reported such an incident, Caroline thought. Who would believe it?

"What about Mary?" she said. "Can you remember what happened on the night she was—on the night she died?"

"How d'you mean?" Liza asked.

"I mean, did anything unusual happen? It was Sunday—" Only last Sunday; it seemed much longer.

They thought about it. "The police already asked us," Katy said.

"I know they did. But perhaps by now you remember something you didn't tell them. What did you tell them, by the way? Anything?"

"No, miss. Nothin' to tell. It was Sunday night, like you say. We had our supper. Matron went out to her service, like she always does."

"And Miss Montgomery was out, too, so Miss Cox was in charge."

"That's right."

"Mary was working in the office."

"Yes."

"Did you see her go out?"

"No. We was at Bible study with Miss Cox, up in the readin' room, an' then we went to bed."

"What time was that?"

"Well—" Katy hesitated, working it out. "The rest of 'em went up about half past eight. But I had to stay back with Miss Cox because I was bad."

"Bad? How were you bad, Katy?"

She glowered, remembering. "I laughed."

"You laughed. At—?"

"Samuel Two, eleven."

"I see." David and Bathsheba. Caroline smothered a smile herself. Jane Cox, lacking the character to be faithful to Agatha, also lacked a sense of humor.

"So you stayed behind with Miss Cox—"

"An' when I was goin' out, after a while, I saw Miss Montgomery comin' in."

"And did you speak to her?"

"No, miss. I was goin' up to bed, an' I heard the door an' I looked down into the front hall. She came in all wet—soakin', she was. She had her bag with her"—her carpetbag, which she had carried, Caroline knew, for as long as she'd run the Bower. In former times, she would carry food in it, or shawls, or bottles of one patent medicine or another, to give to girls on the streets—"an' she just stood there, like she was too tired to walk up the stairs. I didn't think she'd want to speak to me."

"I see. Well, that was thoughtful of you, Katy. I imagine that she was exhausted, and what with the rain—"

"She was drippin', miss. I thought for sure she'd be taken with the pleurisy, but she wasn't."

"All right. So much for Sunday night and Mary. Now, what about Bridget? Did you know her?"

"Some."

"And? Did she have any enemies? Anyone who might have wanted to harm her?"

They couldn't think of anyone.

"And you saw her last—?"

"Monday," Liza said. "She wanted to go out, an' Miss Montgomery didn't want her to."

"No, of course she didn't want her to. But Bridget was disobedient, and she went out anyway?"

And learned the grim lesson: Disobedience brought swift and certain punishment. In Bridget's case, death.

"Yes."

"Can you remember anything else about Bridget that day?"

Liza's glance wavered as she looked away.

"Well? What is it?"

"She—she an' Garrett—"

"Yes? What about Garrett?"

"He was pesterin' her, like."

Worse than pulling teeth, Caroline thought.

"How do you mean, pestering her?"

"I don't know. I don't know what he said. But he said somethin' to her and she said, 'Leave me alone!' She was cryin'."

"This was before she had her argument with Miss Montgomery?"

"Yes. Just before."

"Did you ever see them talking another time? Garrett and Bridget?"

"Yes, miss. Once or twice. I think—"

Katy's brow creased with the effort to articulate her thoughts.

"I think she was afraid of him," she said at last.

"Afraid? Of Garrett? But why?"

"I don't know, miss."

There seemed nothing more to be said. The two girls sat quietly before her, humble, deprived, rescued here temporarily by Agatha Montgomery but destined soon to go out into the world again to try to survive. Caroline felt sudden tears prick at her eyes, and she blinked rapidly to banish them. Crying would do no good—not for them, and not for Mary or Bridget either. It was information that was needed—and after all, these two had given her some of that.

She thanked them for their help and watched them as they rose and went out. For a moment she sat alone in the empty dining hall. All the tables were laid for supper, crockery and cheap tin flatware, row after row of empty places that soon would be filled with the Bower's girls taking their evening meal. The food at Agatha's was hardly lavish, but Caroline knew it was nourishing enough, meat and potatoes and porridge and milk. Most girls, after their three-month stay, were considerably healthier than they'd been when they came.

Garrett. Why had Bridget been afraid of him? What had he wanted from her?

And who was the man Mary had spoken of? A man she'd thought might marry her—who could that have been?

Would a typewriter salesman take up with one of the girls from Bertram's Bower?

And as for the Reverend Montgomery—no, it was unthinkable. Surely Katy and Liza were mistaken about him.

It was time to talk to Cook.

The Bower's kitchen, a vast space taking up most of the basement, was in full battle mode as the evening meal was being prepared—mutton stew, from its pungent smell. In a far corner, by the back door, Caroline saw a man—dirty, dressed in rags—wolfing down a chunk of bread. As he saw her come in, he slipped out. Cook, who had no other name that Caroline knew, was berating one of her slaveys for not properly scouring the pans. Her broad red face was redder than usual, and her voice rained down on the unfortunate girl's head like so many blows. She broke off abruptly as Caroline came in.

"Good afternoon, Cook."

" 'Afternoon, miss."

"I was wondering—could I have a word?"

The woman hesitated, but then she relented. With a curt order to the slavey, she led Caroline into a small pantry at the back.

"Now, miss, what is it?" She stood facing Caroline, arms akimbo, her stout torso swathed in a vast white apron.

"Garrett?" she said when Caroline asked about him. "No, I haven't seen him all afternoon. He was here earlier though."

"Do you see him often?"

"Often enough."

"Do you—might he have some attachment to one or another of the girls, do you think?"

Cook stared at her. "Attachment? I don't know what you mean, Miss Ames. He's a good boy, minds his business. Miss Agatha was kind to give him work here, and he knows that," she added grimly.

"You have been here—how long?" Caroline asked.

"Miss Agatha hired me from the Intelligence Office the

first week after she set up here, and I've been with her ever since."

"She is fortunate to have you," Caroline murmured.

"I am fortunate to have her, miss." Cook's face revealed nothing. "She took me on when I needed a place, I don't mind telling you. Not that I haven't worked hard for her. I always have, and I always will, because Miss Agatha is the best woman in the world and she needs all the help she can get."

"Yes," Caroline replied. "She is. She does. And this dreadful business—"

"Hurts her. Yes. It hurts all of us. It hurts her brother too. Miss Agatha is a wonderful woman, and he's just the same—the best man in the world."

"Yes, I—"

But Cook had warmed to her subject now and was not to be stopped. "I feed him up, poor man. He comes in here nearly every day—he lives alone, y'know, no one to care for him. Get yourself a housekeeper, I say to him. Someone to look after you. But he won't—doesn't want the expense. Wants every penny he gets to go either to his church or to this place."

But he doesn't spare himself on his wardrobe, Caroline thought.

"So he comes in here," Cook went on, "and we talk, and he gets something to eat. He's a fine man, a good worker for the Lord. And the Lord will reward him in the end."

"I think all of you here will find your reward," Caroline replied, "if we can just get past this terrible business. Matron has told me—"

"That one." Cook's mouth clamped shut.

"Mrs. Pratt? What about her?"

"I don't like to tell tales, miss."

Oh, but do, Caroline thought. Tell me anything. Everything. What do you know, Cook?

"What about her?" she said again. "She is very strict with the girls?"

"Well, she has to be, don't she? But it's different with her, isn't it?"

"How do you mean?"

"I mean—" Cook struggled with it. "I mean—she don't care about the girls here. Not the way Miss Agatha does, nor the reverend neither."

True, Caroline thought. But please explain.

"Sometimes I think—"

"What? What do you think?"

"I don't like to speak out of turn, miss. But I s'pose you heard one of my best knives is missing. The police wanted to know all about that, I can tell you. I don't know, I said. All I know is, all my knives was here on Saturday night when I left—I spend Saturday night till Monday morning with my cousin in Brighton—and when I came in on Monday morning, one of 'em was gone. I always sharpen the knives before I go on Saturdays, lay them out in the drawer, each one in its place. So when I came in to work on Monday morning I went right to the drawer like I always do, and right away I saw someone had taken one."

"No chance you misplaced it?"

"No, miss. I'm very careful with my knives. Have to be, don't I?"

"Yes. Of course you do. But are you telling me you think someone here took it? Someone at the Bower?"

"Well, who else?"

"I saw a man just now—a stranger. Men come to beg food here?"

"Yes." Cook threw her a defiant look. "I feed them when I can. I know what it is to be hungry."

Not recently, Caroline thought, taking in the woman's ample girth.

"Could someone have broken in while you were away?"

"No. Not with Her Nibs up there keeping watch."

"You mean Matron."

"Snotty old bitch," Cook muttered. "Don't care a thing about these girls. Spends all her time smarming up to Miss Agatha—oh, I tell you, miss. We've had some run-ins, Matron Pratt and me. She comes down here, ordering me about like I was some kind of servant to her—which I'm not. Miss Agatha gave me full charge of the kitchen and there's no one can tell me what to do. But Matron comes down, tells me I'm putting too much food out. Too much food—too expensive, she says. Cut back, she says. But how can I do that? These girls need feeding up. They come in all worn down to nothing, I don't care that they've come off the streets, they're flesh and blood just like you and me. I'll feed them as much as I can, I says to Matron. Miss Agatha is the one to tell me if I'm spending too much on provisions, and she never has told me so yet. So go about your business, I says, and leave me to mine."

Caroline nodded. "Good for you, Cook."

Cook leaned in close, and Caroline caught a whiff of liquor on her breath. "You want to know what I think, Miss Ames?"

"Yes—tell me."

"I think—" Cook looked around, although they were quite alone in the pantry, well away from the activity in the kitchen. "I think the police maybe should ask Matron a few more questions."

"Why do you say that?"

"Because. She's a mean one, make no mistake. I heard—mind you, I didn't see it for myself—but I heard a while back she was saying she would beat one of the girls. Beat her, can you imagine? Lord knows she's as strong as a bull. And has a nasty temper to boot. Where was Matron on Sunday night, I ask you."

"She was at her religious meeting, I believe."

"Hah. Religious meeting."

"And when Bridget was killed—"

"I don't know about Bridget. But on Sunday night—the night Mary was killed—Matron was coming back from her meeting, wasn't she? Could'v' done it then, couldn't she? Could'v' taken my knife on Saturday night or any time on Sunday, couldn't she?"

"Well, I—"

"I have to get back to work, miss. I don't know if I've helped you at all, but you just think about what I'm telling you, and see if it makes any sense."

With that, she pushed open the pantry door and went back to the kitchen. As she did so, Caroline caught sight of a tall, thin youth in conversation with one of the slaveys.

He knew who she was, of course, and now he met her gaze and even smiled a bit as she approached. As always when she saw him, she was struck by his looks: He was extraordinarily handsome, with a wide brow, a strong jaw, black hair, and sapphire-blue eyes. He had, as well, a good, decent, intelligent look to him. She thought he was perhaps nineteen or twenty years old.

"Garrett."

"Miss Ames."

"How are you?"

"Not so bad." As he edged away from the slavey and toward her, she saw and remembered his limp. Childhood meningitis, someone had told her; he was fortunate that he wasn't crippled altogether.

"Garrett, I was wondering—" How to put it, that she was nosing about in the Bower's affairs?

She tried again. "I was wondering if you—ah—ever had any dealings with Mary Flaherty?"

He'd been smiling at her—a bit too familiarly?—but now his smile faded, and as his finely chiseled features subtly changed expression, his eyes became cold. "Dealings, miss? How d'you mean?"

"I mean—" Well, what did she mean after all? She could hardly put it to him plainly. "I mean, did you know her?"

"Yes, miss."

"How well?"

"Not well. I knew who she was."

"Did you ever speak to her?"

"Yes, miss. Now and again, I did."

The Irish were reputed to be a mysterious race, hard to fathom. She didn't know any Irish well except for Desmond

Delahanty. I should have asked him to accompany me, she thought; Garrett will never tell me anything on my own.

"But you weren't—ah—friends with her?"

What was it she saw in his eyes? Contempt? Surely not. "No, miss."

"So you wouldn't know about any—ah—particular friends she might have had? Apart from here at the Bower, I mean."

"Particular friends? No, miss. I—" He broke off, as if he'd been about to tell her something and had thought better of it.

"What, Garrett? Please tell me." Do you know that Inspector Crippen suspects you? she thought.

"Well, I was goin' to say, I don't think she was a friendly sort of girl, if you know what I mean."

"No. I don't."

"Well—" He lifted his thin shoulders in a shrug. He was wearing a faded, tattered jacket and mismatched trousers, but even his ragged clothing, even his extreme thinness (and why did not Cook feed him up along with the reverend and all the Bower girls and the occasional tramp?) could not detract from his striking good looks. In another lad, those looks might have made his fortune, but for him they were no help at all. Oh, Garrett, she thought, life is so very unfair. Help me to keep it from being even more unfair to you than it has been already.

"You mean, she gave herself airs?" Caroline asked.

"Yes."

"Thought she was too good for most of the people here?"

"That's it. She never would have bothered with the likes of me."

She'd have done better if she had, Caroline thought.

"You didn't like her?"

Again he shrugged, as if the matter were of no importance. "I suppose I didn't. What of it?"

"Nothing. Nothing at all. And you weren't here on Sunday, of course."

"No, miss."

"You don't really have any contact with the girls here, do you?"

He looked faintly puzzled. "No, miss. It's not my place to do that."

"Of course not. So you don't know any of them particularly well, do you?"

"My ma would have my hide, miss. She thinks it's bad enough I work here. She says—" A faint flush rose to his thin cheeks. "She says they're bad, these girls."

"So you've never become friendly with any of them?"

"No, miss."

"You didn't know Bridget at all?"

"No, miss."

"Never spoke to her?"

"No, miss."

He was getting restless under her questioning; no doubt he wanted—needed—to be about his work.

"Thank you, Garrett. I won't keep you. Oh—just one more thing."

He had turned away with a respectful nod to her. Now he stopped short, but he didn't turn back.

"Garrett?"

He faced her. "Yes, miss?"

She was scrabbling in her reticule, where she kept a small store of useful pamphlets, timetables, and the like. "Can you—could you just read this railway schedule for me? I seem to have forgotten my spectacles."

He looked at the little scrap of printed paper she held out to him, but he didn't take it. "I don't read, miss."

She felt a little stab of astonishment even as his admission told her what she wanted to know. "You mean, you can't? You never learned?"

Some people would have been ashamed to admit it, but he was not. He regarded her coolly, and with dignity.

"That's right, miss. Most of us don't, at home. Only Michael, in the primary school. He's learning."

"I see. Well, thank you anyway, Garrett."

"Yes, miss."

As he made his way out of the kitchen, she watched him go. There was a settlement house in the North End, with classes in reading and writing English. Perhaps she could persuade him to sign up. His limp was one thing; not to be able to read was far worse.

Or perhaps he could read after all. Perhaps he'd lied to her.

As he'd lied about Bridget. Liza had said that Garrett and Bridget had had words—that Bridget had been afraid of him, had complained that he was harassing her.

Was that true? It must be true. Why would Liza make up such a thing?

So while Garrett might deny harassing Bridget—probably he would, in fact—why would he deny ever speaking to her at all?

CHAPTER 14

"AND YOU BELIEVE HIM, CAROLINE?" AMES ASKED.

"I don't know what to believe. But that he can't read—yes, I believe that."

She sipped her tea, thought about taking an iced lemon cookie, and decided against. Her warm-weather wardrobe, such as it was, would never fit if she didn't lose ten pounds. She hadn't worn it last spring because she'd still been in mourning for her mother. Now, with the passing of another year, she was sure she'd have to take every single item to the dressmaker to be let out.

She had come home from Bertram's Bower half an hour ago, a little later than usual, and both Dr. MacKenzie and her brother had been quick to tell her they'd been worried about her. Never mind what she'd been able to learn at the Bower, Ames said, the city was a dangerous place just now.

"I saw a man being set upon in the Public Garden as we came home," he told her. "Poor chap—he'd stopped to ask a lady if he could assist her, and she started to scream about the Ripper. In no time, half a dozen men had tackled him. Lucky the fellow got away with his life."

"Chadwick did us all a bad turn with his mischief-making," MacKenzie said.

"He might at least have warned us," Caroline replied indignantly. "Do you know, Addington, I feel as though he—"

well, as though he betrayed us somehow. I mean, how could he come here to dinner, and sit among us all for the entire evening, and not warn us what he'd done?"

"He did warn us, in a way," Ames said. He was standing at his usual place by the hearth; as he spoke, he stared into the simmering flames as if there he would find the answers that eluded him.

"How do you mean?" Caroline asked.

"Well, he told us about the theory that the Ripper had escaped to America. To Boston, in fact."

"That is hardly the same as warning us that he was about to set the city on its ear and throw people into a panic. Really, Addington! The nerve of the man! To write such an irresponsible piece—and in that trashy newspaper."

He half turned to throw her a smile. "No, it isn't the same. But still, it gives Crippen something more to chew on. Perhaps it will deflect him from the Irish boy. Who else did you speak to at the Bower besides Garrett O'Reilly?"

She recounted her interviews with Matron Pratt, with Liza and Katy, with Cook. When she finished, they were silent for a time. Darkness had long since fallen; the shutters on the lavender-glass windows were closed, keeping them safe against the night.

Suddenly, involuntarily, Caroline shivered—so violently that MacKenzie, noticing as he noticed everything she did, took a crocheted afghan from the sofa and offered it to her.

"No—no, I am not cold, Doctor, thank you." Just the opposite, in fact; what with the fire and the closed pocket doors, the room was uncomfortably warm. She wished she could unbutton the long, tight sleeves of her dress and loosen the high collar that, just now, threatened to strangle her; she wished she could be rid of her corset, remove the binding whalebone stays that constricted her waist.

And yet, so warm, she shivered—with fear, with dread of what the dark might bring. Yes, Matron was right to be strict with the Bower's girls, and tonight she must be stricter still. Tonight she must forbid them—literally on pain of death—to leave the safety of the Bower, to venture out into the shadowy, menacing streets of the South End, where lurked a nameless, faceless shadow of a man who had killed two of them already, and who might kill a third.

Like Jack the Ripper.

No. Impossible. It was too horrible even to contemplate—that here in Boston, this sane, safe, neatly compact and tidy little city, was harbored the homicidal lunatic who had terrorized all of vast, dark London three years before.

Ames approached the tea tray, took a brandy snap filled with whipped cream, and sat down. "We had a talk with Professor James this afternoon," he told Caroline.

She brightened. She liked Professor James, particularly since he had once confessed to her that he preferred the sensation novels of Diana Strangeways to the weightier works of his brother Henry.

"Was he helpful?"

Ames shook his head. "I don't know yet, but it is always enlightening to talk to him all the same. If nothing else, it helps me to sort out my own thoughts." He swallowed the last of the confection and sipped his tea. "And in fact I have been thinking, Caroline"—when do you not, dear brother?—"about what it is that connects those two girls, Mary and Bridget."

He'd set down his cup, and now he ticked off his points one by one on his long, slender fingers.

"Both were Irish. They were roommates. Is either of those facts pertinent to their death? Or—"

He cocked his head at her. His eyes were fixed on her, but she realized that he did not see her. He had the look that he wore when he was sorting something out in his mind—his clever, even brilliant mind. Caroline had long since accepted the fact that of the two of them, Addington was the brilliant one. She didn't much care. Brilliance in a woman would be a hindrance.

He was speaking and she was missing it.

". . . the fact that they were both residents of Bertram's Bower? Is that what connected them?"

"I don't know, Addington."

"No. Nor do I. But consider: If it is Bertram's Bower that connects them, then we must take into account not only the Bower itself, but its surroundings."

Restless, he got to his feet and began to pace.

"But perhaps more to the point," he said on his second turn back and forth from the shuttered windows, "has it struck you that Agatha Montgomery is the only person we have encountered who seems to believe that Mary Flaherty was a paragon of—well, I can hardly say virtue—but of many other admirable qualities?"

"You mean, Agatha was the only person who liked her," Caroline said.

"Yes. That is exactly what I mean."

"Perhaps Bridget liked her too."

"Perhaps she did. But no one has told us that, and Bridget, now, cannot tell us either. So as far as we know, Mary Flaherty was heartily disliked by all who knew her."

"I hadn't thought of that," Caroline said.

"It might be significant, don't you think?"

He had paused by the fire, but now he started to pace again.

"Consider what we have," he said. "We have a number of people who disliked Mary Flaherty. The girl Verna more than disliked her, she threatened bodily harm to her. But in light of the fact that she is ill, unable to rise from her sickbed, I believe we can safely eliminate her from our speculations.

"Then we have the other girls at the Bower. Apparently none of them liked Mary, but we have discovered no one there who seems capable of carrying that dislike to the extent of murder."

"Garrett?" murmured Caroline.

"Yes. Then we have Garrett O'Reilly. Whom Crippen seems to have settled upon as his perpetrator."

"But, Addington, he cannot—"

"I know. He cannot read, and so undoubtedly he did not concoct that ciphered note. Which in any case Crippen does not believe has anything to do with Mary Flaherty's death. But you have told us, Caro, that Garrett denied speaking to Bridget, while the two girls you spoke to insist that he did. So that leaves him with a cloud of suspicion hanging over him, despite Delahanty's and Martin Sweeney's vouching for him."

"I don't believe that he is capable—" Caroline began.

"Possibly not. But the cloud is there, and there it will remain until he is cleared. Now. Who else do we have to consider? Matron?"

"She is certainly strong enough," MacKenzie offered. "And filled with—how would you describe it, Ames? Hate?"

"Yes. She is that—filled with hate for the very girls who are in her not-so-tender care. But why would she do it? Why would she be moved to kill not one but two of them?"

"If she'd learned that Mary was in the family way, and thus might bring disgrace on the Bower, perhaps she thought to eliminate her."

Ames snorted. "And Bridget as well? That is going a bit far, is it not, even for a woman like Mrs. Pratt. To risk not one but two murders, thus twice putting her own neck in jeopardy? I agree with you, the motive may have been there, but still. She is hardly a sympathetic figure, but whether she is a murderess—hard to say."

"The typewriter salesman," MacKenzie said. "Remember that he had an argument with Mary the day before she was killed."

"Yes. I think we cannot eliminate him—or not, at least, until we have a chance to speak to him. A traveling salesman already has points against him, given the reputation of the breed."

Caroline shifted in her chair. Her shoulder was aching again, undoubtedly because of the weather. She'd ask Margaret to get her a hot water bottle tonight, and she'd retire early and read a Diana Strangeways in bed.

"We still don't know very much about Mary," she said. "Perhaps the person who killed her is someone we never heard of—someone from her past, someone with a longstanding grudge against her."

"Yes." Ames nodded. "That may be our answer after all. But then, once more, we are left with the question of why that same person—if it was the same person—killed Bridget also. I am convinced that the two deaths are connected, so this hypothetical person must have known both girls. And they had different backgrounds, so they probably did not know each other before they came to the Bower. No, I do not believe that our man is someone from either girl's past. He is someone who knew them both here and now, and for whatever reason found it necessary to . . . eliminate them both. I believe absolutely that Mary's condition led to her death—someone wanting to get rid of incriminating evidence, if you will. Mary and her unborn child being the evidence. But the second girl . . ."

"Who may have known about Mary's condition," MacKenzie offered.

"Yes. Probably she did. And so to silence her—"

"You are forgetting Nigel Chadwick's theory," Caroline said. She heard the bitterness in her voice; she couldn't help it. All the triumph of her dinner party had vanished, replaced by righteous anger at Chadwick's betrayal.

"Jack the Ripper? Here in Boston?" Ames's mouth curved into a sour smile. "An interesting idea, but despite all the journalistic to-do, not likely."

"Why not likely?" MacKenzie asked. "The method is the same, the type of victim, the locale—"

"The South End of Boston is not Whitechapel, Doctor."

"No. But still, it is the haunt of a number of dubious characters—riffraff off the rails, single men in rooming houses—"

"Some of the houses there are very fine," Caroline said in a small surge of hometown pride. "Just as fine as any in the Back Bay. It is just that—well, the district never quite caught on. And the population there is not all riffraff. There are a number of churches in the South End, and all of them well attended. Why, the Reverend Montgomery regularly preaches every Sunday to an overflow crowd. He is a splendid preacher, so they say; I've never heard him myself."

The Reverend Montgomery. She hadn't told Addington all that Katy had said about him. It was hard to believe, but still—

"Addington," she began.

"For the moment, I think we must continue to believe that the two deaths are connected," he said. Something was nagging at the back of his mind, but he could not call it up. "Or that Bridget knew something, perhaps, about the murder itself. The only other possibility is that she was murdered in copycat fashion to muddle the case. Which, I grant you, is a distinct possibility, but hardly helpful."

Caroline tried again. "Addington, about the Reverend Montgomery—"

"Yes? What about him?"

"One of the Bower girls told me this afternoon that he—"

But how could she say it? It was too awful to think about, let alone speak of in mixed company.

She'd caught his attention, however, and he stared at her, waiting, his expression one of wary anticipation.

"Yes, Caro? That he what?"

"I can't believe it. It is too grotesque—"

"Grotesque? What are you talking about?"

"Katy told me that she'd seen the reverend—oh, I don't know what to call it! *Molesting* seems too strong a word, but—she said she'd seen him with one of the Bower's girls—and with Mary too—behaving in a—an improper way. A too-familiar way, I mean. And she said—as I've told you—that Mary threw herself at him in a most forward fashion. She even saw Mary coming out of the rectory one time, looking—disheveled. And I wonder if—"

She broke off at the sound of the door knocker and, a moment later, Margaret hurrying to answer. Let it not be Inspector Crippen, she prayed.

The pocket doors slid open. Margaret appeared, followed closely by the bulky, imposing figure of Cousin Wainwright.

Caroline's heart sank. Cousin Wainwright might be even worse than Elwood Crippen. Undoubtedly he had come to reprimand Addington—to warn him once again to stay clear of this case. Her face felt stiff as she smiled at him. She'd promised to deal with him, and she hadn't. Well, now she would.

He greeted them with a brusque word and declined Caroline's offer of tea. Nor would he sit; he stood menacingly before them like a hanging judge.

"Good evening, cousin," Ames said cordially, just as if their last interview had not been an unpleasant one. "To what do we owe this—"

"No time for chitchat, Addington. I've just come from a meeting with the mayor."

"Ah. And how is he?"

"Not good. I don't have to tell you why. This confounded notion that we have that Ripper fellow here in our midst has given him a bad turn. He's been literally a prisoner in his own office ever since that story came out today. Sheer speculation, I said, no need to panic, but every ward heeler in the city has been hounding him to take action. So he's putting the screws on the police pretty tightly, I can tell you."

Wainwright's small eyes flicked from one to another of his listeners as if he might find the answer to his dilemma from one of them. As indeed he might, Caroline thought. Still, she was glad he hadn't heard their discussion of a moment earlier; they were no farther along than Crippen.

"Crippen tells me he has his suspect," Wainwright went on, "but if he's wrong, there will be what-all to pay. The Irish in this city have no love for the police as it is, and if Crippen railroads an Irishman to the gallows and then it comes out that he was mistaken—"

"Crippen will not railroad anyone, cousin," Ames interrupted.

"Let's hope not. Have you seen him?"

"Not since this morning."

"Hmmm. Well, I saw him not an hour ago. He is determined to make an arrest before the week is out, mistaken or not. He's a good man, Crippen, but sometimes a trifle—shall we say—overenthusiastic."

"When it comes to the Irish," Ames said.

"When it comes to the Irish, yes. I don't mind telling you, Addington, we have a delicate situation here."

"To say the least," Ames murmured.

"And tomorrow morning Crippen has scheduled a lineup. I'd appreciate it if you could come."

"Really, cousin? But I thought you wanted me to stay out of it."

Wainwright glared at him. "So I did. But that was before this English scribbler stirred everything up with his foolish speculations. I can't understand the fellow, throwing a bomb into our midst like that. A Red revolutionist couldn't have done worse."

Bomb-throwing revolutionaries were an ever-present threat, but mostly they operated in Europe.

"So you'll come to it?" Wainwright added. "Tomorrow at ten in the Tombs."

"Certainly. If you wish it."

"I do. We can't put an end to this matter too soon, and perhaps, in the lineup—well, we will see. D'you know, on my way here I took note of people passing, particularly the women. They were afraid—terrified, even—and the men looked ready to riot at the drop of a hat. That's what one irresponsible journalist—"

"And newspaper," Caroline put in.

"And newspaper, yes—what one irresponsible journalist and newspaper together can do. They can put an entire city into panic. Destroy the public's confidence in the police. Give rise to vigilante justice, men being snatched up off the street and beaten—lynched, even. And we can't have it. Not while I sit on the board of commissioners."

He drew himself up to his full height and stared at them as if they were personally responsible for the city's fearful state. And perhaps I am, Caroline thought guiltily. After all, I entertained Nigel Chadwick in this very house, not twenty-four hours ago. Did Cousin Wainwright know that? She hoped not. And if I had not held that dinner, perhaps Chadwick would not have felt emboldened to write his sinister little screed. . . .

Cousin Wainwright was saying good-bye. ". . . find out what you can, Addington. I was wrong when I warned you off the other day, and now I'm asking for your help."

And with that he was gone, leaving the astonished little trio in his wake. As Caroline met her brother's eyes, she thought: Cousin Wainwright doesn't seem to consider that someone aside from Addington—herself, for instance— might also be of help in this case.

CHAPTER
15

THERE WERE SEVEN MEN IN CRIPPEN'S LINEUP. THREE looked harmless; two looked like the tramps they were; two looked thuggish, murderous, capable of any misdeed.

" 'Morning, Mr. Ames." Crippen was even more puffed up than usual, strutting around the little room with its window looking onto the lineup. Present also were Agatha Montgomery, Matron Pratt, and three Bower girls.

"Good morning, Inspector. You have a couple of prize specimens today, I see."

Crippen winked. "Just a couple, Mr. Ames. Gives it a little interest, like."

"Of course."

Ames stepped to the back, to stand beside MacKenzie. Agatha Montgomery and the others from the Bower moved to the front, where they had the best view. The men in the lineup were sitting. Now Crippen gave the order, and more lights went up so the men's faces were brightly illuminated.

"Look front!" called a police functionary.

The men did, and then, as ordered, to the left and right.

"Stand!"

They stood. One of the thuggish ones was muttering to himself, but he broke off on a short command from the functionary.

Crippen turned to Miss Montgomery. "Well, miss?" he said. "D'you see anyone likely?"

She was peering intently at the lineup. "No," she murmured after a moment. "I don't recognize—" Her face was contorted as she scrutinized the seven men. "I don't believe I've ever seen any of them, Inspector."

Crippen grunted. "You, miss?" he said to Matron Pratt.

She did not deign to look at him, but after a moment she said, "Third one from the left. I've seen him once or twice."

Crippen nodded and turned to the girls. "Well?"

They were cowed, obviously intimidated. All their young lives they had tried to avoid the police, and now here they were, in a basement room next to the infamous Tombs, and the police were questioning them.

It was too much for one of them. She began to cry, bowing her head on the shoulder of one of her companions, who comforted her. "There, Meg! Don't take on! You ain't done nothin', they won't hurt you."

She meant, Ames understood, the police rather than the seven men in the room beyond.

"Come on, girls," Crippen barked. "We don't have all day."

But they were useless. They stared, transfixed, at the lineup, but they were unable to say if they had ever seen any of these men lurking near the Bower or anywhere else.

After a moment Crippen gave up. He ordered his men to detain the man Matron Pratt had singled out, and to release the others.

"Now, Matron, can you tell us more? You've seen this man near the Bower?"

"I—yes."

"When?"

"I'm not sure. Sometime in the last few weeks."

"Lurking? Or walking past?"

"I—I think I saw him when I went to my Sunday evening meetings. Twice. Yes, I'm sure of it."

"All right." Crippen motioned to an officer. "Let's have

him upstairs. See what he has to say for himself. You're free to go, ladies. I'll be in touch if this fellow looks promising at all."

As Miss Montgomery and Matron Pratt shepherded the three girls out of the room, Crippen turned to Ames.

"Wait here if you want," he said. "I won't be a moment." In less than five minutes he was back.

"Nothing," he said. But he didn't look as disappointed as he might have, Ames thought.

"You mean, he denies being near the Bower?"

"I mean, he was pulled off the street this morning to fill up the places. He's a clerk at Goodwin and Hoar. He lives in Cambridge. Says he's never been near the Bower, and I believe him. Says he had nothing to do with the murders, he can account for his time both Sunday and Monday evenings. So there you are. We've released him."

"Well, Inspector, I am sorry this little exercise turned out to be a waste of your valuable time."

Crippen gave him a sly look. "Not a waste, Mr. Ames. It was just a formality in any case. Some little sop to throw to my superiors—and the newspapers, who are on me now like a pack of jackals. Had to toss one of their men out of my office this morning, if you can believe it."

"How do you mean, just a formality?" Ames asked.

"Why, I mean I'm getting closer to the man responsible in this case—closer every day—and I put on this little show simply because my superiors told me to. I knew before we began that it was all for nothing, but there it is. You have to know how to play the political game in this business, Mr. Ames."

"You mean you not only have to do your job, you also have to give the appearance of doing it."

Crippen allowed himself a small smile. "That's it. We have to look as though we're right on top of the matter. And we are, Mr. Ames. We are."

"How so, if I may ask?"

"I am not at liberty to say."

"I see. But—" Ames leaned in to speak close to the little

inspector's ear. "I couldn't help but notice that you did not have a certain young Irish lad in that lineup."

"Aha. Indeed I did not." Crippen's eyes grew cold. "Didn't need to, did I? I mean, they all know him at the Bower. Don't need to see him in a lineup to identify him, do they?"

Ames thought of Caroline's discovery that Garrett could not read. "I wonder if we could impose upon you, Inspector, to have another look at that coded note? I'd like to see the original again."

"I told you, Mr. Ames, that note has nothing to do with this case."

"Nevertheless. Are you returning to your office now? We would take only a moment of your time, I promise." The Tombs had recently been moved to the basement of the new courthouse in Pemberton Square, not far from police headquarters in City Hall.

Crippen shrugged. "If you like, yes, come along. I just need to speak to my sergeant and then I'll catch you up."

Outside in the rain, MacKenzie said, "Inspector Crippen stacks his deck, don't you think?"

"What?" Ames replied. "Stacks his deck? Worse than that, I'd say. That lineup was no better than a charade. I will speak to Cousin Wainwright about it when we are done with all this. I shouldn't be surprised if they get a complaint or two, hauling men off the streets in that fashion."

An omnibus lumbered by, and then another. Then came a break, and they made their way across. The air was damp and chill, heavy with the odor of horse dung and burning coal, and the muck underfoot had congealed into an icy mess that made walking treacherous. MacKenzie trod cautiously, careful of his newly healed knee.

"And another thing," Ames went on as they proceeded down School Street toward City Hall. "I can think of someone else—another familiar face if you will—who wasn't present for that lineup."

"Who?"

"The Reverend Montgomery."

MacKenzie was taken aback. "Surely you do not mean to imply—"

"I mean to imply nothing. I am merely saying that the more I think about that man, the more I suspect him—of what, I am not sure. But he is a trifle too smooth for my taste—remember what Caroline told us about him—and he had both the opportunity and the means to kill both Mary and Bridget."

"And his motive?" MacKenzie asked.

But to this Ames did not reply.

At City Hall, the door to Crippen's room was closed. In the outer office, the harried-looking secretary blinked nervously and ran his hand through his hair as he explained to them that the inspector was not in at the moment, but if they cared to wait—

He glanced apprehensively at the corridor, from where they could hear footsteps and a man's voice—not Crippen's—raised in anger. Ames could make out a few words: ". . . city in fear . . . panic in the streets . . . your responsibility . . ."

"It sounds as though our friend is in some kind of trouble," he murmured to MacKenzie.

Suddenly a rather shaken-looking Crippen appeared in the doorway. Behind him they glimpsed a tall, white-haired man who did not come in but went on down the corridor.

"Perhaps we should come back later?" Ames said to the little police inspector.

"What? Oh—no. Come in, come in." Crippen was pale, his voice unsteady. Without looking at his clerk, he hurried into his office and Ames and MacKenzie followed.

"Trouble?" Ames asked solicitously.

"That was my chief."

"I know. I recognized him."

"He—"

"Wants results." Ames nodded. "I imagine he is feeling pressure not only from the mayor, but from certain of the commercial establishments. Eben Jordan and his like, yes?

No one will come into the city to shop or do business if the public panic keeps up."

"That's it in a nutshell, Mr. Ames. Public panic. They lean on him, and he leans on me. He has threatened to take the case away from me if I cannot make an arrest."

"But you believe that you will—"

"Oh, yes." Crippen's ugly little face was grim, his mouth set in a hard line. "Just as soon as I—well, never mind about that. You wanted to see that note again, did you?"

"If you wouldn't mind, yes."

"I have it here." Crippen turned to the tall oak filing cabinets behind his desk. In a moment he produced the note and handed it to Ames, who studied it briefly before handing it back.

"Yes. Thank you, Inspector. I just wanted to refresh my memory."

"But I told you, Mr. Ames, that note doesn't signify. It doesn't have anything to do with the case."

"All the same, I—"

"And if you're going to go after that typewriter salesman, you can think again. He isn't in the city."

Ames hesitated, mindful of Crippen's touchy vanity. "Have you considered a night watch, Inspector? If people assume that the killer will strike again, I would think that public confidence would be bolstered by a show of force. A massive police presence in the South End, an operation for the next two or three nights, letting it be seen that you have put every available man on the job—"

Crippen shook his head. "Every available man, Mr. Ames? But we are close to moving in on the Copp's Hill gang. I need every warm body I have for that, so where am I going to get the men for a display of force in the South End?"

He was sweating, MacKenzie saw. Disgusting.

"Well, now, that is a question," Ames replied. "You are being squeezed both ends against the middle. But I have every confidence that you will find a way. Come, Doctor."

Outside once more, they made their way up School

Street to Tremont. Across the way, at the Parker House, newsboys were crying their wares. "Ripper in Boston! Police hunt killer! Public warned!"

"Damnation," muttered Ames. He plunged across and, throwing down his coins, snatched up a *Herald* and a *Post*. As he turned away, his foot slipped on something.

He looked down. It was a printed paper, muddied and wet. Still, for the most part, it was legible. He picked it up.

THAT MORNING, WHILE AMES AND MACKENZIE VIEWED Crippen's lineup, Caroline went to see her friend, Dr. Hannah Bigelow. She would be an inconvenient visitor, she knew, for mornings were Dr. Hannah's time to see scheduled patients. Nevertheless, Caroline told herself, this was not a casual call but something much more important. Since Dr. Hannah treated the Bower's girls, it was possible she'd heard something that might be helpful. Probable, even, Caroline told herself, remembering what she'd heard about the Reverend Montgomery from Katy and Liza.

Shortly after ten she set off from Louisburg Square, walked briskly through the rain down the hill, and took the Green Trolley to Dartmouth Street, where she disembarked. Coming into Copley Square, she passed shouting newsboys, and she stopped.

Jack the Ripper. They were caterwauling about Jack the Ripper.

Feeling as though she was about to do something very daring, she approached a boy selling the *Post* and bought one. Her eyes scanned the page. She could hardly believe what she read. They were stating flat out that Jack the Ripper was in Boston. The morning *Globe* had carried an article about the Bower killings on an inside page, but nothing like this.

She stood as if rooted to the ground, hardly noticing when people jostled her to get a newspaper for themselves.

The Ripper. But surely Nigel Chadwick's article had been

only speculation. Why had the *Post*—and the *Herald* too—taken up his poisonous fantasy?

She looked around. People were snatching up papers, reading avidly. She started to walk again, past the foundation of the building that would be the new Boston Public Library. It would be a Renaissance palace, as fine as any building in Europe. Boston deserved such a palace of learning, a kind of temple to the arts. But what good would a grand new Renaissance palace do for a city forever stained by its association with the notorious, the black, evil Jack the Ripper?

But the Bower killer wasn't the Ripper. He couldn't be.

She passed the S. S. Pierce castle and came into the South End. Here she saw poor-looking women hurrying by, heads bowed; three or four men clustered at a corner. They eyed her, but at least none of them spoke to her or made rude noises the way men sometimes did.

By the time she came to Columbus Avenue, where Dr. Hannah's clinic was, her sides were hurting from her lacings, and she longed to take a deep breath. Perhaps the women of the Sensible Dress League had a point, she thought. The next time one of them offered her a pamphlet, she'd take it.

The clinic was housed in a tall brownstone that like all the others hereabouts had seen better days. The waiting room was full, as it generally was; the woman at the reception desk was someone Caroline did not know. She received Caroline's request to see Dr. Hannah with a cold stare. She would see, she said.

Caroline took a seat on one of the hard wooden benches along the wall. The room was warm, smelling of garlic and unwashed bodies. A few babes in arms wailed listlessly; one small girl of about five stood at her mother's knee and stared fixedly at the newcomer.

Poor mite, thought Caroline, what lies ahead of you except years and years of drudging work punctuated at frequent intervals—too frequent—by the arrival of yet another mouth to feed?

A door opened and Dr. Hannah's assistant came out. The woman at the desk spoke to her, glancing dubiously at Caroline as she did. The assistant, whom Caroline knew, nodded and beckoned.

"I'll just get Doctor a cup of tea," she said when they were in the corridor. "She needs a rest. She's been on her feet since six this morning, and the day isn't half over yet."

Dr. Hannah's office was neat and spare, like the doctor herself. She came in at once, smiling to see her friend.

"Caroline! What a pleasant surprise."

They greeted each other with a kiss and an embrace. Dr. Hannah was a small, thin woman with graying hair and luminous gray eyes. She smelled of some chemical mix, and since she did not wear corsets, considering them unhealthy in the extreme, Caroline felt her body through the thin gray stuff of her dress, her bones quivering like a captive bird's. Quivering with fatigue, Caroline thought. She is working herself to a shadow here, and no matter how hard she works, or how long, her work will never be done.

The assistant brought in a tray of tea and biscuits, and Dr. Hannah, sinking onto a wooden chair, asked Caroline to pour.

"What brings you?" she said, smiling as she accepted the steaming brew.

"It is this business about Agatha's girls."

"The murders?"

"Yes."

Dr. Hannah arched a skeptical eyebrow. "Don't tell me you are involved in that nightmare."

"I have known Agatha since we were children. You know I go to the Bower regularly to teach. I don't have to tell you how important Agatha's work is. And now, because of this madman, she is in danger of losing everything she has worked for all these years. People will no longer support her—"

Dr. Hannah raised a hand as if to ward off further expostulations. "I understand. How can I help you?"

"I wondered—you tend to the girls there."

"Yes."

"And I thought perhaps you might have heard something, or—did you know Mary and Bridget? Agatha told me that Mary was quite ill when she came to the Bower. Did you treat her?"

"Yes, I did." Dr. Hannah frowned, remembering. "Sometimes I do not recall a particular girl—there are so many of them, you understand—but I do remember Mary. She was pretty and bright, and once she'd begun to recover her health, she was the kind of girl who—I hardly know how to put it. She was the kind of girl who seemed determined, after her bad start, to make something of herself. Of her life."

"That seems to be the general opinion. You saw her—when? Months ago, when she first came to the Bower?"

"That's right, and for some weeks afterward."

"But you haven't seen her recently?"

"No."

"Nor Bridget either?"

"I can check the files, but I don't believe so."

"And you don't know of anything that might help us—Addington—to learn who killed them?"

Dr. Hannah shrugged. "You know as well as I do that girls like that—the girls who go to the Bower—are more vulnerable than your neighbors up on Beacon Hill."

There was no censure in her words, and yet Caroline caught a faint hint of—what? Reproach? For Caroline and her well-off neighbors? No, not that, not anything so strong. But something.

"Yes, I know that."

"And so they are often put in the way of—shall we say—unwelcome advances. Such girls are not treated with the respect that men show to what the world calls 'decent' women. I believe that most of the girls whom Agatha rescues—there is no other word for it—truly want to begin a new life. A decent life, away from the streets. But sometimes they fail. A man will try to press himself upon them, make advances. . . . And the girls fall—or fail—all over again."

"Do you think Mary welcomed such advances, assuming she had them?"

"Mary? I don't know. She might have. But she was obviously determined to rise in the world—as far as a girl like herself could rise, which might not have been very far."

"She was expecting a child," Caroline said abruptly.

Dr. Hannah stared at her. "Are you sure?"

"The medical examiner said so."

"I see."

"So perhaps someone did press himself on her, as you put it. But not on Bridget. Poor Bridget was not the kind of girl who would have had many overtures."

"And yet someone found it necessary to kill her too," Dr. Hannah said.

"Yes."

"Probably because she knew something that the killer— if it was one man and not two—could not afford to have revealed?"

"Addington thinks so. Perhaps she knew Mary's condition."

"Yes." Dr. Hannah met her eyes. "And she may have threatened to tell—"

"Yes. Perhaps."

Dr. Hannah swallowed the last of her tea and shook her head when Caroline offered her the plate of biscuits. She frowned and looked away, obviously working something out in her mind. Then she met her friend's eyes again. "Do you know Agatha's brother at all?"

"The Reverend Montgomery? Why, yes, I do."

"How well?"

"Not very. He came to dinner on Wednesday night, as a matter of fact, part of a group of a dozen or so."

"Was that the first time you ever invited him?"

"Yes. As you know, I have not entertained for the past year and more, not since Mama's last illness. But before that—no, I'd never invited him. Why do you ask?"

"Because." Dr. Hannah's expression turned hard, her eyes grew cold. "I am going to tell you something I have not told before. I never thought I could tell it—not to you, not to anyone. Not even to the police," she added bitterly.

"The police! What are you talking about?"

"I am talking about the Reverend Randolph Montgomery. He is widely admired, is he not, for his devotion to the Bower, for helping his sister maintain the place by his ceaseless fund-raising?"

Caroline felt a small warning tremor at the back of her mind. "Yes," she said faintly, "he is."

"And yet," Dr. Hannah went on, "perhaps he is not the paragon of virtue that he pretends to be."

"Pretends to be? What do you mean?"

"I mean"—Dr. Hannah leaned forward, fixing Caroline intently in her gaze—"that he is a fraud."

"What are you talking about?"

"I am talking about the girls who come to me here. They are filled with remorse, some of them—for their pasts, for what the world would call their shame. But some of them, seeking shelter and help from Agatha, are subjected to new shame, new degradation—and from the very place that is supposed to be their refuge."

Caroline stared at her, dreading what would come next.

"He molests them," Dr. Hannah said flatly.

"Who?"

"Whom are we speaking of, Caroline? The Reverend Randolph Montgomery. That paragon of virtue, that man of the cloth who parades himself before the world as a man of God, a man dedicated like his sister to the salvation of the outcasts of this city. Oh, yes, she rescues them all right. And then he moves in on them, preys on them—a bad pun, is it not? He prays for them, and with them, and then he preys *on* them. Poor things, they are terrified to tell. They confess to me only after I have built up their trust in me, and even then I must pry it out of them. They don't want to be dismissed from the Bower, you see. They are afraid that if they tell what he does to them, they will be thrown back onto the streets before their three months with Agatha are up. So they keep quiet, and it is not until I see signs of distress that have become all too familiar to me, and I begin to question them, that they tell me—about him."

Caroline's heart was beating so fast that she found it difficult to breathe. Katy had told her this, and now Dr. Hannah was telling her all over again. The Reverend Montgomery—oh, but how could he? How could he betray Agatha like that?

"Have you spoken to Agatha about this?" she said.

"I tried to, once. She would not listen—would not believe me."

"No, I imagine she wouldn't. Well, what about the police, then? Surely he is breaking the law, to—to molest them?" Caroline's knowledge of exactly what molestation might entail was scant, but it was enough for her to understand what Dr. Hannah meant.

"The police?" Dr. Hannah's voice was filled with contempt. "And how far do you suppose I would get, complaining to the police? Who would believe me? Who would believe the girls from the Bower? The man is not a fool. He knows it is his word against theirs—or mine."

"I can't believe it myself," Caroline said, and then, seeing her friend's expression, quickly added, "Oh, I didn't mean that. I do believe you—of course I do. As a matter of fact—"

"What?"

"I spoke to two of the Bower girls yesterday. They told me that he—something like what you have just said."

"Well, then."

"But it is just so—so *dreadful*."

"To think that the Reverend Montgomery uses the Bower as his own private hunting ground? Yes, it is dreadful, isn't it? But not so unbelievable, I think. Many men of the cloth are not the monuments to virtue they pretend to be."

Caroline knew that Dr. Hannah did not go to church. Occasionally, in the past, she had invited her to her own church, the Church of the Advent, but Dr. Hannah had always declined. She had little time to rest, she said, and Sunday mornings were precious hours to sleep. Caroline believed that Dr. Hannah, in her own way, did the Lord's work, and so, after a few refusals, she gave up. Dr. Hannah's religion was her work, her work her religion. Caroline was sure God understood that even if her fellow mortals might not.

She sat silent for a moment, absorbing what Dr. Hannah had told her. Surely, she thought, there must be some way to stop him. He must be spoken to, admonished, warned. . . . But then she realized the truth of what Dr. Hannah had said. Who would believe it—that a man of the cloth, brother to one of the best-known and most widely admired benefactresses of the city, was in fact a monster of depravity?

No. She flinched from the vision of Dr. Hannah—or, worse, her own self—trying to make that case. Dr. Hannah was right. They would not be believed, and they would themselves become the objects of derision or, worse—scorn, calumny—oh, what to do with this most unwelcome information? Hearing it from Katy had been one thing, but from Dr. Hannah . . .

She would have to tell Addington, of course. But what would he do then? Go to Crippen? To other ministers? But Addington, like Dr. Hannah, was not religious; he had no friends and few acquaintances among the clergy.

Still, she was glad Dr. Hannah had confided in her. Where that confidence might take her she had not yet begun to sort out. She would tell Addington and let him deal with it; he would know what to do.

It was nearly noon when she left Dr. Hannah's clinic, and now, having walked briskly over to the South End an hour earlier, she felt too tired—too crushed by the knowledge she carried away with her—to walk home. So she hailed a herdic-phaeton and sat limp and brooding as the little vehicle jounced along the rainy streets.

The Reverend Montgomery—a duplicitous, even an evil man. A man who turned one smooth, bland face to the world, and showed another to the poor, helpless girls in his and Agatha's charge.

What did it mean? What could it mean?

She peered anxiously out the cab's little window. They were nearly home; she felt the herdic tilt as the horse turned up the steep slope of Mt. Vernon Street. Suddenly, urgently, she wanted to unburden herself to Addington, and she hoped he would be home.

He was, and MacKenzie with him. They rose when she entered the parlor. As always, she was heartened by the smile on the doctor's broad, honest face, and by Addington's acknowledgment, a nod, a half-smile, that meant: Here you are safe again, Caro, and we are here to protect you. She didn't always *want* to be protected, but just now she did.

"How did it go?" she asked her brother, meaning Inspector Crippen's lineup.

He told her.

"But—" She absorbed it. "You mean he deliberately did not include Garrett because he has decided that Garrett is guilty?"

"It would seem so."

"That is ridiculous. Yes, Margaret, we're coming."

She led the way into the dining room, where their lunch awaited them: vegetable soup, a plate of cold ham, Cook's good whole wheat bread.

"And what have you been up to, Caroline?" Ames asked. He spoke not without a small tremor of apprehension. She was his own good, obedient younger sister who would never intentionally act to rouse his disapproval. Yet she had a way of following her conscience that sometimes led to trouble.

She told them about her visit to Dr. Hannah Bigelow, and what Dr. Hannah had told her about the Reverend Montgomery.

MacKenzie received this information with a muttered oath—"damnable rascal!"—for which he instantly begged her pardon.

Ames was silent, his dark, brilliant eyes fixed on her. Then: "We can assume that Dr. Hannah would have no reason to lie."

"Lie? Of course not! Why would she lie?" She put down

her soup spoon and met his gaze as she said softly, "What are you thinking, Addington?"

"I am thinking that Crippen is about to make a colossal blunder."

"One wonders what—or how much—Miss Montgomery knows about her brother," MacKenzie offered.

"Dr. Hannah said she spoke to her about his behavior some time ago, and Agatha would not listen."

"Of course she would not listen," Ames said. "Aside from everything else, it is her brother who keeps the place afloat financially."

"Addington, really! You don't believe that Agatha would sacrifice those girls—the girls to whom she devotes her life—to her brother's lechery?"

"No. I do not. Not when you put it like that. But still, we must keep in mind that he serves her well."

"So what if he does? At the same time, he undermines her work—violates it."

"Yes." Ames nodded. "He does that also."

"I would venture that Miss Montgomery cannot—literally cannot—bear to believe such things about him," MacKenzie said. "It is more properly the province of Professor James, this partitioning of the mind to avoid the pain of unwelcome knowledge, but from what little I know of human nature, I would say that in order for her to survive, she is compelled to deny her brother's behavior. For her to acknowledge it would be impossible."

"Yes, I imagine it would be," Caroline agreed. "Her life's work—and at the very heart of it, a hideous rot. Oh, Addington, you don't think that the reverend had anything to do—"

"Yes. I do think he had something to do—with this case."

It was the world turned upside down, she thought. The good man was bad, the shepherd of the flock was the wolf in sheep's clothing. She was still struggling with it, as she had been struggling ever since she listened to Liza's and Katy's revelations, when Ames pushed back his chair and stood up.

"What are you going to do, Addington?"

"I am not sure." He was reaching into his pocket for his handkerchief, when his fingers touched the sodden paper he'd found on the street. He pulled it out.

"We must still fit this into the puzzle," he said. He handed it to her.

"What is it? Oh—a Christian Science tract. Where did you get it?"

"It was lying on the sidewalk in front of the Parker House."

"And how do you mean, fit it in?"

"The type," he said. "It matches exactly the cut-out letters on the coded note found on Mary's person."

"But what—"

"I don't know, Caro. Not yet. Crippen refuses to listen to me, refuses to believe the note has anything to do with Mary's death. But I believe it does—and now that I have this, I believe it all the more." He glanced at MacKenzie, remembering the doctor's suspicions of the forbidding female who guarded the girls at the Bower. "We must keep in mind that Matron Pratt is a devoted member of this sect."

"Where are you going now, Addington?" Caroline asked. For he was going someplace, that was obvious. He hovered by the door, restless, preparing to take his leave.

"Out."

It was raining still, but not heavily. The walk down the hill and across the Garden would be nothing; in less than a quarter of an hour he could be at the Berkeley Arms. It was early afternoon, too early for her to be at the theater. Unless she had some other engagement—at her dressmaker's perhaps—she might be at home. As if she held him by an invisible cord of memory—of desire—she drew him to her even as he warned himself away.

But yes. He would go to her. Ever since he'd spoken to her, two days ago, he'd felt that she'd left something unsaid. And now, with this fresh information about the Reverend Montgomery, he was sure of it: She had something more to tell him after all.

CHAPTER
16

"IT IS SIMPLY OUTRAGEOUS, CAROLINE," SAID AUNT EU-
phemia Ames, "that an entire city must be terrorized—
terrorized—because of one man's behavior."

A small, elegantly dressed figure, she tucked her hand
more securely into Dr. MacKenzie's arm. The three of them
were walking down through Boston Common to the Music
Hall on Tremont Street, where Euphemia and Caroline had
season tickets for Friday afternoon Symphony. Ordinarily,
Euphemia's niece and Caroline's cousin, Valentine, accompanied them, but in her absence over the past several weeks,
Dr. MacKenzie had agreed to go in her place.

"Yes, aunt," Caroline said. "I agree with you. It is outrageous. But—"

"Where are the police in this matter?" Euphemia went
on impatiently. She was a formidable woman of some seventy-five years, tiny, intense, a terror to anyone who aroused
her wrath and to many who did not. "I am going to speak to
Cousin Wainwright. It is intolerable that the police cannot
apprehend this man."

Caroline had a brief image of Euphemia speaking to
Cousin Wainwright, and, worse, upbraiding Elwood Crippen. If Euphemia scolded Inspector Crippen, he would simply arrest Garrett O'Reilly all the more quickly.

"They need a little time, aunt—"

"Time! Don't talk to me about time, my girl." Caroline would turn thirty-six in May, but to Euphemia she was and always would be a mere slip of a girl, giddy and heedless and needing a firm hand to guide her.

"In my day," Euphemia went on, "such a situation would never have been tolerated. Why, it is only because we have a man with us today that I agreed to go to Symphony. And I am not easily intimidated, as I don't have to tell you."

She didn't. Over Euphemia's bonnet, Caroline and MacKenzie exchanged a smile. Euphemia Ames was a legend in her own lifetime, a fervent abolitionist in her youth, a perpetrator of lawless acts like shepherding escaped slaves along the Underground Railroad, one stop of which was on the back of Beacon Hill. Aunt Euphemia had been a scourge of all that was proper and sedate, and had never been intimidated in her life as far as Caroline could tell. It was strange to hear her now, going on about her fears.

As they waited to cross at Tremont Street, Euphemia suddenly turned on her. "I trust that Addington is not involved in this case," she said. "I know you have some connection to the Bower, Caroline, but that needn't mean he must get mixed up in it."

For all Euphemia's lawlessness in her youth, she was grimly law-abiding now, the most proper of Bostonians; she had reared the orphaned Valentine with what Caroline had thought was far too heavy a hand. Nevertheless, Val had turned out splendidly, and Caroline seized upon her now as a way out of any discussion of Addington's activities.

"I had a letter from Val the other day, aunt," she said brightly. An omnibus lumbered by, followed by two more and a steady stream of carriages and cabs following.

"And how is she?" Euphemia asked. "I haven't heard from her in two weeks. I hope she isn't in with a fast crowd. You never know about those foreigners, but one thing you can be sure of is that they're not reliable."

"Oh, she's very well. I think she's having a grand time."

Having a grand time was not Euphemia's notion of the

way to recover from a broken heart. "There, we can cross now," she said. "Worth your life to go out these days. I never come downtown anymore."

Safe across, Euphemia paused to settle her bonnet, which had come slightly askew. She cast a shrewd glance at Caroline. "Someday, niece, you must tell me the real reason why Valentine threw over George Putnam."

It was a shot intended to stun, and it did.

"Why—aunt—I believe that she—ah—"

"Never mind about it now," Euphemia said. "But he always seemed to me to be a perfectly good match for her. I grant you, he is a trifle dull, but there are worse qualities in a man than dullness. And his people are as steady as a rock. Not a weakness anywhere in that family tree. So why did she decide to create that little scandal by giving him back his ring?"

To avoid a larger scandal, Caroline thought, but she could never have said so. Euphemia knew nothing about Val's being blackmailed by the late, unlamented Colonel Mann, and let's keep it that way, Caroline prayed.

At the Music Hall, people were streaming in. In this crowd, Caroline did not see the anxiety abroad on the city's streets, for this was a solid Brahmin crowd, the Friday afternoon regulars, safe and secure in their tight little world. Not even the advent of Jack the Ripper himself could unsettle these folks.

Nodding left and right, for both she and Euphemia knew nearly everyone here, she led the way in. They settled themselves in their seats and began to peruse their programs.

MacKenzie stifled a sigh. Truth to tell, he was not overfond of classical music. Before he came to Boston, he'd never even heard any, and since he'd been to Symphony a few times with Caroline, he couldn't say he was any the better for it.

Except for the fact of her company: for that, he was very grateful. But the music—heavy, lugubrious stuff produced under the energetic baton of the Symphony's German maestro—

no, he wasn't terribly fond of that. He preferred the martial tunes of John Philip Sousa, or the lilting melodies of the Waltz King, Johann Strauss.

As if on cue, the audience quieted. Herr Nikisch strode onstage, bowing to the applause that greeted him. He lifted his baton, and with a mighty crash of sound, the afternoon's concert began.

I WILL HAVE YOU YET, REVEREND, AMES THOUGHT AS HE strode down Commonwealth Avenue. He passed a woman he knew, tipped his hat to her, and kept on going. He seldom stopped to chat, and just now he certainly would not do so. He needed to keep going lest his nerve—his steady, steely nerve—fail him. Ordinarily he was the coolest of men, always calm while others grew excited, always quiet and thoughtful while others chattered without thinking.

Now, however, he was disconcertingly unsettled.

He didn't need—he really didn't need—to see Serena Vincent again, and unannounced at that.

No matter. He was sure she had something more to tell— something important—and now, having geared himself up to it, he meant to find out what it was.

She did not seem surprised to see him. She wore a tea gown of flowing green velvet, and her glorious hair was not completely up. Seeing it halfway down her back was like seeing her partially undressed.

"Mr. Ames," she said in her low, seductive voice.

She gave him her hand and let it linger a bit in his. Then, motioning him to a seat, she arranged herself gracefully opposite and smiled at him. "And to what do I owe this unexpected pleasure?" The Yorkie was growling at him, and she snapped her fingers to quiet it.

He hesitated. Chitchat was not his style, and yet what did he expect her to say? Something rude—dismissive?

"I am sorry to trouble you again so soon."

"No trouble. I was just reading manuscript plays. It is a tedious job at best, and this week's offerings are worse than usual. You have no idea how difficult it is to find good material."

No. He did not.

"Might you try some of the classics, perhaps?" he ventured.

"You mean Shakespeare? Oh, but that is not my forte. Even the comedies are beyond my reach, I fear. His plays always seem to have—how shall I put it? Too many words."

This was not Ames's opinion of the Bard of Avon, but he let it pass. He had not come here to discuss dramaturgy.

"About Miss Montgomery—" he began.

"What is the news from the Bower?" she broke in. She seemed genuinely interested.

"Not very much, I am afraid."

"And all this business about Jack the Ripper does not help, I am sure."

"No. It does not. My sister entertained that fellow Chadwick at dinner on Wednesday evening, and his thanks to her was to publish that irresponsible piece in the *Star*."

She did not quite smile at that. She was wearing face paint, he was sure, but on her it did not look cheap and artificial but exactly right. Her beautiful eyes lingered on him, and he saw a question there beyond the one she had voiced.

"My cousin, who sits on the board of police commissioners" (and how pompous and stuffy that sounded) "asked me at first not to involve myself in the case. But then, when he saw the degree to which the public has become exercised over the matter, he changed his mind and asked me to—ah—make such inquiries as I can."

"That was very clever of him."

He felt himself flush a little. "And so, since you asked me also, I have come back today to say—"

"What?" She leaned toward him as if she wanted to help him sort out his thoughts. He had a sudden, startling glimpse of her bosom, and he felt himself flush more deeply.

"To say that when I spoke to you before, I went away with the sense that perhaps you had not told me all that you might."

She lifted one exquisitely arched eyebrow. "How very perceptive of you."

"Then you do have something more—"

She sat back, and suddenly her beautiful face—the face that had thrilled a thousand male hearts—ten thousand—went blank.

"I am not sure that I do," she said. "Have something more to tell you, that is."

"Because?"

She contemplated him. "Because it is not the kind of thing you might believe."

"I believe all kinds of things, some of them very strange."

She went on looking at him. A man could drown in those eyes, he thought.

"Mr. Ames, you know this city as well as I do. Better, perhaps. You know what Boston people are like. They are a starchy lot, with very definite ideas about what is proper and what is not. I am living testament to that. No—you needn't make excuses, not for them, and certainly not for me. But what I am trying to say to you is that people believe what they want to believe. And here in Boston they want to believe that I am a—what? A loose woman, a woman who has gone upon the wicked stage, a woman who was cast out of decent society—oh, yes, I committed the sin of adultery, I do not deny it, but the fact that there were extenuating circumstances never seemed to have entered people's minds. They cast me out, and that was that. The fact that I have survived has probably offended some of them. Not that I care—of course not. But you understand what I am trying to tell you. People's minds are set in a certain way, and it is very difficult to change them."

She paused to offer him a cigarette. As before, he declined; as before, she took one and allowed him to light it for her.

She inhaled deeply two or three times, staring into the fire. Over the murmur and hiss of the flames, he heard rain spatter against the window. He felt as if he were caught in the spell of some enchantress. Because it was this particular enchantress's spell, he did not want to break it.

"It is . . . the Reverend Montgomery," she said at last.

He felt no surprise. It was almost as if he had known what she would say.

"What about him?" he asked, but he knew what she would say next as well.

"He is . . . a predator."

"Yes."

"You know that? How?"

"I—my sister has her own informants."

She nodded as she tapped off the ash from her cigarette. "If they told her that he makes advances," she said, "they have informed her correctly."

"He made advances to you?" He felt a sudden stab of anger.

"Advances—yes." She frowned at the memory. "More like an assault. And most unwelcome, I can assure you."

The sight of it in his mind's eye sickened him. "When?"

"Years ago, back when Agatha took me in. I suppose he thought I was vulnerable—which I was, but not to him— and therefore, like all men of that kind, he made his move."

"And what did you do?"

She smiled. "I sent him packing, of course. Fortunately I was not wearing corsets at the time, and I had full freedom of movement. I gave him a knee in the place where he would feel it most."

Such plain talk from most women would have appalled him, but from Serena Vincent it did not. Because she has been coarsened by her years in the theater, he thought, and therefore I expect her to speak coarsely? Or because she has paid me the compliment of speaking frankly, as if we were much better acquainted than we are?

"Did you tell Miss Montgomery?"

"No, of course not. She worships him. She would never believe anything bad about him. But when I read of Mary Flaherty's death, I thought of him at once. If he made advances to

Mary, and perhaps more than that—do you know if she was in the family way?"

"Yes. She was."

"Well, then, perhaps—do you not think—the reverend may have been responsible for her condition?"

"I think it is quite possible. I even think it is possible that he may have killed her. Unfortunately, what I think and what can be proved are two different things."

"And then there is the matter of the second girl," she said.

"Yes. Even if the case could be made against the reverend for Mary's death, we would still need to account for that other one."

"Unless she was killed by someone else, an imitation crime?"

"That is not likely, I think. I believe the same man killed both girls."

She extinguished her cigarette. "And I believe that you are correct. So what will you do now?"

"I don't know."

She stood up, and he did also.

"I am glad to have seen you," she said. "I have been wondering, ever since I spoke to you the other day, whether I should have told you what I know about the Reverend Montgomery. It is almost as if you read my mind, coming here this afternoon."

She was walking him to the door. When they reached the little entrance hall, he saw her maid hovering in the background. Mrs. Vincent held out her hand and he took it.

"I cannot imagine what will become of Agatha if it turns out that the reverend is the man the police—and you—are searching for," she said. "I adore her, and her work is so terribly important. She must continue it. But to have that man by her side, supporting her with his fund-raising and yet betraying her in that dreadful way—it is a difficult thing, Mr. Ames."

"Very difficult."

"Good luck," she murmured.

She had allowed her hand to remain in his, and now, for

an instant, he gripped it so hard that her eyes widened in surprise as, reflexively, she tried to take it back.

At once he released her. She stood so close to him that he was nearly overcome by her heavy, sensuous scent. He didn't know what to do. He'd been in the act of leaving, but now, if he'd had one word from her—only one—he would have stayed.

And she seemed to understand that—his sudden, devastating need for her.

She lifted her hand and with her fingertips lightly traced the line of his cheek—an amazingly daring gesture far beyond the bounds of propriety. Deep within himself he felt his body—his very soul—respond to her touch. As delicate as it was, it nearly scalded him. She was looking deep into his eyes, but he could not read her expression.

"I will be thinking of you," she said.

And I of you, he thought. But when he tried to speak, he could do no more than utter a curt—too curt—farewell.

In minutes he was out on the street once more. It was raining hard now; he looked for a herdic, but of course there was not one to be had, not in this weather.

It was mid-afternoon. Caroline and MacKenzie would not be back from Symphony for another two hours. Usually he wouldn't mind being at home by himself, but today the last thing he wanted was to sit in his study, his mind going around and around, picking over what Serena Vincent had told him, her words like a festering wound on his soul. And, worse, to remember the brief, intoxicating sensation of her touch—No.

He was on Boylston Street now, across from the Hotel Brunswick. He sheltered for a moment in the doorway of Boston Tech. Pulling out his pocket notebook, he flipped through the pages until he found the address he sought; then he set off again in the rain.

FAYETTE STREET WAS A STREET OF SMALL BRICK HOUSES, miniature houses really, set along its narrow length behind the Boston & Providence station. Here the air was thick with smoke, and the city sounds of horses' hooves and iron-rimmed wheels on cobblestone streets were drowned out by the cacophony of the engines, their shrill whistles, their ear-shattering snorts and *chuff-chuff-chuff* explosions of sound.

Halfway along, Ames stopped. Yes, this was it: the ad-dress he'd gotten from the fellow's employer. He yanked the bellpull and heard, faintly, the corresponding sound within. After a moment, the door was opened by a slick-looking young man in shirtsleeves and without a collar; a sparse growth of hair decorated his upper lip.

"Yes?"

"I am looking for Fred Brice."

The young man looked him up and down. "And who are you?"

"My name will mean nothing to him," Ames replied coolly. "Is he in?" He is you, he thought.

"He might be. What's it about?"

"Are you Fred Brice? We might speak more comfortably inside, if you could give me a few moments of your time."

Ames had been standing on the narrow granite stoop. Now he moved in, and the young man backed away.

"Say, mister, I didn't—"

"Just a moment or two is all I need."

Ames pushed the door shut behind him. They were standing in the front hall of what appeared to be a boarding-house; he could see a list of rules and regulations framed and hanging on the wall. The wallpaper was faded and stained, the air stale and reeking of burned potatoes. From somewhere above, he heard a woman's scolding voice.

The young man had assumed a belligerent look, but he made no further protest as he opened the door to a small parlor furnished in a cheap suite of horsehair sofa and chairs. The grate was cold, the air only marginally less offen-sive than that of the hall. Although the light was dim, the young man made no move to turn up the gas.

"Now," he said, shutting the door. "What's this about?"

"It is about the murder of Mary Flaherty."

The young man's gaze wavered for a moment and then held steady again. "And what does that have to do with you? Who are you anyway? The police? Let's see your badge, then."

"No, I am not the police. You know about her death?"

"I saw it in the papers in Worcester. And your name is—"

"My name is Addington Ames. Although I am not the police, I am working with them." A small untruth, not stretched too far.

"And?"

"You knew Mary Flaherty, did you not?"

"Sure. I knew her."

"We have been told that you visited her at Bertram's Bower last Saturday, and that you argued with her."

The young man's narrow eyes narrowed further. "If you're trying to stick me with what happened to her, mister, you're barking up the wrong tree."

"Oh? Why is that?"

"I don't mind saying I had a few words with her. She— Well, never mind about that. But I left for Worcester right after I saw her, and I just got back not an hour ago. So you'll have to look elsewhere for your man."

"She was your friend," Ames replied. "And yet you seem remarkably unconcerned about her death. Considering the way she died."

"Friend?" Brice sneered. "Mary wasn't no friend of mine."

"You became acquainted with her because you sell typewriting machines, isn't that so? And Bertram's Bower was in the market for one."

"That's right."

"You hadn't sold it to them yet?"

"No. Tight with their money, they are, over there."

"But Mary bought a manual from you?"

"Yes. Well—she didn't buy it herself. The Reverend Montgomery was the one who actually paid for it. It was his idea to get them a machine."

"Correct."

"Look, mister, I don't know what you want of me." In a nervous gesture, Brice wiped his hand across his mouth. Then, speaking more firmly: "I had nothing to do with Mary's death. And when I left her on Saturday, I made up my mind I wasn't going to see her again."

"Why?"

"Because. She told me to my face that I wasn't good enough for her. She had her sights set on someone better than me, or so she said. Can you believe it? A girl from the Bower, and she had her sights set above me? I have prospects, you know. I won't be a drummer for much longer."

"Drummer" was the popular name for traveling salesmen, who, in their travels, tried to drum up business.

"Indeed," Ames remarked dryly.

"That's right. I've got my eye on a share in the firm. This time next year, I'll be pretty well set up if everything goes according to plan."

Very little in life goes according to plan, Ames thought.

"Who was this person whom Mary spoke of?" he asked. "Did she mention his name?"

"No."

You are lying, Ames thought, but he kept silent.

"I don't mind telling you," Brice went on, "I was put off by the way she acted. Perhaps we had words—yes, I suppose you could say that. Words. We spoke sharp—of course we did. What d'you expect, when she gave herself airs like that?"

"But you have an idea of who the man was," Ames replied. It was not a question.

Brice hesitated. "I don't want to get into no trouble," he said.

"You will be in very great trouble indeed if you withhold evidence in a murder investigation. Did you know that she was pregnant?"

At this, Brice's mouth dropped open, and for the first time, Ames saw fear in his eyes.

"Is that a fact?"

"You didn't know?"

"No." Brice tried to pull himself together. "Look, mister—"

"Who was the man Mary spoke of?" Ames persisted.

"It sounds foolish, what I'm going to tell you. She'd got way above herself, Mary did, and I told her as much. 'You'll come to grief in the end, my girl,' I said. But of course she wasn't about to listen to me. Who was I? Nobody, as far as she was concerned."

Ames waited. After a moment, struggling with it, Brice burst out, "All right! You want to know who the man was, I'll tell you. But you won't believe it. I didn't believe it myself. But she did, didn't she?"

"Who was it?" But he didn't need to hear the name; he already knew what Brice would say.

"It was the Reverend Montgomery." Brice spoke sullenly, as if guarding himself against Ames's disbelief. When Ames merely nodded, Brice added more confidently, "She thought he was going to marry her. I tried to tell her he never would, but she wouldn't listen. 'He'll have to,' she said. 'Why,' I said. 'Because,' she said, and she wouldn't say more. Now you come here and tell me she was in the family way. Well, I didn't put her there. And I'd be surprised if the reverend did. Him a man of the cloth, and her an Irish girl, and from the streets? Even as handsome as she was, and she was that, I don't mind telling you. A very fine-looking girl."

He leaned in to Ames, speaking confidentially, one man of the world to another. "Now, here's the way I see it. She got herself into trouble, see. And she went off loony, the way some girls do when they find themselves in that condition. And, being loony, she had it all settled in her mind that she'd get a fine gentleman like the reverend to marry her. Crazy, isn't it? I'd say you have to find the man who got her into trouble in the first place, and then you'll find the man who killed her."

Yes, thought Ames. That is my notion exactly.

He nodded, then reached into his jacket pocket and took out his card. "If anything else occurs to you, I can be reached here."

Brice glanced at it, plainly impressed at the address. "I'm off to Providence on Monday," he said. "But, yes. If anything else occurs to me." He slipped the card into his trouser pocket. "She wasn't a bad girl, you know."

"No, I don't suppose she was."

"She just had—ideas above herself, if you know what I mean."

"Yes."

"She didn't know her place, like."

"I gather she didn't."

Ames turned to go, but then he remembered something else—unimportant now, but something that should be checked all the same. "Are you a Christian Scientist, Mr. Brice?"

"What's that?"

Ames shook his head. "It doesn't matter."

All the way back to Louisburg Square, as he thought about his conversation with Fred Brice, typewriting machine salesman, the young man's words echoed in his mind: *You have to find the man who got her into trouble in the first place, and then you'll find the man who killed her.*

CHAPTER 17

IT WAS FRIDAY EVENING AFTER DINNER. IN THE PARLOR AT No. 16½, Ames was sunk into his chair, his chin on his chest, lost in thought. MacKenzie had pulled a straight chair opposite Caroline's, and now he sat with his arms extended, a large skein of dark blue yarn looped over them. Her hands moved with amazing speed as she rolled the yarn into a ball, glancing at him from time to time, her soft brown eyes reflecting the pleasure she took from his company in this humble work.

And he saw something else there as well—a shadow of pain, of fear, that reflected the events of the past few days. This was not a normal, peaceful evening at home, and they both understood that. Their surface calm covered the knowledge of the brutal death of two girls from Bertram's Bower, and until the killer was found, no evening at home would ever be normal or peaceful again.

"Ah—just a moment," Caroline said. She put down the rapidly growing ball and ran her fingers along the yarn. "It is imperfect just here—you see how it is thick and then thin? I will just knot it—so—and then break it and knit it in when I get to it."

"What will you make with it?" said MacKenzie. He never ceased to be amazed at her skill; only last Sunday she'd finished the third of a set of twelve petitpoint seat covers for the dining room chairs. They were the handsomest seat covers he'd ever seen (not that he'd seen many), and he couldn't imagine actually sitting on them.

"Oh—I haven't decided. A shawl, perhaps."

But she had enough of those, and so did every female she knew. She'd thought of something a little more daring: a muffler for him. He needed a new one; his old one was very shabby. Probably it was army issue from when he'd first joined up, and never having had a wife or any other female to look after him, he'd never acquired another. Of course, a muffler was a personal thing, perhaps too personal. She'd have to think about it.

"There." Rapidly, her hands moving so swiftly that he could hardly see them move, she finished up. He relaxed his arms and reached for his pipe.

"Now," she said perhaps a shade too brightly. "What would you like to do this evening, Doctor? Shall we read?"

His thoughts were far too unsettled to concentrate on reading. "How about a game of draughts?" he replied. "I beat you very soundly last week, if I recall correctly."

She laughed. It was the kind of laugh a woman gives to a man when she knows he admires her.

"I was off my game, as you well know," she said. "Perhaps we should have a hand of vingt-et-un—but it is no good with only two. If Addington would play—"

She glanced at him. He still seemed oblivious.

"No," she said. "Addington is thinking. He won't want to be disturbed."

"Dominoes, then?" said MacKenzie. He moved toward the cabinet where they kept their games and decks of cards. Most of them were well worn, relics from childhood. Like everything else in this house, the cabinet held the sense of a family who had long lived here, and would continue to do so for years to come. His own life had been constant moving from one place to the next, first with his widowed mother when he was a child, living on the charity of relatives, and then with the army, going from one post to another. He'd never had a proper home.

Until now.

Ames looked up, and Caroline, noticing, said, "A game of vingt-et-un, Addington?"

"What? Oh—no, thank you. I want to walk a bit."

Something in his eyes made her uneasy.

"Where, Addington?"

He felt, superstitiously, that if he told her, he would jinx it. On the other hand, probably she and MacKenzie should know where he was bound, just in case.

"I am going over to the South End," he said. "To the Reverend Montgomery's place."

"You mean the rectory?"

"Yes."

He hadn't told her about Serena Vincent's run-in with the reverend. Hadn't wanted to—hadn't been able to. In some odd way, he'd felt he was protecting Mrs. Vincent by not telling. She hardly needed protection, from him or anyone else, but still.

Randolph Montgomery. He felt his pulse quicken in anger. Respected, widely admired man of the cloth—and duplicitous predator, preying on helpless females. And what further crimes had he committed? Fornication? Rape? Murder?

Yes, what he knew about Randolph Montgomery sickened him, and yet he did not know enough. He needed to know more.

Over dinner, he had passed along what Fred Brice had told him about Mary Flaherty's ambitions. Caroline had been appalled.

"Marry—the Reverend Montgomery? But that is ridiculous. The reverend would never marry a girl from the Bower."

"Of course he wouldn't. I am merely telling you what this young man told me."

"And now the reverend is engaged to a woman from New York, apparently. So even if he did have some kind of—of friendship with Mary, he would never admit to anything more than that."

"No. He would not. Therefore, if it was more than that, somehow I must persuade him to confess it. If I can."

Now, as he took his leave, she watched him with anxious eyes. After a moment, she heard him gathering his cloak and hat; then the front door slammed and he was gone.

She turned to MacKenzie and, for his sake, put on a smile. "Well, Doctor, it seems we are on our own for a bit."

AMES WENT ALONG THE SQUARE TOWARD MT. VERNON Street, his long legs striding fast over the uneven brick sidewalk. It had stopped raining, but the night air was raw and misting, a night to be at home beside one's own fire. Through partially opened shutters he could see lighted parlors, families gathered around. The sight held no charm for him. Tonight he wanted cold air in his lungs, he wanted to stretch his legs and pump up his blood for the confrontation—surely it would be that—with the Reverend Montgomery.

Serena Vincent's face rose up in his mind. He remembered how her eyes had met his, how her voice had enchanted him as it must enchant her audience every night, how he'd felt at her touch.

And how he'd sickened as she told him of her unwanted encounter with the reverend.

So it was not for Caroline, not for Agatha Montgomery that he ventured out this night, but for Serena Vincent. The reverend had accosted her—would probably have raped her if she'd not been a woman of his own class. If she'd been a poor, frightened girl off the streets, unable to resist a man of authority, a man who held power over her, who could deny her shelter at the Bower—oh, yes, Ames thought bitterly. Then the reverend could have had his way with her and none the wiser. Had he done that, many times, with the Bower's girls? Had he done it with Mary—had his way with her, and then, panicked at her condition, had he killed her?

He turned down Charles, crossed Beacon—traffic, for once, was light—and plunged into the Public Garden. The misted haloes around the lamps, widely spaced apart on their tall posts along the winding paths, gave little light; the lagoon, its ice partly melted in the thaw, glimmered fitfully. Between the lamps were stretches of darkness where an unwary pedestrian, on a night like this, might be set upon by footpads. But he had spent years at Crabbe's Boxing and Fencing Club. He would give any man who accosted him a fight for his life, and the fellow would go away the worse for the encounter.

He emerged from the Garden across from the Arlington Street Church, whose tall brownstone spire was lost in the darkness and mist. He crossed and went on down Boylston Street. There were not many people about, and of those, few were women. Now, loping along, he overtook a lone female; as she realized that a man approached her from behind, she threw him a terrified glance over her shoulder and tried to walk faster. But she was encumbered by twenty pounds of clothing over a tightly laced corset, and she made no headway.

"I beg your pardon, madam," Ames said, hurrying past and doffing his hat. She stopped short, staring after him, her face a pale blur.

He strode on, over the railroad tracks to the South End. There were even fewer pedestrians here, but at the corners, and in doorways, he could see the dark shapes of men. Menacing, threatening shapes, and might one of them be the man he sought?

No. He swerved to avoid a creature slithering across his path—a cat? a large rat?—and went on. None of these tramps and drifters was his man. He was sure of it—more sure with every passing hour.

At Columbus Avenue, he turned toward Bertram's Bower. His footsteps echoed as he went, giving him an unaccustomed sense of vulnerability. And if he felt vulnerable, what must a lone young woman feel? Anyone could step out from one of those sheltering doorways and set upon her, and she would have no defense.

He was not far, now, from the Reverend Montgomery's place. With luck the man would be at home. He was stepping off the curb to cross, when out of the night a figure appeared and seized his arm.

"What the—"

"Police, mister," said a voice. "Hold on now, or we'll have you in for a look-see." An Irish voice.

Ames drew himself up. They were standing under a streetlamp. In its feeble glow, he could see that the man who had accosted him wore a policeman's uniform, but he could not make out his face.

"Have me in, by all means," he said. "My friend Inspector Crippen will vouch for me."

The hand on his elbow relaxed a bit. "Himself, is it? Well, he's hereabouts. Let's see if we can find him."

With his free hand the policeman took out his wooden clacker and whirled it furiously. In the quiet night, the rat-tat-tat seemed very loud.

"You might let go of me," Ames said. "I won't run."

"Yes, well, we'll see about that," the policeman replied gruffly. He did not take away his hand. Ames made a mental note to speak to Cousin Wainwright about teaching a few rules of common courtesy to the police force, but then he reminded himself that this was the night watch he and Crippen had spoken of, and the man was only doing his job.

A herdic clattered by, and then another, followed by a four-wheeler. Inspector Crippen, it seemed, was elsewhere.

"Look here, Officer," Ames said, "I can assure you that Inspector Crippen knows me well. I am late for an appointment as it is, and I see no reason why I should be detained unless you intend to arrest me."

"Not yet, I don't." Ames noted that the man had not yet called him "sir." "But we have to ask you your business hereabouts," the policeman went on. "We're questioning every man abroad in the district, and—"

He broke off at the sight of a trio of men hurrying toward them. Two were tall, and one was short, rotund. Crippen. The little inspector was panting as he came up, but when he recognized Ames, his ugly face broke into a grin.

"Well, well, well, if it isn't Mr. Ames! Getting a breath of air, are you? It's all right, Devlin, I know him."

Ames felt the pressure on his arm fall away, and he shook his cape into place.

"Your night watch is most thorough, Inspector," he remarked dryly. "I consider myself fortunate not to be loaded into the paddy wagon and taken downtown for a night as a guest of the city."

Crippen was not in the least disconcerted. "We have to be thorough, Mr. Ames. We have our work cut out for us, and I don't mind telling you, we need to do it quickly."

"I thought you were on the verge of making an arrest, Inspector. Or has the situation changed?"

"No." Crippen tipped back his bowler and rocked back on his heels as he peered up at Ames. "No, it hasn't changed at all. I still know what I know. This little exercise here tonight won't change that. But as long as we're undertaking it, we have to make it look good, don't we?"

"You mean, this is like the lineup—strictly for appearance's sake?"

"Well, now, I wouldn't say that exactly. But what with my superiors breathing down my neck, so to speak, I want to give 'em their money's worth. I have my men on every block in this district, and I'll be surprised if we don't have a fine good haul down at the Tombs come morning."

"But nowhere in that haul will be the man you seek?"

"Probably not, no."

Ames thought of the drain on the city's treasury from the overtime paid this night, but he said nothing. The drain on the city's treasury was not his concern.

"May I take it that I am free to go?" Ames said, his sarcasm lost on Crippen.

"Of course you are, Mr. Ames! And you can tell your cousin who sits on the board of commissioners that we are doing our job right and proper."

"Good hunting, Inspector." Ames nodded to him and set off once again, aware that they still watched him. Well, that was their job, and he couldn't fault them for performing it.

His lips twitched as he thought of Caroline coming down

to the Tombs to vouch for him in the morning. What with her eagerness for him to involve himself in this case, there were aspects to the business that she probably hadn't anticipated. She'd not let him into the house, he thought, if he'd spent a night in the city jail.

He rounded a corner and saw, across the street, the grim stone building that was the Reverend Montgomery's rectory. A single light shone from a downstairs window.

He crossed, opened the wrought-iron gate, and went up the path to the door. As he lifted his hand to grasp the knocker, he paused. His repugnance for this man was so great that he wondered if he could speak to him and remain civil.

But then he reminded himself that it was imperative to speak to him; this was no time to allow his feelings, no matter how strong, to keep him from doing what he must.

He lifted the knocker and brought it down sharply, twice.

No sound came from within. Perhaps the light was a ruse to ward off burglars.

He tried again, three raps this time.

Suddenly the door opened, startling him; he'd heard no footsteps approaching.

The Reverend Randolph Montgomery stood before him.

"Yes?"

"Good evening, Reverend."

"Who—?" Montgomery peered out at him.

"Addington Ames."

"Ah! Mr. Ames! I could not make out who you were. What brings you to our humble neighborhood on such a night?"

"I wanted a word with you."

"I see. Well, I—Yes, all right. Come in." He stepped back to allow Ames to cross over the threshold; then he led the way into the parlor, which, as before, was drab and dingy, messy, none too clean. Whatever else the reverend did with all the money he collected, Ames thought, it was not used on this house. He put his hat and gloves on a chair by the parlor door, removed his cloak, and hung it over the back.

"Now," said the reverend, rubbing his hands as if to

warm them. There was a tiny fire in the grate, not nearly enough to make the room comfortable. "What can I give you? Brandy?"

"Nothing, thanks."

Ames would in fact have liked a drink, but he did not want to accept Montgomery's hospitality.

"You don't mind if I do?" the reverend asked, moving toward a monumental Jacobean sideboard that took up much of one wall.

"Not at all."

"Take a chair, then, and I'll be with you in a moment."

On the large round table in the center of the room lay sheets of writing, illuminated by the dim light of a gas chandelier overhead. As Ames pulled out a chair, he glanced at the scattered pages.

"Sorry about these," the reverend said, returning. He put down his brandy glass and scooped them up, putting them in a pile upside down at the far edge of the table. "Hard to sort out my thoughts sometimes, you know. But people come to services expecting a good, rousing talk, and I have to give it to them."

Ames nodded. "I imagine you find a way."

"Oh, yes. I do. And they are so appreciative, don't you know."

The reverend took his seat and sipped his brandy. In the gaslight, his face looked smooth and bland, and his well-manicured hands—large, strong-looking hands—were steady as he held his glass.

"And what will your text be this Sunday?" Ames asked.

"This Sunday? Oh, I won't preach this Sunday. I have a substitute coming in. That sermon"—he nodded toward the pile of manuscript—"is for the week after."

"You will be out of the city?"

"Over in Cambridge, yes. For the annual meeting of the Congregational ministry. Members come from all over the Northeast, and we get together and say a prayer and have a good confab."

"All day Sunday?"

"Tomorrow and Sunday, actually. We used to begin on Fridays, but some members found the lodging charge too expensive, so we've cut it to just the two days."

"I see."

The reverend took another sip of his brandy, and now in his pale eyes Ames could see the question: Why have you come here?

"That was a fascinating time, the other night at your place," the reverend said. "Please tell your sister again for me how much I enjoyed myself."

Ames inclined his head. "It was good of you—and Miss Montgomery—to come on such short notice."

The reverend smiled unctuously. "We are not proud, Mr. Ames. And for Agatha, particularly, I felt that the change of atmosphere, even just for an evening, would do her good."

"Yes."

An easy introduction of the subject of Bertram's Bower, then, without any awkwardness.

"How does she do, your sister?" Ames asked.

The reverend looked grave. "Well enough, I suppose. No—that is not true. I do not suppose that. I suppose—I *know*—that she is very nearly overcome with grief, with guilt, call it what you will. She feels very strongly that she has somehow betrayed those two poor, unfortunate girls— that she has betrayed her own mission by not keeping them safe. She has always been her own harshest critic, and in this instance it is no different."

Ames nodded. "It is a most distressing case. I must say, the police are doing heroic duty. Coming over here just now, I was stopped and very nearly arrested."

"You? Arrested?" The reverend appeared sincerely shocked. "For what?"

"For being abroad in the nighttime, I imagine. They have put out a watch in the district tonight, in response to the public's panic."

"Well! Good for them. I only hope they have some success. Have they spoken to that typewriter salesman?"

"I don't know. But I did myself this afternoon."

"Did you indeed? And?"

"He left for Worcester on Saturday, just after he'd had the argument with Mary. He returned this morning."

"I see. Well, then, that would seem to eliminate him, would it not?"

"It would, yes."

"Which leaves—who? The Irish boy, I'd say."

"Or one of the neighborhood riffraff."

"Yes. Well. Not likely that one of them would kill both girls, is it? One, perhaps, but not two."

"Even less likely that one of them would have put Mary into the family way."

"Yes. There is that to consider." The reverend frowned, seemingly considering it.

You fraud, thought Ames. You knew Mary's condition; probably you caused it. His revulsion toward this man was so great that he found it difficult to keep his anger in check. You may fool the world, Reverend, he thought, but you no longer fool me.

"But if we are dealing with something more than riffraff," Montgomery went on, "if, as your guest proposed the other night, we are dealing with Jack the Ripper, either the man himself or some demented creature who seeks to imitate him—"

"It was most unfortunate that Mr. Chadwick chose to unburden himself of his theories, Reverend. And even more unfortunate that he chose to publish them. I do not believe for a moment that we have Jack the Ripper in our midst."

Instead of replying, Montgomery rose to refill his glass. "You're sure about that drink?" he said.

"Quite sure."

Ames waited until he had returned. Then: "I wonder if you could tell me, Reverend—"

"Yes?" Suddenly Montgomery was wary, sensing danger.

"Where you were last Sunday evening." Even as Ames spoke the words, he understood how they would sound to Montgomery. They would sound impertinent—unforgivably intrusive, ill bred, rude, and altogether intolerable.

The reverend could not quite hide his shock—his anger at Ames's blunt question. He swallowed a large gulp of brandy and with great care and precision set his glass on the table.

"You told me that you were—ah—assisting the police in their investigations, Mr. Ames." The reverend's eyes were cold now, and his voice, ordinarily so rich and mellifluous, had gone very soft.

"Yes."

"So must I assume that your question has some kind of—ah—official sanction? Did the police tell you to come here to interrogate me—"

"I would hardly call it an interrogation," Ames broke in.

"I repeat, to interrogate me. Or did you take it upon yourself to do so?"

"I am merely doing what I can."

"I understand that your sister, too, is poking her nose into this regrettable affair. I was told that she spent some time, yesterday, questioning people at the Bower."

"Yes."

Montgomery lifted his chin and stared down his fleshy nose at Ames. "I will tell you quite frankly, Mr. Ames, I think you are seriously out of line. This is a matter for the police. Leave them to deal with it. I cannot imagine why you have concerned yourself about it in the first place. Surely a man who lives on Louisburg Square does not need to come slumming over here in the South End to keep himself amused?"

Ames smarted under this calculated insult, but he clenched his teeth and forbore to respond in kind. Of course Montgomery resented him. Probably he resented everyone who had not suffered, as the reverend's family had suffered, the humiliations of bankruptcy and consequent loss of standing in the small, circumscribed world of Boston Society into which they, like the Ameses, had been born.

"No," he replied quietly.

"Then why do you trouble yourself, man? Two girls you never knew, never would have known, girls who came from the lowest, the humblest rung of society, who could have had no importance to you? Their deaths were admittedly horrendous crimes, but still, why do you care about them?"

Montgomery leaned forward, his eyes searching Ames's face as if he truly wanted to know the answer to his question. And perhaps, Ames thought, he did.

But I cannot tell you, Reverend. I can tell you part of the truth but not the whole of it, not the most important part of it, which is that a woman who has begun to haunt my thoughts—my dreams—asked me to involve myself in this case, and the reason she did so has partly to do with you.

And with this reflection, all his anger and disgust with the man sitting before him returned to sicken him once more, and he was forced to look away lest he betray himself.

"My sister pleaded with me—" he began.

"Ah, but *my* sister did not, did she? I cannot imagine that Agatha has welcomed your—I must say it—your meddling in this affair."

"No," Ames admitted. "She has not."

"Well, then. Why persist, when the one person who has been most affected by these deaths gives you to understand that she does not wish you to do so? Great heaven, man, leave it to the police, and go and find something else to occupy your time!"

With that, he shoved back his chair and stood up. He was a tall man, nearly as tall as Ames, and much heavier. But I could best you in a fight, Ames thought as he stood also. You may be strong enough to overpower some poor frail girl, Reverend, but you are not in condition. You could not, if it came to that, overpower me.

"You will not tell me?" he said quietly, referring to the question that had so aroused the reverend's ire.

"Tell you what? That I can account for my time when poor Mary was being set upon and killed in the most horrible way?" The reverend's mouth was set in a hard line, and his budding jowls quivered ever so slightly. "Very well, Mr. Ames. If you insist—yes, I can account for it."

Ames waited.

The reverend sniffed. "I was at the home of Mr. and Mrs. Lawrence Norton. Three-something Beacon Street, I forget the exact address. They were kind enough to hold a reception for me, with the understanding that the guests who came would be people happy to contribute to the Bower."

"And you arrived at the Nortons' when?"

"About four o'clock."

"And you spent the rest of the afternoon there?"

"Yes, and part of the evening as well."

"Until?"

The reverend's nostrils flared slightly, and he sniffed again. "Until nearly ten."

"I see."

"You had better see. How on earth, man—how can you come here, into my own home, and insult me by demanding that I account for my time? Which, mind you, I have already done for the police. I am under no obligation whatsoever to answer to you—none!"

The voice—that rolling, basso-profundo preacher's voice—was in full flower again as Montgomery excoriated him.

"No," Ames replied quietly. "You are not. But—"

"And now I suppose you will want to know where I was on the following night, when the second girl was killed."

Ames waited.

"I was here, Mr. Ames. It is none of your business, but— Yes. I was right here in this room."

"Alone?"

"Of course alone! I live very simply, and I never entertain."

Wrong, thought Ames. You entertained Mary Flaherty on more than one occasion.

The Reverend Montgomery stared at him belligerently, as if he could read his thoughts. "Now, you listen to me, Ames. You come here unannounced, you make the most monstrous accusations—"

"I have accused you of nothing, Reverend."

"Not directly, no. But it is obvious that you believe me to

be implicated in this dreadful affair. And I warn you, I will—"

"You knew Mary Flaherty fairly well, did you not?"

"How do you mean?"

"I mean, from what I have heard, she seemed to look upon you as a special friend."

The reverend frowned, drew down his mouth. "I am not sure I understand you."

"It is simple enough. Were you particularly friendly with Mary Flaherty?"

"No."

"She seemed to think otherwise."

The reverend shrugged. "I can hardly be held accountable for what she thought."

"Ah, but it was more than what she thought. She told Fred Brice, for one, that she hoped to marry you."

Montgomery started back as if he'd been slapped. "Marry me? But that is preposterous."

"That is what Mr. Brice thought. But Mary, apparently, had some reason to believe it. I would remind you that she was three months gone with child."

"Now, wait a moment." Montgomery stood and put his hands flat on the table as he leaned toward Ames in a menacing way. "Are you trying to implicate me in that as well?" His face, which had been pale, had turned pink, and his eyes, which had been cold, suddenly blazed with anger.

"I am not—"

"Get out!" Montgomery roared. Straightening, he advanced a step, and quickly Ames stood and stepped back.

"Reverend, if you will just—"

"*Out!*" As Montgomery suddenly raised his fist, Ames put up his own to defend himself.

"And stay out!" Montgomery came at him and struck a blow that Ames easily deflected. Montgomery stopped. He was breathing heavily, and a little trickle of saliva showed at the corner of his mouth.

There seemed nothing more to be said, and so, in the

next moment, with a curt farewell, Ames took his leave. He had done himself no good, he thought, and probably a great deal of harm. The reverend was on guard now—more than he had been before—and would not only refuse to help him, but would also do what he could to impede him.

So be it, Ames thought grimly as he strode down the walk and let himself out at the gate. The night was colder than before, the freezing mist turning to ice underfoot. The street was quiet, not even a passing cab to break the silence. Next to the rectory, the reverend's church stood massive and dark.

Ames crossed the street and stopped at the first doorway. From here he could see the rectory clearly, the single light still showing from the front room where he had had his unpleasant interview with the Reverend Montgomery.

It was a sizable house, built no doubt for a minister who had a large family. Double windows on either side of the front door with its small porch; a row of smaller windows on the second floor.

And above those, a third story with three gables protruding.

Ames took a few steps and then turned to look at the rectory again.

Martin Sweeney of the Green Harp Saloon would know of a man who could do the job—a sharp-witted cracksman who was not only skilled with locks, but tight-mouthed as well.

I will have you yet, Reverend, he thought as he strode rapidly away into the night.

At No. 16½, THE FIRE BURNED LOW IN THE GRATE AND THE grandmother clock in the hall struck the hour: ten o'clock.

Locked into fierce combat with her opponent, Caroline lifted her eyes to his and smiled. She was winning, but only just, and not, she thought, because he was allowing her to do so.

"You have put yourself into a difficult position, Doctor,"

she said. But still, she was smiling; he heard no censure in her words.

He cleared his throat. She was right: He was going to lose. Somehow, he didn't mind.

"I seem to have done, yes," he replied, staring at the pieces on the board.

While he considered his situation, she listened for the sound of Addington's return. What had he learned, if anything, from the Reverend Montgomery? And if a homicidal lunatic stalked the streets of the South End, looking for another victim, had Addington encountered him? What if that same lunatic decided to use his knife on a man instead of a woman? Addington was strong, and well trained in the martial arts from his years at Crabbe's, but still. An encounter with an assailant who had a weapon was hardly a fair fight. Dr. MacKenzie owned a gun. She should have insisted that he accompany Addington. Perhaps—and it was a weapon of her own that she had employed only a few times in her adult life—she should have begun to cry. Addington would have had to listen to her then.

Dr. MacKenzie was staring at her. He seemed to have forgotten about their game.

She felt a little quiver in the region of her well-protected heart. Once, long ago, she'd felt something of the kind for a young man who, in the end, had gone away. Her heart had been broken, and she'd promised herself she would not allow that to happen to her ever again. But now, in the company of this quiet, kindly man who had come so unexpectedly into their lives, Addington's and hers, she felt her heart tremble once more as she met his eyes, and she did not want to subdue it.

She held his gaze, and when she spoke, her voice was soft and (it seemed to him) resonant with meaning.

"Your move, Doctor."

CHAPTER
18

BEACON STREET, THE NEXT MORNING, WAS BUSY WITH COM-
mercial traffic, but it was still too early for the day's parade
of landaus and four-wheelers, delivering the Back Bay's
fashionable ladies to make their calls.

Ames and MacKenzie, having taken the Green Trolley to
Gloucester Street, mounted the tall flight of brownstone
steps at the home of the Lawrence Nortons.

"Not a propitious hour," Ames murmured as he grasped
the bellpull. "But I know Norton. He'll not be put off."

Admitted by a surprised-looking butler still adjusting his
jacket, they waited in a small room off the spacious foyer. In
a moment they were shown up to the library at the front of
the second floor. Norton, a lanky, loose-limbed man with
gingery sideburns, greeted them cordially enough, but without troubling to hide his curiosity about their visit at such an
hour.

"What's the trouble, Ames?" he said, motioning them to
comfortable leather chairs before the fire. "Since I assume
this is not a social call. How do you do, Doctor?"

In a few words, Ames stated his question: Had the Reverend Montgomery attended a gathering here last Sunday?

"Why, yes," Norton said. "My wife, you understand, is a
staunch supporter of the Bower. We hold a fund-raising social for the reverend two or three times a year."

"And this one lasted into the evening?"

"Not very late. Until about seven."

Ames leaned forward, his keen gaze fixed on his host. "Can you say for certain what time the reverend left?"

Norton thought about it. "I think I can, yes. I remember because my son broke his curfew that evening. He'd gone out in the afternoon but promised to be back by six to do his lessons. He's at the Latin School, and they work the boys pretty hard there. Just when the reverend was leaving, my son came in and I looked at the clock. It was quarter past. I was thoroughly put out with him, I don't mind telling you."

MacKenzie had a fleeting moment of sympathy for Norton Junior, facing his father's wrath.

Norton cleared his throat. "If you don't mind my asking, Mr. Ames, why it is that you want to know?"

"I am trying to account for his time," Ames said simply.

"For the entire evening?"

"Yes."

"Because?"

"Because on that night, one of the Bower's girls was murdered."

Norton nodded vigorously. "Yes. Terrible business. And then a second girl—"

"Was killed the next night. But for the moment, I am interested in Sunday, when the first girl was killed. I spoke to the reverend last evening, and he told me that he left here about ten on Sunday night. Now you tell me that it was quarter past seven."

Norton pursed his lips. "I believe your sister, like my wife, is active in helping Miss Montgomery in her work."

"She is, yes."

"Mrs. Norton is of the opinion that this scandal will hurt the Bower."

"That is what my sister thinks also."

"But—" Norton's face was a study in puzzlement. "You cannot possibly believe that the Reverend Montgomery had anything to do with these murders?"

"I do not believe anything. I am merely trying—at my

cousin Wainwright's request—to assist the police in their inquiries."

"Wainwright sits on the board of commissioners."

"Yes. And the longer it takes for the culprit to be apprehended, the more the police suffer in the public's trust. Naturally he wants the case brought to a conclusion as soon as possible."

"Of course." Norton pondered for a moment. "And all this business about Jack the Ripper does not help matters."

"It certainly doesn't."

"Mr. Ames, I will be frank with you." Norton tapped a nervous little tattoo on the arm of his chair. "I hold these fund-raisers for the Bower because my wife asks me to. And of course I cannot deny that Miss Montgomery performs a worthy service. Worthy—and, unfortunately, necessary. Do you know Miss Montgomery? Of course you do. She is a most worthy female herself, if a trifle offputting. These people who have a mission in the world are very often offputting; they cannot help it. Still, I admire her."

He was obviously building up to something, MacKenzie thought. Get on with it, man.

"But I will tell you this as well, Mr. Ames. Even though her brother is widely admired for his own part in keeping the Bower afloat, I personally have a mental reservation about him."

Ames cocked his head. "And what would that be?"

"He is . . . duplicitous."

"How?"

"He . . . does not always behave well. In fact, he sometimes behaves very badly."

"Do you believe him capable of murder?"

Norton blinked. "Murder? Well, now, I don't know about that. I suppose anyone is capable of murder if he's sufficiently threatened." He leaned forward as if to impart a confidence. "But the man is not what he seems."

No, thought Ames, he is not. "How do you mean?"

"I mean, my brother-in-law is active in the Watch and Ward. You know of their work?"

"Yes."

The New England Society for the Suppression of Vice, popularly known as the Watch & Ward, was a group of men who had taken it upon themselves to guard the public morals of the city. In pursuit of their goal of absolute moral purity, they visited bookstores to demand that objectionable titles be removed from the shelves, they shut down—mostly in Scollay Square—risqué theatrical presentations, they raided houses of ill repute, they monitored the sale of indecent postcards and other pornographic material, and generally made themselves busy about minding other people's business. Privately, although Ames deplored the general coarsening of the culture, he thought the Watch & Ward was the Puritan impulse run amok, a subject perhaps for William James's studies of psychological aberrations, but he forbore to say so now.

"And what I have to tell you must be kept in absolute confidence," Norton went on, glancing at MacKenzie.

"Of course. You may rest assured of Dr. MacKenzie's complete discretion."

"I am sure I can. Well, my brother-in-law went with a few other men last month on a surprise visit to the Black Sea, down in South Cove. You know of it?"

"I do."

"A district of the foulest vice if ever there was one. Disorderly houses, gambling parlors, fancy bordellos, what have you. The police make regular raids, of course, but as I don't have to tell you, a little baksheesh goes a long way with some of those officers, particularly the ones who walk a beat."

"I imagine it does, yes."

"In the course of this particular visit, a few so-called respectable men were discovered at one or two of the houses."

"And among them was the Reverend Montgomery?"

"Yes."

Ames was silent, and after a moment, Norton said, "You do not seem surprised, Mr. Ames."

"I am not. To be frank, I have the same impression of him that you do—that he is not what he pretends to be. But if you knew about this—ah—discovery, may I ask why you entertained him here? Surely a man who frequents the Black Sea should not be welcomed into any decent household."

Norton's gaze wavered, then came back. "You are right, of course, Mr. Ames. But I had already given my wife permission to hold the event, and in all honesty, if I had demanded she cancel it, I did not feel I could tell her why. One cannot speak of such things to a lady, after all."

"No. I suppose not. And she knows you well enough to detect it if you made up some falsehood as an excuse?"

Norton rolled his eyes. "Yes."

MacKenzie smothered a smile.

"So if you are looking to discover where the reverend was on Sunday evening after he left here—earlier than he said he did—I am sorry to say, Mr. Ames, that you may have to pay a visit to the Black Sea yourself."

THE BLACK SEA WAS A DREARY AREA OF TENEMENTS AND small commercial establishments, saloons, dingy cafés, and, on the narrow side streets, three- and four-story row houses. Here and there could be seen the three gold balls of pawnbrokers' shops, and small hand-lettered signs announcing the premises of crystal-ball readers and dubious healers. Some places, lacking any advertisement, looked more prosperous than their neighbors; these, presumably, housed the area's active flesh trade.

To MacKenzie's astonishment, Ames seemed familiar with the neighborhood. Since he was sure his landlord was far too fastidious a man to frequent such a district, he had to assume that Ames was operating on hearsay and clever guesses.

The first three places they visited, while assuredly disorderly houses, had no knowledge of the Reverend Montgomery. Ames did not use the reverend's name; instead, sure that Montgomery would have come here under an alias, he described him.

At the fourth house, he found what he was looking for: a

woman who said—after Ames intimated that the police might wish to pay her a visit—that yes, such a man was a regular customer.

"But who are you?" she asked. She was middle-aged, hard-looking, with dyed black hair and pouchy eyes. "Not the police, I know that for sure."

"No," Ames replied. "Not the police. Now, tell me, my good woman, did this man visit you last Sunday night?"

She squinted, as if the daylight hurt her eyes. "Last Sunday? I couldn't say for sure."

"Try."

She sniffed. "I can't."

"I believe you can," Ames said. "And my friend, Inspector Crippen, will—"

"All right!" she said quickly.

"He was here?"

"Yes."

"What time?"

"I couldn't say."

"No? Of course you could."

She thought about it. "Around nine, nine-thirty."

"And he stayed until?"

"He's always quick about it, that one," she said with a sour smile. "Not after ten."

As they turned to go, she cried, "No trouble from the police, now, mister!"

When they were on the sidewalk once more, Ames gave himself a shake as if to slough off a film of dirt.

"I don't hold with the Watch and Ward, Doctor, but I must say, sometimes I don't object to their activities if they can rid the city of places like this."

But they can't, MacKenzie thought, and they never will.

Ames hailed a cab on Washington Street and gave the driver the Bower's address. Despite the admission he had wrung from the brothel's owner just now, he felt oddly deflated. He'd hoped to find that the reverend had no way to account for his time on the night that Mary was killed, and now, perhaps, he had done so. That is, if Crippen would take the word of a whore. If Norton had been correct in his estimation of the hour when Montgomery had left his house. If, if, if—

The medical examiner had put the time of Mary's death at between seven and midnight—a span that easily could have allowed the reverend to leave the Nortons', make his way back to the South End to deal with Mary, and then visit the Black Sea.

But why, if indeed he had killed Mary, had he killed Bridget also?

"SHE CAN'T SEE YOU," SNAPPED MATRON PRATT. SHE STOOD in the hall, hands on her hips, eyes slitted nearly shut with animosity. "She can't see anyone. Why don't you leave her alone? She's near out of her mind with worry, and you come here to pester her—"

Ames inclined his head. "I understand, Matron. I will not take up one moment of her time more than I need, I assure you."

The Bower was quiet. From the dining hall at the rear of the building, where the girls were presumably at their noon meal, came the odor of boiled cabbage.

"She's resting," Matron Pratt replied through clenched teeth. "She hasn't slept a wink since—since it happened, and now for once she is, and I won't—"

She broke off as they heard voices rising, high and piercing, from the dining hall. In the next moment, they heard curses, and then the sound of what might have been someone's head hitting, very hard, a bare floor.

At once, Mrs. Pratt whirled and went at a half-run toward the back of the house.

"Stand guard," Ames muttered to MacKenzie. In the next instant, he was inside the office. Lifting the glass door of one of the bookshelves, he took down the account book for the previous year, 1891. Quickly he scanned the pages that held the record of income and outgo for the last three months.

In a moment more, he was out in the hall once again, just in time to greet Agatha Montgomery coming from the dining room, giving the lie to the matron's excuses.

"Mr. Ames."

"Miss Montgomery."

"How can I—what do you want?"

She looked worse than ever, MacKenzie thought: pale and tense, and her voice strained and thin.

"We want a few words with you, no more," Ames said.

"You are not fit—" Mrs. Pratt growled at her, coming up behind.

"It's all right, Matron."

Miss Montgomery opened the door to the office and went in, Ames and MacKenzie following. She sat in the chair behind the desk—Mary Flaherty's chair—and the men seated themselves opposite. They caught sight of Matron Pratt's angry visage at the door before she slammed it shut.

For a moment, Miss Montgomery seemed to be trying to summon up the strength to speak. She sat rigid, her hands clenched on the desk before her, her long, equine face tight with strain. Her hair was straggling out of its knot, and the collar of her dark dress was crooked.

Then at last she said, "Now, Mr. Ames. What do you want?"

He reminded himself that women were the weaker sex. He reminded himself that Agatha Montgomery, although hardly weak in the way that most women were, was nevertheless a female herself—and, more, that during the past few days, she had been through a great deal of emotional turmoil and devastating loss. She must, he thought, be particularly vulnerable just now.

So. This was his chance, and he must take it.

"Miss Montgomery, were you aware that Mary Flaherty was expecting a child?"

Her mouth dropped open, and her pale eyes widened with shock—at what Ames had told her? MacKenzie wondered. Or at the fact that he would mention such an unmentionable thing?

Ames waited for a moment. Then he pressed on. "Did you know that, Miss Montgomery?"

"No." She spoke so softly that they barely heard her.

"I believe you did. Or you suspected it at least. And since your brother was friendly with Mary—"

"He—I don't know what you mean by friendly."

"He knew her rather better than he knew most of the girls here, didn't he?"

Her eyes shifted away, to the file cabinets and bookcases lining the walls, to her clenched hands, to the ceiling, back to her hands.

"Didn't he, Miss Montgomery?" Ames persisted. "He had to see to the account books, after all, which Mary kept here in the office. He was in and out at all hours, and he would have met her here as she worked."

"Yes. I suppose so."

"And so, being friendly with her, he would have listened to her troubles."

"What troubles?" She looked up sharply.

"I think you know."

No answer.

"Didn't you know about Mary, Miss Montgomery? That she was expecting a child?"

"No."

"But you must have suspected it?"

"Never. She was— No. I don't believe it."

You are lying, MacKenzie thought.

"The medical examiner is quite sure," Ames said.

She blazed up at him. "Then the medical examiner is mistaken! She couldn't have been—she wouldn't—"

"No, Miss Montgomery. The medical examiner is not mistaken," Ames said softly. "And I believe you know he is not."

She made no reply. She sat immobile; after a moment, they saw tears begin to slide down her thin, sallow cheeks. She made no move to stop them or to wipe them away. She simply sat, without speaking, without making a sound, letting her tears fall—and what bitter tears they must be, Ames thought. It was almost as if she were mourning, not Mary's death, or Bridget's, but the whole wreckage of her life, all her years of effort and toil to establish this place, this "bower" of refuge for girls who might, in the end, throw that effort back in her face. Other girls had left the Bower because they'd been pregnant, but those other girls had not been Mary Flaherty: her pet, her prize girl.

Gently, Ames said, "Did you ever talk to Mary about her condition, Miss Montgomery?"

She shook her head. Then she fumbled in her cuff for a handkerchief, withdrew it, and wiped her eyes. She looked old—older than she did ordinarily, and somehow beaten.

"But you knew," he said.

"I did not!" Suddenly she was infused with a dreadful energizing anger. She sat up straight and glared at Ames as if he and he alone were the source of all her woe.

"But if I had known, I can assure you I would have expelled her at once! At once! To have allowed her to stay— and with a bastard child—never! To see her, like *that*—! No, Mr. Ames. If what you say is true, she would have gone at once."

"It is true," he said. "Believe me. And what I am trying to discover is if you have any idea who the man might have been."

She stared at him as if he had taken leave of his senses. "How can you ask such a thing, Mr. Ames? How would I know that? The girls are strictly monitored—"

"Ah, but Mary was not, was she?"

They watched, fascinated, as a series of emotions passed over her face: anger, bewilderment, a kind of cunning. And finally, once more, that look of defeat.

"No," she said. "She was not. Let it be a lesson to me, never again to allow a girl to be so free. I thought I could trust her."

"But she betrayed you."

"If what you say is true—yes, she did."

"With whom, Miss Montgomery? That is what I need to know. Who was the man?"

She shook her head. "It seems impossible. For her to—"

She caught herself. "What about that typewriter salesman? He was hanging around, making a nuisance of himself. If anyone got Mary into trouble, I would wager on him."

"I agree with you that at first glance he would seem a likely candidate, but I have spoken to him, I have asked him that very question, and he denies it. For the moment, at least, I am inclined to believe him."

"Well, then, who?" She thought about it. "There is a boy who works here—"

"Garrett O'Reilly? I don't believe it was he."

"Why not?"

"I have character references for him which lead me to believe that he would not be so rash as to—ah—become intimate with one of the girls here."

Miss Montgomery's mouth twisted in a bitter smile. "Because they are not good enough for him? An Irish boy?"

"For the moment, at least, let us eliminate him. Can you think of anyone else?"

"No."

"And your brother—?"

She sucked in her breath with a loud hiss. "My brother! My *brother*? Are you suggesting that my brother, who is the very heart and soul of this establishment, had anything to do with Mary's condition? You come here to insult me, to insult him—"

A sedative, thought MacKenzie; she needs a strong dose of chloral hydrate and twenty-four hours in her bed.

"I am not trying to insult anyone," Ames retorted. "I beg you to believe that. I am merely trying to help the police—"

"Where you are not wanted! I told you before, I do not want you interfering—"

"Miss Montgomery, do you realize the seriousness of this situation? The Bower is in danger of losing its support if Mary's killer—and Bridget's as well—is not swiftly apprehended."

"Then go and apprehend him, and leave my brother out of it! It is outrageous that he must be dragged into this affair when he is the best man in the world, devoted to us, to our work! He has been my strong right hand from the beginning, and to have you insinuate such things about him is more than I can bear!"

She turned her head away from them. When, after a moment, she had quieted a little, Ames said, "He might, in fact, know something that can help us."

"If he does, he would have told it to you—or to the police—already."

Although she had calmed, still she twisted her hands, hard, until MacKenzie thought they must hurt her.

"My brother, Mr. Ames, is a very different person from me. Yes—I know it. I accept it. He was always, from the time he was born, a charming, personable boy. Everyone always liked him. They didn't like me particularly—charm is not one of my virtues—but they liked him. He has always made his way in the world on the strength of that charm— his ability to bring people over to his side. That is why he is so successful at raising funds. People naturally want to help him, and, by extension, the Bower."

She paused, distracted by her thoughts. For a moment, the ghost of a smile flitted across her face.

"It is not Randolph's fault that people find him attractive," she went on. "Women in particular seem to throw themselves at him. Oh, yes. More than one woman has tried to befriend me in the hope that I will connect her to him. I never do, of course. Why should I?"

"And yet, one woman has—ah—connected herself to him on her own, has she not?" Ames asked. "Just the other evening, at Caroline's dinner party, we learned that he is engaged to be married."

Miss Montgomery's face darkened, her mouth tightened—with anger, MacKenzie thought—but she made no reply.

"Did we not?" Ames persisted. He felt, just then, like a bully—something he never wanted to be—but he was coming close to something, he didn't know what, and he needed to keep on until he found it.

"We did—yes," Miss Montgomery replied reluctantly.

"You were not aware of it before Wednesday evening?"

"No."

Why not? Ames wondered. Why did your precious brother keep it secret? To avoid your wrath?

"You do not know the lady?"

"No."

"Nor anything about her?"

"No. Except that she is a widow. Randolph told me that later. And quite wealthy."

"I see." Ames's pulse quickened at the thought of the Reverend Montgomery, a wealthy widow within his grasp. And if a girl from the Bower—a girl who was inconveniently in the family way, and perhaps by him—threatened to be an impediment to that match, what would the reverend have done to get rid of her?

"It will be a splendid marriage for him." Miss Montgomery seemed to have forgotten her anger, her distress. She spoke now in a singsong voice, her eyes gazing into the middle distance, seeing, perhaps, the advantageous match that her brother had achieved. "And when they marry, they will live here in Boston, they will not go to New York. Randolph would never leave me here alone. He always promised me—"

"He promised you what?"

They had not heard him open the door. Now he came in, closing it behind him.

Miss Montgomery started. "Randolph!"

"Good morning, sister." His eyes raked Ames and MacKenzie, but he did not greet them.

"We were just—Mr. Ames came to—" Suddenly, she was afraid. Of the reverend? Ames wondered. And if so, why?

"Mr. Ames came to—what?" Montgomery's voice was soft, but they heard the threat in it.

"To ask Miss Montgomery—" Ames began.

"To harass her, you mean." Montgomery was breathing hard, as if he were trying to contain anger he did not want to reveal. "To hound her—to pester her once more, when in fact you have done enough pestering already, sir."

He glanced at his sister, who sat immobile. Only the

rapid blinking of her eyes showed that she, too, labored under some considerable stress.

"And so, Mr. Ames—Doctor—I ask you to leave. At once."

Ames rose, and MacKenzie did likewise. "Of course," Ames said. "Since you request it. But as long as you are here, Reverend, I wonder if I might prevail a trifle more upon your patience—"

"My patience is at an end, sir! I told you that last night! I order you to leave. Now!"

They were moving toward the door, and the reverend stepped aside to allow them to go out. But as Ames passed by, he murmured, "Only a moment, Reverend."

In the hall, Ames and the doctor continued on to the front door, opened it, and went out. Montgomery stood by the office door, glaring at them. At last, as if he had come to some difficult decision, he joined them.

The three men went down the tall flight of brownstone steps to the sidewalk. At first glance, the square was deserted, only a lone grocer's wagon trundling down the opposite side. Then MacKenzie saw a rather slovenly looking man leaning against a tree, facing the Bower. A neighborhood tramp? Doubtful, he thought. The fellow seemed to be waiting for something—or someone.

"Well?" Montgomery demanded.

Ames walked a few doors down, MacKenzie and the reverend behind. Then Ames stopped and turned to face Montgomery.

"I have spoken to Lawrence Norton," he said.

Montgomery's eyes, meeting his own, did not waver. "And?" he said.

"And he told me that last Sunday evening you left his house shortly after seven."

"Perhaps he is mistaken."

"I do not believe so."

A dull red had begun to spread over the reverend's fleshy face, and his eyes, so pale, so cold, seemed no more than two chips of flinty stone.

"What business of yours—I ask you, Ames—what earthly business of yours is it at what hour I left the Nortons'? You barge into my home, you come here, you harass my sister, you poke and pry—"

He raised his clenched, gloved fist and shook it under Ames's nose. "Get out!" he said, his voice choked with fury.

"This is a public walkway, Reverend."

The man leaning against the tree straightened.

"I do not care what it is! Get out! Or by God I will have you arrested for trespassing at the Bower!"

"The Black Sea, Reverend."

This threw Montgomery off guard. "What?"

"The Black Sea. I believe you know it. They certainly know you."

Montgomery's face was bright red now. "Get out!" he shouted. A woman just emerging from an areaway across the square stopped in astonishment as she heard him.

"I warn you, Ames!" Montgomery advanced, fist raised. "Once and for all!"

Ames held up his hands, palms out. "We are going, Reverend. Do not excite yourself further. Good morning to you."

He turned and walked swiftly toward the end of the square. MacKenzie, hurrying to keep up, saw out of the corner of his eye the man who had been leaning against the tree begin to head in their direction. And now he thought he recognized him.

"Excuse me—"

Ames looked around, but he did not pause. He knew this man: Babcock, from the *Globe*.

"Mr. Ames, is it? I wonder if I could have a word—"

"No."

"But I'll pay—"

"*No.*"

"Make it worth your while, sir, if you'd just give me—"

With a snarl, Ames dismissed him. The journalist stood in the middle of the sidewalk, staring after them, shaking his head.

It was not until they had turned into Columbus Avenue that Ames spoke. His face was taut, his eyes flashing with anger.

"A—what would you call him, Doctor? A mountebank? I don't mean that damned scribbler back there. I mean the reverend. Yes. That is what he is. A perfect charlatan. I smell fraud about his person—stinking fraud, and worse besides."

"Nevertheless, he has his prospects," MacKenzie replied.

"Indeed he does. And, having them—her, rather, that wealthy widow—he would not want his plans spoiled by the inconvenience of a poor girl at the Bower who presented herself to him in a scandalous condition."

"You mean a condition for which he was responsible?"

"Exactly, Doctor. A condition into which, if I am not mistaken, the good reverend put her."

"His sister will never believe it."

"No, she will not. Her faith in him is absolute."

"To the point that if that faith were destroyed, her world would come crashing down around her."

"Yes. Precisely." Ames lifted his arm, and a herdic-phaeton veered toward them. "I have another errand, but you, I imagine, will be glad to go home. Tell Caro that I will be back at some point, I do not know when. She is not to worry."

The last MacKenzie saw of him was his tall, dark-clad figure loping at a rapid clip down the avenue in the rain.

CHAPTER 19

MACKENZIE GAZED THROUGH THE LAVENDER GLASS AT THE purplish winter-dead greenery behind the black iron fence of the oval. The rain continued unabated, the gray skies emptying sheets of water onto the square. Already now, at two o'clock, the afternoon was growing dark. Soon the streetlamps would glow, casting their pale illumination through the downpour. Lights would go on in the windows of the houses ringing the square; people would hurry home to the peace and comfort of their firesides.

But not here. Here was tension and worry, no hope of peace. As he turned back to the room, he saw that Caroline had picked up her knitting. After completing a row or two, she put it down, took up one of her beloved Diana Strangeways novels, and tried to read. He did the same, seating himself in his Morris rocker and opening the pages of the life of Lincoln that he seemed unable to finish. The words danced before his eyes in a senseless jumble, and he kept going over the same sentence, the same paragraph, without understanding what he read. A half hour passed; three-quarters. At last he put the volume aside and looked up to find her watching him.

"Where is Addington?" she said.

He saw the worry in her eyes, he heard the tension in her

voice, and he longed to find the words to reassure her that her brother was safe.

"I don't know."

"But surely he should be back by now? I wish he'd told you where he was going. It isn't prudent to go who-knows-where, and possibly—"

A knock at the front door interrupted her. She broke off, her hand flown to her bosom, listening—hoping—for a friendly voice instead of word of some disaster. They heard Margaret hurrying to answer. When, after a moment, she did not announce the caller, Caroline stood up.

"Who do you suppose—" she began, but just then the pocket doors slid open to reveal Margaret, her face unwontedly grim.

"Yes, Margaret? Who is it?"

"It's an Irish, miss," the maid said disapprovingly.

"Well, who, Margaret? Does he want to see Mr. Ames?"

"Him—or you, miss."

Caroline pushed past her. The vestibule was empty, the front door closed. She opened it.

On the front step, shivering, hatless, wearing only a thin jacket and soaked to the skin, stood Garrett O'Reilly.

"Garrett! What on earth—come in, you'll catch your death!"

He dripped puddles onto the tiled vestibule floor, and his teeth were chattering so badly, he could hardly speak. When Caroline turned to lead him into the hall, she confronted Margaret's scowl.

"It's all right, Margaret. Would you bring tea, please?" But tea hardly seemed adequate to Garrett's condition, and so she added, "And would you go up to the fourth floor, to the box room, and see if you can find any of Mr. Ames's old clothing?"

Not that there would be much to choose from, she thought; Addington, like so many men of his class, wore his things year in and year out. He didn't have many castoffs.

"Yes, miss. But you remember—"

"What, Margaret?"

"I'm catching the train, miss. To my sister's."

"Oh, yes. I'd forgotten. But the train doesn't leave until nine o'clock, does it?" Even in the present emergency, Caroline hadn't the heart to forbid Margaret's long-anticipated visit.

Margaret disappeared, and Caroline led the shivering young man into the parlor, where MacKenzie was pulling up a side chair to the fire. He shoveled more coal onto the low flames, stirred them up, and said, "Well, my lad, you're a candidate for pneumonia. Come here and warm yourself."

"Yes, sir."

Caroline introduced them, and Garrett limped across the rug, shedding water as he went, to take MacKenzie's outstretched hand—with no hesitation, the doctor noted. Once seated, Garrett held out his thin, chapped hands to the flames. He couldn't seem to stop shivering.

Caroline gave him a moment, and then, unable to contain her curiosity, she said, "What is it, Garrett? Why have you come?"

He looked up at her. He was trembling, MacKenzie thought, from more than cold.

"It's the police, miss."

"What happened?" Caroline asked. "Did they question you?"

"Yes, miss."

"Just now?"

"Yes. It was that inspector—Crippen, is it? He thinks—" His voice broke, and he swallowed hard. "He thinks I did it. He was that nasty, miss."

"I'm sure he was."

"He wanted to know—like, did I know the girls. Did I talk to them. Where was I on Sunday night."

"Well?" said MacKenzie. "And where were you?"

Garrett shot him an inscrutable look. "At home, sir. Where else would I be?"

"Any number of places, I imagine. Did Crippen believe you?"

"No, sir. He said family alibi isn't good enough. Any mother would lie to save her son, he said."

"Hmmm. True enough, I suppose. What else did he want to know?"

"Just—things," Garrett muttered, shaking his head.

Like whether you had intimate relations with Mary Flaherty, MacKenzie thought. Hardly a topic to discuss in front of Caroline Ames.

Margaret came in, then, with the tea tray. She was still scowling with disapproval, and she put it down with an unnecessarily loud thud and left the room without her usual curtsy.

Scalding hot as it was, Garrett greedily drank the full cup that Caroline gave to him and accepted another. She waited until he had stopped shivering somewhat, and then she said, "Garrett, what did you tell Inspector Crippen?"

"I told him the truth, miss. That I didn't do it—didn't have anything to do with either of 'em."

"But you did," she said.

He looked away.

"You sometimes spoke to Bridget, didn't you? I have been told that you sometimes asked her questions. Is that so?"

And now they saw the first hint of truculence in him. He stared at them as if he were trying to judge the degree of danger they posed to him, instead of being the source of help he'd sought.

"What if I did?" he said at last. "What difference does that make?"

"None," she replied, "except that it gives the lie to your statement that you had nothing to do with her. And that makes people suspicious. Surely you can understand that."

That, and a good deal more, MacKenzie thought. He could almost see the rapid workings of Garrett's mind as the lad considered what to say next.

After a long moment, Garrett said, "I had my reasons to speak to her. It doesn't mean that I—that I did her in."

"Of course it doesn't," said Caroline warmly. MacKenzie

could see that she was genuinely troubled about this boy, and he was touched by her compassion.

"Why did you?" he asked Garrett. "Speak to her, I mean."

Garrett hesitated. Then: "Because I was asking her about the new girl."

"New girl? Who was that?"

"Peg Corcoran."

"And why were you asking about her?" Caroline said.

"I wanted to see if she was getting along." It seemed a tremendous effort for him to get out the words. "She's my cousin," he added, obviously with great reluctance.

"Your—oh, dear. I am sorry."

"It was—you understand—a disgrace to us. To our family. My ma didn't know, y'see. Peg is her niece—her brother's child. They live in South Boston. My uncle Frank near died when he found out about Peg. Last year, it was. She'd gone into service with a family over in Cambridge. But then something happened, I don't know what, and they put her out. She couldn't bear to go home like that—a failure. So she took to the streets. Lived with three other girls in a room. She was arrested once or twice, and one time she was sent up for thirty days. Then she got sick. She went to Uncle Frank for help, but he turned her out. Said she was no daughter of his no more. He told me about it, made me promise not to tell my ma. That must'v' frightened her more than anything, I think—that she was so far gone, her own family didn't want her. She must'v' seen she was headed straight for Potter's Field if she didn't straighten herself out. That's when she came to the Bower."

"Did she know you worked there?" MacKenzie asked.

"No, sir, she didn't. I saw her in the dining room one day when I was washin' windows. I almost fell off my ladder, I can tell you. But I never spoke to her, not once. I wouldn't want her to think I'd let on to the family she was there. Though it mightn't have made any difference, seein' as how they considered her dead. An' anyways, the Bower's better than the streets, isn't it?"

"So it was simply out of concern for her that you asked Bridget about her," MacKenzie said.

"Yes, sir. I just wanted to make sure she was all right."

It seemed an innocent enough explanation, and yet MacKenzie doubted Inspector Crippen would accept it if he had already made up his mind, as he seemed to have done, that the lad was the Bower killer.

"And now with all this goin' on," Garrett added, "how do I know she's safe at all? Any of the Bower's girls might be the next."

"If there is to be another, yes," Caroline replied, suppressing a shudder. Another—but there couldn't be. There mustn't be.

"Inspector Crippen let you go in the end," MacKenzie said.

"Yes, sir." Garrett nodded at him. "But he said I must stay in Boston. I shouldn't think of tryin' to run away, he said, because he could find me anywhere. But where would I go anyways?"

Caroline went to the bellpull by the fireplace and pulled it twice sharply. Then she said to Garrett, "You must stay here."

"Do you not think—" MacKenzie began, but he broke off as she gave him a look. It was not, after all, his affair if she chose to offer shelter to this lad.

"Yes, I do think, Doctor," she said, and that, he understood, was the end of it.

When Margaret came, she still had that stubborn, mutinous look. "Yes, miss?"

"Have you found any dry clothing, Margaret?" The way to deal with the maid's attitude, Caroline believed, was to ignore it.

"Not yet, miss."

"Please do so immediately. And then make up the bed in Henry's old room"—this was the chamber, next to the kitchen, that had once housed the family's butler—"and tell Cook to find something for this young man to eat. He will be staying with us for a day or two."

If not longer, she thought, and she momentarily quailed at the thought of her brother's reaction when he learned of Garrett's presence in the household.

"Cook is gettin' dinner, miss, an' then she'll be on her way home."

Caroline stared at her. "Then tell her to put something out before she goes! Really, Margaret!"

"Yes, miss." Margaret shot a hostile glance toward Garrett as she left the room.

In all Margaret's years with the family, Caroline had never had trouble with her. Well, she'd deal with her when she came back from her sister's; she hadn't time to soothe the maid's obviously ruffled feathers now. "Do you understand, Garrett?" she said. "If you are here with us, we can vouch for you in the event of another—"

"I can't stay, miss."

"But why not?"

"My ma'll be worried crazy if I don't come home."

"We could send her a note," MacKenzie offered.

"She can't read."

"Send it anyway. Where do you live?"

"Salem Street."

A street of tenements in the North End. "Well, then, surely someone in her building can read. Or she could take it to one of the neighborhood shopkeepers, perhaps, to read to her."

Caroline went to the little desk in the corner and took out a sheet of paper. "If you go down to Charles Street, Doctor," she said, "you will find a runner at Bright's Apothecary. Tell them you know me. They always have a supply of boys to run messages, and they won't charge you more than a nickel."

She wrote a few lines, folded the paper, and sealed it into an envelope. "What is the address, Garrett?"

He told her and she printed it large and clear. "There, Doctor," she said, handing the envelope to him. For once, she didn't smile at him, and for once, he didn't mind.

Out-of-doors, he pulled his muffler more tightly around his neck as he made his way down the hill. The rain had stopped, but the air was raw, filled with a tangy, salt-smelling mist that overlay the odor of horse dung.

Charles Street was thronged with Saturday afternoon shoppers and pedestrians; a seller of roasted chestnuts was doing a brisk business. At Bright's Apothecary, the clerk acknowledged knowing the Ameses, but this was a particularly busy day, he said, and he didn't have a lad handy. Could the gentleman wait for a moment while he finished up with this customer?

Impatiently, MacKenzie tapped his fingers on the polished wooden counter. He hadn't thought to be delayed; he needed to get back to No. 16½. He didn't like leaving Caroline Ames alone with that Irish lad, no matter how innocent he seemed to be. Margaret was there, of course, and Cook, but still. Not a good arrangement. And he was certain that Ames would be unhappy when he learned that Caroline had asked Garrett to stay, no matter that he himself had offered to help the lad.

Five minutes passed; ten. MacKenzie stared at the shelves of tall glass apothecary jars containing various colored liquids and powders and bits of vegetation—roots, stems, ugly-looking dried things. The place had a musty, medicinal smell. MacKenzie wanted to be outdoors; he felt confined in here, too nerved up to wait patiently. He spoke to the clerk again: Could a lad be found to take this note?

At last the door burst open and a whey-faced little boy came trotting in. This, it seemed, was the runner for whom MacKenzie waited. He handed over the note and a nickel, and at last the message to Garrett's mother was on its way to the North End. He stepped outside to watch the child set off at a rapid clip, and then he rounded the corner to climb Mt. Vernon Street. He'd been gone almost half an hour, he estimated. Too long.

He was slightly out of breath when he reached Louisburg Square. He lumbered along the uneven brick sidewalk toward

No. 16½, peering eagerly at the welcoming light shining through the lavender windowpanes. She'd be worried, he thought, wondering what had become of him.

But when he greeted her at last, he saw that she wasn't worried after all—or not about him at any rate. She was alone, Garrett presumably having gone down to the kitchen to be fed, and she was standing by the fire, holding a flimsy scrap of yellow paper: a telegram.

"What is it?" he said, still puffing a little.

"The Ladies' Committee at the church."

Not some further crisis at the Bower, then. He was relieved to hear it, but in the next moment his anxiety returned when she added, "They want me to make a visit."

"A visit? To whom?"

"To the family I saw on Monday. Oh, I hope he hasn't come back!"

"Who?"

"The husband." Her sweet, pretty face was suddenly grim. "He has been warned repeatedly to stay away from them, but when he is inebriated, he comes back and beats her. The eldest son is fifteen now, so he can defend her—his mother—fairly well, but still, I must go."

"When? Now?"

"Yes."

"But—late on a Saturday afternoon? Can it not wait until tomorrow?"

"I am afraid not. People generally don't call on us unless it is an emergency. They have no place else to turn, you see."

He was not convinced. "Surely you can ask someone else to go. You should not be burdened with such a request at a time like this." He was pulling at one end of his mustache, a sure sign of his distress.

"Oh, I couldn't do that," she said hastily, looking slightly shocked, as if he had suggested some truly outrageous thing. "This family is mine—assigned to me, my responsibility. I must go."

"Then I will come with you."

"Oh, no, Doctor. Thank you, but no. I won't be long. I

know these people fairly well. The woman is very self-reliant, she wouldn't call on us—on me—if it weren't absolutely necessary."

She tucked the telegram into the pocket of her skirt and started for the door. MacKenzie, seized with a sudden dread, threw propriety to the winds and put his hand on her arm. "Where do they live?"

"On West Newton Street."

He was familiar enough with the city, by now, to know where that was. "In the South End."

"Yes."

Where, in the past week, two women had been brutally murdered. What would her brother do? he wondered. Forbid her to go? Could he act in Ames's place and do the same?

Before he'd decided how to proceed, she had gently removed his hand and was going out into the vestibule to collect her things from the hall tree. Struggling with his rising sense of helpless panic, he followed her.

"Miss Ames, I am sure—I am absolutely positive—that your brother would not want you to go on this—this errand of mercy."

She had been pulling on her overshoes. Now she straightened, one on, one off, and said with no little dignity, "My brother does not need to know about it."

"Yes, but if he should return and find you gone—or if, God forbid, you should come to some harm—"

"I will not come to harm."

"How can you say that?" He was aware that he was shouting. He couldn't help it. "You know as well as I do that a homicidal lunatic is at large in that district! He has killed two women in the most brutal fashion. Undoubtedly, if the police do not apprehend him, he will kill a third. I cannot—I will not—allow you to put yourself in danger like this."

He had maneuvered himself past her as he spoke, and now he stood before the front door. If she insisted upon going out, she would have to push him aside.

Or—

"Very well, Doctor," she said after a moment. She stared at him, outraged. Her voice was cold and hard. Furious, he thought. She is furious with me. In that moment he realized, too late, that in opposing her he had pitted himself against a woman who embodied generations—centuries—of stern New England resolve. Briefly his courage failed him as he saw the wreckage of all his dreams. He would lose her either way, he thought: If she went out, she'd come to harm sure enough, and if—at his insistence—she stayed, she would never forgive him for meddling in her affairs.

"Please, Miss Ames," he begged, his voice little more than a hoarse croak. "Please do not go on this errand, no matter how much an errand of mercy you believe it to be. Are this family's troubles worth your life? At least let me come with you."

"It is far more important, Doctor, that you stay here with Garrett. I will be quite all right on my own. I understand your concern, but this is a summons I must obey. It is my Christian duty to go, can you not understand that? We—the ladies on the committee—are responsible for these families. I have no idea what this summons is about. Perhaps it is simply a problem with one of the children that can be solved quickly. Or perhaps the husband has returned, after all. But whatever it is, I must tend to it. If you insist on barring my way, I will go down to the kitchen and leave from the areaway."

She turned her back to him, pulled on the other overshoe, and lifted down her waterproof and bonnet.

Utterly defeated, and still struggling with himself—should he risk her further wrath by forcibly restraining her?—MacKenzie watched her. She was the only woman who had ever captured his heart, and now—he was sure—he was going to lose her. Probably he had lost her already.

"Good-bye, Doctor," she said. She lifted her chin as she met his eyes. Her voice was quiet—deadly quiet—but still very cold, and her eyes were filled with contempt.

Contempt for him, he thought miserably as the door

closed behind her. He was certain he'd ruined himself in her opinion. She'd never think of him now as anything but a coward.

Raw with self-reproach, his conscience racked with guilt, he lingered by the lavender-glass bow window until she disappeared around the corner of Mt. Vernon Street. Then he turned back to the empty room. Where was Ames? he thought as he began to pace. Up to something, undoubtedly. Why wasn't he here, where he should be, to protect his sister? Ames had the authority to dictate to her which he, John MacKenzie, did not. Fat lot of good it did, that authority, when Ames wasn't here to exercise it.

His knee was aching. He came to a stop by his chair and, with an audible sigh, settled into it. He wondered if he should go down to the kitchen to see how the Irish lad did. Perhaps, after a while, he would.

He rested his head on the antimacassar. Exhausted by the emotional turmoil of the past half hour, he let the warmth of the simmering sea-coal fire envelop him.

He closed his eyes and slept.

He was startled into wakefulness by the sound of the front door slamming. At once he felt a wave of relief: She'd come back, then, safe and sound. He heaved himself up, preparing to greet her, but his welcoming words died on his lips as Addington Ames walked into the room.

"What is it, Doctor?" Ames asked.

"Nothing," MacKenzie stammered. "I thought it was Miss Ames, returning."

"Returning! Where did she go?"

Ames frowned as MacKenzie told him of the summons from the Ladies' Committee. "Confound it! And to the South End—you couldn't prevent her going?" Instantly he corrected himself. "No—no, of course you couldn't. When Caroline sets her mind on something—you don't know the name of the family?"

MacKenzie was embarrassed to admit that he hadn't thought of asking for it.

"Never mind. Even if we went after her we'd probably

cross paths and miss her anyway. Well! Shall we have tea?" He stood before the fire, rubbing warmth back into his frozen hands.

And where have you been, MacKenzie thought, and doing what? But he didn't ask, because tea made him think of the kitchen, and the kitchen made him remember Garrett O'Reilly.

"There is something else you should know," he said.

Ames turned a wary eye to him. "What?"

"The Irish boy came, in a fright because he'd been roughly questioned by Crippen. Your sister told him to stay here. He is downstairs."

Ames had taken hold of the bellpull to summon Margaret, but now he let it go.

"What? Garrett is here?"

"Yes."

Without a reply, Ames turned and swiftly left the room. MacKenzie could hear him clattering down the back stairs; in what seemed too short a time, he had returned.

"Gone!" he exclaimed.

"What? I didn't hear him go out." But you were asleep, his conscience told him.

"He ducked out at the front areaway, no doubt," Ames said. "Damned young fool! I don't like the thought of sheltering him, but even less do I like the thought of him abroad in the city. He will put himself into Crippen's hands by his own foolhardiness if he doesn't watch out."

Margaret appeared, then, bearing their tea. Her face wore an expression that MacKenzie, in his present state of unease, read as "This is what comes of trying to help someone from the lower orders."

"No point in trying to go after him either," Ames commented gloomily as he surveyed the plate of lace cookies and sliced fruit cake. "Tea, Doctor? Help yourself. We are captive here, I am afraid, until either Caroline or that young Irish scamp sees fit to rejoin us. We can do nothing but wait."

CHAPTER
20

IT WAS DARK ON WARREN AVENUE, DARKER THAN USUAL BE-
cause along this stretch, a whole row of streetlamps had
gone out. As Caroline hurried along, she had only the pale
illumination from an unshuttered window, here and there,
to see by. Not so fast, she told herself; the last thing you
need is to trip and fall. At the corner, up ahead, she saw the
welcome glow of a lamp on every side, and she kept her eyes
fixed there, a beacon in this dark night.

Dr. MacKenzie had been right: She shouldn't have come.
The emergency had turned out to be not so very urgent after
all; it could easily have been tended to the following day or
even the day after. Christian charity was one thing; waste of
it was another.

She heard the sound of a carriage behind her, and she
turned to look. It was a four-wheeler—a private carriage,
not a cab. She'd taken a herdic earlier because she'd wanted
to save time, but when she'd left the cold, cheerless room
where the objects of her charity lived, she'd been so annoyed—with herself, with them, with the Ladies' Committee—that she'd thought to punish herself by denying herself
a cab to get home.

But now, on this dark, deserted street, she thought better
of it. If a herdic came by, she'd hail it, never mind the expense.

She started to walk once more. In the silence, her footsteps sounded very loud. Then, from a nearby church, she heard the bell begin to toll the hour: six o'clock. For a moment, a scene from home flashed across her mind's eye: the warm, bright parlor, Dr. MacKenzie—and perhaps, by this time, Addington too—sitting by the fire, awaiting her. Oh, how she longed to be there with them! Why had she come out—and for nothing after all?

A heretical thought came to her: She would quit the Ladies' Committee. She'd served on it for years; surely she'd done her share. Someone new could take her place.

She reached the lighted corner, crossed, and went on. Darkness again. The bell had stopped, but now suddenly, out of the silent night, came the angry screech of a yowling cat. Dear heaven, what a noise! It was an unnerving sound at any time, but particularly now, when she was a solitary female abroad in the nighttime, a foolish female to have come here alone. What had she been thinking of? She should have allowed Dr. MacKenzie to come with her. Better yet, she should have listened to him and not come at all.

The yowling reached a high pitch and then suddenly stopped. *Clomp-clomp-clomp* went her galoshes on the brick sidewalk. *Thud-thud-thud* went her heart, as if in answer. Only a little way now until she came to Dartmouth Street, where she could cross over into Copley Square. It would be safer there, more people, brightly lighted, and well away from this district where those two girls, those poor, unfortunate girls, had been so atrociously murdered.

Someone was following her. Over the sound of her pounding heart, over the sound of her clomping galoshes, she heard footsteps. A man's footsteps, much too heavy to be a woman's. They were gaining on her.

Her heart jumped into her throat, and for a moment, she thought she would choke.

Stop and turn to look? Or ignore him and keep going fast, faster, as if she hadn't heard? If he sees that you are frightened, she told herself, that in itself may spur him to some reckless—some unthinkable—act.

The footsteps ceased. He must have turned a corner or gone into one of the tall, poorly lighted row houses that lined the street. Glancing back, she saw the sidewalk stretching empty behind her. The lights from the street-lamps—those that worked—glimmered on the deserted cobblestones of the street.

Despite the cold, the raw night air, she was perspiring. Sweat trickled uncomfortably down her face and neck. She wiped at her upper lip, but her fingers, encased in her kid glove, did no good. Perhaps she could find her handkerchief in her carpetbag.

She fumbled at it, scrabbled for the scrap of cloth. But she couldn't find it, and now, to her horror, she heard foot-steps again—a man's again, but with a different rhythm to them.

Fearful, terrified of what she would see, she glanced over her shoulder. Coming at her, very fast, was a tall, solid fig-ure. He was no tramp, no riffraff from the rails, but a confi-dent, long-striding male dressed in a tall hat and well-fitting overcoat. He was perhaps half a block away, and gaining rapidly.

Hurriedly she closed her bag and started to walk again, faster than before. But still she heard his footsteps; he was gaining on her. Suddenly seized by panic, she started to run. No, she thought. It isn't possible. Please let him not be—

She thought she heard him call to her, but she ignored him. She was running hard now, pain stabbing at her side, her lungs throbbing, her corset cruelly cutting her. She must draw a full breath or she would faint. But she mustn't faint, she must run—run for her life, because she was being chased by this man who was running, now, himself, and in a moment he was going to catch her.

Her overshoe caught on a protruding brick, and she went down. Her shoulder hit the ground with a heavy thud; then her head hit, but the rim of her bonnet kept her from seri-ous injury.

But she was stunned, what little breath she'd had knocked out of her, and for a long, terrible moment she lay prostrate. Her heart hammered, ready to burst, and her mouth went dry as she heard the footsteps coming closer and closer. . . .

She looked up. Just before she fainted she saw, looming over her, the faceless figure of the man who had pursued her.

CHAPTER
21

SHE MIGHT HAVE BEEN YOUNG, BUT HER FACE WAS FROZEN into a grotesque mask of terror so that it was impossible at first to tell her age. Her throat was slashed, her abdomen ripped open.

At first, when he'd spotted the crumpled heap halfway down the alley, he'd paused in his search, afraid of what he would see. But then, drawn by his need to know, slowly, cautiously, near paralyzed with dread, he crept down the narrow way until he reached the thing lying on the ground. His knees were so weak that he almost collapsed, and for a moment he leaned against the wall to steady himself. With trembling hands he fished a box of matches from his pocket, but it was nearly a minute before he managed to get one lit.

He heard a low, keening sound—a despairing wail of grief and loss—and he knew that it came from him. He sank onto his knees beside her, heedless of the muck and filth of the alley, heedless of her blood, and struck match after match. In the damp, misty night they went out quickly, and so he needed to keep striking them. With a shaking hand he held them close to her face. He still could not believe it. He kept thinking he had wandered into some nightmare, and any moment now he would awake and find himself safe in the Ameses' kitchen.

"No," he crooned, "no, no, no. . . ." He rocked back and forth on his knees, overcome with grief. "No, no, no. . . ."

He never heard the commotion at the end of the alley, never heard the approach of the men's heavy steps. He was startled when they seized him by the arms and hauled him up. He looked wildly around at their stern, accusing faces; in the flickering light of their lanterns, they looked like a trio of executioners.

He started to protest, but they ignored him. As they dragged him away, his shouts echoing off the walls of the alley, they were sure they had found the Bower killer at last.

CHAPTER
22

CAROLINE GROANED, AND THEN BIT HER LIP TO KEEP FROM groaning again. In the parlor of No. 16½, she sat in MacKenzie's chair while he knelt at her feet, gently exploring with his fingertips her swollen—and quite naked—right ankle.

"No breakage," he said, smiling up at her. "But you've had a nasty sprain. You should soak this for a while, and then I will bind it."

From his place by the fire, Ames clucked in disapproval. "I cannot emphasize enough, Caroline, how fortunate you were."

To have been pursued by the man he believed responsible for the Bower murders? How did that make her fortunate?

But she'd been frightened enough, he thought as he saw her disconsolate face. Even as disapproving as he was of her recklessness, he wouldn't chastise her further.

She'd arrived half an hour ago in a herdic. The driver had come to the door to ask assistance because she'd been unable to walk across the sidewalk. When at last she was safe inside, and had gasped out the details of her misadventure, Ames and MacKenzie had been appalled—horrified at her narrow escape.

"The Reverend Montgomery?" Ames had said.

"Yes, Addington. He—I thought he was pursuing me.

That's why I ran. And then I fell, and he caught up with me. He was almost as upset as you are now to find me there. He was very kind. He helped me up, and he stayed with me until a herdic came by. He was going to accompany me here— he insisted upon doing so—but I would not allow it. He told me he was overdue at some conference, and he'd been kind enough already. I didn't want to delay him any longer."

The reverend had said he was to spend this day and the next at a conference in Cambridge. Some urgent reason must have detained him in Boston. And so, stalking the streets of the South End, he had come upon Caroline, alone and defenseless. . . .

Suddenly Ames's throat constricted, and he swallowed painfully.

MacKenzie stood up. They should ring for Margaret to bring a basin of warm water, he said, and meanwhile he would fetch a wrapping from his bag of medical supplies.

A short while later, the soaking completed, Caroline allowed him to bind her ankle. The intimacy of this act had at first given her pause; for a man to see her bare leg and foot protruding from her petticoats would have been, in ordinary circumstances, indescribably embarrassing. But MacKenzie was a doctor, after all, and so kind, so gentle, so thoroughly professional, she hardly minded at all. She reminded herself that he'd seen more of her than her ankle when, two months before, he'd tended to the bullet wound in her shoulder.

"There." He fastened the wrap with a metal clip and gently placed her foot on a low stool. "You'll need to stay off it for a day or two, or possibly longer. But there has been no permanent damage."

"You were fortunate, Caroline," Ames said grimly.

"I know that," she said, and her voice was not sharp, as it might have been, but low, subdued. "You were right, Doctor, to say that I should not have gone. The errand was not truly necessary. I shall speak to the committee, to ask them to clarify the rules whereby we may be called upon. And I am sorry that I—spoke harshly to you."

"Am I forgiven, then?" MacKenzie wanted to clasp her hand, but he did not quite dare.

"Yes. Completely."

He felt an enormous sense of relief, as if a heavy weight had been lifted from his heart. He was not to be banished from her good graces after all. And perhaps, someday . . .

She sat back, suddenly exhausted, accepting the cup of tea that Ames put into her hands. It was hot, reviving; she sipped it gratefully as she glanced around the familiar, welcoming room. How inexpressibly glad she was to be here, with these two men who cared for her—she took Ames's caring for granted; she'd come to appreciate MacKenzie's—safe from the terrors of the night, the dark, rain-swept streets.

Suddenly, although she was not cold, she shuddered.

"What is it?" said Ames.

"I was thinking of Agatha. And the girls at the Bower. Even if the police catch this man—"

"When," he interjected. "When they catch him."

"Yes. When. But forever afterward, for a long time, the girls at the Bower will not be able to go out without the memory of—of Mary and Bridget."

"But in time—" MacKenzie began, looking for some way to banish her dark thoughts. But just then they heard the door knocker—loud, peremptory—and he broke off.

They heard Margaret going along the hall to answer. They heard her startled exclamation, and then a man's voice, stern, demanding. Without waiting for Margaret to announce the caller, Ames strode to the closed pocket doors and slid them open.

"Desmond! What is it?"

Delahanty stared at each of them in turn, as if he were looking for someone. He'd been running; he was breathing hard, and his hair was disheveled and damp, long, straggling red locks falling over his high forehead.

"Is Garrett here?" he demanded.

And when they did not answer at once: "For God's sake, Ames! Is he here or not?"

"He was," Ames replied. "But not now."

"What do you mean, not now? Where is he?"

"We don't know," Caroline said. "He came—at your direction, he told me—but then he went away again."

"Why?" barked Delahanty.

"We don't know that, either."

Delahanty's thin shoulders slumped, and suddenly he looked defeated. He shook his head.

"What is it, Desmond?" Ames asked. He'd never seen his friend so distraught, and he was sincerely alarmed.

Delahanty took a deep breath. "There has been another murder," he said quietly.

There was a moment's shocked silence. Then: "Oh, *no*," breathed Caroline. For a moment, she was back in the dark streets of the South End, fleeing a faceless pursuer.

"The same?" Ames asked. But of course it was the same; Delahanty would not have come here to announce, say, the death of some roisterer down in Roxbury.

"Yes. I had word just now, down in Washington Street. The *Globe* has a line to the police. As I was leaving my office, their men were running out. When I asked them where they were going—it was almost as if I knew before they spoke—they told me that another girl has been killed over in the South End."

Caroline tried to speak, but her throat was dry and she could not get out the words. At last: "You mean, another of Agatha Montgomery's?"

"Yes. Another girl from Bertram's Bower."

CHAPTER 23

TWO POLICE WAGONS STOOD AT THE CURB, THE HORSES' breath rising in small columns in the raw night air. Several uniformed men stood guard along the sidewalk. For what? thought Ames as he stepped from the herdic-phaeton. The damage, once again, had been done, and once again the police were too late to prevent it.

Beyond the police line stood a crowd of restless men: journalists. Damnation! Some of them shouted at him, but he ignored them.

"There's Babcock, from the *Globe*," muttered Delahanty at his elbow. "And Hibbens, from the *Post*—watch out for him, he'll misquote you every time."

"Comment, gentlemen?" shouted a journalist.

"Connected to the case?" shouted another.

"Related to the girl?"

"Give us a statement!"

A brief scuffle erupted as two of them tried—and failed—to break through the police barrier.

"Carrion crow," muttered MacKenzie. He saw Crippen hurrying down the Bower's steps, followed by two plainclothesmen. Behind them, at the open door at the top, stood the forbidding figure of Matron Pratt.

" 'Evening, Inspector."

"Ah! Mr. Ames." Crippen came to an abrupt halt.

"There has been another murder," Ames said.

Crippen allowed himself half a grin. "That's right. But this time, we've got him dead to rights. He's down at headquarters now, being booked. We caught him red-handed."

"Who?" Ames asked, dreading to hear the answer.

Crippen nodded in a self-satisfied way. "Why, the fellow I've had in my sights all along, that's who. That Irish lad. Who else?"

"Impossible!" Delahanty blurted, pushing forward past MacKenzie. "You cannot mean—" He stopped as Ames put a warning hand on his arm.

Crippen turned his gaze to Delahanty, and now his face was grim. "I cannot mean what, sir?"

"He is not your man," Delahanty said.

"Oh? Is he not, indeed? I think otherwise, Mr.—ah—"

Hastily Ames introduced them, but Crippen had no time for social niceties. He had started to move toward his carriage, when Ames said, "Who was the girl, Inspector? Do you know?"

"Oh, yes." Crippen turned back, and again they saw that unsettling half-grin. "We know. Her name was Peg Corcoran."

Peg Corcoran. Who, MacKenzie had said, was Garrett O'Reilly's cousin.

Ames was glad of the dark, glad that Crippen could not see his face clearly. With a word to his companions, he stepped toward the little police inspector and walked with him to his waiting carriage.

"Inspector, I would ask you—my cousin Wainwright, as you know, does not want this case to blow up in our faces."

"Blow up in our faces, Mr. Ames? How do you mean?"

"I mean, the Irish population of Boston is restless enough. The three girls who were murdered were Irish, and now you have arrested an Irish lad in their deaths. If it should happen that he is not in fact guilty—"

Crippen had been walking with his head slightly tilted toward Ames, as if he were listening carefully, but now he came to an abrupt halt and thrust out his chin in an antagonistic way.

"Mr. Ames, you surprise me."

"How is that, Inspector?"

"Because you are an intelligent man. Even, if I may say so, a very clever man, which is something else entirely. Do you think I don't know what you're telling me? I need to be sure when I make an arrest in a case like this, and I can tell you right now I am very sure indeed." He thrust his hand into his inside jacket pocket and took out something small that glittered in the dim light from the streetlamp.

"Have a look at this." He gave it to Ames, adding, "It's some kind of religious medal apparently—and you know how religious the Irish are. The girl had it clutched in her hand, like she grabbed it off him. It's almost like she was trying to identify him."

Ames stopped under the light to look at it, and as he did so, something tugged at the edges of his memory. A small, glittering disc—where had he seen it?

"It is not a religious medal, Inspector."

Crippen's face sagged with disappointment. "It's not? What is it, then?"

"It is a coin—a very ancient one. If I am not mistaken, it is third or fourth century B.C.—the head of Medusa, an idealized version of the dread monster, Gorgo. The later Greeks rendered her as a beautiful young woman facing death, as she is here. Rather appropriate, wouldn't you say?"

He handed it back, and Crippen took it and slipped it back into his inside jacket pocket. "Whatever you say, Mr. Ames. We'll get it all sorted out later." It was obvious that he did not believe what Ames had told him.

Crippen's uniformed driver clucked to the horses to bring the carriage near. On the door, Ames could see the words BOSTON POLICE. With a curt "good-night," Crippen clambered up, and the driver ordered the horses to walk on. Ames stood at the curb, watching the vehicle move away until it disappeared into the darkness. The other police vans followed, and then the square was left with only a lone uniform patrolling. Already the journalists had begun to drift away.

"We must do something about that boy, Ames," said Delahanty.

"Indeed we must," Ames replied. "And quickly. Once Crippen learns that the murdered girl, this time, was Garrett's cousin—"

"What!" exclaimed Delahanty. "His cousin? Are you sure?"

"Fairly. He told Caroline that, at any rate." Ames thought for a moment. "I am going to speak briefly to Miss Montgomery, if she will see me. And I will ask you, Desmond, to run an errand for me, if you will."

In a moment more, he had given Delahanty his instructions, and the Irishman set off at a fast clip.

Then Ames turned to glance up at Bertram's Bower. The place was brightly illuminated, every window ablaze behind drawn shades.

"They must be terrified, poor things," said MacKenzie as he saw the shadow of a female form.

"Undoubtedly," Ames replied. "And Miss Montgomery may be indisposed—I would not be surprised if she were—but let us just see for ourselves."

As they ascended the steps, he thought of Caroline. She was alone at Louisburg Square. He had warned her to admit no one, and he assumed that she had the good sense for once to obey him. And if the house was locked and secure, with the faithful Margaret there, then Caroline would be safe until he returned.

"Yes?"

It was Matron Pratt herself, thinking, no doubt, that the police had returned.

"Good evening, Matron. I wonder if we could impose briefly upon Miss Montgomery."

She started to snap a refusal, but then, to their surprise, she thought better of it and stepped back to admit them. Inside, in the dim light of the hall gas jets, they saw that her face, ordinarily so hostile and belligerent, was sunk into what looked like despair.

"In her room at the back," she said dully, not meeting their eyes. Before they could say anything more, she had disappeared into the office.

Agatha Montgomery sat with two of the Bower's girls. Side by side on the sofa, they were crying—loudly sobbing, their faces red and wet with tears. Across from them, Miss Montgomery sat with her hands folded in her lap. She was leaning toward them as if she had been speaking to them, but as Ames and MacKenzie knocked and entered, she looked up. Her expression was calm, her eyes clear.

"Miss Montgomery," Ames began, "we do not mean to trouble you—"

"It is no trouble, Mr. Ames." She inclined her head toward the two girls. "They were just leaving." And when they did not move, she said in a sharper tone, "All right, girls. Go on, now."

After they had gone, she sat back in her chair and closed her eyes. She was pale but composed. She looked like a woman of a certain age who had had a tiring day, but nothing more than that.

Ames cleared his throat. She opened her eyes and looked up at him. "Mr. Ames," she said flatly.

"I wanted first to extend my sympathy—"

She stopped him with a wave of her hand. "Do you know where I went this afternoon? I went to the Women's Industrial Union. They have invited us to join their sewing cooperative. We will be able to make some money, they tell me, and so we will not need to depend so heavily on charity. That should improve our fortunes, do you not think?" She smiled a small, bitter smile.

It seemed odd, thought MacKenzie, for her to be speaking of sewing cooperatives and charity, when the Bower had just suffered another hideous crime against one of its own. Perhaps she was still in such shock that she could not face the truth of what had happened.

Ames glanced at the doctor, quirked an eyebrow, and tried again.

"I am very sorry to trouble you at this time, but—" He seated himself on the sofa opposite her. MacKenzie cautiously took a chair nearer the door.

"But I understand the police have spoken to you just now," Ames went on.

She came back from someplace far away. "Yes?"

He saw that she had not grasped what he'd said, and so he repeated it.

"Oh—the police," she said. "Yes, I have seen them. Such a tiresome little man, isn't he? That inspector, whatever his name is."

"Crippen."

She nodded vaguely.

Ames gritted his teeth. He desperately needed this woman's help, but she seemed in no condition to give it.

"They have made an arrest, but I believe they have the wrong man. Or boy, rather."

She frowned at him, puzzled, but she did not reply.

"Miss Montgomery, they have arrested Garrett O'Reilly for that girl's death tonight. And I have no doubt that Crippen will find a way to charge him with the murders of Mary Flaherty and Bridget Brown as well."

She shook her head, but she did not reply.

"Miss Montgomery? Are you listening?" Ames hunched forward on the sofa, fixing her in his dark gaze. For a moment, she struggled to come to grips with what he was saying; then, as her eyes met his, some spark of his own energy, his own determination, seemed to leap from him to her, and she snapped to.

"Yes, Mr. Ames. I am listening." She folded her hands in her lap like a dutiful pupil.

"They have arrested the wrong person."

"Yes, I believe they have," she replied.

"You believe Garrett is innocent?" he asked sharply.

"Yes, I do."

"Did you tell Inspector Crippen so?"

She faded again; she shook her head and began to twist her hands in her lap—that restless, obsessive habit of hers, profoundly unsettling to see.

"Did you?" Ames persisted.

"No."

"But why not? It is very important that you, his employer, vouch for him to the police. They intend to convict him—and he is innocent, I am sure of it."

She came back a little. "Yes," she said, nodding. "I believe that too."

"Well, then. You must say so—and as forcefully as you can. May I send word to Inspector Crippen that you will go down to police headquarters?"

"Oh, I couldn't do that!"

He leaned toward her and seized her hands. She started and tried to pull away, but she could not.

"Miss Montgomery, listen to me. Yes—listen! A young man who is probably innocent has been arrested for the murder of three of the Bower's girls. He is poor, illiterate, the sole support of his family. He will be put on trial for his life, and public sentiment being what it is, he will very likely be convicted. If he is convicted, he will very likely be hanged. You said just now that you do not believe he is guilty. Why? Why did you say that, Miss Montgomery? Do you have some suspicion about who is?"

She stared at him. Her mouth worked, but no words came. She blinked several times, as if she were trying to order her thoughts.

Then she began to laugh. It was a horrible sound, harsh and cackling, that made the hair rise on the back of Ames's neck.

He had let go of her hands, and now he rose and stood over her. He glanced at MacKenzie, hoping perhaps for some helpful word. "Doctor—?" he began, but before he could say more, the door flew open and Matron Pratt rushed in.

"There!" she snapped at Ames with some of her former vituperousness. "You see what you've done!"

She bent over Miss Montgomery, put her arms around her, and tenderly embraced her. "There," she said again, but softly now, almost singing, in the tone used to soothe a troubled child.

Miss Montgomery went on laughing for a moment, but then her laughter changed to deep, wrenching sobs that from someone else would have been heartbreaking. From this woman, MacKenzie thought, they were faintly revolting.

But he was amazed at Matron Pratt, who apparently had some human feeling after all. He found that notion oddly reassuring.

Suddenly Matron Pratt reverted to form. Still shielding Miss Montgomery with one arm, she straightened and half turned to the two men. "Go away!" she snapped. "She's in no condition to speak to you!"

Since this was so obviously true, they left. As MacKenzie glanced back, he saw that Matron Pratt had both arms around Miss Montgomery and was bending over her, embracing her, crooning softly to her. He shook his head. Amazing, to see such tenderness from that dragon.

It had begun to rain again. As they went down the steps, the uniformed patrolman was just passing; he nodded to them and touched the brim of his helmet.

"All quiet, Officer?" Ames asked.

"Yes, sir."

They watched him as he walked on. The square was dark, deserted.

"Come along, Doctor," Ames said. "We've work to do."

CHAPTER
24

"THERE HE IS," MUTTERED AMES. "ON MARTIN SWEENEY'S personal assurance, he's the best cracksman in the business."

They had come to a corner a few blocks from the Bower. Briefly, MacKenzie had been disoriented, but now, as he peered through the darkness and rain, across the stretch of wet, glistening cobblestones, he saw that they stood across the street from the Reverend Montgomery's rectory.

"He" was a short, stubby man in a tweed cap and shapeless jacket. He stood a little away from the streetlamp, so that they could not see his face clearly, but obviously he recognized Ames, for he approached them now as they crossed. MacKenzie noted that he carried a dark lantern, unlit. Without a word of greeting he put out his hand, and Ames shook it briefly.

Then Ames led the way to an alley halfway down the block, and they went along the high wooden fence until they came to the gate behind the church property. Ames pushed it open. They were in a small garden whose stone benches and lone marble statue were evidence that someone—the Reverend Montgomery? some of his female parishioners?— cared for it more than for the bleak, inhospitable rectory itself.

In a moment more they were at the rectory's basement

door. MacKenzie waited, holding the dark lantern, while Ames went down the small flight of stone steps with their companion. After a moment, there was the sound of metal scraping on metal. To MacKenzie's ears, acutely attuned to the danger of their situation, it sounded very loud. Hurry, he thought, or Garrett O'Reilly will not be the only one arrested this night.

After what seemed an endless time but was probably no more than thirty seconds or so, Sweeney's cracksman gave a small grunt of satisfaction, and MacKenzie heard the door creak open.

There was a moment's pause during which Ames, after a muttered word or two, slipped a folded banknote to their silent companion. Then the cracksman, without a word, came up the steps, slipped past MacKenzie, and disappeared through the gate, carefully and silently closing it behind him.

"Well, Doctor," said Ames quietly, "shall we proceed?"

As well be hung for a sheep as a lamb, MacKenzie thought as he slipped into the darkened rectory.

"Here," muttered Ames. "Hold the lantern." He struck a match, and the lantern's dim light blossomed in the gloom.

They were in a back passageway. Doors led off it, all closed. Ames tried one and then another until he found the way to the rectory's kitchen. "Come," he said softly—although why he troubled to lower his voice, MacKenzie did not know. Either they were alone in the house, in which case Ames could speak in a normal tone, or they were not, in which case they would inevitably be discovered.

MacKenzie held the lantern high while Ames prowled the room. He stopped by a large butcher's block, above which hung a rack of knives. He pulled them out one by one, examined them closely, and then, shrugging, moved on. He opened a cabinet door and peered at its contents: bottles and jars of various sizes, some labeled—SODA, CINNAMON, SALT—some not.

"The reverend suffers from toothache apparently," Ames murmured, turning away. Glancing in, MacKenzie saw a bottle labeled CHLOROFORM. It was not significant; half the households in America had chloroform on hand.

With a final glance around the shadowy room, Ames motioned for MacKenzie to follow him out into the passageway once more and up a flight of stairs that led to the first-floor hall.

"Now," said Ames. "Just bring the lantern over here, Doctor, if you will." He stepped to a place by the wall, toward the front door, and, crouching, struck a match. Holding it close to the wall, he peered intently at the heavy, dark, leathery paper. When the match had burned down to his fingers, he dropped it into his pocket and lit another, and then another.

"What is it?" asked MacKenzie. His knee was hurting, and although the rectory was nearly as cold as the streets, sweat trickled uncomfortably down his face and neck.

"Or what is it not?" Ames replied. "Set the lantern down, Doctor, and—here—light matches for me."

Ames was on his hands and knees now, his face only a few inches from the red-and-black tile floor where it met the wall.

After MacKenzie had lighted four matches, Ames got to his feet.

"Enough," he said. Taking back the matchbox and picking up the lantern, he led the way upstairs. As MacKenzie followed, his feeling of unease grew with every step, until by the time they had reached the second-floor hall, he was as nervous as a cat in a dog pound. Ames must have believed that they had enough time to make their break-and-entry exploration, or he would not have attempted it; nevertheless, MacKenzie liked to think of himself as a law-abiding man, and this exercise unnerved him. Well-connected though Ames might be to the police and the other power centers of the city, MacKenzie knew that their presence here, if it were discovered, would not be looked upon as anything but criminal.

Ames opened the door to the front bedroom. Like every other room they'd seen in the rectory, this was a bare, dreary chamber with little attempt at adornment or decoration. A sagging bed in an iron bed-frame stood against one wall, a tall chiffonier against another. The blinds and curtains at the front windows were drawn shut, but a dim light from the streetlamp outside shone around the edges.

Handing the lantern to the doctor, Ames went to a door and opened it: the reverend's clothes closet. Rapidly he rummaged among the frock coats and trousers hanging there; after a moment, he turned away. He opened the drawers of the chiffonier, riffled through the contents, and shut them. Nothing.

In the hall once more, Ames turned toward the rear, where, opening a door, he saw not a closet but a flight of stairs leading up.

"Now we may find something of interest," he said, starting up ahead of MacKenzie. The steps were narrow and high-risered; once, MacKenzie stumbled and nearly dropped the lantern.

At the top was a door—locked. There was no landing, so MacKenzie waited behind on the stairs while Ames took from his trouser pocket a small ring of skeleton keys.

"Fortunately I persuaded Sweeney's man to lend these to me for the night," he said. "Now the question is, can I get one of them to work?"

Carefully he inserted one key into the lock, fiddled with it with no success, took it out and tried another, and another. At last, with a small exclamation of triumph, he turned the lock, turned the knob, and pushed open the door.

They were in a large room, richly furnished—how richly they could not at first discern in the dim light of the dark lantern. After making sure that no light would show from the heavily curtained windows, Ames turned the gas jets on the wall sconces by the fireplace, and with the turning rod illuminated the large chandelier in the center of the room.

MacKenzie caught his breath. Richly furnished indeed— an exquisite Turkish carpet woven in shades of red and topaz and indigo; velvet and brocade furniture in the latest, most ornate styles, including a fringed ottoman and a sofa with a high, carved rosewood back; marble-topped ebony tables; lamps with multicolored glass shades in the fashionable Tiffany style.

A tiled fireplace took up much of the wall opposite the windows, while on the other two hung a number of paintings framed in heavy carved and gilded wood. A large table in the center of the room held several books bound in fine tooled leather.

Ames, muttering under his breath, had been prowling the room, but now he stopped before a table on which was propped a small painting.

"Look at this!" he exclaimed.

MacKenzie looked. It was an antique-looking scene of dainty, half-clad maidens cavorting in a misty wood.

"What is it?" he said.

"The Watteau," Ames replied. "Do you remember, just—what was it?—three nights ago, when Caroline had her dinner party for that rapscallion Englishman? He spoke of an art auction in New York. He was beat out by a Boston man, he said, whose name he never learned. I could give it to him now, sure enough. There hasn't been time to find a place to hang it, I assume."

Ames moved to a bookshelf beside the fireplace. "Doctor, look here." He pulled out a large volume and carried it to the center table. "This is the Bower's account book for the last year. I have seen its twin at the Bower's office."

He opened it and began rapidly to scan its closely written pages. "Yes—here—and, yes—why, the man has no shame. None at all."

MacKenzie stepped to his side. He saw columns of names with sums of money entered next to them. Quite large sums of money, and many names.

"Look at the last month of the year," Ames said. "For December—the total receipts are listed as—ah—one thousand four hundred and seventy-five dollars. But I distinctly remember that in the account book at the Bower, the receipts for December were only three hundred and something. And the expenditure column in that book matched the receipts exactly, whereas here, there are no expenditures listed at all. Only the intake."

"One wonders why the man bothered to record it," MacKenzie said.

"This," said Ames, stabbing at the page with his forefinger, "this is the real amount that the reverend has brought in for the Bower. The one at the office is false. And it is from these sums—these moneys given by the good people of Boston—that the reverend affords all this." His angry gaze swept around the room. "The man is a thief for certain. And far worse than that, if I am not mistaken," he added grimly.

He returned the account book to its place and moved to a small rolltop desk. Pushing up the slatted lid, he plucked from among the littered papers there a small manual.

"If I am not mistaken, the reverend used this to compose his coded notes to Mary Flaherty. I wonder if he might have a sample."

He rummaged among the papers—bills from Brooks Brothers, from Locke-Ober's restaurant, from a wine merchant in Brookline—without success. No matter. The manual was evidence enough.

"I wonder—" he began, but MacKenzie never learned what Ames planned to say next, for at that moment they heard, from below, the sound of the front door slamming. The reverberation carried up through the house.

For a fraction of a second their eyes met. Then Ames darted to the gas jets, turned down the lights by the mantel, and reached with the rod to extinguish the chandelier.

In the near darkness, illuminated only by the dark lantern, they listened. They heard a heavy footfall—surely the reverend's—upon the stairs leading to the second floor.

MacKenzie's heart hammered painfully in his chest, and his mouth was dry. They were caught in a trap of their own making, and if Ames could not bluff their way out—but what possible excuse could he give for their being here, having broken into the place, in stealth, by night, if not to burgle then at the very least to pry?

The reverend's footsteps had not stopped at the second floor. Now they were on the stairs leading to this room, and now MacKenzie could hear the reverend's voice, and the soft sound of laughter—female laughter—in reply.

Ames had closed the door when they came in. They heard the reverend insert a key into the lock, turn it, and turn the doorknob to push open the door. But the reverend had not unlocked but locked the door, and he cursed softly now, with a querulous tone to his voice.

The key turned in the lock again, and with a horrid fascination, MacKenzie watched as the door opened.

"THANK YOU, MARGARET," CAROLINE SAID AS THE MAID came in to fetch her supper tray. She leaned back in her chair, comfortably nourished on beef tea and scrambled eggs, ready to pick up a Diana Strangeways until her menfolk returned.

"I'll be leaving soon, miss," Margaret said.

"Yes, of course. Go ahead."

As the maid went out, Caroline heard the grandmother clock in the hall strike the hour: eight o'clock. Surely, Addington and Dr. MacKenzie would be home soon.

Rain spattered on the lavender-glass windows, shuttered now against the dark, and the sea-coal fire murmured soothingly in the grate. Her ankle hurt a bit, but not as much as before. She wouldn't try to walk down the hill to church tomorrow, however; she'd rest at home. She was safe here, she knew that, and yet—

She thought of them now, with Mr. Delahanty, returning to the South End, those dark, dangerous streets where another girl had been caught and killed. Oh, poor Agatha! However would she recover from this dreadful time?

Poor you, she corrected herself. If it had not been the Reverend Montgomery who came upon you . . . if it had been that homicidal lunatic—

Stop it. Addington would deal with it; she could do nothing more. Resolutely forcing her thoughts away from the scene at the Bower, she opened her book.

A short while later, she heard the front door knocker, and she looked up in alarm. Who had come? Not Addington and the doctor, safely home at last, for they had a key. Someone else, then, who might bring bad news, fresh news of disaster—

She heard Margaret going to answer. She strained to hear the caller's voice, but the pocket doors were closed and she could hear nothing.

The doors slid open, but instead of Margaret, it was someone else who came into the room. She was breathing hard, and her eyes were wide—with fear? What had happened? Her cloak and bonnet, wet from the rain, dripped onto the carpet.

Caroline spoke first. "I can't get up, Agatha. I twisted my ankle, and I—"

"There has been another death," Miss Montgomery said abruptly.

Caroline saw Margaret hovering behind. Their eyes met, and Margaret was nodding even before Caroline could ask her to bring the universal prescription for all crises—which this obviously was—a tray of tea and cakes. Somehow, Margaret would manage to produce it before she left. She took a step back into the hall and pulled shut the doors, leaving Caroline and her friend alone.

"Yes. I know," Caroline said to Miss Montgomery.

"You do?" For a moment, Miss Montgomery looked puzzled, but then she went on. "It was another one of our girls."

"I know that too. Agatha, do come and sit down. Take off your things—why, you are soaked! Just put them on that chair."

Caroline thought of the damage her friend's dripping cloak would do to the already well-worn brocade—the dye would run, she just knew it—but this was no time, she chided herself, to be house-proud. Agatha was clearly in a state, and the important thing was to help her through it.

Miss Montgomery did not move at first. Then, as if at last she understood what Caroline had said, she unfastened her cape and let it fall to the floor. Slowly, as if she moved in a dream, she untied the strings of her bonnet, took it off, and dropped it onto the cloak.

"That's right," Caroline said soothingly. "Now come and sit down."

Still moving slowly, one cautious step at a time, Miss Montgomery approached. With great care, as if every bone in her bony frame hurt her, she lowered herself onto the sofa opposite Caroline.

"How did you know?" she asked dully.

"Mr. Delahanty came to tell us. He has his office down in Newspaper Row, and he had word when the reporters were alerted. Agatha, I really do think—"

"Her name was Peg Corcoran," Miss Montgomery said, still in that flat, deadened voice that Caroline found quite alarming.

"Peg— Oh, no!"

This seemed to jolt Miss Montgomery. "You knew her?"

"She was—yes, she was in my embroidery class, but worse than that—Agatha, I don't imagine you knew it, but she was Garrett O'Reilly's cousin."

Miss Montgomery absorbed this in silence, her eyes darting back and forth as if she were trying to adjust her obviously erratic thoughts.

"His cousin?" she said slowly.

"Yes. He didn't want it known, but—"

"They have arrested him."

"Arrested him? Garrett? But that is wrong!"

"They said they caught him red-handed."

"But that is monstrous!" In her agitation, Caroline had shifted slightly in her chair, and she winced at the pain in her ankle. Then she rushed on. "Agatha, I must tell you, Garrett was here earlier. Inspector Crippen interrogated him. He—Garrett—was badly frightened. Mr. Delahanty had told him to come to Addington if he needed help."

"Is he here?" Miss Montgomery demanded.

"Who? Addington? No. Did you want to speak with him? I'm sure he'll be back soon."

They heard a soft rapping at the pocket doors, and in the next moment Margaret came in bearing the tea tray, which she set on the low table beside Caroline's chair.

"I'll be off now, miss," she said. "Cook's on her way too. She says the gentlemen's dinner is in the warming oven."

"Yes, yes, go on, Margaret. And remember me to your sister."

Miss Montgomery did not appear to notice the interruption. She stared at Caroline, blinking, her mouth working, her uncorseted body under her drab black dress as rigid as if she suffered rigor mortis.

Caroline glanced at the tea tray. Margaret had had the sense to supply a plate of sandwiches, thick and meaty. Agatha probably hadn't eaten any dinner. A nourishing cold roast sandwich would do her good, and several cups of steaming Darjeeling, and a piece of lemon pound cake.

"Agatha, you must eat something. And then when Addington gets back, we'll sort this out. I simply don't believe that Garrett is capable—"

She had lifted the plate of sandwiches, and now she held it out to her friend. Miss Montgomery ignored it.

"Agatha, please. You must keep your strength up."

"You are right, Caroline." Agatha wasn't talking about the food, Caroline realized. "Garrett didn't kill that girl tonight—or the others."

"No, of course he didn't," Caroline replied. The plate seemed very heavy, and so after a moment, she put it back on the tray. "So in that case—" She didn't know how to continue. In that case, what? Or, more to the point, who?

"Do you know what that policeman told me?" Miss Montgomery asked.

"No." Caroline cringed a little as Miss Montgomery's

pale, intense eyes fixed on her own. Of course, Agatha was always very intense, very driven, but just now she looked—

"He told me they found something clutched in Peg's hand. He said it was a religious medal of some kind, but it wasn't that."

Not a religious medal. Caroline's thoughts raced. She saw something small and round, glittering on her dining room carpet. She saw Agatha, bending down to pick it up.

Suddenly she felt ill, and the feeling had nothing to do with her injured ankle.

"Agatha—"

"Yes." Miss Montgomery nodded, as if satisfied that Caroline had understood. "It was Randolph's watch fob. If you remember, I told you I would return it to him, after he dropped it"—she looked around with a vaguely baffled expression, as if she had only just realized where she was—"at your dinner."

Caroline swallowed hard, but the lump in her throat did not go away. Earlier that night, she had thought she was being pursued by the Bower killer. *Had she been?*

"When the police realize what it is," Miss Montgomery went on, "they will trace it to him. He will say he lost it, of course. As he did."

"Agatha—"

Suddenly Miss Montgomery's face convulsed into a rictus of hate. "I didn't know," she gasped.

"Know what, Agatha?" Caroline's voice sounded odd in her ears, tinny and faint.

"That he planned to marry that woman in New York. He never told me. If it hadn't been mentioned the other night, I might not know about it even now."

"Agatha, about his watch fob—did you give it back to him?"

"That is what I will tell the police." Miss Montgomery nodded again, as if she had settled something in her mind. "Not that I had it, but that he told me he'd lost it and then that he found it again."

"But—"

"The only person who knows I had it is you, Caroline."

Caroline tried to speak, but for a moment her voice wouldn't come. She tried again. "You did return it to him?"

"No."

The word hung in the air between them, echoing over and over again: Nonono.

CHAPTER 25

AT THE RECTORY, THE TALL, BULKY FORM OF THE REVEREND Randolph Montgomery came into the third floor room, followed by a female.

"What the—" Montgomery's hand went to his coat pocket as if he reached for a weapon, but no weapon was forthcoming. Instead, he called: "Who's there? Who is it?"

"Good evening, Reverend," Ames replied with what MacKenzie thought was admirable calm. He reached up and turned on the gas in the lamps over the mantel. In the sudden, harsh illumination, MacKenzie saw that the female who had accompanied the reverend was young, tastelessly overdressed, and certainly no lady.

For a moment Montgomery did not reply; he stared, openmouthed, as if Ames were an apparition.

Then: "What the devil—Ames?"

"I am afraid so, Reverend."

"But—what are you doing here? How did you get in?"

"I hired a cracksman."

The reverend had gone pale, but now a flush mounted to his cheeks, and his hands clenched and unclenched at his sides. MacKenzie remembered his previous burst of temper—his sudden, alarming loss of control.

Montgomery took the female by the arm and shoved her toward the door. "Get downstairs," he said brusquely.

With a frightened whimper, she obeyed. He shut the door behind her.

"Now," he said heavily, turning back to Ames. "Explain yourself, if you can."

Ames waited for a moment, as if he were trying to gauge the extent of the reverend's anger.

"Another girl from the Bower has been murdered," he began.

The reverend started at that; he blinked several times and ran his tongue over his lips.

"You didn't know?" Ames asked.

"No."

"I don't believe you."

"What do you mean, you don't believe me? Why should I know that?"

"Because I believe you killed her."

Montgomery did not reply at once. His mouth opened and shut, his eyes darted back and forth as if he sought escape—and yet he stood still, rooted to the spot. As if, MacKenzie thought, all his strength had been suddenly drained away, rendering him immobile.

Then at last he said, "You have taken leave of your senses, Ames."

"I think not. I am merely trying to prevent a miscarriage of justice. The police have arrested one of your candidates in the case—"

"My candidate?"

"Yes. The Irish lad, Garrett O'Reilly."

"Well, then, the case is settled, is it not?"

"Hardly." Ames put out a warning hand. "Before you say anything more, Reverend, I should tell you that the police found an incriminating piece of evidence on the girl who died tonight. They believe that it was a religious medal of some kind, but I told them they were wrong. It was a gold coin of the Hellenistic period, a very fine Medusa head."

Montgomery seemed to crumple. He remained standing, but he visibly withered, as if he had had some devastating emotional blow.

"That was your coin, Reverend, was it not?" Ames said quietly.

Montgomery put out his hand, still in its glove, and like a blind man feeling his way, moved into the room until he came to a tall-backed, brocade Queen Anne chair. For a moment, he gripped its back; then he came around and, with a groan, lowered himself onto the seat. He sat slumped, one hand covering his eyes. Ames shot a glance at MacKenzie as if to say, Be ready in case he begins to rage again.

But the reverend did not rage. He sat for a moment more, the picture of miserable dejection; then slowly, deliberately, he began to remove his gloves. They were very fine gloves, MacKenzie noted: soft black kid, looking brand new. He thought of the account book with its record of generous donations, and his mouth twisted in revulsion. Did Agatha Montgomery know of her brother's thievery? Did she know and yet allow him to cheat her so that on the meager funds that remained after he'd taken his lion's share, she could continue to pursue her life's work?

"Brandy," said the reverend hoarsely. "In the cupboard."

Ames nodded to MacKenzie, who went to the sideboard, where he found a half-full bottle of Courvoisier. Pour for one or for all of us? he wondered. All of us, definitely. This night is only just beginning, and we all have a long way to go.

He gave snifters to Ames and the reverend and took his own. His knee was acting up very badly, and he wondered if Ames would mind if he sat. Easing himself onto a chair across from the reverend, he glanced at Ames, but Ames paid him no mind. All his attention was on Montgomery, who, now that he had taken a few restorative sips, seemed more like himself.

"A Medusa head," he said to Ames.

"Yes."

The reverend fiddled at his coat buttons and drew back the garment's edges to reveal his watch chain stretched across his middle. "I had such a coin on this chain," he said slowly.

"I know you did. I saw it."

"But at some point in the last few days, I lost it."

Ames regarded him, disbelief plain on his face.

"Damn you!" The reverend had regained his strength, and now he set down his glass and leaned forward in his chair, glaring at Ames. "Yes—I lost it. It dropped off, I don't know where. I looked all over this place, I looked in the church, and at Agatha's. Finally, I decided it must have fallen off in the street, and I gave up trying to find it."

"Or possibly you lost it when Peg Corcoran was trying to fend you off," Ames said.

"*No!*" thundered the reverend, in full-throated voice once more. "God damn you for the meddling, interfering bounder that you are, Ames!"

Meddling and interfering, possibly, thought MacKenzie, but bounder? No.

"What are you trying to do, man?" the reverend demanded. "Destroy me? Why?"

Ames glanced toward the bookcase. "Not that, Reverend, but I am trying to save an innocent lad from the gallows. I came here tonight—yes, we broke in, I admit it, and you are free to report me to the authorities—to look for evidence against you in the death of the Bower's girls. As I was examining this room, I came upon a set of account books that record the sums you have collected for the Bower. More, I might add, than is shown in the book for the same year in the Bower's office."

The reverend gave a short laugh. "The books here will be destroyed this night, Ames, and where will you find your proof then?"

"By interrogating every person in the city who has ever given a penny to you," Ames said. "And I promise you, Reverend, I will do that if I must."

"A lengthy task," the reverend replied. "You will be lucky to finish—"

"Before you hang," Ames said flatly.

Only a faint tremor around Montgomery's eyes betrayed any reaction to this. "Before I hang?" he replied. "Before *I* hang? Ye gods, man, you most certainly have taken leave of your senses! You come here and accuse me—"

"There is blood on the wallpaper downstairs," Ames said. "And the floor tiles have been freshly scrubbed—but not enough. You missed a place next to the wainscoting."

A sound like a low growl came from the reverend. MacKenzie set down his glass and prepared to rise, ready to spring to Ames's aid when Montgomery exploded.

But Montgomery did not explode. He sat tensed in his chair, that eerie, inhuman sound issuing from his throat, staring at Ames as if by his mere look, he could cause Ames to disappear.

"You seduced Mary," Ames said.

The growling grew louder.

"And, having come upon a rich widow willing to marry you, you could not afford to have Mary inconveniently in the way," Ames went on.

"No!" And now the reverend did explode. He sprang to his feet and faced Ames for a moment, glaring at him. Then with an oath he whirled, as if he were about to run down the stairs. But they could not lead him to safety, not while Ames lived.

He began to pace. Like an animal, MacKenzie thought: growling, every nerve alive with tension, ready to spring, ready to attack . . .

At last he came to a stop in front of the fireplace and put his hand on the mantel as if to steady himself.

"This is the hardest thing I have ever done," he said. His tone had changed once more, as if, now, he were speaking to himself.

He paused, shaking his head as he peered at Ames. "She betrayed me," he said.

"Who did? Mary? Under the circumstances—"

"No, no. Not Mary. Agatha."

Through the heavy draperies they heard the bell in the church next door begin to toll the hour: eight o'clock.

Ames waited until the tolling stopped. Then: "How did she do that, Reverend?"

"She knew Mary was pregnant. She was unable to deal with that fact. Apparently, Mary not only told Agatha about her condition, she named me as the man responsible."

"And were you?"

The reverend's hand tightened on the mantel as if he were afraid he would collapse, but his gaze did not falter.

"Yes."

"I see."

"No. You cannot possibly see." Montgomery shook his head violently, as if he would shake all his bad memories away. "Agatha is so very . . . involved with the Bower. It is all she has—all she needs. She is not afflicted, as I am, with a taste for—" His eyes swept the room. "For all this. I cannot help it, Mr. Ames. I cannot live, as she does, a life deprived of beauty. Of beauty in all its forms—fine paintings, objets d'art, elegant clothes. Agatha can wear the same dress day in, day out, and never notice. She can live in one bare room at the Bower and never really see it, much less hate it. But I—I am different, you see."

Let us get to the point, MacKenzie thought; we are not your congregation, to be swayed by your eloquence.

"And Mary was a very pretty girl," Montgomery went on. "Very pretty indeed. When she came to us, she was quite ill. We—Agatha, I mean—brought her back to health. And then one day, in the late summer, I went to the Bower on some business or other, and it was as if I were seeing her for the first time. She put herself in my way, of course. She wanted me to notice her, and I did. I did. . . ."

He trailed off.

Ames glanced at MacKenzie, and a wordless message passed between them: Say nothing, no matter how long he rambles on, say nothing to distract him from what he will tell us in the end.

"She was not an innocent," Montgomery said. "Oh, no. Far from it. But you know what they are, those girls at the Bower. Their innocence has been destroyed long before Agatha takes them in. It can never be restored, never repaired. But the odd thing is—Mary *looked* innocent. She had that fresh-faced, girlish appearance, as if she'd never known a man in her life. And when she—when she put herself in my way, I thought, why not? It was not as if I were deflowering her, after all. She'd made her living on the streets before she came to Agatha's, and she knew a few tricks too, I don't mind telling you."

Suddenly, horribly, he leered at them.

"So I took her," he said. "Why not? She was a . . . reward, of a kind, for all my years of devotion to the Bower."

Ames thought of what Serena Vincent had told him, he thought of what Dr. Hannah had told Caroline, but he gritted his teeth and stayed silent.

"Yes," Montgomery said. "A reward. It never occurred to me that she would let herself become pregnant. They have ways, don't they, those girls on the streets, of preventing it? Sinful as they are, what is one more little sin like that—interfering with Nature? I thought Mary would do the same. It never occurred to me that she had another agenda entirely."

"Which was marriage," Ames said.

Montgomery grimaced. "Yes," he said. "The slut wanted to marry me. Can you imagine? I would as soon marry that old battle-ax Carry Nation."

"And Miss Montgomery knew all this?"

"Eventually—I suppose inevitably—yes."

"Even the coded notes?"

"Mary must have told her about those. Certainly I never did."

"Why do you say that your sister betrayed you, Reverend?"

"Because—" Montgomery paused, wiped his hand down over his face, and took a deep breath. "The Medusa head," he said simply.

"I don't follow."

"Damn it, man! Don't you see? I didn't kill that girl tonight! And when it becomes necessary, as it undoubtedly will, for me to account for my time, I will do so, no matter the embarrassment. Yes—I was at the Black Sea just now. I admit it. I often take dinner there. Then I find a girl and bring her back here for the evening. The atmosphere is somewhat better here than there." He thought for a moment. "I was on my way there tonight, when I came upon your sister. It was most foolhardy of her to be out alone after dark, particularly in this district. She began to run away from me. She must have feared that I was about to attack her. She tripped and fell. Fortunately for her I am not the Bower killer, or I would have had an easy victim. She refused to allow me to accompany her home, but at least I was able to help her into a herdic. She has told you about it? Yes. After that, I went to the Black Sea."

"And the conference in Cambridge?" Ames asked.

"I planned to join them tomorrow. To be frank, two days in the company of my fellow ministers is more than I can endure."

He peered at Ames, squinting a little, as if his vision had suddenly clouded.

"So you see, Mr. Ames, I did not kill that girl tonight. I lost the coin a few days ago. Someone found it and planted it on the girl's body—someone who knew it was mine, someone who wanted to implicate me in her death."

Ames waited. Then, when Montgomery did not continue, he said, "Your sister?"

"Yes." The reverend's eyes were blank, his voice—his fine preacher's voice—hollow.

"It was my impression that Miss Montgomery is devoted to you. Why would she try to implicate you in a murder?"

Montgomery gave a short, harsh laugh. "You do not know Agatha very well, Mr. Ames. She is—was, I should say—exceptionally devoted to me, yes. Or she always has been, until—what was it? Three days ago? When one of your guests spoke out of turn, and tactlessly brought up the subject of my impending marriage to Mrs. Wilson."

"The wealthy widow in New York."

"Yes."

"Miss Montgomery had not known of your plans?"

"No. I had intended to tell her, of course, but not so

soon. I suppose she felt . . . betrayed, in some sense. Abandoned, perhaps."

"It hardly seems sufficient reason—"

"As I said, Mr. Ames, you do not know Agatha. I suppose she saw the collapse of all her life's work if I should cease my efforts in her behalf. My so very successful"—he swept his hand to encompass the room—"financial efforts."

She saw something more even than that, MacKenzie thought. She loved you for more than your fund-raising, Reverend. Did you know that? Do you know it now?

"And so she took her revenge by making it look as if you killed Peg Corcoran tonight," Ames said.

"Was that her name? I can't place her. But, yes, it was Agatha—it must have been—taking her revenge on me. For my sins," he added sarcastically.

"And the other girls?" Ames said quietly. "Mary? Bridget?"

Montgomery took a deep breath. "I knew nothing of how Mary met her death until the next evening, when the girl who roomed with her—Bridget Brown—came hammering at my door. She had known, apparently, of Mary's condition—and of my part in it. She was overcome with grief, with anger. She came to accuse me, to threaten to expose me to the authorities. But she hardly had time to say more than a few words, when Agatha came." He paused, remembering. "We were standing in the front hall. Agatha came rushing in. Before I realized what she meant to do, she had attacked the girl." He spoke as if he were reciting a dream, thought MacKenzie. A nightmare.

"I must have worked half the night to wash the floor," Montgomery went on. "Fortunately, I do not keep servants, so there was no one to see . . . what I did."

"And the body?" said Ames.

"The body. Yes. Dear God, the body." He drew a deep, harsh breath. "I waited until—until much later that night. Then I took it to—I don't remember. An alley."

"Miss Montgomery?"

"Returned to the Bower. They had seen her run out after

Bridget. She told them she'd searched for her without success. They accepted it."

"Her skirts must have been soaked with blood."

"Yes. She washed them in the kitchen sink here. I imagine that at the Bower, they thought her dress had gotten wet—very wet—in the rain."

"Was it then she told you about Mary?"

"You mean that she'd killed her? Yes. I could not believe it at first, but after seeing how she'd attacked Bridget—in a frenzy, a madness—I did."

"But her murder of Mary was not a sudden frenzy. It was planned. She lured her out of the Bower with a coded note—"

"Yes. She feared that Mary would disgrace me—and the Bower as well. As she might have done in the end, of course. So Agatha was angry with Mary, but even more, she feared her."

"And when she discovered your plans to marry, she felt betrayed by you as well, and turned on you? You believe that she killed a third girl for no reason but to throw suspicion on you?"

"It seems so, yes." The reverend's face was bleak, his voice flat with exhaustion.

"Crippen has arrested the Irish boy," Ames said. "But when I spoke to Miss Montgomery this evening, she said she did not believe Garrett was guilty."

"Did she say whom she suspected?"

"No."

"She means to implicate me. That is obvious." Montgomery looked suddenly afraid. "When the police realize that the coin is mine—"

"We must go to her—we must confront her, insist that she confess—take her to Crippen!"

"But—"

"What, man? Come on, we must go at once!"

"Then I will be—what do they call it? An accessory."

"Yes, undoubtedly you will." Ames threw him a scornful glance. "But the authorities have ways of dealing with accessories. As I understand it, they will treat you gently if you provide them with evidence against her."

Both Ames and MacKenzie were appalled to see the look of relief that passed over the reverend's face.

"All right," Montgomery muttered. "Let us go to her and get done with this miserable business once and for all."

AT BERTRAM'S BOWER, THE WINDOWS WERE STILL BRIGHTLY illuminated behind the drawn shades. As the three men approached, the uniformed patrolman intercepted them and ordered them to halt. He was appeased when Ames stepped forward to identify himself.

"Beg your pardon, sir," he said. "I'm ordered to question everyone, you understand."

They hurried up the steps, and Ames sharply brought down the brass knocker. He had no idea what to expect from Agatha Montgomery: hysterics, denial, an attempt to implicate someone—anyone—else?

The door flew open.

"You've come back—" It was Matron Pratt. When she saw who they were, she collected herself and assumed her normal hostile demeanor. "Mr. Ames," she said curtly. "And Reverend—"

"Whom were you expecting, Matron?" Ames asked, but already he knew, and his heart sank.

"She went out," Mrs. Pratt said, not moving aside to allow them to enter.

"When?"

"I don't know. A while ago."

"Why?"

"I don't know that either. She said she had an errand to do."

"At this hour of a Saturday night?" said Ames. "And after—" He turned to the reverend, who stood on the step below him. "Where could she have gone? Have you any idea?"

"None. I cannot imagine—"

But Ames, suddenly, could. Into his mind's eye had come a vision of the company at Caroline's dinner party three nights before. He saw the ladies in their finery, the men in their more subdued attire. And very distinctly, he saw the Reverend Randolph Montgomery, standing with the others in the parlor before they went in to dinner. He was certain— yes, absolutely—that Montgomery had had a gold disc dangling from his watch chain.

"Reverend, when did you say you first missed the Medusa head?"

He heard the Bower's door slam shut behind them as they descended to the sidewalk.

"I'm not sure," Montgomery replied. "Thursday, I think."

"So you probably had it on Wednesday."

"Yes. In fact, I am sure I did, because someone admired it on Wednesday afternoon."

"So. Between then and Thursday—"

"What are you getting at, Mr. Ames?"

"I am getting at—" Suddenly it came to him in a rush, and he nearly choked on it.

"Doctor—you have your weapon at home?"

"Yes."

"I pray you won't need it, but—you must go there at once. Only hope you arrive in time, before she—"

"Who, Ames?" said the reverend. Already MacKenzie, disregarding the pain in his knee, was hurrying down the square in search of a herdic.

"Why—your sister, man!" Ames was nearly shouting now. "If I am not mistaken, she has gone to Caroline to make sure— Go on! Go with MacKenzie! You may need to deal with her! She is your sister after all. She may listen to you. Go on!"

Finally Montgomery seemed to understand. With an exclamation of alarm, he hurried after the doctor, down to the avenue where a herdic, on this foul night, might be found.

Ames bounded back up the Bower's steps and, ignoring the door knocker, pounded on the wooden panel.

"Matron!" he called. "Open—at once!"

The door swung back.

"What?" Mrs. Pratt began, but Ames pushed past her, into the hall where the Bower's telephone was. He'd never used a telephone, and so now he hesitated, but only for a moment, as he stared at the wooden box and its appendages.

"How does this thing work?" he demanded. Matron Pratt had followed him and stood now at his side, breathing heavily.

"Why?"

"Damnation, woman! Never mind why! This is an emergency, and if you do not tell me how to operate this confounded contraption, I will have you charged with interfering with a police investigation!"

Seeming unintimidated by his threat, still she stepped forward, seized the handle attached to one side of the box, and cranked it hard, four times. Then she lifted a black earpiece attached to a tube and held it out to him. "Hold this to your ear. Speak here, into this. Tell the operator who you want."

In an amazingly short time, Ames was connected, but the connection was so poor he could hardly understand what the person on the other end of the line was saying, and it was obvious that person could not understand him either, even when he shouted. Which he felt he needed to do, else how could someone a mile and more distant—two miles—ever hear him? After a moment more of frustration, he slammed down the earpiece and without a further word to Mrs. Pratt, hurried out.

At the other end of the square, the patrolman was just finishing a circuit. When Ames insisted that he needed to get to Inspector Crippen at once, the man produced his clacker and whirled it rapidly, making a tremendous noise in the quiet night. In no more than a few seconds, a police wagon appeared and Ames clambered in.

"Whip up the horses, man! There is no time to lose!"

CHAPTER
26

IN THE PARLOR AT NO. 16½, AGATHA MONTGOMERY LEANED forward and rested her elbows on her knees, which poked up sharply through the thin stuff of her skirt, not properly swaddled in layers of petticoats as they should have been. But she has no money for petticoats, Caroline thought; she has no money for anything except the Bower. And what money she has, she gets from the reverend.

"Caroline, can you imagine how I felt when I learned of Mary's condition?"

"Her condition?" Caroline repeated faintly. Had Agatha known it all the time?

"No. Of course you cannot. No one can. That girl whom I had rescued from the streets—as I rescue all of them, but—she was different. She was—" Miss Montgomery broke off as if she were remembering what Mary had been. "Do you know, I actually thought that someday, Mary might take my place as directress of the Bower? Can you imagine such foolishness?"

She paused. She was breathing heavily.

Tea, Caroline thought. If only I could get her to drink a cup of tea, and eat something—

"She was a slut!" snarled Miss Montgomery, her pale eyes blazing. "A vicious little trollop who tried to blackmail him into marriage!"

Her voice broke, and for a moment, she clapped her hand over her mouth as if she were ashamed of her weakness.

A cup of hot tea, Caroline thought. And then Dr. MacKenzie, when he comes back, can tend to her professionally, give her a few drops of chloral hydrate to sedate her.

"As if my brother—*my brother*—would ever allow himself to be trapped like that! You have taken leave of your senses, Mary my girl, I told her. She defied me. She threw it up to me—that she carried his child. Can you imagine? She thought she would get him in the end, but she was wrong. I could never have allowed her to do that, could I?"

Miss Montgomery wiped away a tear. "Don't you understand, Caroline? I could never have allowed her to marry my Randolph. It would have been his ruin—and ours. Not that I had any sympathy for him, mind you. No, indeed. Men are so weak, aren't they? So weak, so easily taken in by a scheming female."

The bellpull, Caroline thought. It was only a few steps away, hanging by the mantel. If she could stand up, surely she could bear to put her weight on her foot for just a step or two, and then Margaret would come—

But then she remembered that surely, by now, Margaret had gone, and Cook along with her.

"Bridget knew," Miss Montgomery said. "She confronted me the day after Mary's death. She knew of Randolph's involvement with Mary, and she knew of Mary's condition. She said she intended to go to Randolph and make him confess. Confess! Can you picture it?"

She paused, as if she were reordering her thoughts. A sudden burst of rain spattered against the windows, sounding very loud in the silent room.

Caroline realized that she had been clenching her hands. She looked down and saw the small, bright red half-moon cuts where her nails had dug into her palms.

"Randolph had to work half the night to clean up her blood," Miss Montgomery went on. "We were indoors—in his front hall—and so there was no rain to wash it away. He was very good about it. He never complained. He said it would be our secret, his and mine. No one would ever know, he said. But all the time he had another secret of his own that he never told me."

She had begun to cry. She made small, wheezing, whistling sounds—horrid sounds—while her mouth quivered and tears ran down her long, pale cheeks.

Caroline fumbled in her sleeve for a handkerchief. For once in her life, she didn't have one. A napkin, then, from the tea tray—

"Don't you understand, Caroline?" Miss Montgomery sobbed. "He was going to leave me—to marry that woman in New York and move away! He said he would stay here, but I didn't believe him. I knew he would go in the end. But he won't be able to do that now, will he? Not now. Not after— They will think he killed her, this girl tonight. And they will think that if he killed her, he must have killed the other two as well. It didn't matter who it was, I had to provide a third girl, and I had to make sure that something would connect her to Randolph."

"Agatha, what are you saying? If you did not return that coin to him, then—"

Caroline saw the gleaming metal blade in her friend's hand, and for a moment, before her brain registered it, she did not know what it was. She stared at it, fascinated; then she jumped as the grandmother clock in the hall struck the half hour.

"Agatha . . ."

"You and your meddling brother," said Miss Montgomery. "If only you had stayed out of it, Caroline. Why couldn't you do that? But no. You had to intrude yourselves, you had to poke and pry—"

She raised the knife and lunged.

In the same instant, Caroline seized the hot-water pot and threw its contents into Miss Montgomery's face.

She heard a scream, saw the blade come at her.

"Miss Ames!"

Dr. MacKenzie stood at the open pocket doors, another

man behind him. Not Addington. In one bound the Reverend Montgomery pushed MacKenzie aside, crossed the room, and seized his sister's wrist to wrench the knife from her grasp.

But she was as strong as he—stronger, perhaps, in her madness. Blinded by the boiling water, her face scalded, still she clutched her weapon, and as she wrestled with him, she cried, "Randolph, how could you?"

They fell in a death struggle to the floor.

"Miss Ames!" MacKenzie exclaimed again.

He was at her side, helping her up. She managed to stand, and in the next instant she and MacKenzie were across the room and out into the hall. She felt a sharp stab of pain in her ankle, but she ignored it.

"Hurry!" he said. His knee was on fire, and he didn't know how much longer he could bear her weight leaning on his arm. Pray the elevator was on this floor and not stopped somewhere above. He couldn't remember when he'd used it last, but— Yes. Here it was.

As he pulled open the door, they heard a cry from the parlor—the reverend, he thought—but they had no time to stop, they must get into the elevator cab.

"Can you stand?" he asked.

"Yes."

Her face was as pale as Death, but her voice was steady. He pulled the door shut and grasped the lever. Slowly they began to go up.

"What will we do, Doctor?" Caroline asked. It had all happened so quickly that her mind was a blur.

"We are safe here," he said. Safe—but in this very small space. Already he was beginning to feel trapped—uncomfortably confined. "Your brother will come directly. He asked me to get my weapon. It is in my room. I will—"

His voice died in his throat. Something was on the stairs that curved around the elevator shaft. He could dimly see its dark form, and he heard its harsh and painful breathing. Then he saw the gleam of a knife blade.

Agatha Montgomery.

The knife flashed through the grille, narrowly missing his midriff. With alacrity he stepped back, but he could not step far enough for safety because he needed to keep his hand on the lever.

The elevator kept on rising, but too slowly. Sweat trickled down his neck, down his back. I will not panic, he thought.

What had happened to the reverend? Had she killed him?

The blade flashed again, and this time it nicked his hand just above the thumb. In the dim light he saw the dark spurt of blood, and he fumbled with his free hand for his handkerchief to stanch it.

"Doctor—your hand!" Caroline exclaimed behind him.

He half turned to her. "It is nothing. You must keep quiet."

As they kept on going up, he caught a glimpse of the creature on the stairs. He saw the dark, shapeless mass of her clothing, and for an instant he saw her face, which bore the blistering red wounds from the scalding water. She was muttering, but so low they could not make out her words. Every few seconds she emitted a low moan, as if she were in great pain.

As she is, thought Caroline. She is in agony, and not just from her burns. But her natural feelings of compassion for her friend—for the woman who had been her friend, she corrected herself—were overcome by her terror, for this thing crouching on the stairs was not the Agatha Montgomery she had known. This was an alien creature, all her obsessions—with her life's work, with the reverend—transformed into a murderous madness.

Like the flickering tongue of a deadly serpent, the knife blade flashed through the grille again, this time at their feet. Keep going, MacKenzie told himself. But what would they do when they reached the top? With his game knee, he would never be able to reach his room in time to fetch his pistol, not with Agatha Montgomery hot on his heels, intent on stabbing him to death.

The elevator whined and moaned. Miss Montgomery panted up the stairs alongside them. The blade flashed again through the grille, and then again. Then her dark shape passed them, heading on up.

"She will wait for us above," MacKenzie said in a low voice.

"Then do not go all the way up!" Caroline whispered. "Stop—stop now."

With a little jolt, he did. They were just short of the third story, with the hall floor at eye level. They could see Miss Montgomery's worn boots, the sodden hem of her skirts.

"Go down," Caroline whispered. "We cannot get out while she is there. We must just keep going up and down until Addington comes."

If he does, MacKenzie thought.

He reversed the lever, and with agonizing slowness they descended toward the second floor. As they did so, they saw a movement—a shadow—on the stairs: Miss Montgomery, following them down. She stood a little below the cab, awaiting them.

He stopped. In the sudden silence they could hear Miss Montgomery's breath come heavy and hard. It was her madness that sustained her, thought MacKenzie—that gave her the strength to fight her exhaustion, her pain.

Suddenly she came back and thrust at them again. The blood-tipped blade slipped into the elevator at their feet.

With his good leg, he stepped on it—put his booted foot down hard. He heard Miss Montgomery grunt as she tried to pull the knife free. He started up the elevator again. Miss Montgomery held on to the knife with a death grip. He bore down on the blade with all his weight. Suddenly they heard a sharp *snap!* as the blade broke, and with a cry of anger Miss Montgomery fell back onto the stairs, still clutching the handle. A small portion of the blade was attached to it; the rest lay under MacKenzie's heel.

"We must—" Caroline began, but then she heard a sound on the stairs below. She peered out.

It was the reverend.

He was on his hands and knees, crawling up, trying to reach his sister. They heard his gasping, agonized breath, and when he managed to utter a few words, his voice was weak.

"Agatha . . . stop . . . you must stop. . . ."

She made no reply—not in words—but they heard a snarl like the snarl of a devil hound, and then a strange, high sobbing as if she felt not remorse but some faint memory of remorse.

"Agatha . . ."

Somehow the reverend had managed to get to his feet. He staggered up a step or two, bracing himself against the banister. His sister waited for him. He put out a hand and seized the hem of her skirts, but he had no strength to pull her down. Caroline, craning her neck, saw dark red stains on the stair carpet. Agatha must have wounded him very badly, she thought. He must be attended to, or he will bleed to death.

With a sudden movement, Miss Montgomery pulled away from his grasp and he fell facedown onto the stairs, his arms thrust up in front of him.

And now—most horrible of all, to Caroline—Miss Montgomery began to curse him.

"Damn you, Randolph! Damn you to eternal hell! Why? *Why?*"

He lifted his head. His eyes, caught in the light of the hall gas jets, seemed to blaze with an anger equal to her own.

"It would have been—" he began, but then he broke off, as if he were saving what little strength he had left for his last effort.

Groaning, he braced himself and slowly got to his feet. He took one step up, and then another.

Miss Montgomery backed away.

He went after her.

She turned and scrambled to the second-floor hall. To Caroline's amazement, the reverend kept on.

"Doctor," she whispered, "do you think—"

"Yes," he said. He shifted the lever and they began to rise again. Above them now, they heard Agatha Montgomery and her brother stumbling up the stairs. The sound of their footsteps had an erratic rhythm: She ran up a few steps, then waited for him nearly to catch her; when he had staggered up and was almost upon her, she ran up a little farther.

Caroline heard them even as she heard her heart pounding, pounding, the sound of it mingling in an eerie way with the footsteps, and with the whine and moan of the elevator, until it was all one sound in her ears.

Then she heard something new. "Listen!" she said.

A key in the front door lock, the door bursting open—

"Addington—at last!" she cried, no longer caring if Miss Montgomery heard her. Relief flooded over her, making her suddenly weak, and she clung to MacKenzie's arm.

And pray he is not too late, MacKenzie thought. He was exquisitely conscious of her presence, her touch, but this was not the moment to respond to it. They were nearly at the third floor now; he heard Miss Montgomery in the hall there, the dragging steps of the reverend in pursuit.

"Addington!" Caroline called. "We are here—in the elevator! And the reverend is on the stairs, and he is wounded! Be careful—Agatha has a knife!"

Broken the knife might be, it was still a weapon that could inflict a serious wound.

In no more than an instant, Ames was bounding up, calling to her. "Are you safe?" he cried. "Stay there! Crippen is with me!"

And now she heard someone else, and she caught a glimpse of the little inspector, close on Ames's heels as they raced up the stairs past the elevator.

Footsteps thudded along the third-floor hall. The elevator shuddered to a stop. MacKenzie pulled open the door and stepped out, wincing at the pain in his knee but unutterably relieved to be free of that small, panic-making space. Above, on the stairs to the fourth floor, he heard Crippen's voice: "Halt! Halt, I say!"

Intending to get his weapon, MacKenzie limped to the door of his room. Before he could utter a word of warning, Caroline had slipped past him and was heading up to the fourth floor behind the others.

Please, she thought, gritting her teeth against the pain in her ankle. Please let them stop. Let Agatha not harm anyone—not anyone else.

When she was halfway up the stairs, she felt a sudden draft of cold air. She came into the fourth-floor hall just in time to see Addington and Crippen disappear up the last little half-flight of stairs to the roof.

As fast as she could, she hobbled up behind them. She heard Agatha's voice—"Randolph!"—and his reply—"You fool! See what you have done!"

She heard a warning shout from Addington, a single explosive oath from Crippen.

She came out onto the roof.

She felt the cold night wind on her face, and a spattering of rain. She saw two dark forms grappling near the edge. They might have been lovers entwined in a deadly embrace. They swayed back and forth—they staggered and teetered—they fell, still clutching each other—rolled over—and then—

Agatha went over the edge.

But she did not fall far, because she held on to the reverend, truly in a death grip now, both hands grasping his above the wrists while he sprawled flat on his stomach. She had dropped her broken knife; it lay, gleaming dully, halfway across the rooftop.

In two steps, Ames reached them. With a warning cry, he seized the reverend's legs. Caroline started to shout—"No, Addington!"—but then, afraid of startling him, she bit back her words.

They will all three fall to their death, she thought. Please, Addington, let him go, let Agatha go—

Ames hauled back on the reverend, and for a moment it seemed that Agatha could be saved as well.

But she could hold on no longer. They heard her scream—a sound that would haunt Caroline to her grave—and then she was gone.

CHAPTER
27

EARLY THE NEXT AFTERNOON, A COLD, CLOUDY DAY WITH
the wind strong from the north, Ames strode purposefully
across the Public Garden and exited through the tall iron
gates at the Commonwealth Avenue Mall. The city was Sun-
day-quiet, which suited his pensive mood.

How could he tell her what had happened? She was convinced of Agatha Montgomery's near sainthood. How could
he find the words to say that far from being some kind of
saint, the proprietress of Bertram's Bower had been a
woman who, tormented by her demons, had committed
murder three times over and possibly four?

He paused to allow a brougham to pass at Arlington
Street, and then, buffeted by the wind, crossed and strode
on down the avenue. Snow by nightfall, he thought. Well, he
didn't mind snow. Winter in New England wouldn't be
right without it. Some of his friends had taken to wintering
in the South. He'd had jolly notes postmarked from
Charleston and Savannah. Unnatural, he thought: a winter
of sunshine and mild breezes, weather warm enough to sit
outdoors.

He rounded the corner and crossed in the middle of the
block to the Berkeley Arms. He hadn't thought to send a
telegram warning her of his arrival, but surely she'd be at
home.

The concierge announced him and he went up. She'd opened the door before he reached it, and she welcomed him with a heart-quivering smile.

"Mr. Ames," she said softly, giving him her hand. She wore a dark green velvet tea gown and a necklace of baroque pearls. Her eyes were shadowed with sorrow, and her lush, beautiful mouth trembled a bit. "What has happened?"

"I cannot stay long. But I wanted to—I did not want you to—"

Already he was bungling it; he should not have spoken so abruptly. He deposited his cloak and hat and gloves with the maid and followed Mrs. Vincent into her warm, expensively elegant parlor. Her little dog, who was apparently becoming used to him, lifted its head and yawned.

"Can I give you lunch, Mr. Ames?"

"No, thank you." He looked around. He saw a stack of Sunday newspapers on a low table. "You have seen the news?"

"Yes. But the news is not the whole story, I imagine."

"No. The whole story— Perhaps you had better sit down."

Her eyes widened in surprise, but she did as he suggested, and with a graceful gesture waved him to a seat opposite.

He hesitated, wanting to get it right, conscious that he had her fixed attention. Many men, he knew, would have given much for that. As he always did in her presence, he felt awkward, like a gawking schoolboy.

"Well, Mr. Ames? What is it? I cannot believe that Agatha Montgomery is dead, and yet the Sunday *Herald* prints it, so it must be so."

"Yes. She is dead."

"Did she really fall from your roof? Or . . ."

She held his gaze, wanting him not only to finish her question but to answer it. But when he kept quiet, she said, "Or was she pushed?" Her voice—her splendid actress's voice—was low and throbbing and filled with emotion. As it always did, it set his pulses racing even as he reminded himself that this was a woman beyond the bounds of polite society. Polite society be damned, he thought. If he was going to cause her pain—and he was—he wanted that pain to be as brief as possible.

"She was not pushed," he said curtly.

"Then—how did she fall?"

"She was struggling with her brother—trying to kill him."

Mrs. Vincent was obviously shocked at that, but quickly she collected herself and said, "So she found out about him at last?"

"You mean about his—ah—tendency to take liberties?"

"Yes."

"At least one person—Dr. Hannah Bigelow, a friend of my sister's—tried to warn Miss Montgomery about that, but Miss Montgomery would not listen. This episode last night occurred not because of his liberties, however, but because he planned to marry a woman from New York. And perhaps—so Miss Montgomery feared—to move there. Thus, in her view, deserting her."

"But surely—" She broke off, trying to make sense of it.

Ames leaned forward, his elbows on his knees. He wanted very much to take her hand, but he did not quite dare. He hated to distress her with what more he had to tell her, and yet he must do it; he couldn't let her learn it from the newspapers.

"Mrs. Vincent, I came here today to tell you what all the city will know soon enough. I didn't want you to see it first in the public prints, because I know how much you admired Miss Montgomery, and I know it will hurt you to learn that she . . . was capable of . . . what she did."

"What she did?" she repeated.

Make it quick and clean, he thought. "She was the Bower killer."

She went quite pale, and her face—her beautiful face, beauty beyond men's dreams, beauty a man could die for, and had—froze as she absorbed what he'd said.

Quick and clean, and tell it all. "She killed all three of those girls, and she may have killed her brother. He is at Mass General now, near death."

"But—*why*?"

"I don't know. I don't really know, I mean. The facts of the case—" He spread his hands in a gesture of futility. He saw the rapid rise and fall of her bosom, and he wished he could comfort her somehow, make it up to her for shattering her faith in the woman she'd called a saint.

Failing that, he tried to explain it to her: Mary's pregnancy, Bridget's threats, Peg Corcoran's bad luck to be at hand when Miss Montgomery needed a third victim to avenge herself on her brother.

She heard him out in silence, her hands folded in her lap, her eyes never wavering from his—very strong, she seemed, and yet he could not help thinking that even as he spoke, he was watching some part of her wither and die: the part that had believed in Agatha Montgomery.

At last he came to the end of it, and he fell silent. I have failed her, he thought. She asked my assistance, and instead—

"I owe you a debt of thanks," she said softly.

"Not at all. I merely tried to help."

"And you did. It is not your fault that things turned out rather differently than either of us expected."

Abruptly she rose and went to the hearth, where a seacoal fire simmered with a steady warmth. After a moment he realized, with a stab of dismay, that she was weeping. At once he was on his feet and at her side, and then, without knowing how it happened, she was in his arms and sobbing against his shoulder. He felt her shuddering, trembling body all down the length of his own, and he realized with another sharp little stab that she was uncorseted.

Holding her was unlike anything he'd ever experienced. For a long moment, as he rested his cheek against her glorious hair, he breathed in her scent—some heavy, sensuous scent that no proper Boston lady would wear—and he murmured to her he didn't know what, anything to ease her grief, her very real heartbreak.

Gradually her sobs quieted, and after a moment more she pulled away from him a little, but without leaving his embrace entirely. With no embarrassment she gave him a small, tremulous smile. He reminded himself that she was accustomed to displaying all kinds of emotion to perfect strangers, all the time. He reminded himself that she had a string of lovers, a supply of men eager to be where he was now, with her in his arms.

None of that mattered. What mattered at this moment was that he must leave her, and he had no idea when he might see her again.

Could he ask her to call at Louisburg Square? No. Impossible. Caroline would never—

"I must go," he said.

"Yes," she said.

"I am sorry if I—"

She shook her head, dismissing any apology he might have made. She stepped back, free of his embrace, and his empty arms dropped to his sides. "You were kind to come, Mr. Ames."

Kind. Was that what he wanted to be to her?

"It was—I felt that I—" He cleared his throat, trying to recover his equilibrium. Having her stand so near, with the memory of her in his arms, was an assault on his senses that made it difficult to think.

"Will you stay in touch with me?" she said.

In touch. What did that mean? "Yes, of course."

"Thank you." She held out her hand, sending him on his way. In her eyes he thought he saw not sorrow, not pain at what he'd had to tell her, but a curious kind of understanding. Beyond understanding. Sympathy, he thought as he went out into the cold once more, heading home. Not for Agatha Montgomery, but for him.

Yes. Sympathy—and something even more than that. Why? Because she knew how he felt about her? He didn't know that himself. Because she knew he was in danger of falling in love with her?

She was right. He was in danger of that. And now at last

he realized what he'd seen as she'd said good-bye to him: not understanding, not sympathy. What he'd seen in her beautiful eyes—and how the realization galled him!—had been pity.

WINCING AT THE PAIN IN HIS KNEE, MACKENZIE HEAVED himself up from his chair, seized the poker, and stirred up the coals in the hearth. He heard the grandmother clock in the hall strike the half hour: three-thirty, nearly dusk. When he turned to speak to his companion, he saw that she was gazing up at him, and because of what they'd recently endured together, because of the fate they'd narrowly escaped, it seemed to him that in her face he saw some feeling for him that had not been there, or at least not so strongly, before their harrowing adventure last night. Affection? Perhaps. Or, at the very least, a comforting kind of trust.

She is still afraid, he thought. But surely they were done with it now; she need fear nothing more.

Until early that morning, and all the long night before, they had had chaos: curious neighbors, swarming police, medical teams, ambulances, hordes of reporters tipped off to a sensational story.

But now at last they were at peace. Ames had gone out and had not yet returned. He was all right, he'd said; he merely wanted an hour or so of quiet. Caroline agreed: quiet was what she wanted, too, more than anything.

"Would you like tea, Doctor?" she asked.

"If you would," he replied. "Shall I ring?"

"Please."

The household might have been severely discommoded because of Margaret's absence, but their neighbor across the square, Dr. Warren, had kindly sent one of his servants to assist.

After they were alone once more, MacKenzie carefully lowered himself into his chair. His knee was throbbing; he could only imagine what Dr. Warren would say to him about it.

Although it was growing dark, he had not wanted to turn

up the gas. He liked sitting in this shadowy room with Caroline Ames. He liked knowing that when he spoke, she was there to answer him. That in the normal routine of their lives, when he went out, she would be there to greet him on his return.

Suddenly he shuddered, thinking of what had happened in this room last night: Agatha Montgomery in a murderous fury, wielding her knife.

"Are you cold, Doctor?" Caroline asked.

"No. Not—not cold." He searched for the words to tell her what he felt, but they eluded him.

The pocket doors slid open, and Ames stood there, surveying the quiet domestic scene. MacKenzie, just at that moment, would not have dreamed of asking where he'd been, but he could guess. She will cause you to suffer, my friend, he thought but did not say, and then, for fear his thoughts showed on his face, he looked away.

Ames turned up the gas a little and took his accustomed place by the hearth, one slim, booted foot resting on the brass fender. "I must send to the hospital to see how the reverend does," he said.

"And if he lives—?" asked MacKenzie.

"If he lives, I suppose he will tell his story to Crippen. Whether he will be believed is another matter."

"I wonder what he will say about the account books," MacKenzie ventured.

"What can he say? At the very least, the man is a thief—and a blackguard." Ames's long, lean face drew down into lines of disgust. He felt dirty even thinking about the reverend, never mind talking about him.

"Poor Agatha," Caroline murmured. She caught MacKenzie's eye and added, "I know, Doctor. I know what she did. But she was driven to it."

"She lived in a fantasy world," Ames said sharply. "She believed in something that bore no relation to reality."

"She loved him," Caroline said. And when both men looked at her sharply, she raised her chin and added, "Well, she *did*."

"Unwisely—and far too well," Ames said. "And until she turned against him, she would have been willing to allow an innocent lad to be hanged for murders he did not commit."

"Yes," she replied softly. "I know."

So much for Miss Montgomery's putative sainthood, thought Ames. Serena Vincent's face rose in his mind, and with an almost physical effort, he banished it.

They heard the front door knocker, and when the borrowed servant did not answer, Ames went himself. They heard him in the vestibule welcoming the caller, and Caroline could tell from the sound of his genuine pleasure that it was not Inspector Crippen. Thank goodness, she thought. She did not feel strong enough, just yet, to deal with him.

In another moment, Ames ushered in Desmond Delahanty.

"Miss Ames—Doctor—what a time of it, yes?"

As usual, he was hatless, his hair windblown, his long blue muffler wrapped around his neck.

"Mr. Delahanty, how good to see you," Caroline said, giving him her hand. "What news?"

"Well, the lad's free, and that's something."

Delahanty shook hands and then went to the fire to warm himself. "And it took them a good long time to do it, mind you. I went down to the Tombs myself to speak for him. You wouldn't believe the paperwork they had to go through just to release an innocent boy."

Their tea came then, and the men helped themselves to Sally Lunn and lace cookies while Caroline poured. Then Delahanty, perched on the edge of the sofa, looked around at them and they knew that not all his news was good.

"What else, Desmond?" asked Ames.

"The Reverend Montgomery died just after noon."

"Ah." Ames realized he was disappointed that the reverend had so easily escaped the law. "Hardly surprising, considering his wounds."

Good riddance, thought MacKenzie, and yet he found Delahanty's news somewhat disturbing. Despite his aching knee, he heaved himself up once more and went to stand at the lavender-glass bow window. It was dusk; the streetlamps had just come on. In the oval behind the high iron fence, the purplish trees thrashed in the wind, and a few snowflakes whirled in the lamplight. Across the square, he could see lights in the houses opposite—a comforting sight, the blessed tranquillity of ordinary lives.

And yet—

"Will the Bower continue, do you think?" Delahanty asked.

"I don't know," Caroline replied. They heard the sadness in her voice. "Agatha was its heart and soul."

"It is a very worthy cause. Surely some other dedicated female might be found to keep it going."

"Yes." Caroline thought of the Bower's girls, of Liza and Katy. She would talk to Edward and Imogen Boylston, she thought, and perhaps— "Perhaps," she said.

MacKenzie looked back at the little group in the parlor. The firelight illuminated the men in their dark clothing, edging them with light; it gilded Caroline's hair and played over her face, her dress. It was like a painting, he thought: The Angel of the Hearth.

His Angel?

Perhaps. With luck—and time.

He left the window and went back to her, back to the warmth and the light, and she turned up her face to smile at him. And then, gladdening his heart, she gave him her hand, and eagerly he grasped it.

A gust of wind blew down the chimney, causing a shower of sparks. The thaw was past; winter had come again.

AUTHOR'S NOTE

"BOSTON," WROTE AN ANONYMOUS COMMENTATOR IN 1879, "in spite of the organized efforts of thoughtful and good people, and the annual expenditure of large sums of money, has its full share of unrelieved suffering and want."

In an age without modern-day "safety nets," the Victorian impulse for doing good, in Boston as elsewhere, found many outlets. Most of them were bluntly, even crudely named: orphanages, workhouses and almshouses, lunatic asylums, homes for "aged females" and "children of the destitute," and, as in *Murder at Bertram's Bower,* refuges for "fallen women."

There really was such a place in Boston in the late nineteenth century, a "bower" in the South End.

Today we might ask, "Fallen? From what? Into what?"

From virtue into sin, the Victorians would have replied. And for them, sin, particularly women's sin, was almost always sexual. In that age, so similar to and yet so different from our own, women were ruled by a social code far more constricting than the corsets that crushed their bodies into unnatural shapes to please the eyes of men. High on the pedestals where men put them and tried to keep them, women perched so precariously that one slip could cause them to fall into a chasm of ostracism and shame.

To our somewhat jaded modern sensibilities, the Victorian code of conduct for women, both written and unwritten, seems faintly ridiculous, not to say inhumane. But it ruled the lives of women then, as well they knew, and they violated it at their peril.

As for Jack the Ripper, the most famous criminal of all time: He haunts us still. The faceless, nameless killer stalking his female victims in London's nighttime streets is the very image of terror. Despite more than a century of sleuthing both amateur and professional, he is still a mystery. Who was he? Why did he kill in such a dreadful, bloody way? Why did he stop? What happened to him? Probably, now, we will never know.

One thing we do know, however, is that Scotland Yard believed he might have escaped to America; they even sent a man here to search for him. And so I took that intriguing possibility, together with the fact of a home for "fallen women" in Boston's South End, and combined them to make this tale.

What if . . . ? I thought.

What if, indeed?

—Cynthia Peale

ABOUT THE AUTHOR

CYNTHIA PEALE is the pseudonym of Nancy Zaroulis, author of *Call the Darkness Light* and *The Last Waltz,* among other successful novels. She lives outside Boston, and is currently at work on the fourth book in her Beacon Hill Mystery series.

Please turn the page for
an exclusive advance preview

THE WHITE CROW

A BEACON HILL MYSTERY BY
CYNTHIA PEALE

Available from Doubleday Books in
March 2002
wherever books are sold

CHAPTER 1

IN A DARKENED ROOM IN A HOUSE ON LIME STREET, ON THE flat of Beacon Hill, Caroline Ames sat at a table clasping the hand of her friend, Dr. John Alexander MacKenzie, and tried to speak to her mother, who had been dead for a year and a half.

There were six other querants in the room. The medium, Mrs. Evangeline Sidgwick, was in deep trance. Her control, a temperamental entity named Roland, had spoken some minutes before in answer to a question—not Caroline's— but since then he had been silent for what seemed a very long time.

Caroline shifted in her chair. Her back itched just below her waistline, but her corset made the place impossible to scratch. The room was very warm—too warm, the windows closed and the curtains drawn against the bright May afternoon—and filled with a scent she could not identify: some heavy, musky odor that smelled the way she imagined incense might smell.

As if in answer to her movement, Dr. MacKenzie squeezed her hand. Impulsively she squeezed back. Improper, she knew, but she didn't care. Dr. MacKenzie, over these last months, had proved to be the best friend she'd ever had, and she realized that she had grown perhaps too fond of him. What would she do if he decided to move on, to return to his position as a surgeon with the army in the West? Well, she would worry about that when it happened. For now—and particularly now, at this moment—he was here, with her, and that was all that mattered.

It had been a daring thing, to come here this afternoon. She'd had to swear Dr. MacKenzie to silence, make him promise not to tell Addington where they were going. Addington—her older brother, the guardian of her life—disapproved of mediums. Very probably he would have forbidden her to attend this séance today. In which case, she'd have had to engage in a deception even more blatant than the one she'd devised. We are going to walk in the Public Garden, she'd told him, such a lovely day, the first really good spring day we've had. He'd accepted it and gone about his business.

And now here she was, and after all her maneuvering, she'd failed. Her mother hadn't come through.

Dear Mama. Where was she? Was she happy? Busy about her work, up there in the ether or Heaven or wherever she lived, now that she had passed over? Surely she'd gone to Heaven, Caroline thought, where all good souls went.

She blinked back her sudden tears. Her mother's death had left a terrible emptiness in Caroline's life that hadn't eased until Dr. MacKenzie had come to board. She hadn't missed her mother so much, these last months, and she knew that the doctor's presence in the Ames household was largely responsible for that.

But still, when the opportunity had presented itself to attend one of Mrs. Sidgwick's séances, she had been unable to resist. Mrs. Sidgwick was reputed to be the best medium in Boston, and Caroline had heard intriguing, even astonishing reports of her abilities to contact loved ones who had left the earthly plane. Meeting her for the first time today, she'd been surprised, for the medium was a small, modestly dressed woman, soft-spoken, even seeming rather shy, nothing about her to make one suspect she had such extraordinary powers.

But despite her powers, she—or, rather, her control, that irascible "Roland"—hadn't managed to reach the late Mrs. Ames.

Other spirits, yes. Many of the people here today had had the satisfaction of speaking to their loved ones. Before the séance had begun, they'd gathered in this room and had gotten to know each other a bit. That nice Mrs. Ellis, for instance, an elderly widow who said she'd been trying for years to reach her son, killed at Gettysburg. He'd come through for her loud and clear, with fulsome assurances that he was doing splendidly, no pain, no sorrow, living in harmony with the hundreds—thousands—of other spirits like himself, no bodily ills, choirs of angels. . . .

And Miss Price, a fortyish spinster, here to contact her brother who had died years ago when they were children. Miss Price was still weeping now—weeping from happiness, they all understood—a full half hour after Roland had relayed her brother's message. Essentially it had been the same message as that of Mrs. Ellis's son: a happy existence on that ethereal plane, no troubles.

And Mr. Theophilus Clay, poor man, here with his daughter, both of them trying to reach the late Mrs. Clay, who had died, Caroline knew, a very painful death.

Although "poor man" was hardly the way to describe Theophilus Clay, Caroline thought, since he was not only one of the wealthiest men in Boston but also one of the most generous and therefore loved, a liberal philanthropist widely known for his good works. So he was rich in friendship as well as money, and not to be pitied.

Still. All the money and all the friends in the world couldn't bring his wife back to him, could they?

Clay sat on Caroline's left. He'd clenched her hand tightly as he'd asked his questions and Mrs. Clay had answered them through Roland. She'd told him her agony had ceased and she was happier now than she'd ever been.

The late Mrs. Clay's sister was here as well, but her questions had not been answered. Caroline had heard the woman's voice choked with tears as she put her queries to

Roland, but for some reason Mrs. Clay's spirit had chosen not to respond.

Despite that disappointment as well as her own, Caroline had to admit that it had been a successful—amazingly successful—afternoon. Whoever Roland was, he was very knowledgeable. He transmitted information that Mrs. Sidgwick herself could not possibly have known. She could never have studied up on the family histories of everyone here today to prepare herself, as some mediums—fraudulent ones—were reputed to do.

That Mr. Jones, for instance, sitting on Mr. Clay's other side. He was a small, nondescript-looking man who had mumbled his queries as if he had a speech impediment. But Roland had understood him well enough and had answered him promptly. Perhaps Roland had mind-reading capabilities, and didn't even need to hear the questions spoken out loud.

No, thought Caroline, despite Addington's scoffing at mediums and séances and making contact with the "other side," this exhibition today was genuine enough to make a believer out of anyone.

She tensed. Mr. Clay's daughter was asking another question.

"Is Grandmama with you in Heaven, Mother?"

"Yes." Roland's voice, coming through Mrs. Sidgwick, was deep and rasping, very different from the medium's own.

"Is Grandmama there with you now?"

"Yes."

"Might I speak with her?"

"I am here." A different voice, higher. The voice of an older woman? A grandmama, in fact?

"Oh, Grandmama, I am so glad to speak to you!" cried Clay's daughter.

"Good works."

"You mean—what Papa does?"

"Laying up his treasures for Heaven."

Caroline heard Mr. Clay clear his throat as if he were embarrassed at this praise. Was "Grandmama" his mother or his late wife's?

"Oh, Grandmama! How we miss you!"

Clay's daughter had married a young-man-about-town, dashing and handsome—a bit of a rake, some people thought. She and her husband were among the young fashionables, with a magnificent new mansion on upper Commonwealth Avenue and a lavish lifestyle that was looked down on, Caroline knew, by some of the older, less affluent Boston families. But the girl was Clay's only child, and he had always indulged her freely. Her coming-out had been the most extravagant that Boston had ever seen, and now she and her husband entertained regularly and expensively and traveled widely, with apparently none of Clay's concern for doing good.

"Grandmama! Are you there?"

No answer.

"Mama! Mama! Don't go yet!"

Caroline heard the girl's voice break. For a moment there was silence in the room as they all strained to hear, but Roland apparently had nothing more to transmit.

Then she heard a new sound, like a pencil scribbling and scratching, papers shuffling. She looked in the direction of the sound, toward the medium, but in the darkness she couldn't see anything. Amazing, how on a bright, sunny May afternoon this room was as black as a moonless midnight.

They make the room dark so as to deceive their credulous clients, Addington had said, his long, lean face drawn down into an expression of disdain. If you go there, you can expect to see a glowing phantom appear. It will be the medium's accomplice, shrouded in a sheet covered in luminescent paint. You can expect to hear weird music coming from afar. It will be another accomplice, hidden away in the medium's cabinet, playing a harmonica. It is all a cheap carnival trick, Caroline.

Well, he didn't need to know she'd come. This would be her secret—hers and Dr. MacKenzie's, whom she knew she could trust. And in any case, none of those things Addington predicted had happened. There had been no glowing phantom, no music. Too bad she wouldn't have the satisfaction of telling him that.

The scratching stopped. Her neighbor on her left, Theophilus Clay, started and made a sound like a grunt, as if something had bumped into him. He kept hold of her hand, however, so she assumed he was all right.

From the place where Mrs. Sidgwick sat, Caroline heard a low moan, as if the medium were in pain. And perhaps she was, Caroline thought; who knew how these mental voyages into the beyond strained the physical body?

Another moan, louder. Then the door opened and the maid appeared, as if that sound had been a signal. Moving briskly around the room, she turned up the gas and twitched back the heavy draperies. Caroline blinked as her eyes became accustomed to the light. All around the table people were shaking their heads, clasping each others' hands.

With a small, final pressure, Dr. MacKenzie removed his hand from hers.

"Are you all right?" he said in a low voice, smiling at her. She'd been disappointed not to contact her mother, he knew; he hoped she wouldn't take it too hard.

"Yes, I'm fine."

As she spoke, turning toward him, she flexed her left hand to release it from Mr. Clay's grasp.

Mr. Clay's hand didn't move.

She turned to look at him as she pulled hers away, shaking it a little. Mr. Clay's arm dropped and fell straight at his side.

And then, to her horror, he began to tilt toward her, his rather heavy torso threatening to fall onto her, and it would have done so if Dr. MacKenzie hadn't quickly risen and stepped around to straighten him.

"What is it, Doctor?" said Caroline, not caring if anyone overheard her. "Is he—what's wrong?"

MacKenzie was grappling with Mr. Clay, fumbling with his cuff to get at his pulse, with his shirt-studs to reach his heart.

Across the table, Clay's daughter sprang to her feet.

"Papa!" she cried. "What is it? What is wrong?"

Dashing to her father's side, she pushed MacKenzie away as she slapped at Clay's face and squeezed his hands. The other people in the room, not realizing what had happened, stared at her in amazement.

"Papa!" She was screaming now, shrieking and sobbing. "Speak to me! Papa! Papa!"

But she was too late. Theophilus Clay, who had apparently been too greatly excited at contacting the spirit of his late wife, had gone over to the other side to join her.

CHAPTER 2

"HE WAS DEAD, ADDINGTON! AND I—I WAS HOLDING HIS hand, and I never knew!"

It was evening, after a dinner Caroline had been unable to eat. She hadn't minded not eating; she was too plump as it was, and if she'd had the willpower, she would have fasted often. She reclined now in the parlor at No. 16½ Louisburg Square, her sweet, pretty face, ordinarily rosy with good health, still pale and drawn, her fair, curly hair escaping a little from its Psyche knot. Her feet were propped on the cricket before the fire. Ordinarily the Ameses stopped their hearth fires on the first of May every year, not starting them again until the end of September, but on this chilly night Ames had ordered that sea coal be brought and the parlor fire lit, as well as one in Caroline's bedroom.

Caroline had told him what happened at Mrs. Sidgwick's séance. She couldn't seem to stop telling it. Dr. MacKenzie hovered by her side, his broad, honest face a study in worry and concern. He was twisting the ends of his mustache—always, for him, a sign of distress. He longed to help her, but he didn't know how. Although he was a medical man, his entire experience had been with the army on the western plains; he knew very little about women, and nothing at all about their often mysterious vapors and swoons. And so now he could only stay by her, ready to offer brandy or *sal volatile* in case she fainted.

But to her credit she had not fainted—not here at home, nor at Mrs. Sidgwick's either. What a to-do that had been! In the immediate aftermath of the discovery that Theophilus Clay had died, old Mrs. Ellis had uttered a loud cry and had toppled from her chair, causing a little sideshow. Clay's daughter had carried on with her hysterics, shrieking and sobbing like a madwoman. But Caroline had been cool and clear-headed. She had gone at once to Mrs. Sidgwick, who, still weak from her exertions, had not at first understood what was happening. An ambulance, Caroline had said; we must send at once to the hospital.

Dr. MacKenzie had gently reminded her that the unfortunate Clay was beyond medical help; the police, he said, were surely the ones needed now?

Mrs. Sidgwick had a telephone. MacKenzie himself had placed the call; Caroline had heard him shouting in the front hall below. Clay's daughter had collapsed at her father's side while her aunt, Mrs. Briggs, tried to calm her. Mrs. Ellis had been cared for by Miss Price. Jones, the small, quiet man who mumbled, had moved from the table to sit by himself in a corner, his lips moving as if he were caught up in prayer.

Mrs. Sidgwick, after her first horrified reaction, had sat quite still, allowing Caroline to hold her hand but uttering no word. The maid who came in to open the curtains had retreated to the hall, where they could hear her sobbing.

"And then the police came?" Ames said now. He spoke gently, prompting her to go on because he understood that talking about it was helpful to her.

"Yes."

"But not Crippen?"

They were well acquainted with Deputy Chief Inspector Elwood Crippen, a fussy, officious little personage who got some things right but many wrong.

"No. Thank heaven."

Ames tolerated Crippen; Caroline disliked him; MacKenzie loathed him.

"And they went through some kind of pro forma interrogation?"

"Yes. Well, there wasn't much they could ask, after all. I mean, what could we tell them?"

"Heart attack, Doctor?" Ames asked MacKenzie.

"As far as I could tell, yes. I thought when I met him, before the séance, that he looked unhealthy."

"Poor fellow," Ames replied. "I hope he had his affairs in order."

"Did you know him, Addington?" Caroline asked.

"Not well. I've seen him occasionally at the Somerset."

That was one of Ames's clubs, a handsome granite neoclassical building on the rise of Beacon Street across from the Common.

"He didn't strike me as the kind of man who would go in for séances," Ames added. He gave his sister a look.

"I know you don't approve, Addington." She bit her lip; she was not in the habit of apologizing to him, and doing so came hard to her now. "And perhaps I was wrong to deceive you, but I so wanted to see if I could contact Mama." Her voice broke, and she turned away.

"I understand what you wanted, my dear." He didn't wish to bully her; she'd had a scare, and perhaps it had taught her a rough lesson. "And I was perhaps too harsh in my judgment of Mrs. Sidgwick," he added kindly. "If it gives you some comfort to—but you didn't, did you?"

"Make contact with Mama? No." Suddenly she was very tired. "I tried, but she didn't—couldn't—come through. Although—"

"What, Caro?"

"That's odd. I'd forgotten all about it. Dr. MacKenzie, do you remember, just at the end, Mrs. Sidgwick seemed to be doing some kind of writing. And in fact I saw it afterward, when the lights came on—sheets of paper on the table."

"Writing?" Ames asked. "About what?"

"I don't know. I didn't examine it. Just scrawls. It looked illegible."

"Perhaps she was taking dictation from her control," MacKenzie offered.

"Yes. I'm sure that's exactly what she was doing. What are you smiling at, Addington?"

"I was thinking of the Oracle at Delphi. It is a wondrous place, Delphi, high in the mountains—a fitting place, near the gods, to receive a message from the beyond."

Ames was an amateur of archaeology, among other things. Several times he'd accompanied expeditions led by his former professors at Harvard. He'd traveled to Italy, to Greece, to Persia.

"The Oracle was always a poor girl from the village," Ames went on. "The priests would give her laurel leaves to chew, to intoxicate her. Then they would take down her babblings and transmit them, always suitably ambiguous, in perfect dactylic hexameter—Homer's meter."

"Are you saying that Mrs. Sidgwick may have been intoxicated, Addington? I can assure you—"

"No, my dear, I am not saying that. I am saying that like the Oracle at Delphi, Mrs. Sidgwick may—wittingly or not—have been transmitting nonsense. Although not, I imagine, in dactylic hexameter. And if people want to deceive themselves by patronizing her, it is none of my affair. Poor old Clay got his money's worth, though, didn't he? He reached the other side with a vengeance." He just managed to keep from smiling; sometimes he had a rather mordant sense of humor, which he knew his sister did not appreciate.

"She is a private medium, Addington. She does not advertise, nor does she charge a fee."

"Hmmm. Then I wonder where she gets her living?"

"I so wanted you to be with us," Caroline added plaintively. "Not for the séance—of course not—but afterward, when the—when we found him. If I could have telephoned to you—"

She broke off. They had occasionally discussed—had

argued about it, even—subscribing to the telephone, and although Caroline thought it a splendid idea, her brother had always said No. This was not the moment to take up the issue once more.

"I could have done nothing," he said. In an unaccustomed gesture of sympathy, he patted her hand. "You know that. And now—" The grandmother clock in the hall had begun to strike the hour: ten o'clock. "I suggest that you retire. You have had a shock, and you need a good night's rest. In the morning, all this will seem nothing more than a bad dream."